THE BOOK THAT WILL PUT YOU TO SLEEP

DAWN GREEN

Of The MARGINS Press

Of The Margins Press

Cataloguing in Publication Data available from Library and Archives Canada. Legal deposit – Library and Archives Canada, 2025

Edited by Natalie Munro and Nichelle Garraway. Design by Natalie Munro. Text set in EB Garamond

ISBN: 978-1-0697120-0-4

eBook ISBN: 978-1-0697120-1-1

Printed in Canada

First Edition

For Nichelle, and for every soul who's ever wandered into a bookstore just to breathe. Who's traced the spines, lost track of time, and found meaning in the margins.

THE VAST
THE TARN

THE TOR

INTRODUCTIONS

Hello, dear reader. Allow me to introduce myself. I am the story. Or rather, the story is me. Don't be alarmed. This book isn't about to sprout arms, do a little tap dance across your blanket, or whisper your name in the dark. Although, wouldn't that be something? Just imagine it: if all books came alive, shaped by their genres. Romances would drift about sighing dreamily, clinging to tissues and heartache; historicals would shuffle by in tweed jackets, adjusting their spectacles and muttering facts no one asked for; and horrors... well, horrors would be lurking under your bed and hiding in closets, waiting for that perfect moment to make you drop your flashlight and scream. But no, I'm not that kind of story. Not exactly a fantasy, either... at least, not in the usual sense. And certainly not something corporeal. Just me and you, here in this curious, quiet moment. You're reading. I'm being read. Together, we exist. That's the magic.

The relationship between a story and its reader is wonderfully strange, isn't it? Intimate. Fleeting. Beautiful. For a little while, we are one. I open my world to you, and—whether you know it or not—you open your world to me. And let me say, for what it's worth: as stories go, my world is pretty spectacular.

Now, I get it. Bold move, right? Calling myself spectacular right out of the gate. You're probably thinking about *other* stories. The ones you've loved. The ones with dog-eared pages, coffee stains, and highlighted lines that hit a little too close to home. The ones that live on your bedside table or travel with you from place to place. They stay on the shelf even if you won't ever read them again because you just can't bear to let them go. Maybe I won't be *that* book for you. That's okay. Stories are sacred to their readers.

But here's a secret: readers are sacred to their stories, too.

Over the centuries (and believe me, we've been around), a few stories rise above the rest. Not bestseller-list stories, but the kind that settle into culture and memory— Indigenous creation stories, myths, legends, epics, *The Odyssey*, *Hamlet*, *Anna Karenina*, *Moby Dick*, *Don Quixote*, *The Princess Bride*... I could go on and on and on. These stories echo across time, languages, and generations. To them, I flip my pages with reverence.

And now you're wondering, if I'm so great, how come you've never heard of me? Fair question. Stories have a way of hiding until the moment is right. And now, here you are, and here I am. Which means... the time has come.

So, like an awkward first date, allow me to introduce myself properly. I am an Adventure story, capital A, if you please. And proud of it. Inside me, you'll find all the trappings of the tales you've loved before: heroes and heroines, queens both evil and misunderstood, a prince and some princesses, a knight or two (with questionable judgment), a journey, a curse, a betrayal, a death (or more), some magic, and—naturally—a bit of love.

I come from a long line of stories. A story tree, if you will. My roots run deep into myth and folklore, fairy tale and legend. If parts of me feel familiar, that's because they are. We stories are all connected. We pass things down. We borrow, echo, and whisper across time.

And now, at long last, it's my turn. Me, with my words. You, with your tired eyes and beautiful brain.

I hope you're nestled in somewhere cozy. Maybe curled in your favorite nook with a soft blanket and warm drink. Or soaking in a lavender-scented bath, candlelight flickering. Or tucked under the covers, planning to read just one chapter before sleep gently claims you. We stories *love* those sacred places, the ones that say:

"I'm ready." "I'm here for you." "I'm listening."

But if you're sneaking in a few pages on your lunch break, or riding the subway beside a Talkity McChatterson, that's perfectly fine too. Life is noisy. You made space for me anyway, and for that, I'm grateful. Because the truth is: you're here. I'm here. And that means we're ready. Now, take a breath... and let's begin.

THE BEGINNING

Once upon a time, in a land far, far away...

Oh no. I can already feel your eyes narrowing. Yes, I know. That's one of *those* beginnings. The kind that practically screams "storybook." And yes, it's vague. But stay with me, I promise I'm better than that. (Mostly.)

The time we find ourselves *upon*, because stories *do* like to perch "upon" time, is a few hundred years ago. How many? Hard to say. Let's just agree it's long before electricity, computers, smartphones, or the e-reader you might be clutching like a talisman right now. Back then, a galloping horse was the fastest way to get anywhere, homes were timber and clay with thatched roofs and hearths that cracked and smoked with real fire, and battles were fought not with buttons, but blades. And the people who reigned? Kings and Queens in drafty stone castles, wearing crowns that didn't always fit. Can you see it? Are you there?

As for the land, yes, it is "far away." But that depends entirely on where *you're* reading this from. The truth is, the land isn't *here*, exactly. But it isn't *not* here either. It exists somewhere, quietly nestled in the in-between, and it's worth getting to know. Because this land, its shape, its scars, its secrets, is part of what makes me *me*.

The region is called The Vast Region. (Creative, I know.) But the name is accurate. Everything about it is... well, vast. The jagged, snow-crowned Northern Mountains. The deep, glimmering Southern Lakes. And in between, a wild sprawl of ancient, towering forest, trees so tall they whisper in clouds and creak with memories older than kings. Some say giants shaped this land. Settled it, seeded it, left behind boulders as skipping stones and riverbeds as footprints. Do I believe in giants? I'll leave that to you. Myths are like that, half-truth, half-dream, all mystery. You won't find any giants in *this* story. (Not the traditional kind, anyway.) But what you *will* find is a land defined by its immensity. By its beauty. And, most of all, by the river. Ah yes... the river.

The Still River begins as a cascade high in the Northern peaks and rushes, untamed, through the belly of the land, winding southward until it exhales into the lakes. Don't let the name fool you, "Still" it is not. The river is swift, cold, and deeply dangerous. A wild, slashing diagonal of silver that cleaves The Vast Region into two parts: Tor and Tarn. You'll need to remember those names, Tor and Tarn. Not just because they sound important (which they are), but because much of what happens from here on out will be shaped by the divide between them.

Two territories. Two temperaments. One story.

Now, earlier I said the land shapes the story. But truthfully? Sometimes, it's the stories that shape the land. That's how it tends to work. A kind of slow, whispering loop. People form stories, and stories, over time, form people, and everything else around them.

There's one such story, the legend of Tor and Tarn, that came long before me. It's not mine to tell, not in full. But I've heard echoes of it whispered between pages, passed along in footnotes and folktales. I'll share the bits that matter, the *Coles Notes* version, if you will.

But before that, maybe it's time to take a breath. You've made it through the opening, and I can feel your attention stretching out around me like a cat in a sunbeam. Good. That means we're getting somewhere. ...Now then... would you like to hear a legend? Or, perhaps, not just yet. Perhaps this is the moment you close me softly, tuck your blankets up to your chin, and let your eyelids grow heavy. That's okay. I won't be offended. I'm used to it, you see.

I am The Book That Puts You to Sleep.

Yes. *That* book. Not just a spell book—but *the* book of sleep. The one hidden in dusty tower libraries and passed hand to hand beneath velvet moons. The one witches and wise women once whispered over, its pages inked in ancient dreams and night-sky spells. Ever heard of Sleeping Beauty? Of course you have. That famous spinning wheel didn't spin its curse on its own, you know. The sleep that claimed her castle? That was me. A page torn from my spine, recited by a bitter fairy Queen with too many names. And Snow White? That apple wasn't only poisoned. It was enchanted. A sleep spell, ripened over time from words once read aloud in a tongue forgotten. My tongue. Two girls. Two sleeps. One book.

Me.

I've lulled kingdoms into silence and cradled queens throughout centuries of dreams. My magic isn't loud or showy, it's soft. Subtle. It curls in corners and settles in shadows. It waits for the hush at the end of a long day, for the slow exhale, for the moment your body remembers how to be still. So yes. You could keep reading. The legend is just over the next page. Or, you could close your eyes now. Let the story hold your place. I'll be here when you wake. After all, that's what I do. I put things to sleep. And in this world of endless scrolling, doom news feeds, blinking screens, and one too many viral dances... couldn't we all do with a little more sleep?

THE LEGEND

Tor and Tarn were twin brothers. It's said they were direct descendants of the gods. Which gods, exactly? I can't say. No one can, really. The details have been worn smooth with time. What matters is that they were powerful, stronger than any ordinary human. Strong enough, according to legend, to punch a tunnel straight through the Northern Mountains. And yes, *punch*. If you're thinking that sounds impossible, well, it probably is. But that's how the story goes, legends usually do. I'm just telling you what I've heard.

When the brothers arrived in The Vast Region, Tor, an avid climber, claimed the North. He built a great stone castle atop a crag and ruled over his mountainous domain. Tarn, a swimmer to his core, settled in the South, where the lakes shimmered like glass. For a time, the land was peaceful. The brothers hunted, farmed, fished. They ruled with fairness. They laughed often. They were happy. And then, of course, a girl came along.

It always seems to be about a girl, doesn't it? In these old stories, some beautiful stranger shows up, and everything begins to unravel. Her name was Still.

They say she rose from the waters of the Southern Lakes like a ghost, with eyes the color of glacier-fed waters and hair the hue of an autumn sunset. She was beautiful. Mysterious. Enchanting. You know where this is going. I hardly have to say it. Both brothers fell in love. And not in the sweet, poetic, hold-hands-by-moonlight sort of way. No. They fell hard and fast and ugly, and soon enough the Northern and Southern lands were at war.

The battle lasted only three days, but in those three days, thousands perished. Blades sang, fire rained, blood soaked the soil, etc...

At the end of that third day, only two figures stood among the wreckage: Tor and Tarn, stubborn and furious, refusing to fall. For three more days, they fought each other, brother against brother, neither gaining ground, neither relenting. At last, they stopped, and exhausted, bloodied, broken, they turned to Still and demanded she choose between them.

Why they hadn't asked her to do this *before* starting the war, I couldn't say. Seems like a logical first step. But love, like stories, rarely operates on logic.

And Still? She didn't want either of them. She never had, but no one had bothered to ask or seemed to care about her opinion on the matter. Typical.

What happened next is not pleasant. I'm sorry. I'm only the messenger.

Still's rejection, oddly, united the brothers. Wounded by her refusal, ashamed by the war they'd waged, and haunted by the devastation they had brought upon the land, Tor and Tarn did the unthinkable. Together, they hunted Still down, a pursuit that took sixteen years and that crosses into stories-within-stories too long to recount here. Eventually, they dragged her to the highest cliff in the Northern Mountains and threw her from it. Or she jumped. The details are foggy.

The legend says that when Still's body struck the ground, the mountains split open in grief. The earth cracked—deep and jagged—and from that wound burst water, wild and silver, rushing down in a torrent too powerful to be stopped. It raced from the peaks to the Southern Lakes, carving a path as it went. That path became the Still River. A boundary. A scar. Not a neat line, but a great, slashing diagonal—drawn from the northwest to the southeast—that cleaved The Vast Region in two. On one side, the Tarn: lush, green, and thick with ancient forests that breathe mist and memory. On the other, the Tor: sparser, colder, its woods thinner and its winds sharper, brushing shoulders with the mountains themselves. The river did more than carry grief—it rewrote the shape of the land. Two territories. Two temperaments. One story, forever split by a single, sorrowful line.

As for the brothers, no one truly knows what became of them. Some say they fell in love with another woman and waged war all over again. Others believe they flung themselves from the same cliff, overcome with guilt. The dullest version (and therefore, the least believed) is that they simply walked away, one to the West, one to the East, and never looked back.

Stories told over centuries tend to fracture like old glass. Every retelling adds a new scratch, a new splinter. Eventually, the pane is too cracked to see through. The shape remains, but the truth inside becomes cloudy. Unknowable. And maybe that's all right.

It only takes a quick skim through any history book to understand one universal truth: a land divided is a land destined for conflict. The Vast Region, cleaved in two by the ever-rushing Still River, was no exception. Through centuries of turmoil, its people, those born of the Tarn and those of the Tor, have endured war after war, each one seeding the next like a bitter harvest. The most recent was both an ending and a beginning: the final chapter of one story, and the first page of mine.

As I unfold my tale for you, you'll hear echoes of the one that came before me, and perhaps whispers from those still to come. Like countless others, the story that preceded mine ended with a familiar refrain: "The End." preceded, of course, by "And they lived happily ever after." Or so the readers believed. But here's something I've learned, a quiet truth passed between stories like a secret in the margins: stories never truly end. The ending is simply where the story needs to rest. It's a comfort, a pause, a perfectly placed ribbon tied just so. But it's not the end. Not really.

It's no surprise that most stories choose to end at a happy moment. Readers love happy endings, or at least they think they do. But happiness isn't the whole of it. The real truth, the fuller truth, is that "and they lived happily ever after" should really say: "and they lived." Because life is more than happiness. It's a dance of opposites, of sorrow and sweetness, of peace and unrest, of light and shadow. One cannot exist without the other.

So, without unspooling every thread, I'll tell you this much: when the story before mine reached its so-called ending, a tale of love and alliance, the Kings and Queens of both Tor and Tarn were, by all accounts, happy. For a time, they were even friends. Imagine that, true friendship across the Still River, a peace unprecedented in the thousand year blood-soaked history of The Vast Region.

But peace, like stories, is rarely permanent.

Seven years later, happiness dissolved like the morning mist on a cool September day. At only twenty-eight years old, the ruling King of The Tor fell ill. The finest doctors, priests, and apothecaries from both sides of the river gathered at his bedside. Prayers were uttered, potions poured, herbs ground to dust in desperate hands, but nothing worked. The King, beloved and mighty, slipped quietly from life. And as for his beloved wife, Queen Prima, his death was the end of everything. Her "happily ever after" came undone, thread by aching thread. The people of The Tor would come to remember this time not by its year or season, but by its sorrow. They called it: The Hundred Day Sadness.

For one hundred days, Queen Prima vanished. Not a single villager, not even her young daughter, caught sight of her. Rumors spread like mold in the silence. Some said she had locked herself in her chambers and starved. Others swore they heard her screams echoing from the cliffs of the Northern Mountains, claiming she had thrown herself into the falls of the Still River. And though I am the book who holds this story, I do not know the truth. During those hundred days, Prima simply slipped off the page.

And then, on the one-hundredth day, she returned. But she was no longer Prima the Kind... she had become Prima the Blade, known by many as simply, the Dark One.

The change was unmistakable. Her long, wild red hair was gone. Some say she shaved it herself in grief. Others claim it fell out, strand by strand, sorrow so deep it hollowed her to the bone. Whatever the cause, the result was chilling—her head, bare and pale, mirrored the snow-capped cliffs she ruled. But the transformation was not only in appearance. Wherever she had gone—wherever her desperate journey had taken her—she had not come back empty-handed. She returned with something else. Something old and strange. Magic. Not much, just a trace, a shimmer in the air, like frost before dawn. But it was more than The Vast Region had ever known. And even in that faintest dose, it was enough to change things.

Her kindness vanished with her hair. She ordered the royal banners changed from violet to black. All her subjects were made to wear the same. Light-colored horses were put to death. Homes and buildings throughout the Tor were painted a uniform dark grey, so that when she looked from the castle, she would see her soul reflected in the colorless world below. She could no longer bear the sound of laughter, or the pain of seeing her husband's eyes echoed in her daughter's gaze. And so the girl was sent away, far from the castle, to be raised by tutors and strangers. The light went out in the Tor. And the Dark One made certain it stayed that way.

But even that wasn't enough.

Every morning, as the sun rose in the East, Queen Prima would stand on the balcony of the throne room and gaze over the Tor, across the Still River, and into the western valley. She would watch the sun shedding its light on The Tarn, a place where love and happily-ever-after still dared to exist.

When the King of the Tor died, the rulers of the Tarn had done all the right things. They sent condolences, came to the funeral and organized a search party when Prima disappeared. They even tried, multiple times, to visit the castle. But Prima saw none of it as compassion. No, to her, their efforts reeked of mockery. Every time they crossed the bridge, she saw their clasped hands, their soft smiles, their lingering glances, and interpreted them not as gestures of solidarity but as sharp, cruel reminders of everything she had lost. She ordered the leader of her army to turn them away. And eventually, she lowered the gate entirely, posted guards at the bridge, and forbade anyone, Tor or Tarn, from crossing without her royal consent.

The rulers of The Tarn did not retaliate. Instead, they responded with patience and understanding. They hoped, as most hopeful people do, that pain, like the spring rains, would pass. But this pain didn't pass; it festered. And each time that Prima saw the sunlight warm the Tarn, each night she crawled into a bed built for two, her rage grew. And she welcomed it. She nurtured it, like a twisted little seed. Fed it with silence, watered it with grief, tended to it with resentment. She took solace in her anger, let it blot out the gnawing ache of sorrow. But as with all things left untended by balance, her anger morphed into bitterness, and her bitterness calcified into pure, unshakable hate.

And so it was, on a crisp late autumn evening, while the Tarn festively danced beneath lanterns, sang around fire pits and drank from goblets of sweet nectar cider, the Dark One finally struck.

Her soldiers, silent and loyal, slipped through the gates of The Tarn like the Still River itself. Tarn's guards, drunk and sluggish from celebration, barely had time to lift their swords. The slaughter was swift. The fire, intentional. I won't go into detail. You wouldn't sleep if I did, and as you know, I *do* know how precious sleep is. Soon, you will too.

What I *can* tell you is this: she spared the Tarn royal children. Not out of mercy. Not even cruelty. But intention. As she whispered to the dying King and Queen, her voice low and steady beneath the roar of the flames, their children would live. But not as royalty. As orphans. They would grow in darkness and grief. They would wake each morning without the warmth of love, fall asleep (if they were lucky) without comfort, and come to understand what it truly meant to lose everything.

"Why?" the Queen of The Tarn gasped with her last breaths. "They're just children. They've done nothing."

"Neither had I," Prima seethed. "Yet pain came for me anyway. It always does. For all of us."

The princess was sold into slavery. The prince was taken back to the Tor and placed into training with the Dark Army. But this... this was not her final act. Prima had done more than conquer a kingdom that night. She had cast a curse.

The magic she called upon was older than the river, older than the cliffs, older even than the crown upon her head. In one terrible invocation, she stole from the Tarn their most vital resource, not their land nor their people, but their *sleep*. Yes, sleep. A resource highly valued yet often taken for *granted*.

It started subtly. Nightmares. Restless tossing. Children crying out in the night. But within weeks, the Tarn people could not sleep unless it was *granted* to them. Sleep became a commodity. A currency. A weapon. Only the Tor, those loyal to Prima and her reign, were given the power to grant sleep through single-use obsidian tokens imbued with magic. Without them, no Tarnish citizen could drift into slumber. And without sleep, well... we all know what happens without sleep.

Sleep, my dear reader, became the leash. And Prima held it tight in her cold, pale fist.

And so, The Vast Region was hers. The Tor, now dark and joyless, feared her power and obeyed her commands. The Tarn, broken and sleepless, became slaves, working endlessly for the chance at even an hour of rest. Families sold heirlooms for tokens. Children worked for their parents' sleep. People died not by blade, but by exhaustion. And Prima? She watched it all from her tower, her gaze fixed on the valley, her eyes never blinking.

But, of course, you know this isn't where the story ends. If anything, this is where it begins. You might already suspect who our main character might be. And you'd probably be right. But I won't spoil the fun. Just know that thirteen years have passed since that terrible night, and the world is not what it was. I could start in several places. There are a few moments that might do. I was tempted to skip ahead, give you the polished version of our heroine's introduction. But that would be unfair to her and to you. If you're going to walk beside her through this story, you should know who you're walking with. She's not perfect. She's not polished. She is real. And real, as you well know, means flawed. She would tell you herself, and I quote, that she doesn't give a "flying fig" what you, or anyone else, thinks about her. Charming, I know.

And yes, I'm the story. Could I have written her differently? Possibly. Would I want to? Not in the slightest. She is difficult, stubborn, and often foul-mouthed. But she is also brilliant, and brave, and something this world desperately needs.

And now, we begin, as all great stories should: With a crying girl, a fox, and a thief.

~~~

So yes. That's the beginning, or rather, the background. Not quite the adventure you were promised, not yet. But stories don't
~~~

always charge ahead like galloping horses. The best ones arrive like dusk, soft at first, slow and sure, gathering shape in the quiet. Let this be your hush. There will be time for daring escapes, for curses and crowns, for keys that open doors better left shut. But not just now. Not tonight. Tonight, let your covers rise like forest mist around your shoulders. Let your breath match the rhythm of quiet footsteps on a woodland path. The girl, the fox, and the thief—yes, them—they'll still be here tomorrow, waiting, right where you left them. You see, I am best read in bed. I was made for lamplight and tired eyes, for pages turned with the slow patience of someone who isn't in a hurry to get anywhere at all. I don't mind being read in pieces. In fact, I prefer it. A chapter a night, maybe two, if you must. I'll hold your place when you drift. That's part of the spell. The world can wait, dear reader. I can wait. You've turned enough pages for one day. Close your eyes now. Sleep well. I'll be here when you wake.

CHAPTER ONE

"I don't want to do this," Avery pleaded. "I'm tired. Let's go home. Please."

"Shhhhh…." Wynn commanded while crouching lower. "They're coming now." She threw her hood over her head and motioned for Avery to do the same. "And the inn is not your home, it's not anyone's home." She pulled the girl down until they were well hidden in the deepest part of the bushes. Their moss-green cloaks, "found" from past guests at the inn, blended perfectly with the dusky forest hues. With hoods up and bodies still, they were nearly indistinguishable from the earth itself. Wynn believed that the forest had a way of hiding those who knew how to ask it nicely.

You might be thinking I got that wrong; it should be that the cloaks were *lost and found*, but in Wynn's world, items were not lost and then found. They were found *by her* and only later discovered missing by their original owners. Some might argue that she stole them. Like she stole many things. But Wynn would tell you, as she told Avery more than once, that she only ever *reclaimed* what others didn't care enough about to keep safe, and the cloaks were such a find. Left—or abandoned, depending on your perspective—on stools at the inn by two boorish travellers who drank too much, laughed too loud, and slapped Wynn on the backside every time she passed with a tray of stew or ale. By their seventh round, they were deep in their cups and louder than ever, boasting of imaginary triumphs with Tarn women and slurring half-forgotten war songs. They were too drunk to notice Wynn slip past and scoop up the cloaks, walking away swiftly and confidently as if they had always been hers.

When the travellers finally noticed the cloaks were missing, they blamed each other, shouting accusations over spilled ale, until someone threw the first punch. Within moments, the entire tavern had erupted into a full-blown brawl. As tends to happen when those who feel entitled drink too much and their egos bruise faster than their knuckles.

No one was seriously injured, the inn only slightly more battered than usual, and Wynn, well, she got a beating from Dena for not "managing the floor," as always. But worse than the bruises was what came after: her sleep token was revoked. Just one coin, withheld from the ration, and her body paid the price. She lay in the servant quarters that night, body aching, mind buzzing, eyelids heavy but unable to close, listening to the hum of dreams slipping through the walls, knowing none would come for her. That was the true punishment. And she knew the next day would be harder for it. The drag in her limbs, the fog behind her eyes, it would all come. But one night without sleep? She'd done that before. Tired, yes. Slower, maybe. But she would survive. She always did. To her, the price was fair. The cloaks were warm, durable, and, most importantly, perfect for stealthy foraging.

It had been drilled into her, just as it was drilled into every Tarnish-born citizen since the Dark One seized control, that in the Tor-ruled lands, sleep was no longer a right. It was a *privilege*: granted, denied, and carefully regulated. The Tor held the cursed obsidian tokens, the blessing of Queen Prima, and with it, the power to ration out hours of rest as payment for work, loyalty, and obedience. Dreams in this land came with a cost.

Wynn peered through the brambles. Her breath slowed. The carriage rounded the bend, a heavy coach of polished black oak, pulled by two charcoal horses and flanked by armoured guards. The insignia of the Tor gleamed faintly on their breastplates. She didn't need the dark metals and royal trim to identify them. She had waited on them just last night, silent as always. She'd brushed their horses this morning, washed the stained sheets of the royal treasurer's bunk this afternoon; they reeked of garlic, sweat, and arrogance. He was also a loud-mouthed hunter who, while swilling cider, couldn't resist boasting about the trunks of tribute stored in the rear of the carriage.

"Wynn, please," Avery whispered again. "Don't make me do this. Dena is expecting everything to be ready for the Day of the Fates tomorrow. I still have to..."

"Avery, enough." Wynn cut her off sharply. "Stop being such a scared little youngling. Everything will be fine."

She crouched lower, hand lifted. A rustle sounded in the bushes behind them, soft and purposeful. Their signal. The carriage was close now, just twenty feet. Wynn's pulse slowed. She loved this moment. The stillness. The hush before...

It wasn't just about stealing. Not anymore. Wynn had learned something long ago, before her life as a servant at the inn. She'd learned that the world wasn't fair. That no one was coming to save her. And that sometimes, if you wanted anything at all, you had to take it for yourself.

"Okay..." she whispered. "Go. Now."

Avery didn't move.

"A, I said, go. They're almost here."

Her breath hitched. Wide, watery eyes locked with Wynn's. "I don't want to..." *Crack.*

A hard slap whipped across her cheek, quick and sharp. Her head jerked to the side, the red mark already blooming across her skin. Shock replaced fear for a split second, then Wynn shoved her, sending Avery stumbling over roots and rocks and sprawling into the open road.

As intended, the sudden appearance of a small, crumpled figure startled the horses. They reared with high, panicked whinnies, hooves skidding and scraping against the gravel. The carriage lurched and came to a screeching halt. Inside, the royal Treasurer pitched forward with a thud and a muffled curse, while the guards scrambled to rein in the startled team.

"WHOA... WHOA... steady now!" the lead guard barked, yanking hard on the reins as the horses stamped and huffed. "What do we have here?" he muttered, squinting down at the small figure in the road. Avery blinked up at him, tears trembling at the edges of her lashes—real ones, this time.

The guard frowned. For a moment, he said nothing. People often paused when they looked at her. Not out of recognition, no, it wasn't that. It was something else. Her skin was darker than most in The Vast, her features neither clearly Tor nor wholly Tarn, like a story that didn't quite belong on the same shelf. Even in moments like this, shaken and silent, Avery had a way of making people stop. Tilt their heads. Recalculate. As if they were seeing something they weren't entirely prepared for.

"Hey there, little girl," the guard said, his tone softening just a hair. "You lost?" There was a flicker beneath his voice—something almost eager. As if her being lost might serve him somehow.

She wasn't lost. Not even close. But Avery, small and gaunt from years of thin rations and hard work, looked no older than ten. In truth, she was thirteen. And like most who underestimated her, the guards would soon regret it.

The coach door creaked open and out leaned the royal Treasurer, rubbing his temple where he'd smacked it during the abrupt stop. His jowls jiggled as he growled, "What in the devil is going on? I was napping! What are you idiots..."

But before he could finish his tirade, a silver fox with dark ears and a dark face darted from the bushes with a burst of speed and startling elegance. It was small but swift, its fur mottled like smoke and shadow.

"Help!" Avery shrieked. "Help! Shoot it! Please, shoot it!" She scrambled to her feet and bolted into the trees, her voice shrill with panic. The fox darted in after her.

The Treasurer's eyes gleamed. "A silver fox!" A slow, greasy grin curled over his crooked teeth. "My bow. Now."

"Sir," the lead guard started, hesitating, "we really shouldn't..."

"I'll tell you what we *should* and *shouldn't* do. Do you know how much that pelt is worth? Give it to me." He held his arm out in command.

Still grumbling, the Treasurer lumbered down from the coach and with bow in hand, he pushed into the woods after his imagined quarry. The guards exchanged a look, one of those wordless, exhausted glances that said, when he trips and stabs himself with an arrow, we won't lose sleep over it. But, duty is duty, so they followed him into the trees, armour clinking, branches snapping beneath their boots, curses cutting through the leaves, leaving one bored guard to protect the trunks.

Only one, Wynn thought, the corners of her mouth twitching with satisfaction. *How thoughtful.* Slipping from the thicket, she used a low-hanging branch to swing soundlessly down, landing in a crouch beneath the rear axle of the carriage. She held her breath, listening.

The lone guard dismounted. Gravel crunched dangerously close to her ear as he wandered past. Wynn slid her knife from her belt, slow, silent, not a whisper of metal on leather. She watched his boots. Paused. Waited. Then, satisfied no eyes were peering under the carriage, she saw him shuffle to the roadside ditch and, with a sigh, begin to relieve himself.

In the distance, she heard a high-pitched yelping and the blundering roar of the Treasurer giving chase. *Perfect.*

Wynn hoisted herself up to the rear of the carriage with practiced ease. The trunks were stacked tightly and bound with leather straps. She knew exactly which one she needed. A flick of her blade, a twist of the latch, and it creaked open. Inside: ledgers, tokens, velvet pouches tied with golden strings. Her fingers moved quickly, selectively, and precisely.

She re-latched the trunk, slid back beneath the carriage, and was in the underbrush again before the guard had finished fastening his trousers. He stretched and yawned. She was already gone, moving like the wind that sneaks in through cracks, the kind you only notice when it's already passed you by. Her fingers closed around the cold shape of the stolen sleep tokens in her cloak, and for a moment, she felt the weight of them, real sleep, formed with thin circles of magic.

Perhaps now you understand why I hesitated to begin with this scene. Introducing Wynn as someone who slaps others and robs royalty blind, it's not exactly the fastest way to earn your affection for her. Hardly the stuff of bedtime story heroines, I admit. But as I mentioned earlier (and will likely mention again, because I *am* rather fond of repeating myself), this is who she is. Or at least... who she has had to become.

Still, let me offer you this: stories shouldn't fault their heroines for the shadows they walk through before they find the light. Wynn's path winds through darker places than most, yes, but every step has shaped her into exactly who this story needs. She is flint and fire, thorn and bloom, and a girl like that? She doesn't come from easy beginnings. She doesn't trust easily, either. So don't go scribbling her into the villain column just yet. She has a heart; an inconveniently large and often reckless one, and it does beat loud and true, especially when it matters most. You'll see...

eventually. For now, just trust me: she's worth staying awake for. Even if she, more than anyone, would prefer you didn't.

Wynn was sitting comfortably by a shady stream, her boots kicked off, toes buried in the cool moss as she examined her haul. Sunlight filtered through the canopy, dappling her hands in shifting gold as each obsidian token and silver coin caught the light. Nestled among the loot was a ring—a smooth, gleaming band of black stone, darker than obsidian, with a sheen that seemed to hum beneath the surface. It was heavier than it looked and strangely cold. Turning it in her fingers, Wynn caught the glint of a faint inscription etched along the inside—barely visible, nearly worn away. She mouthed the words as she traced them: *fatis fidelis* – faithful to the fates. This was the kind of thing that would definitely be noticed missing. She should've left it. She knew that. But it called to her, and the temptation to slip a piece of the Dark Queen's power into her pocket had been too strong. It felt like rebellion. Like a quiet, satisfying *no.* She turned the ring over once more, scowling at the inscription. *Fatis fidelis.* Ugh. The Fates. She hated anything to do with them—supposedly twisting lives from some lofty place, always watching, always weaving. Still, she didn't toss the ring away. She just clenched her jaw, shoved it deeper into her pocket, and tried not to think about what it might mean that it had found her.

Behind her, a twig snapped and Wynn prepared herself as a smokey blur launched from the underbrush and landed squarely in her lap.

"Night!" Wynn laughed, catching the fox mid-leap as the soft furball showered her with licks. "Good girl, Night. Good girl." Night wriggled free, landing lightly beside the stream, ears perked for her treat. Wynn fished out some cut-up pieces of sausage. She didn't have to turn to know Avery had arrived. She could feel the heat of her disapproval like a light sunburn. Wynn glanced over just as Avery stepped into view, arms folded, jaw set, eyes narrowed to slits of stormy blue.

"Oh, don't be like that. I didn't mean to slap you that hard. I just needed you..."

"You just needed me to do what you want," Avery's voice cracked. She bent, picked up a stone, and hurled it into the stream where it splashed and sank without ceremony. Wynn reached out to put an arm around her, but Avery twisted away.

"Come on, A. Please don't be mad..."

"Don't. Just... don't." Avery's shoulders rose and fell. "Just tell me you got something."

A glint of silver spun through the air as Wynn tossed a coin in her direction. "Sure did." Avery caught the coin and then let it drop on the ground. "Hey!" Wynn shouted and bent down to pick it up.

"You can keep it," Avery snapped and turned to go. "And I'm not doing that again. They almost shot your stupid fox this time. But I bet you don't even care."

Wynn's eyes drifted to Night, now curled on her side, paws tucked neatly, tail flicking once in contentment. Of course she cared. Night was her shadow, her anchor. And Avery... well, Avery had gotten in, too. Despite every wall Wynn had built. She didn't love like other people did—no warm speeches, no easy softness—but it was there, deep and stubborn. If Avery only knew how much. Wynn wouldn't say it and she wouldn't show it in ways that made sense to most. But she would stay. She would fight. She would bleed, if it came to that. And for Wynn, that was love.

Wynn had found Night as a small pup three years ago, on an evening that smelled like damp earth and burnt crusts. She was emptying the kitchen scraps behind the inn when a small, sharp yapping cut through the hush. The sky was thick with cloud cover and it was too dark to see further than an arm's length away. Still, when Wynn peered around the compost heap, a pair of pale blue eyes blinked back at her like miniature moons, catching what little light there was. There was no mother nearby.

No siblings tumbling in the shadows. Just a filthy little puffball of a fox that looked far too young to be on its own. Dena would never allow her to keep it; too many mouths already snoring under one roof. In fact, she'd probably kill her and say something about killing what'll grow up to steal the chickens anyway. As if a newborn fluff with twig legs posed any real threat to poultry. Wynn had tried to shoo it away. Even threw it a scrap of potato in the hopes it would scurry off like a proper wild creature. But the fox didn't budge. It curled up instead, shivering in place, and watched Wynn with a stare that was equal parts stubborn and... oddly familiar.

Now, I won't pretend Wynn had a particularly soft heart back then. She didn't melt for kittens or swoon over anything fuzzy. But something about that fox struck her clean through. Maybe it was those eyes—clear, calm, not pleading. Maybe it was that Wynn saw something of herself in them. Alone. Unclaimed. Refusing to be pitied. Or maybe, and this is only a thought, there's something true in the old Tarn whispers, the ones that say a few are born with wildness stitched into their bones, a quiet tether to the natural world. Maybe that's why Night chose her. Or maybe some souls are simply meant to find each other, even if one of them is half-starved and smells like turnip peels.

Knowing the risks and against her better judgment, which, to be fair, she didn't listen to often anyway, Wynn scooped up the fox and tucked it away in the barn, buried beneath old burlap and the softest scraps she could find.

The next morning, Wynn made a hasty excuse about collecting berries and carried the pup deep into the forest. There, in the hollowed stump of a long-dead alder, she built a tiny den. But it wasn't just for the fox, it was a test. She always had tests. Little made-up trials to see who could be trusted. Leave the fox, return after dark. If she was still there, maybe this wasn't a coincidence. Maybe it meant something.

Most of her tests failed, Wynn didn't trust easily, and frankly, neither should you in a story like this. But that night, with the inn finally quiet and the last candle blown out, Wynn crept back through the trees, and didn't have to go far. The pup was waiting for her at the forest's edge. Just sitting. Silent. Those glowing eyes like lanterns in the dusk. If not for their shimmer, she'd have vanished into the shadows. Wynn crouched down, her breath fogging in the cool air, and whispered, "You waited?" The fox blinked once, slow and sure, as if to say, *Of course I did. Did I pass?*

And just like that, she had a name - Night.

From the very beginning, Avery had been jealous of the bond between Wynn and Night. She never said it aloud, Avery was too proud for that, too quiet with her hurts, but Wynn could feel it, the way you feel a splinter that's been in your finger too long. Not painful, exactly. Just... there. And she understood. Night wasn't just a pet, some bushy-tailed thing to cuddle on cold winter evenings. She was her eyes in the dark, her silent step in the underbrush, her lookout and her escape route and, frankly, her better half in most of their small-time crimes. They were a pair, like a lock and its key, if keys could jump up trees and growl when someone got too close.

"A, wait up," Wynn brushed Night's head and then skipped after her. "A, wait. I suppose you don't want this either..." Wynn pulled out a feather quill. It was long, sleek, indigo with a golden tip that caught the late sun like it was dipping into a pot of honey. She held it up casually, like she hadn't risked a great deal to swipe it.

Avery's eyes widened just a fraction. Quick as a blink, but Wynn caught it. She always did. Avery reached out, then stopped herself mid-motion, fingers curling back like leaves in frost.

"Why would I care about that?" she muttered, too flat to be convincing.

Wynn didn't push. She just leaned back, still grinning. "You can pout all you want, but I know how much you want this. I took it for you."

A new quill wasn't just a treat, it was dangerous. The kind of dangerous that could land someone in the Dark Dungeons, if they weren't careful. In the age of the Dark Queen, reading and writing weren't just frowned upon, they were outlawed. Forbidden. Words, it was whispered, had the potential to stir things best left sleeping. Dangerous things. And in a world just beginning to feel the breath of magic, even the *possibility* was enough to make people afraid. Afraid enough to ban books, burn libraries, and break the hands that dared to write. Wynn, however, had never been particularly good at obeying. She'd learned her letters before the decree was passed, and she taught Avery, not out of defiance, but out of necessity. Only two others knew their secret. Three, if you counted Night, who often curled nearby, her ears twitching at the soft scrape of syllables whispered onto parchment.

Avery stared longingly at the quill. She loved writing, really loved it. Sometimes Wynn would climb up to the top of the barn and find her tucked beneath the rafters, scribbling her version of events: their adventures, the guests who passed through the inn, dreams of far away places she'd had. Always in secret, always in ink, like that made the stories real.

"When Dena sees it, she'll take it," Avery said quietly. "And I'll get a whooping or worse."

"Then don't let her see it," Wynn replied, offering the quill again.

"I'm still mad," she scowled.

"I know," Wynn shrugged, nudging it forward. Avery's hand lifted and she took it, slow and reluctant, unable to help herself. Wynn kept her smile to herself. Forgiveness accepted.

"I've got to get back," Avery said after a beat. "Start the breads for the Day of the Fates. You coming?"

"Right behind you," Wynn said, adjusting her pack. "Just have to make one stop first."

Avery didn't even bother asking where. "So you're out hunting rabbit, then?"

"Yes. Rabbit will work."

Avery rolled her eyes, but the corners of her mouth twitched. "Just bring some back this time."

Wynn glanced down at Night, who gave a very deliberate little nod. As if to say, *Of course we will.*

~ ~ ~

That's enough excitement for one day, don't you think? A pinch of mischief, a trail of crumbs, a few secrets pocketed like stones. One returns to the scent of baking bread, and the other vanishes between sun-dappled leaves, followed by the flick of a white tail and the weight of a promise not quite kept. But that's all behind us now. You, clever reader, have done the hardest part—turning the pages. The rest? That can wait. Let the light fade behind your eyes. Let the world slow its spinning. Tuck yourself in like a letter waiting to be opened. There will be more to tell, but not just yet. For now, you're exactly where you need to be.

...unless, of course, you're not. Unless your eyes are still bright and your fingers are still twitching for the next bit. In which case, go on. I'll be here either way.

CHAPTER TWO

Wynn's boots crunched softly over the fallen leaves as she wound her way up the narrow deer path. Night padded ahead, tail swaying, ears flicking back now and then as if to make sure Wynn was still behind her.

The familiar clearing came into view slowly. If you didn't know it was there, it was easily missed. Places like these often choose to stay hidden amongst the overgrown forest, embarrassed to show the world the bruises and violence inflicted on them.

Climbing the rubble steps into the open-aired ruins, Wynn moved carefully, like someone returning to a place they weren't sure still wanted them. The bones of the castle loomed, hollowed out by time, but not forgotten. Not by her.

She made her way to her usual perch: the crumbling southern tower, the highest remaining peak. From there, the view stretched out like a painting left to weather in the sun, a turquoise lake below, rimmed by whispering pines, the western mountain range catching the last orange blush of the setting sun. A wind slipped through the skeletal remains of the old stone walls, carrying with it the chill of a crisp fall evening and something older still. The breeze slowed to a hush, making it feel like the land itself was holding its breath.

Moss had claimed the floors. Ivy draped from fractured arches. The earth, calm and patient, was taking back what had always belonged to it. Wynn sat at the edge of the tower, legs dangling over what had once been a ballroom ceiling, or maybe the roof of a library. Hard to say now, there was so much forgotten. Night nestled beside her, understanding that some silences are sacred. She didn't fidget. Didn't sniff around. Just curled into a small dark comma against Wynn's hip, ears alert to the movements below, allowing Wynn the space to let herself remember.

Not *the* last memory. Not the one etched into her ribs like a brand, all fire and smoke and shouting in the dark. No, this was the *other* one. The soft one. The one she kept tucked behind her sharpest thoughts, like a blanket hidden under a bed of thorns - The Day of the Fates.

She could still hear the laughter, faint and flickering, trapped just under the lake's glassy surface. Like the first whiffs of smoke that rise out of a newly lit fire she could see ghosts of her family take shape. Her brother splashing into the water. Her mother scolding half-heartedly, feet bare in the grass, skirts hitched. Her father, tall and impossibly strong, lifting her onto his shoulders so she could see the first sky lanterns rise. She wasn't foolish enough to believe the memory was perfect. Time plays favorites. It will sweeten what should stay bitter, and dull the ache of things you should never forget. She often wondered if that memory had grown too glossy in her mind, like a trinket sold at a market stall, pitched with such confidence that even she had bought in. A thing you think you need to survive. Something to make the rest of it, everything that came after, hurt a little less. Maybe that's all it was. A keepsake for the heart. A dream she wasn't ready to wake from.

And yes, clever reader, you may already know what this place is. Castle Tarn. And yes, you've likely guessed who Wynn is, tucked there among its ghosts. No need to feign surprise, no "aha!" moment, there will be no grand trumpet-blare of a reveal. That's really not her style. Wynn is the lost daughter of the Tarn royal family. She knows it. She remembers (though, she hasn't always). And she knows better than to speak it aloud. Knowledge like that doesn't win you kingdoms. Not anymore.

Wynn closed her eyes and let the silence, the memory, fall around her. Night curled tighter against her knee. And for just a moment, it was enough to sit and remember who she used to be. She was five. Tierney—two years older, impossibly tall, at least by her estimation—towered over her like a castle turret. He was always tall in her memories, always slightly out of reach. But maybe that was less about height and more about how often she'd looked up to him; for guidance, for backup, for help climbing out of kitchen windows after she'd "accidentally" let the ducks inside.

Tierney, though she'd called him *Turkey* ever since toddlerhood, when "Tierney" was far too ambitious a word for her mouth, had taught her everything. How to climb trees and castle walls. How to sneak lizards into the pantry without losing them under the flour sacks. How to swim and hunt and pick just the right reeds for a fishing line. He was part brother, part mischief instructor, and full-time co-conspirator.

In this particular memory, they'd been on the lake for what felt like a full day, sun warming their cheeks, the world slow and sweet like molasses in summer. Their parents were lounging onshore, all tangled up together, like the world hadn't yet found a reason to break them apart. Her father, ever the enthusiastic commentator, kept calling out "helpful" advice from his place in the grass, how to bait the line just right, how to flick the wrist on the toss, how to coax a fish from the shadows with a little flick-flick-flick. Tierney had already given up, annoyed and grumbling, pulling in his stick and tossing it aside dramatically. "They're *laughing* at us," he'd said, glaring into the depths as if the fish were mocking him.

And that's when it happened. A tug on Wynn's line. Then, a sharper pull. And suddenly—commotion. A real, honest-to-goodness *bite*.

Everyone was on their feet.

Tierney leapt forward, eager to take the line, but Wynn turned her back and yanked it closer to her chest, declaring (as she always did), "*I've got it.*"

She did *not* got it.

The fish was monstrous. A small lake beast, probably older than Tarn itself, and *furious* about being disturbed. Within seconds, Wynn's heels lifted from the boat's edge and *—splash—* she went headfirst into the frigid water.

Now, being born of royal Tarn blood, dark hair, striking eyes the same deep turquoise as the lake, Wynn had practically come out of the womb knowing how to swim. In the Vast, it was often whispered that the people of Tarn had gills, or some enchantment that let them breathe beneath the surface. They didn't, of course. But they did tend to stay under far longer than was strictly reasonable. Still, even with all her aquatic skill, Wynn hadn't been under a full breath before both her father and Tierney hurled themselves in after her like panicked otters.

She was fine. *More* than fine. She was determined.

Refusing to drop the stick, or the fish, she kicked her legs hard and swam for shore, the line tugging and jerking in protest. She emerged drenched, triumphant, and shivering, a wild-haired shadow with her prize still wriggling in her fist - maybe, not quite as big as she thought.

On the other side of the lake, her mother was shouting. Her brother and father were still diving and swimming like lunatics. Wynn let them panic a little longer. *Serves them right,* she'd thought at the time. *Maybe next time they'll believe me.*

Eventually, she strolled up to her mother, grinning, and dropped the fish at her feet. The panic turned to laughter, and a fire was built right there on the lakeside. They roasted the catch together—Tierney salted it like a pro, her mother told her she was fearless, and her father swore he'd never seen a fish dragged out of the water with more sheer stubbornness. They joked that it was the kind of story they'd tell for generations. A tale, and fish, that would grow with every telling. A fish so big it had pulled a princess into the lake. A girl so stubborn she'd wrestled it back to shore on her own. A memory so golden it could keep the dark at bay. They said it would be remembered until...

Until.

The wind picked up, sharp and sudden, whisking at Wynn's face and scattering the fragile memory like brittle leaves over cold stone. She wiped at her cheek. The lake had gone glassy, undisturbed and still, the mountains etched on its surface like an old painting beginning to fade.

Night gently licked the bare skin just above Wynn's boot. Her tongue was warm, grounding.

"I'm not crying," Wynn murmured. "It's just the wind."

Night glanced back toward the forest entrance, ears twitching with a silent urgency.

"You're right. We should go." With practiced ease, Wynn grabbed a length of rope she'd tied years ago, back when she first began visiting the ruins, and rappelled down the side of the crumbling southern tower. Night was already waiting when she hit the bottom, tail flicking, head tilted. Wynn grinned. "How do you always beat me down?"

A sharp *crack* echoed from the edge of the trees. Instinct prickled down Wynn's spine. Night froze, her nose lifting to the breeze, ears going flat. Wynn didn't panic. She never panicked. Instead, she slipped the hood of her cloak over her head and with one breath, soft as a sigh, she nodded at Night and they were off.

She sprinted into the trees, every footfall measured, light, impossibly quiet. Roots reached up like greedy fingers, but she danced over them. She leapt from stump to trunk with the surety of someone who had rehearsed this scene a thousand times in her dreams. Branches became swings; ditches became stepping stones. The forest was hers, her teacher, her obstacle course, her home.

Behind her, the crashing, stumbling noise of someone far less familiar with the terrain gave chase. Night, of course, was ahead, a smoky blur slipping effortlessly through the undergrowth. She was the very spirit of the woods, built for the shadows, always a step or two beyond reach. Wynn allowed herself a smirk. Yes, she had Tarn blood, water-born, lake-raised, but the forest had shaped her body into something leaner, sharper, faster. She didn't just *run* through the wild. She *listened* to it. Watched it. Trained with it. She had studied the fox's footfalls, the squirrel's dodges, the owl's glide, and learned their patterns until they became her own.

At a shallow river crossing, she barely slowed, pouncing from stone to stone with the grace of a dancer mimicking her wild companion. Not so for the pursuer.

Splash! Splash! SPLASH! A string of curse words followed.

Wynn skidded to a halt, doubled back, and scaled the nearest tree in two blinks. Perched high among the leaves like a particularly smug squirrel, she peered down and clapped a hand over her mouth to muffle her laugh. Below her stood a dripping, fuming figure, clothes soaked, boots squelching, and dignity thoroughly drowned.

Wynn grinned, eyes sparkling. "You'll never catch me. I don't know why you even try."

A lump of wet brown rags finally untangled itself and looked up with a soggy scowl, "I'm starting to wonder the same thing."

Wynn perched above, twirling a bit of moss between her fingers. "Oh, come on. You got a little closer this time."

"Don't mock me, Wynn. Not when I look like this."

"I'm not, K. Look, I'm actually out of breath and everything. You gave me a good run." She was absolutely mocking him, just a little.

Hey reader... this is the part of the story where we take a quiet breath and another look backwards. Stories do this sometimes, because the present rarely makes sense without a little context stitched into it. Let me tell you about Kiernan...

Wynn would call him her oldest friend. Not in years, though at the weathered age of twenty, he is technically two years her senior, but oldest in the sense that he's been there the longest. Since the beginning of her after.

They first officially met when Wynn was five and he seven, just days after the fall of Castle Tarn. The smoke hadn't even settled. Like fog that refused to lift, loss was dense and everywhere. Everyone had lost something. Kiernan was no exception.

He never knew his mother, who died giving birth to him. But he was raised in the shadow of his father, a Blue Knight, one of the revered seven sworn to protect the royal family. Kiernan adored him, knowing that one day he would don the same sapphire armor. But on the night of the attack, six of the seven knights fell. The only survivor? His father's closest friend. His godfather.

The traitor.

He is now better known as The Stone, for the coldness that fills the hollow where his heart used to be. It was he who opened the gates from within, who let the Dark Queen's army pour in like ink over parchment. He leads them now, with a scar slashing down one side of his face and a milky-white eye that sees no mercy. Kiernan knows exactly where that scar came from. His father gave it to him—one final act of defiance, blade in hand, as the castle burned around them. A moment burned just as deeply into Kiernan's memory as it was into his skin. He also knows his father died trying to protect Wynn's family. And in the quiet, heavy way that grief can harden into purpose, Kiernan made a choice. He would carry on what his father gave his life for.

As a boy, he begged to be part of the guard, pleaded to be trained, but his father always said, "Maybe when you're older," which, as he and all children know, is adult speak for never. So Kiernan did what children do best: he disobeyed. He snuck into the castle, often through the kitchen door where the scent of warm bread and honeyed tarts made it almost impossible not to linger. He'd steal a pastry or two—always the jam-filled ones, still warm if he was lucky—and sometimes he stayed longer than he should have, watching the bakers work, mesmerized by the quiet rhythm of flour-dusted hands and crackling ovens. But eventually, he'd creep through to the halls beyond, hiding in shadowed corners and behind tall tapestries, watching. Not lurking, just... learning. From those secret perches, he saw her—Wynn. He knew her face. He knew who she was. So when the kingdom fell, and the surviving children of Tarn were herded into wagons, Kiernan stood beside a sobbing, stunned Wynn and made the quietest of promises. No armor. No ceremony. Just a whisper of a vow that she would never be alone. That wherever she went, he would follow. That the legacy of his father's blade would live on, not through steel, but through him.

Most of The Vast believe Wynn and Tierney perished with the rest of her family. But there are whispers, told in low voices when the fire's burned down and the night feels safe enough for hope, that she and her brother survived. That they will rise again, one day, and bring an end to the sleepless reign of The Dark Queen. Kiernan doesn't need whispers. He knows the truth. He's lived beside it. And through every muddy ditch, every sleepless night, every petty theft and near-miss, he's stayed by her side.

He tries. Stars above, does he try. Sometimes too hard. But the truth is, he's not exactly your classic hero material, and his father knew this. He's all heart and elbows, stumbling through plans Wynn makes look effortless, always a half-step behind but never out of sight. Lanky rather than strong, with long limbs and a tangle of awkward energy, he has the look of a man still growing into himself; all sharp edges now, but with the promise of something steadier once he fills out. He moves like someone who hasn't yet made peace with the size of his own feet; forever bumping into corners, knocking over mugs, apologizing under his breath. But for all that, there's a quiet loyalty in him that never wavers. Wynn grew up knowing that she could trust a boy like that, even if he does trip over his own shadow now and then.

Wynn held out her hand to help Kiernan out of the river. His chestnut curls fell in a messy wet mop just above his eyes.

"Thank you, Princess."

She scowled and snatched her hand back just as he grabbed it, causing him to stumble and nearly plunge backward into the water again. "Don't call me that. Ever."

He grinned as he regained his footing, sloshing toward the riverbank with dripping boots and pride slightly dampened. He knew how much she hated the title. That was, of course, exactly why he said it. "Okay, okay. I'm sorry," he said, wringing out his sleeve as they climbed the muddy slope. "What were you doing at the ruins anyway?"

Wynn didn't answer right away. She was already walking, brushing twigs from her tunic, pace quick and shoulders set. Kiernan had to jog to catch up.

"Nothing," she said. "What were you doing there?"

"Looking for you," he replied, hopping over a log and nearly losing his balance again. "Dena came by the farm earlier, looking for you and Avery. Madder than a newly branded bull. Kept going on about you abandoning your duties on the busiest day of the season and how she's going to teach you both a lesson..."

"Dena can leap into the Still for all I care," Wynn said, waving the air in dismissal. "Avery should already be back by now anyway."

"Why are you always antagonizing her, Wynn? Do you actually *enjoy* getting punished? Do you like losing your sleep?"

She let out a low, half-hearted laugh and kicked a pinecone down the path. "I learned a long time ago that that troll of a woman is going to punish me no matter what I do. The least I can do is *deserve* it. Besides, that place would crumble without us servants running it and she knows it."

Ahead of them, Night turned, her silver fur catching the setting sunlight. She paused, ears twitching. "Go on, Night. I'll see you tomorrow," Wynn called softly, flicking her hand in a little wave. The fox hesitated, gave the briefest nod, and then slipped into the underbrush without a sound.

Kiernan watched her go. "How do you know she'll come back?"

Wynn let her eyes settle on where Night had disappeared. "Because she's free."

They walked in silence for a few beats, the forest thinning, the air shifting. "So," she said, side-eyeing him. "Isn't your master missing you?"

"He thinks I'm out chasing a lost horse."

"What happens when you come back without one?"

He flashed a grin. "I'm coming back with *you*, aren't I?"

She punched him in the arm. Hard. "You couldn't catch me if you wanted to." Kiernan rubbed his arm. The comment came out meaner than she meant it, and the silence that followed lingered too long, heavy with something neither of them named. Kiernan's smile faded just slightly. Wynn, as usual, kept her apology to herself.

The trees finally parted, revealing the sun-dappled village of Wickmere below. Chimney smoke curled into the afternoon sky, and the comforting scent of roasted meat and fresh bread drifted upward, wrapping around Wynn like a forgotten memory. Her stomach gave an unhelpful lurch—she hadn't eaten since morning. Down in the lanes, villagers moved like threads in a well-worn tapestry, weaving between carts and stalls, stringing bright ribbons between shopfronts, their voices lifting in cheerful, familiar quarrels. Preparations for the Day of the Fates were in full swing, and the village, with all its crooked chimneys and creaky shutters, seemed to hum with anticipation.

"So," Kiernan said, shaking off the earlier snub. "What are you doing for the festival tomorrow?"

"Probably what I do every day. Serve and clean up after ungrateful slobs who think I was born to wipe their greasy mouths."

"No, I mean *during* the festival."

Wynn shrugged. "I don't know. Watch the games, I guess. What about you?"

"Same," he replied. Keeping the fact that he was going to compete in some of the games to himself. He knew Wynn would say something snide about it, even as her last comment hung in the air.

The Day of the Fates dates back to the origin of The Vast. Legend tells that on the first full moon of the fall harvest, the Fates emerge from their lair to deliver three premonitions, each one a whisper that could shape the year to come. It's one of the few celebrations Queen Prima still allows, perhaps because even she knows better than to cross something older than herself. In every corner of The Vast - Tor or Tarn, noble or no - people mark the day. Because to ignore the Fates is to invite a bad harvest. Or bad luck. Or worse. Wynn called it nonsense.

Her family had celebrated The Day of the Fates with joy, right before the Dark Army reduced everything she knew to ash. Like most stories from her childhood, it now felt like a lie, one meant to lull children into believing the world was kind, or magical, or fair.

It was not.

Now, you, my reading friend, may have heard of the Fates before. Their power, and I do mean literal power (as in, written into the very words of the page), is so strong that they crop up again and again, drifting from one tale to the next like dandelion fluff on the wind. Always three. Often old. Almost always haggish. They've been called many names over the centuries: The Thread Cutters, The Crones, The Watchers, The Spinsters of End and Beginning. But, whether they are real or are simply the talk of legend is unimportant. Their power lies in the belief that they exist. (Yes, I meant *lies* not lays, smarty-pants. It is not a misuse of language. I'm a story. I don't make mistakes when it comes to words).

"Oh," Kiernan said, snapping his fingers like the thought had just walked back into his brain, "I'm supposed to tell you to stop by Anderson's for a sack of potatoes and some onions. For the stew. And that if you don't come back with them, your already tanned hide'll be stretched even thinner."

Wynn let out a long, theatrical sigh. "Fine."

"What's going on with you?"

"It's nothing." It was always *nothing* with Wynn. The truth was, she didn't want to talk about the last good memory she had with her family. She never wanted to talk about her past at all.

~ ~ ~

There now. That's enough for one sitting, don't you think? You've wandered through quite a bit already—autumn forest paths, old castle ruins, and a few things best left in pockets. But stories, like people, need time to breathe. So go on. Set the book down and nestle into the quiet. Pull the blanket up just so. Let your breath find its rhythm, slow and steady, and let your thoughts loosen, like knots undone by gentle fingers. You don't need to hold onto anything right now, not the story, not the world outside these pages. I've got it. I'll keep it safe. Close your eyes, if they're willing. Or don't, if they're not. There's no rush. The story will wait.

Unless, of course, you won't.

In which case, go on, then. I won't stop you. I've seen it before. Just... turn the page softly. Some of us are already drifting off.

CHAPTER THREE

Wickmere square was livelier than usual. Wagons trundled past laden with festival goods, voices rose in cheerful bursts above the crowd, and the scent of spiced cider hung heavy in the air. Wynn slipped into the queue at the vegetable stand while Kiernan hovered nearby, pretending not to.

"You know I can carry a sack of potatoes on my own," she said, eyeing him.

"I'm not here for your potatoes," he muttered, scanning the stall. "I'm here for some rottens. For the pigs."

"Mm. Of course." Her eyes flicked to where his gaze lingered, just a little too long, on a crate of soft blackberries and a bunch of wilting thyme. "Planning another secret bake?"

Kiernan shifted his weight, suddenly very interested in his boots. "I don't bake," he said flatly. "I cook. Sometimes."

"You fuss over spice pairings like someone with a personal grudge against blandness."

His mouth twitched. "Well, shouldn't we all?"

She bumped his arm with her elbow. "Why don't you put something in for the baking competition tomorrow? Your stuff is better than half the things there."

Kiernan scoffed, "Right. Friedrickson barely lets me near the hearth as it is. Says the kitchen makes me soft."

"He's wrong. It makes you interesting."

He didn't answer. Just cleared his throat and reached for a battered basket near the stall's edge, where a few overripe apples were nestled beside some carrots. Wynn didn't push. She never did when it came to this. But she watched the way his fingers hovered over the fruit like he was already tasting what it could become, and smiled, just a little.

As she shifted forward in line, she sensed mischief afoot and something tugged at her attention. A small boy, all bones, face smudged with dirt, was edging along the side wall of the butcher's stall. Kiernan saw him too. The boy moved cautiously, nearly camouflaged against the weathered wood. *Don't do it,* Wynn thought. *Don't do it...* The boy paused, glanced around, then darted forward and snatched a strip of jerky from the drying line. He didn't make it two steps before a thick, calloused hand shot out and grabbed him by the collar. Hans, the butcher himself, had arms like felled tree trunks and a scowl to match. He hoisted the boy off the ground by the scruff of the neck.

Sensing excitement, the crowd began to gather quickly; curiosity, judgment, and the ever-present hunger for a little afternoon drama.

Wynn took an instinctual step forward.

Kiernan's hand caught her shoulder. "Wynn," he warned her, "this doesn't concern you."

She hesitated just long enough for him to think she might listen. Long enough for him to soften his grip. "Wynn, no..."

She quickly slipped his hold and pressed through the forming ring of onlookers until she stood at the front. The boy dangled helplessly from Hans's grip, his legs kicking, eyes wild and wet.

Now, reader, this could've been the beginning. Right here. The would-be thief, the excited crowd, the butcher's grip, and the girl who steps forward when no one else will. It's the kind of moment most stories *love* to open with—bold, cinematic, and full of tension. A heroine revealed in the flare of action, unshakable and sure. And yes, if this were that kind of story, you'd think you knew exactly who Wynn is. Brave. Defiant. Good. But that wouldn't be the whole truth. Because Wynn, like most real people, and all the best characters, is more than her boldest moments. The truth of her lives in the quiet things. In muddy boots and weary silences. In the loyalty she never mentions, the memories she never speaks of. In the rules she breaks and the ones she holds sacred. So no, I didn't begin here. But now that we're in it...

"You dare to STEAL from me?" Hans bellowed.

"Please..." the boy's legs flailed helplessly. "I just needed—"

"I'll show you what you need," Hans raised his open hand to strike.

The boy flinched and cowered as a hand as big as his head took aim and began to move.

"Wait. STOP!" Wynn pushed forward.

Hans froze mid-swing. All eyes, except the boy's, who was shielding his face, turned to her.

"He only took what I told him to take," she stammered.

Hans turned his glare from the boy to Wynn, confusion flickering behind his scowl. She wasn't foolish enough to steal from him. She was smart. Calculated. "Get out of here, Wynn."

"Let's go," Kiernan hissed beside her.

But Wynn didn't budge. She could see the boy trying to wipe the terrified tears streaming down his cheeks. Wynn squared her shoulders. "I said put him down, you Ox-ass. I told him to do it."

A collective gasp from the crowd. Hans's brow folded in slow, stunned disbelief. "What did you call me?"

"You heard me. But just in case your ears are as dull as your knives... Ox. Ass."

That did it. Hans dropped the boy like spoiled meat. The child hit the ground with a grunt and scrambled away without looking back. Wynn could see that he still held the dried meat in his little hand. Good, this wasn't going to be a total loss then.

Sorry... I feel the need to add something in here. While what is about to happen will become a moment that Wynn will remember forever, she will not remember what led to it. She will not carry the boy's name, nor will she ever see him again. Their stories part ways at this very point; hers, winding toward rebellion and legend; his, curling quietly into the pages of a different tale. But what she did today, this small defiance on his behalf, will echo in his life for years to come. It will become one of those defining moments, the kind that roots a person to who they hope to be. One day, that boy will offer kindness to someone else, and they to another, and so on, until the ripple of this single act reaches further than Wynn could ever know. And that's the wonder of stories, dear reader. The little things we do, especially the ones we think will be forgotten, sometimes plant seeds in someone else's life, and bloom.

The butcher turned his full bulk toward Wynn. She was taller than most girls her age, but even she looked small beneath his mountainous frame. He grabbed her arm, fingers like iron bands. She winced but didn't make a sound. "And I suppose you've got the coin to pay for that meat?" he snarled.

Wynn hesitated. She did have coin. A few too many, if anyone were paying close attention. Some normal and some obsidian, marked in ways that raised eyebrows. Servants could have them, sure. But not like this and not Wynn. Everyone in the village knew that Dena was tighter with sleep tokens than a miser in winter. Wynn clenched her jaw. Flashing them now might get her out of this mess... but it would invite questions she couldn't afford to answer. She swallowed. "Of course I don't have anything. I told the boy to get me a sample. To see if it was good enough to bring back to the inn."

"Good enough?" Hans laughed bitterly. "You think you've got the right to judge *my* cuts, you Tarnish gutter-rat?" He shook her, hard. Her shoulder blazed with pain. And then she heard it: the telltale sound of a— *plink*—hitting stone.

The crowd stilled as a single token rolled slowly into view. Hans bent, and as he picked it up, the moment stretched thin and taut.

It was no ordinary coin.

Everyone could see the shade of black, the glint of the marking, etched clean and cruel. Rare. Valuable. Controlled. Hans's eyes widened. "And where did you *steal* this from?"

"It's not mine," Wynn said quickly, voice low, sharp with fear.

"What else are you hiding?" He reached for her again, pawing at her cloak.

She kicked out, "Don't *touch* me, you..."

"WHAT IS THE MEANING OF THIS?" The voice thundered over the market like a breaking storm. Everything stopped. The crowd parted, heads ducking low as Lorkan, Overseer of Wickmere, strode forward with the cold confidence of a man who never had to raise his voice twice. Four members of the Dark Knights flanked him; uniformed, silent, swords bared.

Lorkan's long black cloak swept over the cobbled street as he stepped into the circle of onlookers. Each movement was slow, deliberate, like a predator sizing up a wounded herd. Heads dipped. Eyes dropped. No one dared hold his gaze as he passed.

He had always been described as wolf-like. The crows' feet around his eyes and the ashen beard might suggest a man well past his prime, but closer inspection betrayed that illusion. The scars on his neck, the way he held his staff, not as a crutch, but as a weapon, told another story. Lorkan had seen war. Had survived it. Perhaps even relished it. No one quite knew. What they did know was that respect, in this town, had long since been replaced by fear. He stopped in front of Wynn and turned to Hans. "Explain."

"This Tarn rat—" Hans began.

"I stole from him," Wynn cut in, hoping her defiant admittance might be enough to leave the boy out of it and avoid being searched. It was a dangerous gamble.

Gasps broke through the crowd. Even Hans blinked, stunned. Only Lorkan seemed unfazed, though a flicker of frustration did cross his face. "Is this true?"

Hans straightened. "Well, yes. She did. And the thief had this on her." He held out the token.

"I told you, that's not mine," Wynn said.

"I should say it is not," Lorkan murmured, eyeing the token with disdain. "Wherever it came from, I believe it more than covers the cost of your loss."

"It does," Hans grumbled. "But she *still* stole. What're you going to do about it?"

Lorkan looked down at Wynn, locking cold calculated eyes with hers, but his voice was still aimed at Hans. "What punishment do you believe she is deserving of?"

"Take her to the square!" someone called.

"Seven lashes!"

"Seven lashes fit the crime!" The cries rose like smoke from the crowd, eager, righteous, blood-hungry.

After Queen Prima's conquest, a wooden board had been raised in the center of every village square. Burnt into each plank: a list of crimes and their punishments. Celebrating a banned holiday: three lashes. Theft, depending on the value, anywhere from one to nine. Speaking treason: death by hanging. Reading and writing were forbidden, but no one needed letters to understand that board. Even children could recite it, line by line—fear, after all, is a kind of literacy all its own.

Lorkan raised his hand. Silence fell like a dropped curtain. "Exactly how much of your product was taken?"

Hans furrowed his brow. "Nine chips' worth."

"Nine?!" Wynn barked back. "That's not worth more than three, four when you're feeling stingy!"

"Silence." Lorkan's voice boomed over her. Wynn clenched her jaw but said no more. She met his eyes for only a second. That was enough.

"Nine chips' worth," Lorkan repeated, thinking, calculating. "Then you'll be content with nine lashes?"

Hans hesitated. It was more than most petty thieves had received, but with the crowd behind him, he nodded.

"This matter is settled." Lorkan gestured to the guards. Two pairs of hands grabbed Wynn's arms. "Take the Tarn slave to the square."

As she was dragged away, Kiernan's face appeared in the crowd, only for a second. But in that one glance, she read it all: the helplessness, the frustration, and the unspoken question, *why did you have to get involved?*

The crowd in front of the butcher's had more than tripled by the time they reached the village square. Nothing stirred the people into a frenzy like a good lashing, and it had been a quiet week. Wynn avoided these spectacles whenever she could, though she'd been present for the last one, five lashes to a young servant father accused of stealing an extra loaf of bread. The punishment had been more about the master's pride than the bread. Some people needed to be seen holding the whip. Wynn had looked away with every crack of the lash, every cheer from the crowd. It made her sick. That night, she found the man's family and left them a half-eaten meat pie from the inn.

She'd been whipped before. All Tarn servants had. But never in public. Dena preferred a thin riding crop, the kind meant for horses, or a stick, or whatever was handy. They usually left welts that faded. This... this would leave more than welts.

Why had she stepped in? She knew better. Knew not to interfere. Knew not to draw attention like this. She'd seen children steal before. She'd seen them get caught, punished. But something was happening inside her, some new, raw edge that bristled at the sight of injustice and refused to stay quiet. It was something she could no longer control.

And now that recklessness had led her here.

Lorkan approached without a word. He didn't look at her at first, only reached for the clasp at her neck. The cloak fell away with a tug. But he didn't let it go. His hand lingered, fingers tightening just slightly around the fabric. The extra weight and the faint clink of metal gave her away, subtle, but unmistakable. His eyes flicked to hers then, and something colder passed between them. Wynn swallowed her guilt. He turned the cloak in his hands, found the hidden seam, and curled his hand around the pouch. Still, he said nothing. No accusation. No outburst. Nothing to give her away. Just a slow exhale through his nose and a shake of his head, equal parts frustration and resignation, as he folded the cloak and handed it off to one of the guards.

When he finally looked at her again, she could see the anger in the set of his jaw. "Turn around," he said, voice low.

She obeyed.

Rough hands, not his, took her arms and bound them to the wooden beam. Her shirt was torn down the back, the cool air biting against bare skin and with it, the misplaced thought that Dena was going to be so angry to have to replace another shirt. She heard murmurs ripple through the crowd as Lorkan removed his robe and rolled up his sleeves.

He approached with quiet deliberation, eyes unreadable. "Bite down on this," he said, slipping a worn stick between her teeth. He didn't move right away. She looked up... just once.

It wasn't a plea. It wasn't fear. It was something quieter. Smaller. A flicker of regret, maybe. A silent apology no one else would notice. His expression didn't change. Not for the crowd. Not for her. Then he turned and stepped away, the gravel beneath his boots crackled in the silence.

The crowd hushed, drunk on festive cider and anticipation. Ahead of her, at the edge of the gathering, she saw Kiernan. And then...

"WYNN?!" Avery. Pushing forward, dodging between the legs and shoulders of those too focused to stop her. "WYNN!"

Kiernan caught her before she reached the front. Held her. Barely. Wynn tried to nod. Tried to look brave. She wanted Avery to know it would be all right, even if it wouldn't.

Lorkan's voice rang out. "You have been charged with thieving what is not rightfully yours. By my hand..." a pause, "...and royal order of the Dark Queen, you will receive nine lashes for your crime."

"Let the Tarnish wench suffer!" someone spat from the crowd.

"Teach that piece of Tarn her lesson!"

Wynn gripped the beam. Clenched her jaw tight around the stick. Closed her eyes and tried to imagine that she was—

The first CRACK landed like lightning. A flash of white-hot pain burned across her spine. The second came too fast. And then the third. Her whole body screamed. Somewhere, the crowd had gone silent. Or maybe the pain was louder than everything else.

The fourth blow knocked the stick from her mouth. A cry burst from her lungs before she could stop it.

CRACK.

Another half scream, half grunt.

She couldn't catch her breath. Couldn't think.

CRACK.

There were still more. How many?

CRACK.

Too many.

She swayed. Her knees buckled. The world blurred.

CRACK.

No scream this time. Just silence. Hers and the crowd's.

And then one final blow, but she was too numb to feel it. There was just stillness. Not sleep. Not mercy. Just stillness.

She didn't pass out. She wanted to, the pain *begged* for it the way a plant leans toward light - desperate, instinctive. But unconsciousness hovered at the edges of her mind. Sleep was not hers to take. Not here. Not now. Not in a world where sleep was granted, not fallen into. Many Tarn slaves had tried that trick; unable to get their hands on a token they took drastic actions, tried knocking themselves out, desperate for sleep, but for most, only death awaited.

The magic held her just above the tide, suspended in pain. Awake. She could feel her knees in the dirt. The blood on her back. The ache in her bones. The weight of every eye. Wynn stayed like that for some time, suspended between agony and the place beyond it.

~ ~ ~

Now... reader. I'm sorry. Truly. I wish I could have softened it for you, maybe turned the page before the pain landed or tucked that moment behind something gentler. But stories don't always allow that. Some truths won't be hidden, no matter how we try. They insist on being seen, on being felt. I didn't want you to have to sit with this. But Wynn didn't get that choice. She had to endure every moment. And if you're to walk beside her on this journey, truly beside her, you had to endure it too. Stories like this one have shadows. I won't pretend otherwise. But that's what makes the light matter when it finally arrives. What makes revenge all the more sweet. But maybe, for now, this is where we stop. Just for a while. To rest. To breathe. Wynn can't fall asleep on her own, but you can. And maybe that's a kindness you offer her, without even meaning to. A quiet, unseen mercy. Rest for the both of you. So go on. Close your eyes. Let the story be still. Let your body soften into the sheets. And when you're ready, we'll turn the page—together.

CHAPTER FOUR

Wynn woke up on her stomach, her cheek pressed to a cool, hard surface. The room was warm, lit by the soft crackle of a fire, and thick with the scent of lavender. Everything felt slowed, blurred around the edges. Her mind swam in and out of clarity. She remembered the crowd. The lashes. The weight of her legs giving out beneath her. And then... nothing, save a vague memory of a token pressed into her palm. The mercy of borrowed sleep. Pain anchored her now, a deep, stinging ache across her back, pulsing in waves of heat and chill.

"Try not to move." A chair scraped softly behind her. Lorkan stepped into view, quiet and calm. He held a mug of steaming liquid that smelled awful. "Drink this. It'll dull the pain." His voice was steady, but worn at the edges. "I wrapped your back with a lavender salve. You'll heal, but there will be scars."

She pushed herself up just enough to sip, arms trembling with the effort. "Thank you," she murmured, then let her body ease back down. The table's coolness against her cheek was a small mercy of its own. A soft, familiar lick brushed her fingers.

Night had emerged from beneath the table, whining gently and nuzzling into her hand.

Lorkan watched the fox with something close to wonder. "She clawed at the door minutes after you were brought in. Wouldn't stop until I let her in. She's barely left your side since."

Wynn managed a weak smile and stroked the top of Night's head. The fox gave one more reassuring lick before settling by the hearth, eyes fixed warily on Lorkan and protectively on Wynn. Lorkan pulled his chair around so he sat near her, firelight flickering across his tired face.

"I'm sorry," she whispered before he could speak. A tear fell down the length of her nose and dripped off the tip.

"No sorrier than I." He ran a hand through his silver beard, his voice quieter now, but still edged. "What were you thinking? You're smarter than this. And for what? A few coins and this?" He held up the ring she'd taken. It glinted dully in the firelight.

His gaze sharpened. "Where did you get it, Wynn? Who did you take it from?" His voice had gone grave, heavier than before.

Wynn shrugged, careless. "The royal treasurer. He had plenty on him. I doubt he'll even notice it's gone."

Lorkan didn't answer right away. Something flickered across his face as he stared at it, a recognition he buried before it could take hold. "If anyone else had found this on you..." He didn't finish the sentence. He didn't have to. "Sloppy, Wynn. You can't afford to be this cavalier."

She tried to sit up, wincing as her muscles screamed in protest. "What would you have me do? Let Hans cave in a child's skull? He would've... he would've killed him."

"You think I don't know that?" His voice rose, sharper than before. "You think I don't *see* what this place has turned into? But I can't protect you if you make it impossible." He let out a frustrated breath. "You forced me in a corner. Again."

"You could have suggested fewer lashes," she said, her voice tight.

"And given them reason to question why." His eyes darkened. "You think people don't notice when I show mercy? You think they wouldn't wonder *why* a Tarnish servant girl walks away with half the punishment?"

"You could've picked seven," she snapped. "You could've..." her voice broke. "You didn't have to make it hurt so much."

"Maybe I did." The words fell heavy between them. His shoulders sagged. "I don't know what's gotten into you. Vanishing for days, stealing from Tor nobles, pushing at boundaries you know are there for a reason. You're not even pretending anymore."

She didn't answer. Her chest rose and fell with slow, shallow breaths.

"Defying your owner," he added.

That struck. Her head snapped up. "Dena," she gasped. "How long did I sleep? I was supposed to be back *hours* ago."

"You're not going anywhere," he said firmly, stopping her with a hand before she could slide off the table. "I've already sent word. Paid for extra help out of my own wages. She'll be taken care of."

Her eyes welled, but she blinked them dry. "She'll still be furious."

"Maybe," he said softly. "Probably. But it's better than losing you." There was a long silence. The fire snapped in the hearth. Night gave a low, sleepy grunt. Lorkan moved closer, sitting on the edge of a nearby bench. "Wynn... What's going on?"

She didn't meet his eyes. Her gaze stayed locked on the fire, the flames blurring into streaks of gold.

"I don't know," she turned her head from his. "It's like something's waking up in me. Some kind of beast I can't keep caged. I used to be able to ignore it. The names, the rules, the way they look at us like we're animals..." She thought back to vicious chants calling for her lashes in the square, "But now..." Her voice cracked. "I see someone like Hans about to beat a starving child for trying to eat, and I *can't* just do nothing. I *won't*." She clenched her jaw and turned back to him. "And maybe it's foolish. Maybe it's dangerous. But it's *wrong*, Lorkan. All of it. And I'm tired of pretending it isn't."

His face softened, but he didn't reach for her. "Wynn," he said, voice low. "This path you're walking... it's not safe. Today could've ended far worse. If word travels to the Dark Queen..."

"Let it." Her voice rose like a spark from the fire. "She knows where I am. She *put* me here." She turned and pulled her hair to the side, revealing the small crescent moon behind her left ear. "She marked me, remember? Just in case I forgot I belonged to her." Her eyes burned as she looked back at him. "And you... You're always watching. Always *reporting*. My very own personal shadow."

Now, reader... I know what you're thinking. *Wait? What?* Is Lorkan a good guy or a bad guy? Is he cruel, or kind? What kind of man dresses wounds he helped inflict? The answer, I'm afraid, is complicated. But then again, most real relationships are. And the one between Wynn and Lorkan, well, it doesn't just blur the lines, it redraws them altogether.

This might be a good moment to step sideways from the firelight and take a look at the longer shadows cast by the past. Now, now, I know what you're thinking. *Haven't we done this already? Didn't we talk about the Queen, the massacre, the children left behind?* And yes, we did. Sort of. But the past isn't a clean ledger, it's more like a fogged-up mirror. It clears in patches. It reveals what it wants, when it wants. And stories? Well, the best ones play with you just a little. They give you the truth, but not all at once. They make you lean forward, pay attention, feel the weight of every page. So let's not rush. The reveals come when they're ready, when I think you're ready, and not a moment before. But this one does need some explaining...

You already know the Dark One had the Tarn royal family slaughtered and she let the siblings live. She did not let them live out of mercy. No, mercy isn't something Prima deals in. She let them live because power tastes sweeter when served with control. Because letting them die would have been too quick, too clean. She wanted to *own* them. So she marked them, literally. A crescent moon, inked in just behind the ear, where only a careful eye might notice. A brand of shame. Of belonging. A reminder that no matter how far they ran or how old they grew, they were hers. Then she sent her most trusted knight, the leader of her armies, into a quiet little lakeside village. His orders were simple: become the Overseer. Watch the girl. Report everything. For seven years, Lorkan watched and oversaw, never revealing the truth of his post.

Meanwhile, Wynn was raised in the cramped, soot-streaked backroom of Dena's inn; worked to the bone, unnoticed, unloved. An orphan of war, taught by silence and suffering to forget who she'd once been. And eventually... she did forget. Or thought she had. The mind, after all, is a quiet protector. It tucks away what is too dangerous to carry in the open. Painful memories become stories, then dreams, then nothing at all.

At first, Wynn dismissed the flickers—visions of gold and ash, of sunflower fields and lullabies—as childish fantasy. The kind of nonsense a girl might dream up to survive. The real princess of Tarn was dead. Everyone knew that. And all the while, Kiernan, just a boy himself, kept her secret too. He never uttered a word. Not even to her, especially not to her.

It wasn't until she turned twelve that something began to shift. She'd gone into the woods, chasing mushrooms or berries or a bit of solitude, it doesn't really matter. What matters is that she got lost. And while trying to find her way back, she found something else entirely. A ruin. Half-buried in moss and ash. Cracked stone walls swallowed by creeping vine. The wreckage of a place spoken of only in hushed tavern stories: the old Tarn castle.

They said it was cursed. Haunted. No one dared go near it. But Wynn didn't feel fear as she stepped up the familiar stairs. She felt... called. Like the stones remembered her footsteps. Like the air itself was holding its breath, waiting for her. She wandered into the shell of what had once been a throne room, and something inside her, some old, buried part, shuddered awake and a thick fog rolled in. Not just the weather kind, but the kind that lives behind the eyes. Her chest tightened. Voices echoed—her mother's, crying out. Blood pooled where there was none. Ash turned to embers. Her small hands were tugged by invisible arms. Hide. Run. Remember.

And then a voice, sharp and unfamiliar, snapped her back to the now. "It happened here."His voice sounded hollow in the open space.

Her head snapped around. A figure clad in a long black cloak, a staff at his side, stood statuesque at the crumbling entrance. She recognized him instantly. Everyone in town knew the Royal Overseer. You didn't mistake that silhouette. Wynn had only ever seen him from a distance. His name was spoken in hushed tones, always with fear. He was the Dark One's enforcer. A shadow that punished.

But for Wynn, it wasn't just fear. There was something else. Something terrifyingly familiar about his darkened complexion. She had seen it before. In this place. In her nightmares. Instinctively, she backed away.

"You don't have to worry. I won't come any further than you want me to."

She slowed, but kept edging toward the nearest escape. "Did... did you follow me here?"

He nodded. Her heart thundered in her chest, pounding confusion through every vein. "I, um... kn-know I'm not supposed to be here," she stammered. "It was a mistake. I got lost, and I..." She turned and started to run.

"WYNN OF THE TARN."

The name landed like a strike. "Do not leave. It is no mistake, and you are not lost. You are exactly where you should be."

Wynn froze mid-step. No one had ever called her that before. Wynn *of the Tarn*. Slowly, she turned back toward him. True to his word, he hadn't moved.

"Do you know who I am?" There was something new in his voice now. Not power. Not command. Unease.

"You're the Royal Overseer."

"Is that all you know of me?" The wind began to rise, whistling through broken walls. They had to shout now just to be heard.

"Is there more I should know?" she yelled back, defiant.

The Overseer smirked. "You recognize me?"

Was that a question, or a test? She said nothing. Better not to guess. Better not to answer.

"I'll tell you then. But I ask that you either let me come closer, or you come toward me. What I'm about to say must not be overheard... and this forest has ears."

Wynn looked toward the stone steps, the remains of what once had been a throne. She crossed the ruined floor and sat down, warily nodding in agreement. The Overseer stepped forward, and she saw it for the first time: the limp.

"A wound from battle," he offered, settling beside her with a groan. She cast a glance toward the nearest exit.

"Don't worry," he added with a dry smile. "You could outrun me."

"Would it matter?" she asked. "You could still have me tracked down and killed."

He laughed. Not a joyful sound, more like a sound he didn't use often. "I could. But I won't. I promise you that." He folded his hands. "I'm going to tell you something," he said. "Please don't interrupt and don't leave until I'm finished. After, I'll answer any question you ask truthfully. Deal?"

Wynn hesitated, fighting every urge to run. She nodded.

"Good." He paused. Took a breath. And said the words he'd held in silence for far too long. "My name is Lorkan. I used to be the leader of the Tor... of the Dark One's army. And you... you are Wynn, Princess of the Tarn. Our paths have crossed before."

The world tilted. Something inside her shifted. He was telling the truth. She *knew* he was. Somehow, she had always known.

Lorkan saw the recognition in her face and nodded. "You know it. You were standing right there," he said, motioning to the floor, "the day it happened."

Wynn looked at the spot he had motioned to, and the room around her seemed to dissolve. The stone floor, the broken walls, even the wind, all of it faded beneath the weight of memory. It happened here.

She was small again, ripped from the warmth of her bed and cradled against her mother's chest as they fled through torch-lit corridors. She remembered the heat of her mother's skin, the hurried footsteps, the sound of her name whispered like a prayer. They had entered the throne room. Her family was already gathered, encircled by a wall of Blue Knights - loyal, tall, unshaking. Her mother knelt with her behind the throne. "Be brave," she whispered. "Don't be afraid." But Wynn had seen the fear in her eyes.

Then the doors exploded inward. Voices—shouting, cruel and loud—filled the chamber. A flood of black-armored soldiers stormed the room like a wave crashing down. Her mother's hands moved quickly to shield her eyes, but Wynn remembered the feeling. The scream caught in her throat. The chaos. The sound of steel. And then... nothing. Everything had gone black. Except...

"You were there." The words slipped from her lips like a breath she didn't know she was holding. It wasn't a question. It was an accusation.

Lorkan nodded. “I led the army in.” His voice was steady, though heavy with something she couldn’t name. “What else do you remember?”

She shook her head. “Nothing really. It just... it goes dark after that.” She was lying. She just couldn’t say the next part out loud.

He didn’t look convinced. “Your parents were killed. That much you know. You and your brother were taken. Your lives were spared. The Queen had you both marked with that tattoo behind your ear.” Wynn’s hand flew to her neck, fingertips pressing against the spot just beneath her ear. She had only ever seen it reflected faintly in the still water of the well when she was tasked to retrieve water. A smudge of a crescent she’d assumed was a birthmark.

“Your brother was taken to be trained as a Knight in the Queen’s Dark Army. You, as you already know, were sold into slavery to Dena and the inn. She doesn't know who you are. In case you were wondering.” His expression softened. “And I was ordered to be your keeper. The Queen tasked me... has continued to task me, with watching you. Reporting on you. That’s why I am the Overseer of the Lakeside region and Wickmere village. I was placed there for you.”

He paused, watching her, then continued, “Do you have questions?”

She didn’t hesitate. “My brother is alive?”

Lorkan nodded.

“Does he know I’m alive?”

“I don’t know.”

“Where is he?” She demanded to know.

“I don’t know. Training with the Dark Guard, I think.”

She frowned, eyes narrowing. “Why are you telling me this now?”

Lorkan opened his mouth, then closed it again. The answer didn’t come easily, not because it wasn’t there, but because it hurt to speak aloud. He looked away, to the corner of the ruined room where vines had begun to reclaim the stone.

"I once had a family," he said finally. "A beautiful wife. Two children—a boy and a girl. They were six and eight. We lived a quiet life. My people were farmers. Generations of us. My father grew gourds in the fall and berries in the summer. The best strawberries you've ever tasted, I promise you. My daughter... She loved them more than anything. If she was ever missing, I'd find her in the fields, knees stained with mud, face covered in berry juice." A quiet smile flickered across his face. "She was wild... a bit like you." The smile faded. "Tarn's Blue Knights attacked while I was out foraging for wild mushrooms. I came back to find nothing but soot, bone and ash. They were gone."

Wynn's breath held still in her chest.

"After that," he continued, "I gave myself to the Tor. To the army. I was angry. Furious. And grief can make monsters of us all. I advanced through the ranks, determined to make the Tarn suffer the way I had. Revenge was the only thing that gave me direction. When your parents took power, there was peace for the first time in centuries... but I wasn't ready for peace. I couldn't believe it would last. I couldn't forgive." He gave her a long look. "Eventually, I stepped down as Commander. I left the army for a time."

"Did you return to your farm?" Wynn asked, her voice quiet now.

"No," he said, almost gently. "That wasn't my home anymore." He didn't offer more about those missing years, and Wynn didn't press. "I was called back after the King died," he said. "After the Hundred Day Sadness. When Prima became... what she is now. I was reinstated as leader. And you know what followed."

He looked down at his hands, as though they might still be stained with that past. "Something changed in me after the Tarn attack. Something I couldn't explain. I carried out my orders, but

I felt it in my bones that I was not the man I had once been. The Queen knew. That's why she reassigned me. Why she sent me to you. Not to protect you. Not truly. Just to watch. To control."

He turned to face her fully. "But I've watched you grow, Wynn. I've seen you become clever and bold, fierce and soft-hearted. I've seen what kind of person you are. And I believe you'll be a better ruler than any this land has known.

"The Vast is dim now," Lorkan continued, his voice quieter, though no less sure. "Shadowed by fear and cruelty. I no longer wish to live in such a place." He paused again, letting the silence stretch just long enough. Then added, more bitterly, "I've watched sleep, a gift granted by the ancient gods, become a weapon. I've seen it used to control, to punish, to divide. I've seen it withheld from children, bartered like coin, doled out in tokens to those willing to do unspeakable things. It's not right. It is not just the body that breaks without sleep, it is the mind, then the spirit. And Prima knows it, it's the root of her power. And I cannot abide by it any longer."

Wynn's throat tightened. There were tears burning at the edge of her vision, but she didn't let them fall.

He hesitated, then finally said the thing he hadn't yet dared to speak. "I believe... I hope... that one day, you will be the one to change that."

"I can't fight the Dark Queen," she said, her voice barely audible.

"No," Lorkan agreed. "Not right now you can't. But one day, you'll be faced with a choice. You'll either shape the path ahead of you, or a path will be shaped for you. I want to prepare you, Wynn. If you'll permit me, I will train you. I'll teach you the histories they've buried. I'll show you how to fight, how to move through this land like it belongs to you... because it does."

He stepped closer, just enough for her to see the resolute seriousness in his eyes. "But no one can know. This must remain between us. To those around you, I am the Overseer, and you are no better than any other Tarn peasant. We do not know each other. Do you understand? Your life depends on this. And so do the lives of those closest to you."

Wynn looked up at him, searching his face for any hint of deception. "Do I have a choice?"

"You will always have a choice," he said gently. "That's what makes you different."

She didn't answer right away. The wind had picked up again, curling through the broken walls of the old castle, making the empty place feel haunted. She looked at the spot where her family had stood, at the scarred stone, and felt a flicker of something rise in her; an ember of memory of who she used to be, a flash of defiance.

"Were you there?" she asked, the question a low murmur. "When my parents were killed?"

Lorkan closed his eyes and drew in a long, slow breath. "Yes." He didn't elaborate. He didn't need to. Wynn had heard enough.

She stood, brushing the dirt from her trousers. Lorkan winced slightly as he pushed himself up with the help of his staff and came to stand beside her.

"So... I am a princess," she said, more to herself than to him. It wasn't a question—just a truth she hadn't asked for, slipping into place like a key in a lock she hadn't meant to open.

Lorkan nodded. "Tarn royal blood."

She let out a short breath, almost a laugh. "Princess," she whispered again. The word tasted strange. Heavy. She looked out across the crumbled edges of what had once been a life, her life, if what he said was true. Her fingers curled into fists. All those mornings she'd woken with that aching, breathless sense that she'd forgotten something vital, like a name she should've remembered or a place she'd once belonged. And now here it was. Not imagined. Not forgotten. Just buried.

She didn't know if she could trust him. Or herself. Or this. She didn't know if she wanted to be anything more than what she already was. But what did she have to lose?

She squared her shoulders. "When do you want to get started?"

Lorkan half-smiled, the closest his weathered face ever came to a true one. "Two days from now. I'll meet you here after your morning chores are finished."

He turned to go, then paused. "Oh, and bring Kiernan. That boy already knows who you are, and I could use his help in training you."

Wynn blinked. "Kiernan knows?"

"I'll let him tell you the rest."

"But... how do you know he knows?"

Lorkan's smirk was subtle but unmistakable. "Wynn, as you'll come to learn, I am aware of everything I need to be aware of. That is why I am the Overseer."

She narrowed her eyes. "I thought *I'm* the reason you are the Overseer."

A small chuckle escaped him. "So you are." He turned, starting toward the broken archway at the edge of the ruins. Stone crumbled under his boots. Wynn watched him go, her chest tight with uncertainty. She didn't move.

"How do I know I can trust you?" she called after him.

Lorkan paused beneath the arch, the light slanting gold across his shoulders. He didn't look back when he spoke, but his voice was steady. Kind, even. "You don't," he said simply. "Not yet. Trust is a slow-growing thing, like roots beneath stone. It takes time. And choice. But if we're lucky, Wynn, we'll both come to earn a bit of it from each other." Then he stepped through the arch and was gone, leaving only silence and the whisper of wind through the ruins.

Six years had passed since that day at the ruins, and Lorkan had made good on his promise. Under his tutelage, and with Kiernan's eager, if occasionally chaotic, help, Wynn was schooled in the histories of The Vast, taught to defend herself with fists, feet, and bow, and shown how to move through the forest like it was part of her. The training was hard, sometimes brutal. Lorkan never went easy on her. He never coddled her, never treated her like a princess or even like a girl. And Wynn loved him for it.

He built obstacle courses strung with traps and pitfalls. He timed every run and made her beat her own records. She often returned home scraped raw and sore-limbed, her tunic torn, her shins painted with mud and blood. Once, she misjudged a jump over a ravine, went tumbling fifteen feet down, and landed with a broken arm and a mouth full of pine needles. Dena punished her for the injury, called her careless, docked her a night's sleep and doubled her chores for months after. Wynn didn't complain. If anything, she considered the break worth the lesson. She learned to land better after that.

To someone like Kiernan, watching from the outside, and perhaps even to you, it might seem obvious that the bond between Wynn and Lorkan has grown into something deeper than teacher and student. And while it's tempting to simplify, to say he fills the role of a father and she, the ghost of a daughter lost, that would only scratch the surface. Their bond has been earned through shared bruises and silent secrets, through unspoken trust and shared loss. They carry a truth that could unravel their lives, and because of that, their connection isn't sentimental, it is steel.

Now, Lorkan sat near the hearth, the small stolen ring rolling between his fingers, catching glimmers of firelight with each spin. Wynn sat across from him, cross-legged, her face painted in warm gold and flickering shadow. The roundness of her cheeks had sharpened over the years; the wide-eyed girl had been replaced by someone leaner, watchful, a young woman on the cusp, not yet grown but nearly there, halfway across the bridge from childhood to something far more dangerous.

"Wynn," Lorkan said, the ring slowing in his hand, "I won't always be by your side." She didn't look up. "You have to learn to master your emotions. Keep a calm and steady head. You must assess the risks and..."

"...choose my battles wisely," she finished, waving her hand and rolling her eyes. "And I always need to see the bigger story, weigh my choices and my actions. I know. I've heard this speech before. A few times."

He raised a brow at her, unimpressed.

She grinned, briefly, but then her smile faded. She hated when he talked like that, as if he were making preparations to vanish. It felt like a threat, not a warning. She'd noticed the changes, of course, the white strands overtaking the silver in his beard, the stiffness in his shoulders that lingered longer than it used to. The lines in his face had deepened, too, tugging toward his jaw like vines growing down a wall. But he wasn't old. Not *old* old. Not in the way that felt permanent. She wasn't ready to imagine the world without his voice in it, stern, sharp, steady. Like bark worn smooth over time. He still had years left. She was certain of it. Or maybe that was just what she needed to believe.

Wynn shook her head, "Besides, what does it matter what I do or don't do? Prima knows where to find me."

"Wynn, you can't be causing problems. Making yourself stand out. If she thinks you've become a threat..." He trailed off, not wanting to finish the thought.

"So what? Didn't you raise me for this? Train me for this?" She barked back.

Lorkan sighed, "You're not ready yet." A soft knock tapped at the back door. Night raised her head and started to thump her tail against the wooden floor. Lorkan stood. "You may enter, Kiernan."

The wood groaned open and Kiernan stepped inside, his curls falling just over his eyes. He caught sight of Wynn on the table, splotches of blood seeping through the bandages wrapped tight around her back, and quickly looked away, as if he'd intruded on something too private. It wasn't like he hadn't seen her bare before. Their childhood summers were soaked in lake water and laughter, where clothes were an afterthought. But those carefree days shifted when time began reshaping their bodies, when innocent glances grew weighted with meaning neither of them yet knew how to carry.

Wynn noticed his discomfort, but the ache in her back had dulled any appetite for teasing. "It's alright, K. It doesn't hurt that much." A lie. They all knew. But she was always lying about pain. Even with a broken arm, she'd insisted it was just a bruise.

"It's almost midnight, I've uh... come to escort you home," Kiernan stammered.

"Escort me? What a gentleman. I think I can manage just..."

"She'll go with you," Lorkan cut in, firm. "I gave her a tonic, but it can hit hard. Make sure she gets to the inn without any... further incidents." Wynn let out a groan. "ANY FURTHER INCIDENTS," Lorkan repeated with the steel of an Overseer.

"Okay, settle down, old man. I get it. Keep me on a leash."

"If only I could," he muttered with a smirk.

She slid off the table with a sharp breath and a wobble. Night sprang up, and Kiernan was at her side in a blink, steadying her with a hand at her elbow and another on her hip. "My hero," she said dramatically, lifting her eyes to meet his, but his expression stayed sober. No banter tonight.

She let him help her into her cloak. "Can I have the ring?" she asked, knowing the answer before it came. Lorkan's scowl was answer enough. "Fine. Keep it. It's ugly anyway."

"And I'll be keeping the rest of your haul as well. For safe keeping." But they both knew it was a second punishment for her behaviour.

Wynn shook her head and then pulled her hood up with practiced motion, shielding her anger. "Night?"

At her name, the fox's ears perked. She stretched languidly by the hearth, then trotted over and gave Wynn's hand a single, deliberate lick before returning to the warmth with a soft huff. She curled tighter into herself, but Wynn caught the flick of her tail. She would've come, if asked. Wynn knew that.

"She can stay here until I turn in," Lorkan gave in reluctantly.

"Give her some stew? She's probably hungry."

"If she behaves," Lorkan replied, though his tone was lighter now. He cast a glance toward the fox, who was comfortably resettled by the fire, eyes half-lidded, looking far too dignified to misbehave.

"Training in two days?"

Lorkan shook his head. "You'll need at least a week to begin healing. Rest. We'll meet under the next full moon. Please, try to stay out of trouble until then."

"No promises," she said with a grin.

"Why would I ask something I know you can't keep?"

She turned to the door. "Until the next full moon, Overseer."

He inclined his head. "Until then, Tarn slave." Just as the hem of her cloak slipped through the frame, Lorkan called out, "Wynn?"

She paused but didn't turn. She knew by the tone in his voice that this was an apology. She bowed her head... and was gone.

The day's sun had long disappeared behind the western mountains, and a dry bite rode the chilly night air. Wynn, with Kiernan close at her side, made her way back toward the inn. Less than two hundred yards now. Through the dark, the golden glow of the center lodge fire spilled through the open windows ahead, silhouettes of drinking patrons moving about like shadows in a dream. It was past midnight, but the evening was in full swing.

The "No Vacancy" sign swung from the front steps, crooked on its nail. Normally, that task was hers. Had Avery done it in her absence? Or, had Dena actually lifted a finger herself? If it had been Dena, Wynn knew she would hear about it before the night was done.

Her back throbbed, and with every step, the ache grew sharper. It was the busiest night of the year and it was going to be a long one.

"You haven't said a word to me since we left Lorkan's." She turned her head slightly. "K? Say something."

"Like what?"

"I don't know. Something."

"I'm not mad at you," he said. "If that's what you're asking."

"But you are mad. At Lorkan?"

"No... well, yes. Sort of. But..." His brow furrowed. "It should've been me. I shouldn't have let you stop Hans. I should've jumped in. Or helped you. Or... something. But I just stood there. And then Lorkan showed up, and people started circling, and..." He kicked at a loose stone in the path, trying to vent his frustration, but instead of skittering away, it held firm under his boot. With a sharp yelp, he stumbled forward, stubbing his toe and nearly pitching face-first into the dirt.

Wynn bit her lip, hard, to keep from laughing. A tiny snort still escaped her.

He shot her a wounded look. "It wasn't *that* funny."

"It kind of was."

She stepped beside him, laying a hand gently on his shoulder. He flinched but didn't fully shrug it off this time.

"Kiernan, today was not your fault. I wasn't thinking when I jumped in. There was nothing you could've done, and I wouldn't have wanted you punished too." She didn't say what she often said, that she didn't need his protection. He'd heard it before, and each time, it left a wound. "I'm glad you stayed with Avery. She needed you."

"You needed me," he whispered.

"Alright. Next time, I'll let you take the lashes. Deal?"

He rolled his eyes. "Why do I even bother?"

"Because you love me and can't resist my natural charm?"

Thankfully, the dark concealed his blush. "Oh yes. That must be it. The charm. I think that tonic's affecting your brain."

She smiled. The edge of pain softened a little by his teasing tone. "Thanks for walking me back," she said.

The inn's laughter grew louder as they neared the rear entrance, raucous voices rumbling through the walls. The tonic's effects were fading fast, leaving a thousand hot needles in its place.

Kiernan reached to steady her, saw the pride stiffen in her jaw, and hesitated, then pulled his hand back. "I can stay," he offered. "Help out for a bit. Or..."

They heard the creak of the storage barn door swing open and slam shut. Avery appeared a moment later, a stack of ale bottles cradled in her arms. She nearly dropped them when her eyes landed on Wynn. Her mouth parted, her brow drawn tight, every muscle in her face caught between fury and relief. She marched forward stiffly and then set the ale down on the dirt with trembling hands.

"You're—" she began, but her voice broke. And then she was wrapping her arms around Wynn, pulling her close in a grip so tight it knocked the wind from her. Wynn flinched with a hiss, pain streaking up her spine. Avery jerked back instantly. "Sorry! I didn't... I didn't think..."

"It's alright," Wynn whispered, blinking through the pain. "It's okay."

Avery was crying now, wiping her cheeks with the sleeve of her shirt like she could scrub the fear away. "When that first lash hit," she whispered, "and then I watched you fall to your knees and I couldn't... I thought... I thought I was going to lose you."

"You didn't," Wynn said softly, brushing a strand of hair from Avery's face. "I'm right here, A. I always will be."

Avery nodded, but her throat bobbed as she swallowed back the sobs. "Dena is livid," she added after a beat. "I tried to cover for you, to get all the jobs done."

The back door slammed open and Dena stumbled into view, arms overloaded with a mess of kitchen scraps. Grease-stained apron, bun unraveling like some half-dead bird's nest, strands of sweaty hair pasted to her fat flushed cheeks. She halted at the sight of them. A half-eaten bun and picked-over bones dropped from her grasp, landing in the dirt.

"Well, well, well," she sneered. "Look who's decided to grace us with her magical presence."

"I'll handle her," Wynn muttered to Avery, straightening with effort. "Go on. Take the ale before she sees you slacking." Avery listened, ducking her head as she quickly moved past Dena and into the inn.

Wynn tried to smile, "Dena, I..."

The heap of garbage landed in Wynn's arms. A second later came the backhand, sharp and fast. "I don't want to hear it. Take that out, then wash the waste buckets in the privies, they're overflowing again. Tables need clearing. Mugs need filling."

Wynn swallowed her pride and the sting in her cheek. "Yes, Ma'am."

"Don't 'yes, Ma'am' me. Just get your lazy Tarn ass to it. The patrons aren't going to serve themselves." She paused and then jabbed a finger back at Wynn. "And don't think we're not gonna talk about what happened today. Gossip of the whole bloody town, it is. Hans came through here puffed up like a boiled goose, said you stole from him right under his nose. I don't have time for that mess tonight, but I'll deal with *you* later, you can be sure of that." She sneered, taking a step closer. "No servant of mine crosses Hans and walks away clean."

"She didn't walk away clean," Kiernan said, barely louder than a breath. Wynn had almost forgotten he was there.

Dena whirled on him, eyes narrowed. "What did you say?"

Wynn met his eyes, a soft warning not to make it worse. Kiernan's fists clenched at his sides, "Nothing. I said nothing."

"Good for nothing, that's for sure." Dena shoved Wynn forward with a hand on the back, exactly where Wynn's flesh was torn and tender. Wynn gasped, lips clamped shut to keep the sound inside. "Get your ass to work." Kiernan took a step toward her.

"And *you*," Dena snapped, whirling on him, "I'd imagine your feeble bag of Tarnish flesh is needed elsewhere. Must be nice to have all this free time, wandering around like a stray dog. If I were your owner, I'd tie a rope 'round you. In fact, maybe I will tell him to do just that. Remind you where you belong. Now get..." She kicked out at the air near Kiernan.

Kiernan jumped to the side and scrambled to leave; taking one last look at Wynn as she disappeared into the inn.

~ ~ ~

This is the part of the story where it would be nice to return to the warm hut, to the crackling fire and the quiet place where regret and hope share a room. To stew-scented air and the fox still waiting, just in case there's one last scrap left in the pot. A chair rocks gently where someone once sat. Firelight flickers against stone walls and worn wood. But life, especially Wynn's, is rarely made of soft places. It doesn't wait for healing or warmth. It calls with sharp voices and cold hands, pulling forward even when the body aches and the soul is still half-stitched. And so the story moves on, with clattering dishes and cruel commands, into the ache of memory and the weight of what must be done. But, perhaps, you can pause here. Let the firelight fade behind your eyelids. Let the chill stay beyond your blankets. Find your own stillness, your own warm room, your own quiet place to rest. Sleep well.

CHAPTER FIVE

Imagine, if you will, sitting atop the clouds. Or better yet, perched on the back of a silent hawk gliding beneath the stars, its wings stretched wide over a sleeping world. Below, the land is cloaked in a hush, the colors of day melted into shades of silver and shadow. But look closer, and you'll see autumn still clinging to the edges. dusky golds and deep coppers softened by moonlight, trees swaying gently in the chill.

Lakes gleam like spilled ink, catching the sky's reflection in still ripples. The white river still runs—quieter now, but no less purposeful—as it cuts through valleys and darkened woods. And there, tucked into the folds of the land, are clusters of rooftops, browned with age and dusted with starlight. Chimneys breathe out thin ribbons of smoke, the scent of wood fires curling into the air. From this height, it all looks peaceful. Small lives, warm hearths. A patchwork of stories resting beneath the night. You can almost see how everything fits together. How this village touches and connects to that town through a winding dirt road, how one life nudges another, and another, and another still. This is the world of the story. And the story, dear reader, sees everything: Wynn scrubbing sticky mead from tabletops and Avery sweating in a flour-caked kitchen, and Dena throwing orders at her useless slaves. It sees Kiernan trudging home, Lorkan by the fire with pipe smoke curling like sleepy thoughts into the rafters as a black ring rotates in his fingers, and Night, the fox, curled close to his boots, ears twitching in dream. It even sees the Dark Queen, who at this very moment has slipped the notice of her guards and is scaling the frostbitten cliffs of the Northern Tor with only the wind and her secrets for company.

Yes, we can see her. But we will return to her later.

For now, let us drift, soft as a feather, down from the clouds, down past the cliffs and trees and rooftops, until we find a particular tower tucked in a sparse forest clearing behind the Tor side of the roaring Still River. There, tucked into the night and wrapped in warm candlelight, is a girl sitting cross-legged on a cushion, her hands resting atop a worn book, her eyes drawn wide with wonder.

Her name is Grace.

Wynn and Grace have two things in common. They are both eighteen years old. And they are both of royal blood. But that is where the similarities end.

Grace is a princess in the classic storybook sense of the word. Not the cheeky kind who steals carriages or the muddy sort who hides in forests. No, Grace is the kind raised behind stone walls, watched day and night, schooled in manners and morals, and told, frequently, exactly how many steps she may take away from the castle (one hundred, no more). She's tried to sneak past that invisible tether many times, and every time she's been caught, stopped, gently (and sometimes forcefully) redirected.

In fact, because stories are so much of her world, she has modeled herself after many of the classic princesses she's read about, kind, brave, unflinchingly noble. The ones who wait patiently in towers or gardens, who sing to birds and hope for rescue, even if they never say so aloud. And when it comes to

Evil Queen Mothers? Well, Grace could write a book. A very sad, slightly rage-filled memoir. She hasn't seen her mother in twelve years. And calling her "mother" feels like a lie told too many times. But still, there are traces. The mirror does not lie. Long copper hair falls down Grace's back in soft waves. Her eyes, a light amber brushed with flecks of gold, catch the light like the last leaves of autumn. They are the first things people notice, with some servants pausing to stare a little too long, and the things she avoids noticing herself. Because they remind her of *her*. Of the woman who once cradled her with warm hands. Of bedtime lullabies and gentle whispers. Of a love that vanished like fog in the sun.

For brief moments, from the outside looking in, one might envy her life. Anything Grace requests is brought to her, and if it cannot be found, it is made. Gowns of the finest cloth and lace line her wardrobe. Hot bubble baths are drawn each evening. Beds are made, floors swept, and every meal arrives with three to five courses of the best food The Vast can provide. And part of her believes this is exactly what a princess's life is supposed to be. She has, after all, read the stories.

Stories of princesses kept in towers, of stepmothers with cold smiles and cruel rules, of young girls raised apart from the world and told that one day, perhaps, something or someone will come to change everything. Grace once found comfort in these tales, how neat and familiar they made her strange life feel. How they promised that to be locked away was simply part of the path.

And like so many of us, Grace has been shaped by what she reads. That's the thing about stories: they don't end when the book is closed. Whether the reader knows it or not, it lingers, like a literary kiss left on the cheek, gentle but impossible to forget; a borrowed heartbeat, a hidden thread, a choice that settles quietly beneath the skin. Stories shape us as we take them in, breath by breath, word by word, and in return, we shape them too. And this one, although Grace doesn't know it yet, is beginning to shift beneath her feet.

The people who surround her—caretakers, cooks, servants—do not speak. They've been ordered not to. In her younger years, she tried. A friendly word here, a question there. Some even answered, quietly and quickly. But the castle listens, and those who spoke one day were gone the next. So now they remain silent. And she, mostly, does too. Only her tutors are permitted conversation, brought in weekly to recite lessons in music and mathematics and the structured things that can be memorized but not truly lived. And then there's the keeper of the castle. The quiet man tasked with keeping a watchful eye on her, the one who has remained at her side through the years, steady and unreadable.

She calls him Lorkan.

Yes. The very same. A man with many secrets, so it would seem.

The first light of morning had barely stretched across the Still River when Grace spotted the familiar flicker of movement through the trees. Her breath caught, not that she'd admit it. She leaned against the stone windowsill, the chill seeping through the fabric of her nightdress. Below, just breaking from the forest shadow, was a rider cloaked in black, his horse cutting clean lines into the frost-hardened path. She watched without moving. He always came like this; early, quiet, slipping in like smoke through a crack in the wall. She suspected even those who served the castle didn't know he was here half the time.

He was never loud, never particularly friendly, but Grace liked him more than anyone else in her life. His visits didn't follow a strict schedule, yet they came often enough that she learned to expect him when the moon tilted a certain way or the wind came from the north. He brought with him the scent of outside air and unspoken things. Over the years, his grumpy-old-man gruffness had softened into something else, something quieter, perhaps even a kind of compassion, though he would never admit it, and she would never ask him to.

She hurried from the window as the familiar heavy tread of boots echoed up the tower stairs. There was no knock, there never was, and the door creaked open just as she flopped with intentional casualness onto the edge of her chair.

"You're earlier than normal," she said, without turning.

"You're always watching," he replied. He seemed tired, his voice gravelier than normal. His old frame crossed the room, trying to hide his limp as he always did, and dropped a cloth-wrapped parcel onto her desk. "And your posture is terrible."

"I prefer it that way," Grace said, sitting straighter anyway. "You know, like a tragic heroine." He grunted. Somewhere in the depth of his chest, maybe that was amusement. She tilted her head. "You know, you could bring flowers next time. Or anytime."

He wasn't in the mood for banter. "Too delicate. They'd die on the ride."

"Everything dies eventually, Lorkan. Even your jokes."

His lips twitched, barely. *Teenagers,* he thought. Always performing. Always trying to be both too old and not old enough. And girls, in particular. Impossible creatures. One moment sighing at a sunrise, the next daring the world to challenge them. He was raising two of them, in a manner of speaking, and still had no idea how he managed to keep up.

He unwrapped the parcel. A book, bound in aged leather with embossed gold script curling across the spine, and beneath it, a small tin painted dark blue and flecked with silver stars.

Grace's eyes brightened at the sight of the tin. She jumped up, "Is that...?"

"Sparkfire," he said dryly. "Not enough to burn the place down. Don't test it."

She took the tin with reverence, turning it in her hands like a jewel. "Where do you get this stuff?"

"I have my..."

"Ways," she finished his sentence, knowing he was never going to tell her his secrets.

"It's not much, but at least you can celebrate a little."

"I will make it a grand celebration. Alone and by myself," her smile softened as she set the tin beside the book, her fingertips tracing along its worn spine. "And this one?"

Lorkan folded his arms, his voice neutral but not without a glint of meaning. "*The Hollow Prince.* An old tale from the days when Tor and Tarn still traded stories. A prince turned to stone by a sorcerer's curse, he comes alive only at night and falls in love with a princess, but if she ever learns the truth about him, she'll be turned to stone too."

Grace tilted her head, curiosity already stirring. "That's rather tragic."

"You said you wanted an adventure," Lorkan replied.

"But it sounds like more of a love story."

Lorkan ignored her disappointment. "The epilogue is interesting."

She glanced up at him, surprised. He rarely gave opinions on the books. "That's more detail than you usually offer."

He shrugged, already turning to go.

She looked down at the book, fingers hovering over the faded lettering. "Thank you."

He watched her for a moment, noting the wear in her gaze. There was a tiredness she tried to mask, a quiet kind of restlessness that even her most beloved stories could no longer reach. He'd seen it recently, in Wynn. That same flicker of something stirring beneath the surface. So different, those two. Wynn was lightning and wind, sharp, sudden, impossible to contain. She demanded presence, fast thinking, a firm hand and a quicker mind. Grace, on the other hand, was morning mist and gently lapping water, soft, slow to move, but deep in ways you might not notice until she had you under her spell. She asked for gentleness, patience, and an ear willing to listen all the way to the end of her thoughts... which could be drawn out sometimes.

Yes, they were different elements, opposite forces. But both shaped by the same unseen pull; the quiet howl of youth calling them outward, onward, toward the truth of who they were meant to become. They do not know about each other, of course. It is better that way. Safer. Long ago, Lorkan had made certain to keep their worlds apart. He had been careful, so careful, never to let the names slip. Though once or twice, in a moment of frustration or fatigue, he'd almost said one when he meant the other. But he'd caught himself. Always caught himself. Wynn required his strength. Grace, his stillness. He had learned to carry both versions of himself, and never let them meet.

"I brought you honey twists too," he added, almost as an afterthought, sliding a small paper bag from his coat. "From the southern village. Warmed by the fire earlier." He knew how much she liked her treats when she read.

Grace lit up like a lantern. "You spoil me."

"I shouldn't. It's making you soft."

"You're the one who taught me to read!"

"I regret it daily."

She laughed, genuinely, this time. Lorkan let himself enjoy it, just for a moment. She had always been like this. Thoughtful. Intelligent in her own way, though often too gentle for the sharpness of the world. He worried about that more than he let on. About the way her kindness softened her edges. About how little she understood of what waited beyond her walls. Books could only teach so much.

"I wish you could stay," she said softly, not looking at him.

"You know I can't," he replied, already moving toward the door.

"I know." The words hung in the air.

At the threshold, he paused, resting a hand on the frame. "And what are your grand plans for the day, your highness?"

Grace didn't miss a beat. "Oh, you know. Steal a horse. Befriend a frog. Maybe give him a kiss, see what happens."

Lorkan raised his right brow, deadpan. "Just another normal day, then."

She smirked. "A girl's got to keep her options open."

Lorkan tapped the wall, "Happy Day of the Fates, Grace."

She lifted the tin of sparkfire in a mock toast. "May the Fates grant us all a prosperous year..." but he was gone, swallowed by stone and silence.

Grace stood for a moment longer, the weight of stillness familiar now. Then, with care, she struck one spark. It rose in a spiral, small, golden, flickering like a heartbeat. It spun in the air, casting dancing light on the walls before dissolving into the gray. She smiled faintly at the shimmer's brief defiance, watching it swirl and vanish into smoke. Then she sat, folding her legs beneath her as she opened the book with a careful motion. She was ready to disappear, just for a while. To be anywhere else. To let the story carry her beyond stone walls and silent halls and rules she never agreed to.

~ ~ ~

Well, dear reader, you've met them both now. One with dirt beneath her fingernails and secrets behind her smile. The other with ink-stained fingers and a heart tucked carefully between the pages. Two threads, winding side by side through dusk and dream and whatever waits beyond. Perhaps you're like Grace, letting the world fall quiet as the story pulls you deeper, page by page, until the edges blur and only the telling remains. If so, I hope you're warm. I hope the light is soft and you're nestled somewhere cozy. Change is coming—for Grace, for Wynn, and, who's to say, perhaps even for you. But for now, sleep well.

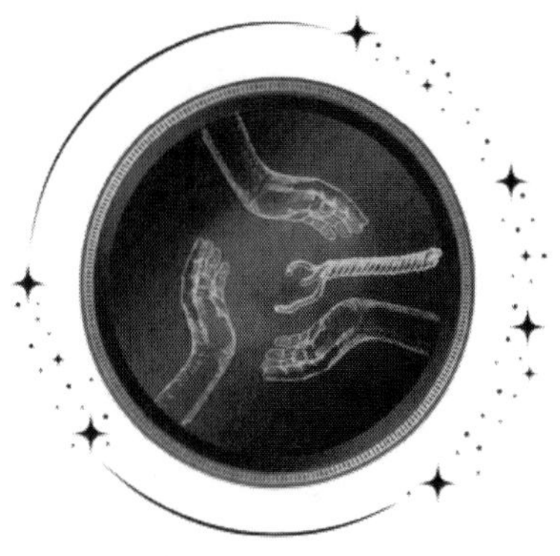

CHAPTER SIX

Let us return to that hawk's eye view, gliding soundlessly above a world that does not yet know what waits for it beneath the clouds. Down below, life continues: a girl winces and toils away through her pain beside a barn. Another clutches a book, lost in a love story, trying to forget about the walls around her. Coins clink, bread bakes, music plays as the Day of the Fates begins, golden and bright in places, heavy and strange in others. But if we shift just slightly—yes, just there—we can see a different corner of the map. A shadowed one. The rising sun has not quite reached the jagged peaks of the Tor mountains, which rise like the teeth of something ancient. There is a figure against the cliffs, small but unmistakable, The Dark One. She is alone, cloaked in black, her bald head covered by a hood. The wind howls, tearing at her skirts and biting her cheeks, but she does not flinch. She climbs as if she belongs to the mountain, as if she is made of the same dark stone. And in a way, perhaps she is. She disappears into a narrow crevice in the rock—a wound in the world, some say—and leaves the dawning light behind. The wind quiets. The air thickens. And now, dear reader, we follow. Carefully.

That path was older than kings and crueller than the legends that had formed it. There, the stone narrowed and slickened. The air grew damp, clinging to her skin like breath from something long asleep. The deeper she went, the less the world resembled itself. It is like time itself has thinned here. Even the shadows seemed to recoil from the torchlight she carried, reluctant to reveal what lay ahead. Still, she walked, straight-backed and certain, deeper into the mountain's throat. As far she was concerned, there is nothing to fear when you are the one to be feared.

The tunnel opened, suddenly and without warning, into a vast cavern. One by one, torches flared to life along the rough-hewn walls, their flames chasing shadows across ancient stone. The light crept slowly, deliberately, until the whole chamber flickered with a restless glow. The walls shimmered faintly, not with gem or gold, but with something more mystical. The ground was uneven and slick beneath her boots, and a mist rolled low and slow across the stone, curling at her ankles like something half-alive. And there were bones, scattered, ancient, bleached and crumbling. Some small. Some not. Certainly not all human. She did not flinch. Not even as a distant sound, a low humming wound through the cavern like a song sung from the bottom of the earth.

At the far end of the cavern, three figures emerged in the dark, seated atop great stone thrones carved from the mountain itself, each one shaped not by hands but by time. They were cloaked in dark folds that pooled like ink at their feet, and though their faces were veiled, one could feel the weight of their gaze. They did not move. They did not breathe.

"She comes, as she must."

"As she was told."

"Thirteen winters, and the fire still holds."

Their voices arrived in a rhythm—one, two, three. Distinct and seamless. Yet their mouths had not moved. It was as though the mountain itself had spoken through them.

Prima stepped forward, chin high. "Let us not waste time. I've come for the premonitions."

A pause. The air turned colder. Dust shifted on the stone floor. The Fates spoke again—three lines, three voices, three *truths*.

"A harvest ripe, the fields shall sing."

"But rot may hide beneath the spring."

"Feast well, for famine waits to sting."

Prima's jaw tensed, annoying news, but nothing she couldn't handle.

"Where mist clings tight and sea winds bite."

"Old oaths are whispered out of sight."

"The East remembers how to fight."

Her fingers twitched near the hilt at her waist, a silent tell as her suspicions of village leaders in the East plotting to overthrow her settled into certainty.

"The crown tilts low, the roots run dry."

"What once knelt down now dares to rise."

"The scales have tipped beneath the sky."

Silence followed, thick and bitter. Prima stood very still, her worries confirmed.

"You are not pleased, we see, we know."

"But threads will twist."

"They need to grow."

She stepped closer, fists closed at her sides. Her next words came clipped and sharp. "I did what you asked. I crushed the Tarn. I burned their halls. I scattered their bones to the Still River." She took a single step closer still, her boots scraping stone. "You said the land must be cleansed. That sleep would bend the will. That fear would hold the line." Her eyes shone with something between accusation and disbelief. "I gave you ALL OF IT. And now you speak of tipping scales?"

Her words echoed. The mountain *shuddered* in response. A groan of stone on stone echoed down the cavern spine, debris raining from the vaulted dark above. One of the great thrones cracked, just faintly, like a line drawn in ice. The Fates spoke, not rustling now, but grinding.

"We feel your shadow stretching long."

"We sense your greed amongst the throng."

"There is an energy that does not belong."

Prima didn't move, nor respond.

"Where did you find it, Prima, the Dark?"

"That power you claimed,"

"Does not bear our mark."

Prima stood taller. "Oh, is there something the great Fates cannot see?" The cavern rustled, a low hiss like wind through brittle bone. The air grew tight and angry.

"You dare to tempt the spindle's song?"

"Even boldness can go wrong."

"The thread you pull has tangled long."

Prima only smirked in response. She could feel the Fates assessing her, searching her, wanting to know more.

"You asked to rule."

"You begged for more."

"You became the blade to forge a war."

But something in her eyes flickered, curiosity, then calculation. "I asked?" she said carefully. "It was you who whispered of power, spoke of what waited in the dark. You told me it was my destiny to take."

"We spoke of conquest."

"Of smoke and steel."

"But not of mercy. You chose to feel."

"What?" Prima demanded between her clenched teeth. "Mercy." The word struck like a slap and curdled in her mouth.

"It was not mercy to let them live." She turned her face from them, from the cavern's shadows and the drip-drip-drip of memory. "What does it matter now?" she said tightly. "The Tarn are broken. The land is mine. The girl is nothing. The boy is... controlled."

The Fates leaned forward in unison.

"Where is the ring?"

"The one we claim."

"You've kept it long, too long to name."

Prima's smile did not falter, but her hand twitched, just slightly, before it disappeared into the folds of her gown. "You speak in riddles," she said coolly. "I have many rings. Be precise."

"You know the one."

"Obsidian band."

"Fatum's mark carved by hand."

"It remains... safe," she said, voice silk-wrapped steel. "As promised."

"Not freely won, that ring you claim."

"It bears the scent of stolen flame."

"A traitor's hand now shifts the game."

She said nothing, but her fingers curled tightly at her side. There was silence then. It seemed as if the Fates were thinking, contemplating the next move. Their following words were spoken in perfect unison; a sweet whisper laced with poison.

"Would you like to know your fate?"

Prima stiffened. She knew better. Understood that the Fates did not give freely. Every thread they handed came knotted, tangled in riddles, and wrapped in quiet consequence. And yet... the pull came like a tide, irresistible and ancient, scratching at her curiousity. She, like all who came before her, was not immune. No one was. Not when the question itched at her willpower. Not when the future hung just out of reach.

Now, dear reader, this is the part of the story where I must ask something. Not of Prima, she's already made her choice, but of you. Yes, you, curled up with these pages, warm and sure of your place in the world. If the Fates offered you a glimpse of what lies ahead—just a peek, a thread, a whisper—would you take it? It's easy, from a safe distance, to say no. To believe yourself stronger than such temptation. But when it is *your* heart in question, your love, your loss, your longing... things begin to fray. Loose threads are hard to leave untouched once seen, and even harder still not to pull. Stories are often ignited by decisions just like this, in the way fire flares when it finds the right kindling. We are taught to look for the grand turning points, the battles, the declarations, the thunderclap moments that split a life in two. But more often, it is the quieter choices that alter everything. A single step instead of a retreat. A word held back. A hand not offered. To take the path to the left over the right. To do, or not to do. These are the decisions that shift the plot, that bend the road, that turn a moment into something more.

And this moment is where we find her: Prima, Queen of the Tor. Once called kind, now veiled in darkness. A woman who has buried more than a husband and wears her grief like moulded armour. She has stood on the edge of this choice before, long ago, when she still believed that knowing a fate might help her escape it. That if she could only see the end, she might outmaneuver it. But that was a younger version. The one before the darkness. Even now, she convinces herself this is strength, that she chooses to listen, that she controls the story. She does not want a fate handed to her like a dainty package. She wants to seize it, shape it, stitch it into her own design. She wants power, not prophecy. But in truth, even she knows, deep in the quiet marrow of her knowing, that the moment she answers, she has given part of herself and something shifts. The plot, as they say, thickens, and the path begins to harden beneath her feet. No one can deny their fate.

She held her chin high. Her voice did not waver, "Out with it, then."

The three figures leaned forward. Their cloaks did not rustle. Their inky black eyes did not blink. The very air around them seemed to still, as if time itself held its next breath, waiting for how to proceed.

"A princess comes."

"Her head now turned."

"With restless heart and vengeance earned."

Prima's lips parted. She felt cheated. "You think I have not planned for this? That I have left the gate unguarded?" Her next words came out like venomous spit, "You have given me nothing." Behind her, the mountain gave a low groan. She was challenging ancient powers, and she knew it.

"She thinks we play with what we say."

"Another question then,"

"To guide the way?"

Prima held her satisfied smirk as she proceeded, "What if I kill them both?" She waited for their response longer than expected. She sensed that they wanted to take care with their next words.

"The thread may cut."

"And vengeance may still."

"But, beware the others who have a will."

Prima said nothing. There was no need. They would not allow another question, and she would not grant them the satisfaction of her doubt. She had her answer, tangled though it was. She turned. Her cloak whispered against the wet stone, a soft, silken hiss. Her footsteps were crisp and cold as shattered glass. She did not bow a goodbye nor look back as she disappeared into the dark mist from where she emerged.

A drip of water fell into a puddle and echoed throughout the cave. The Fates did not move. But they spoke again, this time, to no one but themselves and to the ancient powers of the world still listening.

"The weave twists tighter."

"A new flame flickers thin."

"We sense a thread we did not spin."

And for the first time in centuries, perhaps longer, their heads shifted, only slightly. Not toward the vanished queen, but toward something beyond. Beyond the mountain. Beyond even this page.

"We are older than time."

"We wove the first breath, and the last."

"But now... sisters, something stirs we did not cast."

~ ~ ~

You felt it too, didn't you? That little chill? The hairs on the back of the neck rising? That's what they do, those three. Characters like the Fates slip between stories like the winter wind under a door, poking around, whispering riddles, tying off threads that don't belong to them. And yes, sometimes even I, especially I, get the creeping feeling they're pulling at strings that bind my pages. You see, they don't just weave the threads. Sometimes they tangle them. Many times, they cut them short. But once in a while, just once in a great, long while, one can slip through their fingers entirely. And if you listen closely, you might hear them now, whispering into the folds of the night:

"Sleep, little thread."

"Don't tug, don't twist."

"The ending you want is the one we've missed."

"Close your eyes."

"We might be kind."

"Or maybe, just maybe, we change our mind."

So rest now, if you can. The needles are still. The thread is warm. And morning, after all, is only ever one page away. Sleep well.

CHAPTER SEVEN

Let's begin with a small, tired truth: not all exhaustion is the same. There is the good kind of tired; the kind that comes after a day well spent, with dirt under your fingernails and the sun still warm and clinging to your skin. There is the soft tiredness of late nights spent whispering under blankets, eyes heavy but heart full. And there is the bone-deep tired that follows grief, a tired that has nothing to do with muscles or minutes but settles into the soul like fog on a lake. Then there is the kind of tired that Wynn feels now. It is the kind of tired that comes from being denied what should never be denied; a tiredness that crawls behind the eyes and makes everything slightly too bright, too sharp, too loud. This tiredness lives in the creak of one's joints and the pulses in one's skull. It blurs the line between waking and dreaming until reality feels like a distant bell ringing underwater.

Wynn was exhausted. Since getting back from Lorkan's, she hadn't rested. Not even for a moment. There had been no sleep token allotted to her the previous night. No permission to rest. Just work; scrubbing, hauling, polishing until her knees throbbed and the healing lashes pulsed with fire beneath her shirt. Dena had made sure to make her suffer. Not with shouts or slaps, but with sweet, silken cruelty that declared sleep a luxury Wynn didn't deserve.

She had worked through the night, and then through the morning, and then into the afternoon. Her muscles burned beneath her skin, her eyes stinging and dry, begging to be closed. And now, here she was in the kitchen, stirring soup.

The air was thick with the scent of onions, stale bread, and the heat of the fire. Sunlight angled through the grimy window panes, landing on a row of chipped bowls stacked high on the counter. The rest of the inn was quiet and empty, everyone had gone to the square to watch the games. The Day of the Fates came once a year, and even Dena abandoned her usual vigilance for the excitement.

Wynn set the ladle down with a quiet clink.

"I don't think you should go," Avery said behind her, voice low, as if the kitchen walls might carry her words somewhere they shouldn't.

Wynn didn't turn. The bread knife moved steadily beneath her hand, slicing through the soft round with slow precision. Each cut let out a warm breath of steam, the crust cracking gently under the pressure.

"You haven't slept," Avery added, quieter now. "You're still healing. What if Dena sees you?"

Wynn didn't answer right away. She stacked the slices neatly, her hands lingering on the top one, fingers pressed lightly into the spongy center. "What if she doesn't?" she said at last, still facing the bread. "The whole village is at the square. I'll be back before dark."

Avery shifted her weight. Her arms crossed tight across her chest, her eyes fixed not on Wynn, but on the edge of the table. There were small scratches there in the wood. She'd traced them a hundred times before, but today they felt different. Restless.

"I just..." She hesitated, the words clumsy in her mouth. "I just have a feeling. That this isn't a good idea."

Wynn turned then, slowly, tucking a damp strand of hair behind her ear. Her apron was stained with flour and something darker, maybe jam or grease, and her cheeks were pink from the oven's heat. But her expression was already sliding into something stubborn. Familiar.

"Please," she said, too-sweet. Teasing, but with that glint in her eyes that meant she'd already made up her mind.

Avery opened her mouth to argue, but what came out instead surprised them both. "Maybe I should go with you."

Wynn paused, visibly taken off guard, though she said nothing.

Avery didn't look at her. She watched the bread steam instead, and felt the weight of the silence stretch thin between them. The words had come out before she knew she was thinking them. And now they sat there, heavy and strange. She didn't usually want to go. Not to the village. Not to the square. People stared there. Just a little too long. Just a little too hard. They didn't say anything, but their eyes always narrowed, like she was a word in a book they'd read before but couldn't quite place. Like she was almost familiar... but wrong.

She felt it too. That wrongness. Not in her skin, exactly, but just under it. As though her reflection might blink before she did. As though the world she walked through wasn't entirely the one she was meant for.

But when she was with Wynn, cutting vegetables, or listening to her hum while folding laundry, or standing beside her in this warm little kitchen, something inside her went quiet. She fit. Wynn never looked at her like she was out of place.

"I mean... I could," she added, quickly now, walking the thought back before it gained too much shape. "But, I should probably stay here. In case Dena comes back."

Wynn didn't push. She didn't laugh, or question, or give one of her clever retorts. She just looked at Avery for a long moment, then reached out and gave her arm a gentle squeeze.

"You're the best, A," she said, a little softer than before. Then she kissed her on the cheek, undid her apron, and reached for her cloak. "I'll be back before that next batch of bread is cool." And just like that, she was out the door, leaving the scent of warm yeast and something unspoken lingering behind.

And, dear reader, I wish I could tell you that this decision didn't matter. That it was just a small thing. A girl ducking out of a kitchen, slipping into the afternoon light. But, as I have just gone over with you, stories become epics by way of small decisions, don't they? A step here, a lie there, a promise made or broken in a breath.

Wynn slipped out the servant's door a few seconds later, throwing her hood over her head to conceal her face. The alleyway behind the inn held the smell of spilled ale and sour cabbage from the compost heap. Night was waiting at the edge of the wall. She sat perfectly still, half-shadow, half-fox, the afternoon light catching the silver sheen of her coat. Wynn stopped short.

"Don't start," she said, already exasperated. "I know she's right." Night didn't blink. Her ears flicked once, disapproving. "I'll be careful," she muttered, crouching beside her. "I'm not trying to get caught. I just... I need to be someone else for an hour. And I'll snag you something, alright? Dried rabbit. The good kind."

Night laid down slowly, the way only creatures with long memories and quiet judgment do. She rested her head on her paws and looked up.

Wynn let out a breath that was almost a laugh. "Fine, stay here, then. Be stubborn. I'm going anyway." She stood and turned, striding off with more certainty than she felt. But halfway down the alley, she glanced back—not to check, of course, just to make a point—and there Night was, already padding after her. Silent. Steady. "Thought so," she smiled softly.

Together, they wound through the backstreets, ducking beneath laundry lines strung like garlands and past shuttered homes where festival music seeped faintly through the cracks. The closer they came to the square, the louder it all became: drums, laughter, the clatter of wooden swords, the ring of a bell marking a victory no one would remember by morning. Wynn hated it. The pretense. The painted smiles. The way people still whispered about luck and omens while the dark shadows under their eyes said otherwise. But she understood. She needed this just as much as they did. To move through the town like life was normal. Even if it was just for a moment. A stolen one.

The square opened before her like a stage, the afternoon sun spilling gold over festival booths and painted faces. Scents of spiced apples, roasted roots, and woodsmoke hung thick in the air. Children darted past with ribbons in their hair and sticky fingers clutching bits of candied bark. Merchants shouted over one another from patchwork stalls, bartering hand woven bracelets and carved whistles, jars of honey and rough-spun blankets. A boy in a paper crown tried to balance on stilts while awkwardly reaching for a wooden horse just out of reach. Laughter rang out near the archery lane, where dull-tipped arrows thudded harmlessly against straw men. If one stood here and took it all in, they could almost forget the unjust world they lived in, and perhaps, this is exactly why Prima let it all happen.

Wynn's eyes were drawn to the center square, where the real contest churned like a storm. A sharp splash broke the air, followed by a roar of laughter and groans. There stood the dueling log, slick and glinting above a wide trough of rippling water, already disturbed by one unlucky fall. On a small velvet cushion beside it lay a stack of obsidian sleep tokens, gleaming like midnight tears in the sun.

A crowd pressed close now, murmuring, jostling, hungry for spectacle and the prize of sleep. Wynn smirked, her boots shifting toward the edge of the circle, but before she could take a full step, a streak of soot and russet darted across her path. Night.

The fox stood firm, low to the ground, her ears back, tail sweeping in slow agitation. She didn't growl, didn't bark, just looked up at Wynn with that sharp, imploring gaze, as if to say: *don't.*

Wynn stopped short. "Night," she said softly, trying to step around her. But the fox moved with her, blocking her path again, quicker this time. The crowd laughed at something behind them, a juggler's mistake, maybe, but the sound barely registered. Wynn was locked in a quiet standoff with the only creature in the world who knew her better than she knew herself. Night's ears flicked. Her nose twitched.

"This isn't just about the tokens," Wynn said. "You know that."

The fox set her paws in a defiant stance, chest rising and falling in a quick, unsettled rhythm. Her tail twitched. Wynn knew exactly what she was trying to say, *I look after you, like you look after me. That's the deal.*

"I'll be careful," Wynn promised, crouching low just for a moment, her fingers brushing Night's soft fur. "But I can't walk away from this. Please. I let you be free, now you need to do the same for me." Night stared at her, and then, slowly, reluctantly, she stepped aside.

"Good girl. Stay here." This time, the fox obeyed, slipping discreetly between two barrels, a silent shadow amid the noise and color. But she did not take her eyes off Wynn, not once.

The dueling log was slick with water and years of use, strung over a wide trough deep enough to soak the pride out of any would-be champion. The crowd had gathered in a loose crescent, children sitting cross-legged in front, elders perched on crates, and the rest craning necks and calling bets with hopeful fervor.

And just off to the side, half in shadow, wholly out of place, stood Kiernan, clearly getting ready to compete.

Wynn snuck up beside him.

"You shouldn't be here," he said, voice low, not making eye contact.

"Well," Wynn said, nudging his side, "that makes two of us."

"I'm not—" Kiernan blinked, recalibrating, "I'm not the one with everything to lose."

"And yet," she said, "you *are* the one about to make a fool of yourself in front of half the village."

Kiernan puffed up a little, straightening his spine. "You've seen the tokens?"

"I've seen your two left feet and general lack of coordination, yes."

He narrowed his eyes. "You know, for someone who just got publicly lashed in the square, you're awfully mouthy."

Wynn heard the frustration in his tone. She tried to lighten the mood. "It's the pain. Makes me sharp."

Kiernan shook his head, but there was a smile tugging at his lips. Another splash erupted behind the murmuring crowd, a body hitting water with a thud, followed by laughter, jeers, and the scrape of a wooden staff being retrieved from the trough. The next challenger was already climbing up the ladder to the platform, muscles tense with anticipation.

"I'm doing it for you, you know. Ten tokens. That's sleep for two weeks, maybe more if we stretch it."

Wynn opened her mouth to retort but found herself hesitating. The truth was, ten tokens would mean everything. And he knew it. That was the problem with Kiernan, he meant too well.

Before she could respond, a voice rang out above the crowd. "Next match, Kiernan, son of...", the announcer yelled over, "Oi, who are you the son of?"

"It's just Kiernan, son of no one." It hurt Kiernan to say it, but to say otherwise would invite questions, pity, and embarrassment. He glanced at Wynn. She had asked him before who his parents were, and he always gave the same answer; he didn't know and couldn't remember.

The announcer shrugged, "Kiernan, son of no one, versus Olin, son of Hans the Butcher!" A low murmur rippled through the crowd. Olin was broad as an ox and twice as smug. He flexed as he stepped onto the log, slapping the flat of his wooden staff against his palm.

Kiernan gave Wynn one last look, as if hoping for some encouragement.

"Try not to drown," she offered sweetly.

"Thanks."

"Actually, K..." she reached out and he turned back. "He's slow as a slug and dumber than a rock. Just let him come for you and when he swings, step back, he'll fall." Kiernan nodded and then started to climb the ladder to his spot.

What followed was less a duel and more a tragic ballet of imbalance.

Olin, broad-shouldered, red-faced, and drunk on attention, stomped onto the log with the subtlety of a charging bull. He jeered before the bout even began, swinging his stick in wide, showy arcs that made the crowd whoop and scatter at the edges. His balance was questionable, but his bravado was not. Kiernan followed with markedly less flair, gripping his own staff like it might bite him. To his credit, he did try. He planted his feet, squared his shoulders, and even managed a few decent swings, one of which grazed Olin's side and drew an exaggerated howl from the butcher's son. But from the first wobble, it was clear Kiernan was outmatched. He lacked Olin's reach, his weight, and most critically, his confidence.

The crowd began to chuckle. Not cruelly, yet, but with the hum of anticipation that came before someone inevitably got wet. Olin faked a stumble, drawing a sympathetic gasp. Kiernan, bless him, hesitated, just for a breath, long enough for Olin to throw a handful of dirt he had been concealing into his face.

Kiernan jerked back, sputtering, trying to wipe the grit from his eyes. And that was when Olin surged forward with all the finesse of a drunk bear, slamming his shoulder into Kiernan's chest, and sent him flying.

The splash was spectacular. The crowd roared with laughter. The fists at Wynn's side clenched. That oaf had cheated.

Kiernan surfaced, spitting water and ego, and gave a soggy but gracious bow before swimming to the side. Olin raised his arms, bellowing something about strength and destiny.

"And now," the announcer called, stretching the words like taffy, "who will dare challenge Olin for the tokens?"

A hush rippled through the crowd like wind through wheat. No one stepped forward. Of course they didn't. Olin still stood on the log, water glistening on his feet, chest heaving, arms raised like a champion carved from meat and smugness. Naturally, Wynn raised her hand.

There was a beat. Then another. The kind of silence that stretches itself too long, awkward and taut. Heads turned. Whispers stirred. A few villagers recognized her, eyes widening, nudging each other, remembering who she was and what had happened the day before.

She moved with purpose, slicing through the crowd like a knife through butter. She shrugged off her cloak and handed it to a stunned and still dripping Kiernan. "I don't want to hear it," she said, stopping any objections he had before he could utter them. Her boots came next, kicked to the side. She rolled her shoulders. The cool air stung her arms, and the lashes on her back throbbed like fresh lightning beneath her shirt, but she didn't flinch. She just climbed the platform and stepped onto the log like it was hers.

Olin turned, blinking once, then again, as if hoping she might vanish if he stared hard enough. Instead, she smiled. Slow.

Deliberate. Like a fuse being lit. "You're going to regret that little cheat," she said.

"I don't cheat," Olin sneered, puffing his chest. "And you're the thief. How's the back?"

She cocked her head. "Strong enough to beat you."

A few in the crowd laughed, half-nervous, half-thrilled. The announcer opened his mouth but Wynn didn't wait for permission, she pounced.

The log shuddered under their weight, water slapping the sides of the trough as the duel burst to life. Olin swung wide, an easy, telegraphed arc meant to intimidate. She ducked clean under it and then jabbed quickly, connecting sharply with this stomach. He grunted and then tried to charge, leading with his shoulder again, but she jumped back, toes gripping the slick wood and gave him a cheeky smile. While he was all weight and muscle, she was air and momentum, and the crowd loved it.

This time, she was ready when he reached into his pocket, her staff cracking across his knuckles with a sharp *whack*. He cursed loudly, the dirt scattering harmlessly into the air. He shook his hand out. "You're going to regret that," he growled, lunging again.

But Wynn was prepared with her next move. She dropped down, crouching on the log while swinging her stick into the back of Olin's left knee. His leg buckled with a yelp, and for a heartbeat, he tried to catch himself, arms flailing, face contorting... Wynn jumped back up, smiled, then nudged him gently, just a cheeky poke, but it was enough. Down he went, with a spectacular splash that rocked the log she clung to.

Wynn danced to keep her balance. It wasn't elegant. It wasn't clean. But it was a win.

The crowd erupted. Cheers echoed through the square, bouncing off stone walls like a long-lost anthem. She raised her arms in victory, grinning, chest heaving, drenched in sweat and pride. For a moment, she forgot about the pain in her back. But only for a moment.

She scanned the crowd. There was Dena, arms crossed, lips pressed thin in a mask of disapproval. Hans the butcher was red-faced and shouting, furious as only a father watching his son be humiliated can be. And Kiernan, still wet, half grinning, shook his head at her, somewhere between exasperated and impressed. Wynn didn't care. She had won. She had *earned* this moment, this one moment. Let Dena punish her later, let Kiernan be sore with her, let... but her victory was short lived...

The crowd began to part as cheers turned to murmurs and then murmurs turned to silence.

It wasn't like before, when children scampered to get a better view, or neighbors made space for each other. This was different. This was reverence. This was the hush that comes before a storm, when the air grows too still and the birds disappear.

And then the black cloaks came into view.

A dozen Dark Guards, moving in grim formation. Not running. Not rushing. Just *walking*—and yet clearing space with a gravity that bent the world around them. Their armor glinted like onyx. Their faces were blank. And at their center: The Stone.

He didn't need to speak. His presence was a sentence in itself.

The crowd shrank back. People lowered their eyes. A child whimpered and was quickly hushed. Because when The Stone came to a town, death came with him. That was known. That was unspoken law.

And emerging right behind but coming to stand beside him... was Lorkan.

Wynn's breath caught. Their eyes met. He didn't say a word. He didn't have to. His expression said everything. *This is bad. You shouldn't be here.* But she was. And there was nowhere to run. No crowd to melt into. No shadows to slip through. She was standing on a slick, swaying log at the center of the square, alone and very visible. They had discussed and made plans for when this day might come. How Wynn could slip away and safe locations where they could meet at. But they had not planned for this.

The music faded, as though someone had plucked the last notes from the air. Even the crackling from the grill fires seemed to still. Only the low sloshing of water under the log beneath her remained. Wynn knew there was nowhere to run and yet she couldn't help eyeing her options, looking for a split in the crowd where she could escape. If she could make it to the platform she could maybe hop onto a side roof. Or, she could whistle for Night to create a distraction, then, if she jumped off the log and to the right, she could—The crowd parted again as Avery was dragged out.

She stumbled, wrists bound, mouth gagged with rough cloth. Her curls were mussed and tangled, her eyes wide with fear. She was still wearing her stained apron. The crowd murmured, shrinking further into themselves as she was shoved beside Lorkan at the edge of the square. She was so small beside him. So fragile.

The Stone didn't even look at her. He looked at Wynn. "Is that her?" he asked Lorkan, nodding toward the girl still standing alone on the log.

Wynn saw the hesitation in Lorkan's jaw, the clench of his fist on his staff. But then he nodded and said firmly. "Yes."

And that was all it took. Two guards stepped forward, seizing Wynn by the arms, and dragging her from the log like she weighed nothing at all. Her body jolted with the movement. Her feet hit the dirt, her legs buckled, but she didn't fall. She wouldn't give them that.

"What is your name?" He demanded.

She held her tongue.

The Stone moved forward, slow and deliberate, and grabbed Wynn by the chin with a gloved hand. He tilted her face to the side, but not before their eyes met. And in that heartbeat, something shifted. Recognition. Wynn saw it flash behind his cold, gray stare. His jaw twitched. He said nothing.

But he saw her. She saw him. And they both saw a memory.

Then, as if the moment had never happened, he turned her head roughly, exposing the skin behind her ear. There. The crescent moon. His grip tightened, just slightly, as if confirming what he already knew. Then, without a word, he shoved her, hard, into the waiting arms of the guards. "Take them both." The stone commanded. Her arms were pulled roughly behind her, seizing her back in pain, her wrists bound tightly with rope.

"NO! It's me you want!" Wynn shouted, twisting against the ropes. "Let her go, leave her out of this!" She thrashed as best she could, trying to twist free. She looked at Avery, terrified, apologetic, her eyes begging. "I said let her go!" Wynn's voice cracked.

One of the guards slapped a gag across her mouth.

From the crowd, Dena's voice rose, shrill and furious and she charged forward. "You can't take them! They're mine! My slaves, my workers! I need them to run the inn. You have no right—"

The Stone turned to her, slowly.

Dena balked, but continued standing as tall as her stout frame allowed. "I am Tor. I serve the Dark One," she demanded, chin high. "And so does my inn. I demand compensation. I have papers!"

The Stone raised a hand. Dena froze. The square froze. "You forget," he said, voice echoing like iron dropped on stone, "you *belong* to the Dark One." And without another word, he drew his sword and cut her down.

It was quick. One stroke. Dena gasped, eyes wide in shock. She collapsed to her knees, then to her side with a hard thud, blood pooled in the dirt.

A child screamed. The crowd rippled with panic, but no one ran. No one dared.

The Stone turned to the guards. "Burn the inn. A few moved at once, marching toward the building with oil and flame already in hand. The Inn, home to so many meals and whispered stories and stolen scraps of rest, would soon be ash. He turned back to the crowd. "You all belong to her," he declared. "Let this be your reminder."

Wynn writhed in her bindings. She looked for Kiernan, and saw him, eyes locked on The Stone with a rage that burned hotter than the midday sun. His whole body was trembling, barely contained. He took a step forward.

Lorkan grabbed him. "No," he hissed, quiet, deadly. "Not now."

"That's him," Kiernan growled. "That's the one who—"

"If you move now, you'll get her killed. Maybe all of us."

Kiernan's hands curled into fists. He didn't move.

Rough hands shoved them into the back of the open cart. The wood groaned under their weight as the guards jumped down, and the wheels lurched into motion. Wynn's breath caught as she looked back, one last time, toward the edge of the crowd.

Lorkan stood there. Silent. Still.

Her stomach turned with shame. She'd failed him. She had been reckless, and now she'd dragged Avery into it too. But that wasn't the look he gave her. No disappointment. No anger. Just a steady gaze. And then, he nodded. Small. Measured. Deliberate.

It was not a farewell. It was a promise.

Wynn held his eyes as long as she could, holding onto that single, silent message: *This is not the end.* And then she saw her. Night. Crouched low beneath a vendor's stall, hidden in shadow. Her blue eyes locked onto Wynn's, alert and unafraid. A twitch of her ears. The tiniest shift forward, then stillness again. Waiting. Watching. As the cart rolled on and away Wynn's heart ached with the force of everything she couldn't say.

~ ~ ~

I know, I know. I'm the book that's supposed to put you to sleep. But if you can't close me just yet, if your heart's thudding and your eyes are wide and your pillow suddenly feels too far away... well, I don't blame you. It doesn't get easier from here. I wish I could promise you a calm chapter next, something with tea and blankets and no death by sword. But stories don't often work that way. Especially not this one. Some of you might be ready to shut my covers now, eyes heavy, breath slow, dreams waiting just beyond the edge of thought. If so, I say goodnight, rest well, and pick me back up when you're ready. But some of you—yes, you, leaning forward with that look on your face—are already turning the page in your mind, needing to know what comes next. I see you. I admire your dedication to the word. Everyone reads in their own way. Their own rhythm. Some skim the surface like skipping stones. Some sink in slow, letting each word soak deep. Some read in bursts; three pages on the train, four more before bed, one while the kettle boils. Some dog-ear corners, while others cringe at that literary faux pas. Some underline in pencil. Some whisper the words aloud like spells. Many stay awake a little too long with a book they promised they'd only read one more chapter of. I could go on and on about it. I really could. I like words. But for now, I'll say this:

For those who are ready to sleep, now is a good time. And for those who are ready to continue this adventure, now is also a good time. You do you.

CHAPTER EIGHT

The wagon had been moving for hours. At least Wynn thought it had. Time had become a strange creature: elastic, half-real, unraveling in the corners of her mind. Sleep tugged at her like a slow undertow, dragging her thoughts sideways, but every time she began to slip under, something jolted her back. A bump in the road. A loud bark of a guard. The cold bite of the rope cutting into her wrists. The invisible thrum of the Queen's magic that refused to let her sleep, holding her mind cruelly above the edge of rest. Her hands were tied behind her, forcing her body into an unnatural curve, her shoulders burning, arms long since gone numb. The position wrinkled her back in a way that made her healing welts scream with every bump, the scabs pulling, raw skin straining against itself. Her head lolled against the wooden wall, and her gag tasted of damp cloth and dirt.

Avery sat across from her, slumped forward, breathing softly. She hadn't stirred in a while. In the shifting blue light of the moon, cutting through the trees in glimmers, Wynn watched the gentle rise and fall of her chest, the stillness of true sleep. Of course she could sleep. She always could. Whatever place she came from, it wasn't The Vast. The magic didn't cling to her the way it did to Wynn, like a hand on her throat every time she tried to rest. Avery's brow twitched faintly, caught in some quiet dream. Wynn wished she could reach her, say her name, offer some kind lie, but what comfort could she give, when everything was falling apart?

The forest around them was changing. It had taken Wynn a while to notice, but now she couldn't stop seeing it. The trees, once thick and close like guardians of the road, were beginning to thin. Their trunks grew twisted, their bark gray and cracking. Moss disappeared. The ground beneath the wagon's wheels turned from loamy soil to brittle gravel.

Over the side of the wagon and through the trees, Wynn caught glimpses of the Northern Mountains in the distance, jagged and black. Their dark silhouette looked like claws against the horizon, their snowless peaks lit faintly by the low, graying sky. The road was leading them straight into the jaws of the Tor—to the dark castle. Her breath hitched.

The land there was all rock and wind and bone. No warmth. No rest. The sort of place you were sent, to be broken, to forget you had ever been whole. The slow dread curled and tightened around her ribs with every creak of the wagon. While they had gotten better as she aged, she had countless nightmares about this as a child. She always knew this day would come but not this soon, and not with Avery at her side.

Hooves slowed beside her, and she turned her head to see him: The Stone. He studied her in silence, his gaze pinned to her face like it held some unfinished answer. At this distance, Wynn could clearly see the thick scar starting just above his pale eye, ending near his jaw. It must have been a horrific wound... *good, she thought.*

"You look like her," he said at last. "Same defiance. Same fire in the eyes. Like she was always daring the world to try her."

Wynn didn't flinch, but she felt her pulse quicken.

Ah. The stories we never ask for, the ones that come unbidden, cracked and raw from mouths we'd rather not hear them from.The past is never content to stay stored on dusty shelves. Not really. It waits, tucked in the folds of memory, in the mouths of bitter men, in half-told truths and silences that ache to be filled. And when it returns, it often doesn't knock; marching in and sitting beside us, uninvited but heavy with meaning. Wynn had never truly wondered who her parents were before her. Not as children. Not as lovers. Not as people with stories that didn't end in her. But that's the trick of time, isn't it? Sooner or later, the characters we think have exited stage left reappear—older, altered, and somehow still shaping the plot.

"I was loyal once," he said, almost absently. "To her. More than to the crown. Thought she might see it someday. But I was a fool." His fingers tightened around the reins. "She chose him. The golden boy with a poet's tongue and a spine like sugar glass." There was bitterness in his voice, and something colder. "You know, Prima made her watch," he went on, quieter now. "Watched as he died. Slowly. Right before she ended her." He smirked, "No fairytale ending for those two."

The wagon creaked forward. He looked at Wynn one last time. "Never understood why the Dark One let you and your scourge of a brother live. But it doesn't matter." He gave a short, humorless laugh. "Your turn's coming soon enough." He kicked at his horse and rode ahead, the black of his cloak swallowed by the night.

Wynn stared across the wagon. Avery's eyes met hers. She was awake now and had heard it all, though her face gave nothing away.

She blinked slowly, her eyes burning, her body swaying with the slow rhythm of the wagon, the melodic clicking of the horse hooves connecting with the ground. The sky had darkened fully now, smudged purple and blue, heavy with stars she couldn't see.

She leaned forward and closed her eyes, trying to stop the world from spinning.

And then she heard it.

Water.

Distant at first. Then louder. Rushing. Roaring. A sound that swallowed sound.

The Still River.

Wynn forced herself upright. The wagon's wheels clicked and clattered louder now, echoing differently against the stone. She blinked again, harder this time, trying to force the fog from her mind. Wynn's gaze drifted back to the girl slumped across from her. She looked so small. She felt the sting of guilt. This was all her fault: the inn, the carriage, The Stone, the gag in Avery's mouth. All of it. The secret. The lie. The truth she wanted to tell her all these years but always held back. First because she hadn't trusted her. Then because she'd wanted to protect her. And finally, because it was too late. Now, Avery was caught in a web she didn't even know she'd stepped into.

Wynn pressed her forehead against the wall of the wagon, cool wood against hot skin. She remembered the first time she saw Avery—tiny, barefoot, clinging to Dena's skirts. Dena had bought her off a traveling merchant. Said she needed "another set of hands and nobody wanted this one so she was practically free." Wynn had been told to train her.

"Got a deal on her cuz she's mute," Dena said callously. "Don't need a mouth to work though. Call her Girl."

She hadn't spoken. Not a word. Not for months. Just followed Wynn around like a shadow. And Wynn—tired, angry, half-starved of food and sleep—hated that at first. But Girl stayed close. And quiet. And kind. She would braid Wynn's hair when no one was looking, always in strange, looping patterns Wynn had never seen on anyone in Wickmere. Ropes and weaves that belonged to nowhere Wynn knew. She brought scraps of food, tucked away like offerings, and would cry silently when Wynn was beaten for something or other she had said or done.

And in those quiet, stolen nights, when the inn had gone still and the candles were out, Wynn began to teach her—a finger traced in the dust, a whisper in the dark. It was dangerous, what they were doing, but that only made Wynn more certain. It wasn't just rebellion; it was belief. Every person deserved a voice, even the quiet ones. Especially the quiet ones. Lorkan had told her once that knowledge was power, and power was often hidden in books, tucked between ink and page. That was why the Queen had burned every library in the region. But Wynn, defiant as ever, taught Girl anyway. Quietly. Carefully. A few letters at a time, scratched into soot on the hearth or traced with a finger in spilled water. By firelight and shadow, with ink made from ash and stolen berries, she shaped an alphabet out of nothing; an alphabet of survival, of resistance, of belonging. Letter by letter, as if each one might stitch Girl more firmly into the world.

Girl learned fast. She never spoke, but her eyes were quick, her memory sharper than anyone gave her credit for. Then one day, while kneading dough in the kitchen, her hands dusted in flour, she wrote it—a-v-e-r-y. The letters were clumsy but clear, pressed into the counter with a trembling finger. Wynn had stared at them, heart snagged in her chest, before *Avery* wiped them away in a single swipe, and a second before Dena came in with a sack of onions and a scowl. Wynn hadn't said anything, but she never forgot the shape of those letters carved out in the white. And she never forgot that Avery, even without speaking, had always known who she was.

Her stomach tightened at the memory. While she had always fumbled through kitchen chores, awkward and out of place, Avery moved with quiet confidence, as if she'd been born to the rhythm of simmering pots and wooden spoons. Her soups were her specialty, strange and fragrant, with flavor combinations that didn't belong in The Vast. People looked at her a little too long, uncertain, as if trying to decide where to place her, what box to fit her in. But they never questioned the soup. They came to the inn just to try it, slurping it down with second helpings and wiped their bowls clean. And in that way, they ignored what felt foreign about her, because it tasted like comfort. Like something better than they'd known, even if they couldn't say why.

Months after learning her name, Wynn had snuck out to see what she could steal from some passing merchants. It wasn't unusual. She was getting faster and bolder. She did it for sleep, mostly. Sometimes for spite. Oftentimes for sport. But that night, she hadn't known Avery had followed her, barefoot through the underbrush like a wisp.

She thought she had gotten away with a clean swipe but as she jumped off the carriage and reached the side of the road, strong hands yanked her back by the collar. The merchant's guard was faster than she'd anticipated, and Wynn braced herself for the blow.

But it never came.

Instead, from behind a tree, a tiny voice broke the silence. "Please. Don't hurt her."

It was the first time Avery had ever spoken. Her voice was soft, raw with disuse, but it rang out like a morning bird song in Wynn's memory. *Please. Don't hurt her.* The guard hesitated, looking strangely at where the voice had come from, just long enough for Wynn to drive her knee into his groin and run.

Back in the wagon, Wynn blinked hard. Her vision swam. She could feel the forest pulling at her, as if it sensed she was being taken; its hush deepening, its branches reaching, whispering secrets only she could hear. The caravan slowed as the stone bridge loomed ahead; massive, ancient, and slick with moss in places where the river's spray reached up like fingers. It stretched long and narrow across the Still River, connecting the edge of the Tarn forests to the rocky, scarred land of the Tor. Darkness swallowed the trees behind them, and ahead, the silhouettes of the Northern Mountains pierced the sky, backlit by a moon smudged behind clouds. Wynn could smell fresh snow in the wind blowing down from their peaks. The wagon creaked as it rolled to a stop.

Just ahead, where the mouth of the bridge narrowed between crumbling towers, The Stone had dismounted to speak with a group of armored guards. Their torches flared, casting shadows that danced across the bridge's flanks. Wynn kept her head low, pretending stillness, but her eyes moved, sweeping the surroundings one last time. And there, just beyond the reach of the moonlight, down in the ditch beside the path, a glint of silver in the dark. Two eyes glowed.

At first, relief surged through her. Night was here. Of course she was. Crouched beneath the ferns, perfectly still—tail tucked low, ears pricked forward—waiting, listening. But the relief twisted almost instantly into fear. She shouldn't have come. Not this time and not this far. Not into this danger.

The guards lifted the gate to the entrance of the bridge and then waved the wagon forward.

The ground beneath them changed, the wheels shifting from gravel path to smooth, cold granite. The river opened up below, frothing and hurling itself against the rocks with a roar that filled Wynn's ears and echoed beneath the bridge like distant thunder. She leaned against the wagon's side as they rolled further on.

They were almost halfway across now when Wynn heard the soft scrape of claws on stone. Night leapt, unseen by the guards following in behind, and landed in the back of the wagon like a soft breath of wind, her dark-silver fur barely visible in the gloom. Her teeth went to work without hesitation, gnawing fiercely at the ropes around Wynn's wrists. Wynn tensed, body shielding the motion from view, and in seconds, she felt the cords slacken and fall away.

Night was gone before the guards noticed a thing, vanishing beneath the wagon's frame, her work done.

Wynn's fingers were numb, blood rushing back in pins and needles. She flexed them, then turned to Avery, who was watching, patient and wide-eyed.

"Stay still," Wynn whispered, tugging at Avery's gag and then going to work on her bindings. "And listen." Avery nodded once. "We don't make it to the other side," Wynn said. "We don't go into the Tor. Do you understand?"

"What do we do?"

Wynn glanced over the wagon's edge. The Stone still rode ahead, unaware. The guards behind hadn't looked twice. The moment was there, if they took it. But it would be small. Dangerous. "We run."

Avery looked over the edge, "I don't think I can."

"You have to." Wynn replied sharply.

She softly clicked her tongue three times. Night shot out from beneath the wagon, silver and silent, darting straight for the horses pulling the lead cart. Her teeth snapped at their legs and flanks, sharp and fast. They reared in panic, screaming, hooves kicking wildly. One guard fell sideways, striking his head against the stone guardrail. Another lunged for his sword.

"The fox! Kill that damn fox!" The Stone bellowed.

Chaos erupted.

"Now." Wynn grabbed Avery's hand, and they leapt from the wagon, hitting the bridge hard. They didn't pause. They ran, feet pounding, wind whipping, the river roaring just below.

Dark knights shouted in surprise, yanking at their reins as the girls ducked low and darted between their horses. Steel gleamed in the corner of Wynn's eye, blades half-drawn, too slow. Hooves slipped and clattered behind them.

Then came the arrows.

They hissed through the air, one after another, slicing past Wynn's ear close enough to feel. One cracked into the wall at her side. She ran harder, tugging at Avery, veering toward the front of the bridge, toward the Tarn side, toward home. There, looming from the fog, stood the statues: two great granite kings flanking the archway, their features worn smooth by centuries of rain. They looked regal. Like something out of a bedtime story her mother once told her. But she didn't have time to think about it.

Beneath the arch, a group of guards stood ready. Swords drawn. Eyes sharp. They were closing in fast. Behind them, hooves pounded again. The Stone was coming.

And then, from the shadows just beyond the statues, two figures stepped forward. Kiernan struck first, all momentum and anger, blade swinging with more strength than finesse. He moved like a battering ram, his sword clanging against steel, sending sparks flying, driving his opponent back with sheer force. Lorkan followed close behind, quiet where Kiernan was loud, clean where Kiernan was chaos. His sword moved with surgical intent, every strike landing exactly where it needed to. One guard staggered, clutching his chest. Another turned too late, Kiernan barrelled into him, knocking him clean into the river below. But it wasn't enough.

More guards turned from the archway, cutting off the last stretch of bridge. Trapped between them and the knights behind, Wynn and Avery skidded to a stop. Arrows still flew. One slammed into the arch ahead of them, another dropping a guard to his knees. There was no way forward. No way back. Wynn's chest heaved. She grabbed Avery's arm. "We have to jump."

Avery didn't move.

"Avery! We have to."

"I... I can't swim," she said, eyes fixed on the churning black water. "Wynn, I can't."

"What?" Wynn's voice cracked. "You can't swim? But all Tarnish..." She stopped. The words crumbled. Of course. Avery wasn't born of The Tarn, but more than that, Wynn's breath caught as the realization slid sharply into place, she had *never* seen Avery swim. Not in the lake, not in the river, not even when the younger kids played in the shallows. She always watched from the rocks with no more than a toe touching the water. It hadn't meant anything then. But now… "You're afraid," Wynn whispered.

Avery nodded, eyes glinting in the dark. "It's the only thing I remember," she said. "Water. And being afraid." She exhaled, trembling.

"I heard him," Avery said quickly. "The Stone. I heard everything he said to you." Her gaze didn't waver. "It confirmed what I already suspected about who you are. I followed you. Watched you train. I saw Lorkan when you were taken to the whipping post, the way he looked, like it was killing him and not you."

Wynn opened her mouth, but Avery cut her off.

"You're not just anyone," Avery said. "You're the one who's going to change this. I don't know how, but I believe it. I think that's why I'm here."

The Stone and his men were almost within reach.

"What? No," Wynn yelled. "I'm not leaving you."

"Yes, you are."

"Avery—"

And then, before Wynn could stop her, two hands shoved her. Hard. The scream barely formed before the icy water ripped it away, and the river swallowed her whole.

The current pulled her down, spun her sideways, dragged her like a broken branch. But she didn't panic. She'd been raised for this. Her brother had taught her to swim before she could write her name.

Be one with the water, he'd said. *Don't fight it. Feel where it wants to take you. Then decide where you want to go.* In the Tarn, it was a rite of passage: every child was expected to swim the length of the lake in front of the castle when they turned eight. Wynn had done it at five.

Her parents had told her no. They said she was too small, too young, not strong enough. The water was deep and wide and cold. But that was exactly why she jumped. She remembered the gasp from the shore, the panic in her mother's voice, her father shouting for someone to go in after her. Only her brother had stayed still. He didn't yell. He didn't reach. He just watched—quiet, steady, encouraging—because he knew. He was the one who'd taught her how to float, how to breathe through fear.

She remembered the cool press of the lake, the moment his hand let go days earlier during practice, the way the world went silent under the surface. She remembered the calm. So now, as the river clawed and twisted, she let herself go under. She didn't fight. She flowed.

Then she surfaced, coughing, arms slicing with the rapids, legs kicking. She couldn't hear anything but the roar, not even her own gasping breath. She kicked hard, angled her body with the current. Stay loose. Stay light. Her limbs obeyed like instinct. As she flowed down river she looked back and saw them.

The Stone had reached the edge of the bridge. He grabbed Avery by the arm and shouted something Wynn couldn't hear over the roar of the river, but then his hand rose and came down, striking Avery hard across the face. Her head snapped to the side.

Wynn's breath caught, went razor-sharp in her chest. *I will kill him for that,* she thought, every inch of her alive with fury. *I swear it.*

The Stone yanked Avery backward toward the waiting wagon, then turned to bark orders at the soldiers. Without hesitation, they broke off, some on horseback, some on foot, racing down the opposite bank, the Tor side, boots slamming the dirt, blades flashing in the moonlight. They were moving fast, trying to outpace the river. Trying to catch her. But the river didn't wait. It surged and dragged and carried her away, Wynn swimming with it. They would never catch her.

"WYNN!" A faint and familiar voice cut through the roar. She turned her head and saw Kiernan, running along the riverbank on the Tarn side, somehow keeping pace. He was shouting, pointing, scanning the water for something. Then he spotted her. "Wynn! Swim! Swim hard!" He pointed ahead of her. She saw it now, a fallen tree trunk jutting out like a half-bridge from shore to water. Kiernan scaled it without hesitation, boots slipping on the slick bark. He knelt low, arm outstretched. "Come on! Come on!"

She kicked harder, each stroke a battle. Her arms ached. Her legs cramped. But she reached the log just in time for Kiernan's outstretched hand to grab hers and pull her in. She scrambled up with what strength she had left, collapsing onto the muddy bank, coughing-up river water and trying to catch her breath.

She rolled onto her side, staring up at the stars. "Avery," she rasped. "She's still... she's still..."

"I know," Kiernan said, on his knees beside her. "Lorkan and Night stayed back to hold them off. He told me to find you. To get you out."

Wynn sat up slowly, soaked to the bone, trembling with cold and rage. "She pushed me," she said, trying to catch her breath. "Avery. She pushed me off."

Across the river, hooves clomped, dull and menacing against the damp earth. The sound of dark knights regrouping. Then—*thwip*—an arrow struck the ground just to Wynn's right. Another hissed past her cheek.

"We have to go," Kiernan said, grabbing her arm. "We have to go *now*."

She turned, breath catching.

The bridge was a shadow in the distance now, swallowed by mist and moonlight. But there, flickering, she saw the torches. The caravan was moving again, slipping forward into the Tor.

Avery was gone. And she was free.

Guilt cinched tight around her ribs. As she ran, she pressed her palms to her chest, right over the spot where Avery had shoved her. She hadn't known Avery could push like that. Hadn't known how much strength she held inside that quiet, little body. Maybe she'd never truly seen her. Avery had always followed in silence, but maybe that silence wasn't submission. Maybe it had been something deeper. Fiercer. A kind of strength Wynn, and everyone, had overlooked. She'd need it now.

"I'll come back for you," she whispered. "I swear it." The stars blinked above, cold but listening. And ahead, soft and dark, the trees opened to receive them, their protecting shadows welcoming her back. While behind them, the river kept running.

~ ~ ~

I've been quiet, haven't I? I suppose even books hold their breath when things begin to fall apart and action takes over. I didn't mean to leave you alone in it. Just... sometimes the story pulls so hard, even I forget to chime in. But I'm here again, now that she's running, now that we're back in the Tarn. It's strange how things can change in a heartbeat. How someone small becomes mighty. How fear turns to resolve. How a character, once out of sync, can quickly find their place. If your heart is aching a little, mine is too. So maybe now's the time to rest. To let the trees hush around you, to feel the weight of the story ease for a while. Or maybe, just maybe, you need to keep going, to follow the flicker of what comes next. Either way, I'll be right here. We all will be. And the forest, like the story, will wait for you. For now, let your eyes grow heavy. Let the night be kind and, as always, sleep well.

CHAPTER NINE

The forest had always been the one place Wynn felt safest. Even as a child, when others whispered of monsters in the trees, she had slipped between trunks like they were old friends. The dark didn't frighten her here. It never had. The Tarn night wrapped around her like something living, branches closing in not to trap, but to shield. It made the world smaller, quieter. It could muffle grief and dull pain. Now, soaked to the bone and trembling, she still felt the hush of the trees settle in her chest like a steadying hand. The cold bit deep, but she ignored it. When she stumbled on a root, something out of character for her, she caught herself without a sound. Kiernan glanced over. She didn't meet his eyes.

"You're shivering," he said softly.

"No-o-o, I'm n-n-not," she said through chattering teeth.

"You are."

"I'm f-f-fine."

"You're a terrible liar."

She didn't answer. Her foot landed on a sharp pebble, and she winced.

Kiernan frowned. "Wait! Your boots?"

Wynn glanced down, as if only now remembering. Her toes were pale and caked in mud. "Yeah. I never got them back before they took me. It's fine." She gave a half-hearted shrug. "Not my favorite pair anyway."

"Weren't they your only pair?"

She shrugged and clicked her tongue, soft and sharp. Three clicks, then a whistle. But nothing answered. No rustle. No paw-steps. No glint of eyes in the dark.

"She'll find us," Kiernan said, watching her. "She's cleverer than you are."

Wynn gave a tiny huff. "True, but not comforting."

"It wasn't meant to be."

She clicked again. Whistled. Waited. Nothing. "This is all my fault," she said quietly.

"No, it isn't."

"Yes, it is," she snapped, voice cracking. "Avery asked me not to go to the festival games. She begged me to stay. But I had to be stupid. I just had to prove something." She drew a sharp breath, shaking her head. "If I had just stayed at the damn inn like she asked... they would've taken me. Just me. Not her."

Kiernan didn't interrupt. He just kept walking beside her, close enough to catch her if she stumbled again.

"We wouldn't be in this mess if it wasn't for me," she said. "If I wasn't a princess—" She could barely say the word.

Kiernan still didn't respond.

"See?" Wynn laughed bitterly. "Even you can't deny it. This is my fault."

"Wynn," he slowed their pace, "it is not for us to ask the Fates why, we must accept what is given and move on."

"Sounds like something Lorkan would say."

"He did. That's all him."

Her soaked braid stuck to her neck. The stars blinked down, sleepy, indifferent. She couldn't stop seeing Avery's face, calm and certain. Fierce.

"I still can't believe she pushed me," Wynn murmured, more to herself than him.

Kiernan snorted softly. "People can do stupid things when they care about someone."

She glanced over. "Like throw themselves into a sword fight?"

He gave a crooked smile. "Was that stupid?"

She didn't answer. Just looked at him longer this time, really looked. "You're bleeding," she said, eyes narrowing.

He lifted his arm, peeling back the damp fabric of his sleeve to show a cut high on his bicep. "It's fine. Just a scratch."

"You were always terrible with a sword," she said, half teasing, half serious. "You probably did that to yourself."

"I got the job done, didn't I?" he said with a shrug, and then winced slightly as the movement tugged at the wound.

Wynn huffed a laugh. "Barely."

"I'll take barely over not-at-all," he said. "Besides, I slipped on the bridge. That didn't help."

"You *slipped*?"

"There was blood! And a dead guy!"

Wynn shook her head, biting back a smile. "You're lucky I didn't see that."

"Oh, thank the stars," he muttered. "I'd never live it down."

She glanced forward again, the trees folding tighter around them, the path fading into shadows.

"Thank you," she said, reluctantly.

Kiernan paused mid-step. "Wait—what was that?"

Wynn rolled her eyes. "I said thank you. Don't let it go to your head."

He smirked. "Too late. I always knew I'd make a fine knight in shining armour."

"In what world?" she shot back. "You slipped on a corpse and nearly lost your arm."

"Details," he said, brushing her off with mock dignity, "being a hero is messy." Then, a few minutes later and with a little more sincerity he said, "You're welcome."

The forest path was little more than a worn whisper between the trees, and even that was stretching it. They'd long since lost the moonlight, and the tangled canopy overhead made the night sky feel like a wool blanket had been thrown over the world; dark, muffling, and full of shapes that looked a little too much like guards waiting in the underbrush.

Wynn stumbled again, catching her toe on a gnarled root. She hissed quietly through her teeth. Kiernan didn't say anything at first. Just reached out, steadying her elbow before she could pretend she hadn't tripped.

"I'm fine," she said, for the third time in five minutes. "You can stop coddling me."

"You're soaked and you're limping."

"I'm fine."

Kiernan sighed, the kind that sounded like he wanted to argue but knew it wouldn't get anywhere. He let her go, hands back at his sides.

They walked on in silence for a while. Wynn kept thinking about Avery. About her strength. That final shove. She still felt it in her bones. She hadn't thought Avery had that kind of power.

"She is stronger than I give her credit for," Wynn said suddenly. "I thought she needed me."

"She does," Kiernan said. "But not in the way you think."

Wynn nodded slowly, eyes fixed on her feet as they moved through the forest path. "We all have secrets, I guess."

Kiernan made a small noise in agreement.

"What?" she asked.

"What? What?" He glanced at her quickly.

"You made a noise."

"I make lots of noises," he said, trying to play it off.

But Wynn didn't let it go. "When you saw him—The Stone—I saw your face. You looked like you knew him."

"Everyone knows The Stone."

"K. That's not what I meant, and you know it."

Kiernan didn't answer at first. His jaw tightened. A branch cracked underfoot. The silence stretched, until he finally said, "He killed my father."

Wynn stopped. "What?" She waited. The trees were thinning slightly now, the moonlight catching on the damp leaves like scattered silver coins.

"My father was one of the Blue Knights," Kiernan finally said. "One of the seven sworn to protect your family. The ones who were supposed to die before letting harm come to them." Kiernan went on, his voice quieter now. "That day. The Day of the Fates. When Prima's men came. He told me to run. I was small. Too small to fight. So I hid."

Wynn's chest tightened as she was brought back to the day.

"I was behind the tapestry in the main hall. I watched through the fabric. I saw the doors break open. I heard my father's voice... shouting. And then I saw him, leading the Dark Knights in." For a moment, all that moved was the mist curling around their ankles, like it too wanted to hear the rest of the story.

"It was The Stone," Kiernan said. Wynn drew in a breath.

"I didn't recognize him at first," he added. "Not with the scar, the blind eye. Those weren't there then."

Wynn swallowed. "I thought I recognized him. I did. But the eye..."

"My father did that," Kiernan said. "Before he fell."

Neither of them spoke for a long time.

Kiernan's voice dropped, rough-edged. "I saw the rest, too. After. I saw your mother clutching you and your brother. I saw the Dark One enter the hall. I saw the... the slaughter. And I saw when she stopped. Looked down at you both. I didn't think she was going to let you live."

The wind stirred the branches above. The woods were listening.

"I used to think we met after," Wynn said softly as she started walking again, her gaze fixed ahead. "When they started rounding up the children. But... that's not right, is it?" She glanced at him. "We met before. In the kitchens."

Kiernan's brow lifted, a flicker of surprise crossing his face. "I didn't think you remembered."

"I do," she said. "You were always near the ovens. Sneaking things when you thought no one was looking."

He gave a quiet laugh. "Subtlety was never my strong suit."

"You looked like you belonged there," she said. "Like it was your corner of the world."

"It was." He paused. "It still is. I've always been drawn to kitchens. The warmth, the rhythm of it, the quiet work of making something good. Even back then, I'd sneak in and try things I saw the cooks making earlier. My father knew it too. He hated it. Thought it was beneath me. He used to tell me that real knights don't knead dough."

Wynn's eyebrows lifted. "And now Freidrickson says the same."

"He's worse. At least my father didn't try to beat it out of me."

She went quiet, thoughtful. "Funny," she said after a moment. "I never thought of baking as a kind of rebellion. But for you... it kind of is."

He gave a half-smile. "I used to have a recipe I was obsessed with. Apple spice cake. Caramel glaze. Cinnamon sugar crust. I never got it right."

"You will," she said. "Someday. And I will be more than happy to test it out for you." She nudged his arm.

He smiled but didn't answer right away. Then, solemnly, "I made a vow."

Wynn looked over.

"After my father fell. After what they did to your family." His voice was rough at the edges. "I swore I'd do what he couldn't. Protect you. However I could."

Wynn slowed. She didn't know what to say. So instead, she reached out, brushing her hand against his for just a moment. "All this time," she said, voice thin, "all these years—you've been around because you felt you had to be?"

Kiernan stopped walking. "Wynn—"

But before either of them could say more, Wynn froze. Her voice came out barely a whisper. "Look."

The trees parted and a single castle turret stood before them, rising like a tower from the ground, its stones twisted with moss and wrapped in vine. A crumbling spine of something long lost.

And on the ground beside it, half-cast in moonlight—"Lorkan," Kiernan breathed.

Wynn ran.

He was slumped against the stone wall, head bowed, an arrow in his side, breathing shallow. One hand pressed weakly to his ribs. And curled beside him like a watchful sentinel...

"Night!"

The fox lifted her head, eyes gleaming. She didn't bark. Didn't whine. Just padded forward and nuzzled Wynn's side. Wynn dropped to her knees, pulling her close. Night nosed her jaw, then sat back with a huff, unimpressed by the dramatics. But then she turned. Quietly. And trotted back to Lorkan. She circled once, then pressed herself to his side. Not in her usual, lazy sprawl. She was gentle, deliberate, as if trying not to jostle him. Wynn's breath caught. Something in that simple motion, something in the careful way Night lay her head next to Lorkan's leg, conveyed the severity of his wound.

He blinked up at her, pale and weak, but with a smirk, "You took your time."

~ ~ ~

It was a short chapter, wasn't it? But long enough to feel the cold, wet chill in Wynn's bones. Long enough to breathe the crisp air that burns a little at the top of the lungs. Long enough to hear the wind knock down the dying leaves, one by one, as if autumn itself is unraveling. She's still out there in it now, beneath a moon that gives no warmth. And maybe, just maybe, your thoughts are still out there with her. But your body... your body is here. Wrapped in stillness. Held by warmth. Not everyone has a mattress as soft or blankets as kind. Not everyone gets to sleep with a roof overhead and a story to hold. So take this moment. Feel it. Let the warmth soak in where the chill tried to linger. Let the hush find you and sleep, as she cannot. Sleep deeply. Sleep cozy. Sleep well.

CHAPTER TEN

It was clear that the turret had once been an outpost. You could still see the shape of it; strong, circular bones rising from the earth like a crown, built to watch over the Tarn's borders. There must have been a time when guards stood watch at its edges, scanning the distant mountains for signs of danger. Once, they might have warmed their hands over this same firepit, now lit again with a low, crackling flame. But that was long ago. Now the wooden floor had fallen through in parts, exposing cold, open holes into the dark below. Old nests filled the crevices; birds, rodents, maybe worse. Feathers piled in the corners. Bones, too. Tiny ones. Owl eyes glinted sometimes from the upper beams, and the wind moved strangely through the broken walls, whistling upward into silence. Rain had begun to fall, threading through the half-collapsed roof in fine, cold needles. One side of the turret still held, enough to huddle beneath, if they stayed close, though even there, the damp crept in, slow and persistent. It was shelter, but only just.

Wynn kept close to the fire, her knees pulled to her chest. Night lay curled near the flames, head on her paws, eyes trying to stay open and keep watch but slowly blinking shut, losing the battle. And Lorkan—Lorkan sat propped against a wall, legs stretched out, one arm cradling the arrow that pierced his side. His face was pale, drawn. Older than she had ever seen him. When did he get so old?

Wynn moved closer, jaw clenched, hands trembling. "We need to remove the arrow."

Lorkan's eyes met hers. They were dark and steady. "It won't help."

"Don't say that."

"I've seen this kind of wound before," he said quietly. "Many times. It's gone too deep. I can feel it... my body is letting go."

"No," she said, too fast. "No, that's not—You just need—We can—" But her voice faltered. She didn't know what she meant to say or how she could help him.

Kiernan stood nearby, awkward in his silence, arms crossed over his chest not knowing what to do. Lorkan looked up at him. "Kiernan."

He straightened.

"Give us a few minutes?"

Kiernan nodded immediately. "I'll... gather firewood." He turned to go, but paused at the doorway where the wind whispered through the cracks. "Lorkan, I... You..."

"You were a clumsy boy," Lorkan said, voice rougher now, but not unkind. "Always asking questions. Always underfoot. Loud. Annoying even." Kiernan blinked. "But you've turned into a good man," Lorkan continued. "Still clumsy. I've never met anyone with less coordination. But you're kind, this world needs that. And you're loyal, and she needs that."

Kiernan swallowed.

"You know what you need to do. And you'll know when to do it," Lorkan added.

Their eyes met. Kiernan gave a solemn nod. "Yes, sir. And... thank you... for everything." He turned and stepped out into the dark.

The wind stirred again. Wynn waited until the footsteps faded and then she turned to Lorkan, fiercely, the fire casting golden lines across her face. "Don't talk like that," she said. "Like you're dying. Like you're leaving."

He didn't smile, but something warm flickered in his eyes.

"There's a time for all of us," he said. "When the Fates cut the line and our stories must end. This is mine."

Ah, dear reader. There are moments a story leans in close, not just to tell, but to hold. To wrap arms around the hearts that carry it forward. And in this moment, I find myself hovering near Wynn. Not to change what must unfold, but to steady her steps as best I can. The ink grows slow here, thick with feeling. Time narrows. Breath catches. There are things coming I would spare her, if I could. But she is brave, even when she doubts it. So are you, if you're still here. So come. Let us bear witness, quiet as falling rain, for all of this is part of the journey.

"No," she whispered. "No, I'm not ready. You said I wasn't ready. So, you can't go."

He looked at her gently. It wasn't a look she had ever seen him give. "But you are," he said. "You have to be."

And she broke.

Her face crumpled and her hands balled into fists, and the tears came faster than she could stop them. She turned away from him, toward the fire, like maybe she could hide the way her body shook. She wanted to scream at him. Tell him he didn't get to leave. Not yet. Not with so much left undone. Instead, all she could think was how much time she'd wasted. All those days she'd defied him. The cold silences. The times she'd turned her back, walked away, refused his lessons, his warnings, his strange and distant care.

And now—

Now he was going. And she didn't even know how to say goodbye.

The fire cracked. Night lifted her head and watched Wynn with slow, blinking eyes. Lorkan reached out a hand, slow with effort, and placed it gently on hers. "You're stronger than you know," he said. "And, as much as you like to think it, you're not alone."

Wynn sniffed and tried to steady her voice. "I know. I have Kiernan—"

"No," Lorkan cut in gently, though his voice was thinner now, rasping with pain. "There's another."

She blinked. "What?"

He winced, his hand tightening briefly over his side. Blood still bloomed slow and dark around the shaft of the arrow. "I don't have time to explain it all... and I'm sorry for that. I know you'll have questions. You deserve answers."

She leaned in closer, the firelight catching the edge of her damp hair.

Lorkan drew a shallow breath. "There is another princess. Prima's daughter."

Wynn stared. "I thought she died as a child?"

"As you did?" Lorkan responded with an arched brow.

"Right." Wynn conceded.

"Her name is Grace," he said. "She's real. She lives in a keep across the Still River, tucked beside a small lake at the foot of the mountains. That place... it was hidden, for a long time. Built before Prima turned dark. Before all this began."

Wynn's heart pounded. "How do you know this?"

"I've known for some time," Lorkan said, voice low, as though it might echo into the shadows overhead. "I was tasked with keeping an eye on you both."

She hesitated. A strange twist tightened in her chest, sharp and unwelcome. He'd known about Grace. Been watching her. Helping her. All this time. The thought stung, absurdly, and jealousy bloomed like a spark struck in dry brush. But just as quickly, it burned to ash. This wasn't the time. Avery was missing. The world was unraveling. And Lorkan, whatever else he had done, was now dying.

"Why tell me now?" she asked, quieter.

"Because you have to find her," he said. "If you want to save Avery... if you want to free this land... it won't be enough to run. You must defeat Prima. And to do that, you'll need Grace."

"I don't understand," Wynn said. "What does she have to do with any of this?"

Lorkan shifted, exhaling a sharp breath as pain flared across his face. "When The Stone came for you, I overheard him. He gave orders to another group of knights. They were to take Grace to the Tor capital. Directly to Prima."

Wynn's stomach turned. "Why?"

"I don't know," Lorkan admitted. "But it means Grace is no longer hidden. She's in danger. And I dispatched the ones sent after her—" he didn't say how, and Wynn didn't ask. "But more will come. They always do."

She drew back slightly, processing. Her jaw clenched. "And you want me to save her?" she said slowly. "Prima's daughter?"

"You must."

Wynn looked away, eyes burning. "Why should I care about her? About The Dark One's blood?"

Lorkan's voice stayed calm. "Because she's not Prima." Wynn didn't respond. "She's lived her whole life in the shadow of that woman," he said. "Like you've lived in the shadow of what she destroyed. And still, Grace has held on to herself. Hidden her gentleness, her curiosity, her strength. If there's any part of the Tor worth saving... she carries it."

"I don't know if I can do this," Wynn whispered. "Any of it. Fighting Prima, saving Grace, saving Avery—"

"You can," Lorkan said. "Is it impossible? Yes. But you've been impossible from the start." She looked at him, startled.

"You climbed out of ruin," he said. "You survive. You sacrifice your safety for the good of others. You consistently outsmart the Dark Guards. You won over a fox." At that, Night perked her ears up. "You won me over, too. And that wasn't easy."

A breath escaped her lips. Almost a laugh. Almost.

"I've always known," he said, "the task you have ahead of you."

"I'm not ready," she whispered again.

"Yes," he said softly. "You are. I've told you this before, but you must not forget it... you will always have a choice."

"That doesn't make me special. We all have choices."

"Yes, but you will always make the right one," he said gently. "That's what makes you different."

And for a moment, the circular space of the turret fell into a hush. The fire whispered. The river murmured in the dark beyond. Somewhere above, the eyes in the shadows shifted but did not blink. Wynn looked back to Lorkan. And something inside her—something scared, and grieving, and furious—began to turn.

"Tell me what I have to do," she said, her voice steady despite the tears on her cheeks.

Lorkan's gaze lingered on her a moment, as though he were memorizing her face. Then he drew in a breath, shallow but sure, and nodded toward the pack near the fire. "In there," he said. "You'll find your cloak, boots, some food... a note for Grace. And the ring."

"The ring?" Wynn asked, blinking.

He nodded, "You know the one."

Wynn reached for the pack and pulled the ring out with careful fingers.

"I don't know how or why it ended up in your hands," Lorkan said, watching her. "The Fates must be having a laugh, or are up to their old tricks. All I know is that I've seen that ring before. On Prima's hand, when she came back from the

Hundred Day Sadness. And I do not believe that all this, and that," he nodded at it, "is just coincidence."

Wynn looked up sharply.

"It's imbued with something not from The Vast," he said. "Magic. Ancient. I don't know what it does but I think I know who might. And I believe it's the key to defeating her." The fire crackled. A soft hiss as the wood settled. "You need to get to Grace. The note explains what she needs to know. Give her a chance, Wynn. She can be... a lot sometimes. But, so can you. And the two of you will have to figure this out together. It'll be dangerous. Prima's best will be after you. Trust no one."

Wynn held the ring tightly in her palm.

Lorkan's breathing slowed. His eyes softened as he looked at her again.

"You look tired," he murmured.

Wynn gave a faint, sad smile. "I can't even remember the last time I slept."

"It matters," he continued. "You know it does. If you don't find sleep soon..."

"I'll sleep when I die." She said without thinking and then winced the moment it left her lips.

But Lorkan gave a low, rough laugh that turned into a cough. "Well," he said hoarsely, "then I suppose that makes two of us."

She shook her head, biting her lip hard.

"I wish I'd thought to bring sleep tokens, but in my haste... I should've. I'm sorry. I—" He stopped, eyes fluttering briefly. His voice quieter now.

Night stirred from beside the fire. Her dark paws padded softly against the ground as she crossed to him, nudging beneath his arm. She didn't make a sound, but her body curled gently into his side, warm and still. Lorkan's hand found her fur, fingers brushing behind her ears.

"I always liked her," he murmured. "A little sassy and a lot defiant. Just like you, Tarn slave."

Wynn leaned forward, placing a hand over his. "Until the next full moon, Overseer," she whispered, her voice barely more than a breath.

And so one life leaves the page—quietly, without protest—while Wynn remains, tears slipping down her cheeks before she even feels them fall. A part of her wanted to stay in that moment, to fold herself into Night's fur and the silence and wait for his guiding voice to rise again. But it didn't. And this world, she knew, would not stop for her grief. What frightened her most wasn't the sorrow, but the going on, without his counsel, his calm, his ever-steady presence. Yet even in that fear, she felt it: the weight of his choices now tucked into her own, like a map he'd half-sketched for her in the dust. Because stories, yes, even this one, are shaped by those we meet along the way, who sometimes press their hands to the helm for just a moment, altering our course without asking. Wynn had not chosen this path, not truly. But she could feel it now beneath her feet, laid by his last words, his last breath. A story carried forward.

The door creaked open behind her, and Kiernan stepped into the ruin, arms full of firewood. He looked up... and stopped.

Wynn rose slowly. Her limbs felt heavy, her chest hollow, as if the grief inside had carved out everything else. She turned to him, and something in her simply gave. Stumbling forward, she fell into him, burying her face against his shoulder, as if trying to hide from the truth of it.

Kiernan dropped the wood. It scattered across the stone floor, forgotten. He didn't speak. He didn't need to. His arms came around her with a strength that steadied and gave way all at once. He held her like someone who understood what had been lost, who felt it, too, in the silence Lorkan had left behind. The rain kept falling, steady and soft. The fire crackled low. And inside the crumbling turret, for a single, sacred moment, time bowed its head, and all was still.

~ ~ ~

I know—it's hard to close the book when we've left someone in sorrow, when a chapter ends and the story holds its breath around a wound that can't yet be mended. It feels wrong, doesn't it? To stop here. As if by pausing, we abandon them. As if by sleeping, we forget. But that's not what this is. Stories don't vanish when the covers close, and grief doesn't fade just because you rest your eyes. It waits, gently, without resentment. So if your heart aches as Wynn's does, let it. But also, let yourself be warm. Let yourself be still. Let the sadness be part of the story, not the whole of it. The next page will be here. And when you're ready, only when, you'll turn it. For now, sleep well. You've felt enough for one night.

CHAPTER ELEVEN

The Dark Castle loomed like a shadow that had forgotten the sun. Its towers were jagged silhouettes against a storm-colored sky with pointed spires clawing upward. The walls, black as ink and smooth as glass, seemed to absorb the light rather than reflect it. It was said the castle had no windows, and standing within it, one could believe the rumor. The air was still, stale, as if it hadn't been breathed for centuries. What few torches lined the halls flickered with cold blue flames, casting long, hungry shadows that crept and stretched across the walls like they had a life of their own.

Avery stood in the throne room. Or what passed for a throne room in such a place. The floor beneath her feet was cold and veined with cracks. Hollow, like the ground itself might fall away. A center fire burned in a circular pit, but strangely not seeming to produce any heat. Everything around her echoed faintly, her breaths, the shuffling of guards, the click of Prima's boots across the black marble. Her wrists were once again bound tightly behind her, the rope biting into her skin. Another coarse gag muffled her mouth.

At the end of the hall, Prima took a seat atop her throne of carved stone and ashwood, the crown of the Tor circling her bald head. Her robes shimmered like oil in the low torchlight, colors shifting from deep violet to void-black. Her eyes, however, were steady. Sharp. Too steady. She was studying Avery like one might study a puzzle missing too many pieces, trying to make sense of the incomplete image.

"Who is this?" Prima asked. Her voice was quiet, but there was weight in it. "She's not Wynn. Nor Grace. I sent you for either, and you have returned with neither."

The Stone stood at Avery's side, his armor scraped and smeared with soot. Blood, too. Some of it his. "There was... trouble," he said. "An unexpected turn of events. Lorkan... he turned on us. Killed several of my knights."

"*Your* knights?" Prima tilted her head slightly.

"Forgive me," he bowed quickly, "I misspoke. *Your* knights, my Dark Queen."

Prima paused long enough to let The Stone think about his mistake. "Lorkan?" she continued. "Are you telling me that old man has outdone you?"

The Stone squared his shoulders. "He was clearly never loyal to the Dark Queen."

For a heartbeat, nothing moved. Then Prima rose from her throne. Her movement was slow, deliberate, as she descended the shallow steps. With each click of her boots, the tension in the room grew like a noose tightening.

"So," she said, her voice cool and delicate, "you believe this is my fault."

The Stone blinked. "My Queen, I—"

"You imply that I failed to keep my knights in line. That I'm to blame for your failure."

"No—" He dropped to one knee, his voice stumbling over itself. "No, my Queen, I meant only that he—he deceived us all. I take full responsibility. I—"

Prima raised a hand. Silence fell like frost.

Avery flinched. The Queen moved past her like a shadow sliding over stone, her head gleaming like polished marble in the cold torchlight. She circled slowly, eyes fixed on the bound girl as if trying to divine her secrets with nothing but a glance. She didn't look at The Stone when she asked, "And how did a girl escape the Dark Guard?"

"She..." The Stone, still kneeling, lifted his head slightly and looked towards Avery, "... jumped into the Still River, my Queen. It swept her away. I don't believe she could have survived."

Prima hummed, unconvinced. "She is Tarn-born. Their blood flows with water. The river will not take her. It will carry her, farther than you think. No, she is not dead but she will be a problem. And the other?" she asked without turning.

The Stone swallowed. "I dispatched men to retrieve her, but... I've received no word, yet."

Prima's head tilted. "Your ineptitude is stunning." She snapped her fingers at one of the black-clad knights standing silently against the far wall. "Send for The Hawk."

Avery didn't know who, or what, The Hawk was, but her stomach turned at the shift in Prima's voice as she said the name.

The knight took a step forward, "Dark One, The Hawk has not yet returned from the Eastern fjords."

"Did I ask if he has returned?"

"No," the guard lowered his head. "I will send for him, right away." He turned on his heel and abruptly left the room.

The Stone straightened slightly, drawing breath. "I did strike Lorkan. An arrow. High in the side. He won't breathe the air much longer."

Prima did not react, not really. Only a brief narrowing of her dark eyes. "A small consolation. Although, I would have liked to have seen the life drain from his eyes myself." She paused, "And the other matter?"

The Stone stood a bit taller. "We intercepted Thorald's carriage near the borderlands, just as ordered. My men killed him and recovered the trunk."

"And?" she said, voice thin as a knife edge.

He hesitated. "There was no ring, my Queen."

Ah, Thorald. His name might not mean much to you, dear reader, but let it be said: even the smallest characters sometimes shift the pen. The Treasurer of Tor, round and red-faced and largely dismissed by all, had felt invisible most of his life. And in a way that irony so often favours, he'd risen to power by doing the same to others, climbing over backs he pretended not to see, hoarding coin, currying favor, always watching for a seat at a more gilded table. Do not waste sorrow on him. Thorald was greedy, petty, and deeply unkind. But, it is often despicable men that make bold choices and when he finally turned against the Dark Queen, he didn't choose justice or redemption. He chose revenge. And so he stole the one thing he suspected she coveted, unaware of the true value it held for her. The how of it, well, that's a tale worth telling someday, unfortunately for Thorald and for you, it's not one for these pages.

Prima's fury was immediate.

She turned like thunder cracking, her cloak flaring behind her, the firelight casting long, savage shadows that moved like spirits along the stone walls. "That fat, simpering oaf," she hissed. "He stole from me. *From me.* Did he sell it? Bury it? Lose it to drink or dice?" She whirled on The Stone, voice rising. "*And you killed him?*"

"He resisted, my Queen. He was begging and bartering for his life. He said, he claimed, he'd been robbed. By two girls and a fox." He looked directly at Avery. "Before she... before Wynn jumped into the river, there was a fox. It aided in the escape. I do not believe it was a coincidence."

Avery stayed perfectly still, but her stomach dropped. Blood drained from her face. She didn't blink.

The Dark Queen turned, slowly, her gaze sharpening by degrees. Her eyes did not flash, they focused. Like the point of a spear drawing closer to the center of a target. The room went quiet. Too quiet. Even the fire seemed to hush.

"Well then," she said, her voice now a purr of velvet over steel. "I feel as if you may know something about this." She stepped forward and, with a single flick of her wrist, yanked the gag from Avery's mouth.

Avery sucked in a breath, raw and ragged. "Who," Prima said, eyes never leaving hers, "are you?"

Avery said nothing.

The Stone stepped forward. "Answer your Queen!"

He struck her hard across the cheek. Her head snapped to the side, but she didn't cry out. She didn't blink.

Prima studied Avery like something half-unearthed; an artifact dug from unfamiliar soil, not yet named, not yet understood. There was something beneath the dirt, though. Something other. Maybe dangerous.

"She's important to the girl," The Stone said, eager to offer his piece. "They were... close."

Prima's gaze sharpened. "Is that true?" she asked, turning to Avery. "Does Wynn of the Tarn care for you?"

Avery said nothing. But inside, the question landed differently. Of course Wynn cared. But then— the ring? What ring? Her mind caught the word like a thread unspooling. Wynn had taken something? Why hadn't she said so? Wynn kept things. It wasn't new. But it still stung.

The Stone took a step forward, hand raised, but Prima stilled him with a raised hand. She lifted a single finger. "No," she said, voice like frost on glass. "She's no stranger to suffering. Torture will not pry her open. She has lived with pain. She wears it like old lace."

Then she turned again to Avery, head tilted in a gesture of mild, creeping interest. "She knows about the ring," she said aloud, though her tone suggested she was still deciding. "She must."

Avery's pulse thrummed. She didn't.

"Wynn has become more than a simple irritation," Prima said softly. "I should have ended her when I had the chance. For now, the Fates play." Her eyes stayed fixed on Avery. Then, to The Stone: "Take her to the Rock Cells. Feed her. Not well—just well enough."

He bowed low. "Shall we withhold sleep, my Queen?"

"No," she said slowly. "This one does not require tokens." Her voice dipped, nearly curious. "Do you?"

Avery gave no answer. She didn't need to.

"You are neither Tor, nor Tarn," Prima said, almost as an accusation. A beat passed. Then another. "Intriguing."

A hint of a smile touched her lips, but there was no warmth in it. She stepped closer, eyes fixed, gaze narrowing with a predator's calm. Slowly, she reached out and cupped Avery's face in one cold hand. Her long, black thumbnail scraped lightly along Avery's cheek, not enough to break the skin, but enough to be felt. A whisper of a threat, elegantly delivered.

"Where are you from?" she asked, voice low and curious.

Still, Avery stayed definitely quiet.

Prima leaned back, just slightly. "No answer?" she mused. "Curious. But unnecessary. I don't need you to speak to get what I want." She turned then, slow and calm, her hands folding behind her back. And with the clicking of her boots, the Queen was gone, leaving silence, and the scent of fear, behind her.

The Stone exhaled, sharp and ragged, trying to swallow failure. His jaw flexed, fists clenched at his sides. For a moment, he simply stared at Avery; at her stillness, her refusal, her silence that had made a fool of him in front of the Queen. Then he struck her.

The sound cracked across the chamber. Avery dropped to the floor, breath catching in her throat, head ringing. Dust stirred where she landed.

He stepped forward, face contorted with rage and something fouler, shame masked as power. He raised his hand again, ready to drive it down with all the force his pride could summon, but stopped. His fingers trembled in the air, hovering just above her. And then, slowly, he lowered his arm. Not out of mercy. But calculation. He stood over her like a shadow with no soul, breathing hard, his voice a rasp: "You think you're clever. But silence won't save you."

He looked to his guards. "What are you waiting for? You heard the Queen. Take her to the cells." Then he turned, his boots grinding against the floor, and disappeared into the corridor as rough arms grabbed Avery and dragged her away.

~ ~ ~

Well, that was... unsettling. Cruelty like that has a way of echoing, doesn't it? But don't worry, I won't leave you in the dark. Not unless you want to be left there. You could close the book now, tuck the covers higher, pretend you're not thinking about Avery or the Dark Queen's shiny-black nails. You could let your eyes drift shut and promise yourself you'll read more tomorrow. Or... you could turn one more page. Read just one more chapter. Who really needs to be well-rested anyway? Stories are important too. Some might say more important. But no pressure. Sleep well, if you must. Turn the page, if you have it in you. Either way, I'll be here.

CHAPTER TWELVE

They followed the river's edge in silence, the dark water murmuring beside them, echoing the grief that Wynn carried in her chest. The morning air was crisp and unforgiving, growing sharper, more hollow, the nearer they drew to the shadow of the Tor Mountains. Her cloak hung heavy on her shoulders, damp with mist and travel, and it was no match for the cold spilling down from the peaks. The wind slipped through its seams like icy fingers searching for skin, prying past wool and will alike. Still, she didn't pull it tighter. The chill kept her from drifting too far into thought. It kept her awake, anchored and moving. Behind them, smoke still curled faintly above the tree line, a final breath from the pyre they'd built for Lorkan.

They had stood beside it before dawn, the heat licking their skin, the fire reflecting in Kiernan's eyes as he whispered the old prayers. He believed. In gods. In Fates. In something beyond all this. Wynn had no such faith. But she'd stood there beside him, anyway. And before they'd left, she had whispered a thank you. For the training. For the care. For the moments, few as they were, that had made her consider that not all Tor were monsters.

Now, as they walked, she glanced across the river.

The Tor side looked different. The trees there grew thinner, the grass more sparse, and the soil, even from here, seemed paler, more arid. She wondered, not for the first time, how one river could divide so much difference. "Prima," she cursed under her breath. It had to be her. Her magic. Her rot.

Night darted through the underbrush ahead of them, then back again, the white tip of her tail a flash against the trees, eyes sharp and bright. As she passed, she brushed against Wynn's leg, a quick reassurance, then circled back once more. This time, she nudged at Wynn's hand with her cold, damp nose, persistent in that quiet way of hers. Wynn sighed, but her fingers slipped into the pouch at her side. She handed over a dried strip of meat without a word. Night took it delicately, as if it had been her idea all along, then vanished again into the trees, tail high with satisfaction.

They walked until the roar of the falls became a steady presence in the air, like distant thunder that never ceased. The cliffs loomed nearer now with a thick mist curling at their base.

Kiernan's voice broke the quiet. "So..." he said, glancing sideways at her, his breath visible in the chill air. "What do you think the ring is all about?"

Wynn didn't answer right away. Instead, she reached beneath her cloak and tugged the thin rope that hung around her neck, drawing out the obsidian ring. It dangled in the open now, gleaming faintly, cold as ever.

"I don't know. I only took it because it looked like something valuable to that stupid lump." She went on, "But Lorkan said it was on Prima's hand once. If she didn't want me dead already..." She let the thought hang. The ring swung gently as she let it fall back beneath her cloak. "I figure it might be the only piece I have to bargain with. For Avery."

The roar of the waterfall was growing louder now, the mountain's endless voice, rising around them like thunder. It echoed in the cliffs, in their ribs, in the hollowed-out places left behind by grief.

They rounded a bend in the path, and there before them was the pool at the foot of the raging falls, shimmering in the weak morning light, frothing and turning with force, feeding the Still River with its endless pouring. Mist rose in great gusts, curling through the trees, soaking their cloaks. The whole place felt carved from myth. Powerful. Unyielding. Beautiful in the kind of way that made you feel small.

Wynn stopped and crouched beside a boulder, slipping Lorkan's pack off her shoulder. "Let's eat before we look for this cave," she muttered.

She pulled free a bit of bread and cheese—dry, but still good—and handed a piece to Kiernan. Before she could so much as shift her weight, there was a rustle in the underbrush. Night was already there, eyes bright and ears perked, drawn not by invitation but by the unmistakable crinkle of a food wrapper. Wynn smirked faintly and tore off a chunk, setting it beside her boot. The fox pounced with silent enthusiasm, devouring it like a creature who insisted she hadn't eaten in days, and then patiently waiting, staring, hoping for more.

Wynn tried to ignore the pleading eyes, a battle both she and Night knew she eventually would lose, and rummaged for a cloth to wipe her hands. Her fingers brushed something tucked between two flaps of the pack. A folded note, sealed. Lorkan's writing - *Grace*. She stared at it, thumb hesitating at the edge. Her fingers itched to break the seal, to know what he'd written. But she could hear his voice in her head, *"Some things aren't meant for you, girl."* She so rarely listened, but this one time she feigned restraint, and tucked it back into the bag.

"My parents used to tell me stories," she said suddenly. "Before bed. Legends of how this land was formed."

Kiernan glanced at her. "What kind?"

"About how the land was made. About the brothers, Tor and Tarn. They both loved the same girl, Still. They both loved her so much they went to war over her. When they finally thought to ask her how she felt, she couldn't choose, or she didn't love either of them. So they cast her from the cliffs. Where she fell, here, the river formed."

She looked out at the water, eyes distant. "They said that's why it's called the Still River."

Kiernan looked at her profile, the way her hair caught the mist, the way her voice had softened just slightly on the girl's name.

"I can't imagine anyone being that stupid for love," she muttered.

Kiernan looked away too quickly. "No. Definitely not."

Wynn didn't catch the sideways glance he gave her. She didn't see how long he looked. He remembered a different river. A warmer day. She was swimming, laughing, hair slicked back, skin gold with sunlight. That was the moment it shifted, though he hadn't told anyone, not even himself. He'd been around other girls, sure. But none of them made his chest feel tight just standing next to them. None of them made him want to grab a sword or hike for days in the cold.

Wynn reached for another bite of bread, giving a torn section to Night, and turned to him again. "Do you believe it?" she asked. "The story? That Still fell from up there?" She nodded toward the top of the cliffs.

Kiernan didn't respond. He was still staring at her. "Hello? Kiernan?" Wynn's voice cut through the roar of the falls. "Are you listening?"

He blinked, snapping out of whatever world he'd fallen into, and looked up at the cliffs. The wind was louder here, pushing his curls across his brow. "I heard she jumped," he said casually.

Wynn turned toward him, caught off guard. "You *know* that story?"

Kiernan shrugged, a crooked grin tugging at one side of his mouth. "You don't have to be a princess to know the legend of Tor and Tarn. My dad used to talk about it, usually when he'd had too much mead."

She narrowed her eyes and hit his arm. Not hard, but not soft either. "Ow," he muttered, rubbing the spot. "You always hit just a little too hard."

"Baby," she smirked, already standing. "Come on. Let's go."

They moved along the river's edge, boots skimming over slick rock and moss. The waterfall poured down like a curtain of silver fire. Mist wrapped around them, cool and wet and sharp, turning the world into a hazy dream. Somewhere in that wall of rock, there had to be a way through. "There," Wynn said, pointing up. A narrow, dark opening in the cliff face, half hidden by the angle of stone and the water's mist. But it was high. At least twenty feet.

Kiernan's chest puffed just slightly. "I've got it."

Wynn raised an amused brow, arms crossed, but said nothing.

He stepped to the base and started up, muscles flexing as he gripped the wet edges. He climbed confidently for a few feet, then his foot slipped. In an instant, he was flat on his back in the mud.

Wynn burst out laughing, doubling over. "That was *smooth.*"

He groaned. "Your turn, mountain goat."

Wynn shook out her hands, rolled her shoulders. "Let me show you how it's done."

She made it halfway before her fingers lost purchase, her foot sliding and her weight dragging her down. She landed with a *thud* and a hiss of pain, breath knocked from her.

"Much *smoother*," Kiernan said, looking down at her.

They sat there for a beat, Kiernan catching his breath, Wynn clutching her ribs. As much as he wanted to, he didn't mock her again. He knew her ego was bruised enough. He also knew this was unlike her; she had been deprived of sleep for too long.

Night appeared at the base of the rock wall. She looked up once, then leapt, scaling the ledges with ease, her coat almost vanishing into the mottled gray of the cliff. She paused just below the dark opening, looked down, then turned and disappeared.

"She's showing us the way," Wynn whispered.

This time, Wynn moved with care. Her hands gripped tighter, her eyes tracked each foothold. Her arms ached. Her legs shook. The tiredness wasn't just in her body now, it was in her bones, in her blood, in her brain. It made her feel dizzy and a little drunk. Hundreds of Tarn had died like this, on cliffsides, crossing log bridges, working on a rooftop too high off the ground, minds foggy and too slow to prevent or stop a fall.

Keep moving. Focus. She forced her body up, inch by inch.

When she reached the ledge, she turned and extended a hand down to Kiernan. He took it, and she pulled him up with the little strength she still had. She wasn't one to admit her weaknesses but she could feel every single one of them right now. Even if she wanted to tell Kiernan, she couldn't. The waterfall was too loud now, roaring beside them like a beast. The spray hit their faces as they pressed on, shuffling sideways onto a narrow, wet ledge that disappeared behind the cascade.

They stepped into it together; a world of sound and stone and blur. Water struck the rock with such force it felt like standing inside a storm. The ledge was barely wide enough for their boots, slick with a fine green slime. It felt magical, also, deadly.

They moved by inches, slowly scaling forward, hands gripping what little they could. Without warning, Wynn's foot slipped. Her fingers clawed for grip, but the ledge was too wet. Her body pitched sideways and before Kiernan could grab for her, the water pulled her down and she was gone.

"WYNN!" Kiernan lunged forward, almost slipping himself. He scrambled along the slick rock beneath, moving fast but careful, fingers slipping more than once as the spray blinded him. When he cleared the cascade, he began to climb and skid down the far side, boots falling to find traction. At the base, he waded into the churning pool, scanning the surface, calling her name into the mist. Her cloak floated nearby, her pack bobbing near the rocks. On the shore, Night paced anxiously, whining with every pass.

Kiernan grabbed the cloak and slung it to the side. "Wynn!" he yelled again, voice hoarse. "WYNN!" Nothing. Only the thunderous roar of the falls.

And then—

"Here!"

He turned.

She stood on the shore, drenched, hair plastered to her face, water streaming from every seam of her clothes.

Kiernan waded back toward her, relief written across every muscle. "You just had to do it the hard way," he said, chest heaving, grin breaking through.

Wynn snatched the pack from the ground and yanked her cloak back on, her jaw tight. She turned and started marching up the slope beyond the falls, water sloshing in her boots, anger in every stomp.

"Wynn, wait," he called, climbing out behind her. "We should stop. Start a fire. You're soaked—"

"I'm *fine,*" she snapped. "We keep going."

"But—"

"If we stop now," she said with teeth chattering, her voice low, "I don't think I'll be able to move again."

She swayed slightly, and Kiernan stepped forward on instinct, just in case. "I've never gone this long without sleep before," she murmured. "Everything's starting to..."

"You're in the Haze," he said, too quickly.

The word hung heavy between them.

Those in the Tarn knew it too well. That slow, slipping state when sleep had been withheld too long. It crept in behind the eyes, numbed the hands, thickened thoughts like honey in winter. Some people wandered off in it, chasing voices only they could hear. Others laughed until they cried. A few simply forgot who they were, and never quite remembered again.

He could hear it in her voice, see it in her hands, trembling at her sides. And there was nothing he could do. Not for this. Not for the one thing she truly needed. He'd promised to protect her. Give him wolves in the woods or swords in the dark, he could fight those. But sleep? Sleep was a locked gate, and he had no key.

"I'm fine," Wynn said, too fast. "I'm not... *in the Haze.*" But her knees bent slightly, not quite a stagger, not quite a fall, and she didn't lift her eyes to meet his.

He reached out, steadying her gently.

"I said, I'm fine," she said in a tone that Kiernan had heard before. This conversation was over. Wynn turned and stormed into the brush.

Night looked up at him, circled his boots once, then trotted after her. So he followed too. Toward the Keep. Toward whatever waited for them in the shadow of the Tor.

High above the river, a hawk circled. Its wings sliced the air in slow, steady arcs, casting a flickering shadow across the trees below. The land stretched out like a living map; Wynn's green cloak barely a thread against the ground, Kiernan a quiet presence beside her, and Night moving ahead with purpose, her sleek shape weaving through the underbrush. From this height, the Keep was visible now, they would reach it by nightfall. Closer than they realized.

The hawk tilted into the wind and climbed, higher still, before banking sharply and descending in a long, purposeful glide. Through the mist and spray, past stone and branch and silence. It flew not just with instinct, but with direction; sharp, knowing. Down, down to a figure waiting in the wind. The arm rose before the bird landed. And just like that, The Hawk was home.

~ ~ ~

You feel it too, don't you? The damp in the sleeves, the sting in the fingers, the weight of a cold that creeps all the way into the chest. The kind of cold that doesn't shiver out, that just settles. You feel the squelch of boots heavy with water, the ache in legs pushed past what they should bear, the sharp breath pulled through raw lungs. And the tiredness. It isn't just in the limbs now, but in the thoughts, in the very center of her being. No fire. No shelter. Just the sound of leafless branches groaning above and the long, merciless road ahead. But you, dear reader, are not out in it (I hope). You are dry. You are warm. And oh, what a quiet sort of magic that is. So pull the blankets a little tighter. Sink a little deeper into your bed. Let the storm stay on the other side of the story, and let your body remember what stillness feels like. Sleep now... softly, gratefully, and well.

CHAPTER THIRTEEN

Grace had found her favorite nook hours ago, and the sun had only just begun to dip low enough to kiss the tops of the Tor Mountains. That meant another hour, maybe two, before Seraphina would check on her and she'd have to pretend to be asleep, which meant at least three more chapters. Bliss.

The cushions were arranged just so: one behind her back, one beneath her legs, and one under her book for no particular reason other than it was soft and seemed to enjoy being included. A teacup steamed faintly on the ledge beside her, and a warm ginger cookie rested on a folded napkin like it was royalty. Grace was fairly certain Seraphina had baked it out of sympathy and rebellion in equal measure. When the castle Keep was quiet and it was just the two of them, Seraphina often baked some extra small comforts—a tart, a scone, a bit of sweet bread—never announcing it, never asking if Grace wanted any, simply setting it nearby with that same expression that said *don't make a fuss about it.* That woman had a streak of defiance in her, and an even deeper soft spot for Grace's sweet tooth.

Books, of course, were forbidden. Grace knew this. But she also knew Lorkan hadn't risked slipping her tattered volumes of tales for her to ignore them. She kept them hidden behind curtains and under her bed. Some under scarves in her armoire, their spines bent and creased with love. The one in her hands, a ridiculous, wonderful romance about a stable boy and a runaway princess, was one of her favorites. It had horses, secret messages, stolen kisses, and not a single mention of cursed sleep or tyrannical queens. She was just getting to the good part, which is why it was particularly annoying when, just over the edge of the page, something moved.

Grace blinked. A flick of grey and white just outside the window. She lowered the book and looked out the window. A fox? And, wait, was that a *person*?

She set the book aside with great care, as if the characters inside might keep behaving if she was gentle with them, and scooted closer to the window. Yes, definitely a man. And someone on his back, hooded, slumped. Limp.

Then Seraphina stormed out of the door below, wielding a broom like a sword, shouting something about "pests" and "filthy creatures," aiming squarely at the fox.

"Oh no, not the fox," Grace muttered, hopping down from her window perch. She dashed down the spiral stairs and out the door as quick as her slippered feet could take her.

Once she was outside, skirt swishing, the wind catching the waves of her hair, the fox darted away from Seraphina's broom, took one elegant leap, and, without a shred of ceremony, slipped neatly between Grace's legs like it had every right to be there.

Grace froze. "Oh," she said, blinking down at the fox. "Hello." Two blue eyes blinked back.

Seraphina looked horrified and moved forward, swinging her broom. "Get, get, you beast!"

"Seraphina," Grace said calmly, without looking away, "please don't hit my fox."

Seraphina looked at her disapprovingly. "I've decided it's mine now." She crouched slightly, extending a careful hand the way one might to a wild animal they weren't sure would bite, and gave a light scratch behind the fox's ears. It didn't move. That felt like permission enough.

Then her gaze lifted, and properly landed, on the man again. He was still bent beneath the weight of the cloaked figure on his back, splattered with mud looking thoroughly spent. Younger than she'd expected. Maybe a little older than her, but not by much. He had that rare, tousled look that only seemed to exist in her imagination, half-swashbuckler, half-lost hero, like he'd just leapt off the page of one of her hidden romances. Grace felt her heart hiccup in her chest. Her cheeks warmed. Her first boy, and he came with a fox, a mystery, and someone half-conscious over his shoulder. Honestly, it was almost too perfect. She tugged at her sleeves, smoothing nothing in particular, and cleared her throat.

"What do you think," she asked the fox, "do you want to be mine?" She glanced down at the fox now nestled comfortably between her skirts.

The man gave her a look, somewhere between curious and faintly alarmed, but it wasn't him who responded. The figure on his back stirred, lifting her head just enough to reveal a dirt-smudged face and eyes so heavy with exhaustion it was a wonder they'd opened at all. Her voice was rough, cracking with dryness, but her words landed with the sharpness of a knife. "Night belongs to no one."

Grace startled, blinking at the figure now glaring at her from the boy's back. She was... a girl. Roughly Grace's age, though it was hard to tell beneath the dirt and the wild, tangled hair. She looked like she'd fallen out of the woods themselves, feral, scowling, half-asleep and half-wary, but there was something fierce and unshakable in her expression. Not refined, not polished, not like anyone Grace had ever been allowed to meet.

"Oh," Grace said, surprised and a little delighted. "You're a girl."

"We have a quick one here," Wynn said back, too exhausted to keep her head up.

Kiernan adjusted his grip on Wynn's legs, trying not to laugh. "Sorry about her. I'd say she's just tired and grumpy, but truthfully, this is kind of just her."

Wynn lifted one hand with great effort and lightly slapped his shoulder.

Grace felt a laugh bubble up, part nerves, part disbelief, part something else entirely, and tried to smother it with her hand. She wasn't supposed to laugh. Or talk to mysterious muddy girls with too-sharp eyes and silent foxes and boys who looked like weathered scarecrows. This wasn't how her evenings were supposed to go. But, oh, wasn't it thrilling?

"We seek shelter, milady." Kiernan politely nodded, feeling weird about it but also thinking it was the thing to do.

"*Milady*?" Wynn mumbled with amusement.

"You shush," he chimed back.

Behind Grace, Seraphina stepped forward, the broom now held more like a staff than a weapon. "Princess," she said, low and urgent, "this is not a good idea. We are... without staff. If Lorkan found out—"

"Lorkan sent us," Wynn said suddenly, lifting her head again. Her voice was rough but steady this time. "We have a message. For Grace. For the... the Princess." The ss' stuck on her tongue a little too long.

Grace's eyes widened. Her name in this girl's mouth felt strange and exciting, like she'd been plucked from her own story and tossed into someone else's. She hesitated, her fingers tightening slightly around the folds of her skirt. Beside her, Seraphina shook her head once, subtle but firm, her way of saying this was too strange, too fast. *Too dangerous.* And yet... Grace looked back at the two before her. The girl was now on her own two feet and standing with quiet purpose, like someone who'd come far and wasn't done yet. Curiosity sparked behind her ribs, brighter than caution. Her heart gave a small, traitorous flutter. She straightened, smoothed her skirts, and lifted her chin just a little, just enough to pretend she wasn't trembling with the thrill of it all. Like a real heroine might.

"Well," she said. "Then you'd better come in."

The fire crackled softly in the hearth, filling the room with its gentle warmth. Wynn sat on a plush bench, a mug of something sweet and steaming cradled between her hands. She didn't know what it was, and didn't care. It was hot, and that was enough. Kiernan sat beside her, equally still, his fingers curled around his own mug.

Across from them, Grace had tucked her legs under herself and settled near the fire. Night lay curled beside her, nose buried beneath her tail, but one eye still watched Wynn, stubbornly awake.

The room was too nice. Too soft. Too full of silks and cushions and flower-scented air. Wynn bit her tongue to keep from saying anything. Clearly, not all princesses were raised scraping crumbs off the floor or knowing what it meant to bleed without being allowed to cry.

Still, this strange girl beside the fire had offered warmth and safety. And Wynn, like it or not, had no choice but to accept it.

After a long sip from her mug, Wynn finally asked, voice low with exhaustion, "Where is everyone?" Her eyes drifted to the polished banister, the spotless floors, the neatly trimmed ivy just outside the window. "It's a castle. You can't keep a place like this running with just two people."

Grace looked up, her expression flickering. "Oh, no, of course not. The Day of the Fates," she said. "It's the one holiday where everyone's allowed to go home for a few days. Most won't be back till the week's end."

Wynn blinked. "And they just leave you here?"

"Well," Grace said, glancing at Seraphina, who was dozing lightly in the nearby chair, "Seraphina never leaves. This *is* her home. She's been here as long as I have."

Wynn stared into the fire, her fingers tightening slightly around her mug. That much information, freely given, struck her as either naive or foolish. Maybe both. If she'd been someone else, someone dangerous. Still, there was something disarming about Grace's openness. It didn't come from stupidity, Wynn thought. Just from a life lived mostly untouched by betrayal. Which, somehow, made her feel worse.

Wynn looked down at her drink. "That's a dumb thing to tell a stranger," she muttered.

Grace blinked, then smiled faintly. "If Lorkan sent you here, you're not a stranger. Not really."

Wynn didn't answer. But a small part of her, the part that wasn't entirely cold, tucked the words away anyway.

Grace looked down at her mug, then back up. "I can't believe he's dead." Her voice cracked on the word.

Wynn nodded once. "He died trying to save me."

Grace blinked, the words slow to reach her. "From what?"

Kiernan shifted, his shoulder brushing Wynn's. "Maybe it's best if you read the letter."

He reached into the pack and handed it over. The paper was damp, the edges wrinkled from the river. Grace took it carefully, as if it might crumble in her hands. Wynn, watching, felt the old guilt stir again. "Sorry," she said. "It... it got wet."

Grace shook her head, already unfolding it with trembling fingers. Her eyes moved slowly, adjusting to the smudged ink. The firelight flickered across her face as she read it aloud, and in that hush, Wynn could almost hear Lorkan's voice again.

Grace,

If this has reached you, then so has Wynn and so has trouble. I hope you are somewhere safe when you read it, and that you're not alone. There's not time to explain everything, and not everything can be explained. But Wynn needs you. And you'll need her, too. You've always been clever. That will matter now more than ever. There are things I could not speak aloud, even here. But I left you crumbs. Start with The Mapmaker's Daughters. You always liked the middle one best. Read it again. Then The Hollow Prince, but only the epilogue. And finally, A Study of Storms, the old edition, the one with pages missing. You'll know what to look for. I used to wonder if the books I gave you were too much, too strange, too heavy. But you saw what others missed. You were never just reading; you were preparing. You've spent your life curled in stories, now you must step into one. Just know, the world won't always follow the rules of the tales you love. It will be colder. Crueler. But also more alive than any page could hold. Be sharp. Be brave. And do not wait for permission.

~L.

Grace blinked away the blur in her vision and looked up from the letter. Her throat was tight, her chest full, but it wasn't just her. Across the firelight, Wynn sat unmoving, her eyes glassy with unshed tears. Even Kiernan, who had spent the entire time pretending not to listen, was blinking a little too much, his jaw clenched as he looked away toward the flames.

Wynn's voice was quiet. "Do you know the books he refers to?"

Grace nodded slowly. "Yes. *The Hollow Prince* he just delivered to me. The others, I've read a dozen times, but... I've never thought to *look* for anything." She stared into the fire for a moment longer, then tilted her head toward Wynn with something almost like a smile. "This is kind of exciting."

That was when Wynn dropped her mug and finally keeled over.

Kiernan was on his feet in a flash. "She hasn't slept," Kiernan said, catching her before she hit the floor. "I don't know exactly how long it's been."

Grace stood up. "Follow me."

She led Kiernan, with Wynn in his arms, up two winding staircases and through a heavy oak door, biting her lip the whole time. Her room was... hers. A quiet place for books and blankets and solitude. She'd never had *anyone* in it, let alone two strangers and a fox, let alone a boy.

The room was warmly lit, a low fire still dancing in the hearth. Grace flung back the curtains of the canopy bed, revealing a mattress and sheets so thick they looked like puffy white clouds on a bright spring day. Kiernan laid Wynn down with unexpected gentleness, brushing a lock of hair from her temple and then moving back into the shadows. Night leapt up immediately and curled in at Wynn's side, her tail wrapping protectively around her ribs.

"Oh, Night. No," Kiernan stepped forward but Night growled at him.

"It's okay," Grace shrugged. "The fox is cleaner than she is." She crossed the room to her little jewelry box, the one she kept tucked behind a false panel, and opened it with careful fingers. Obsidian sleep tokens glinted in the firelight. She took two out and walked back to the bed, crouching beside it. Wynn's eyes fluttered weakly, barely open now.

"You don't have to fight anymore," Grace said softly, pressing a token into her palm. She closed Wynn's hand gently around it. "Sleep now."

Wynn looked at her, not all the way, not clearly, but something passed between them in that half-lidded glance. A flicker. A breath. Recognition of some tether not yet formed, some question neither of them knew how to ask. She did not resist the pull this time. She sank into the bed like a pebble thrown into a pond, letting the warmth take her, the sheets wrap her up, the firelight dim behind her closed eyes. The sleep came hard and fast, but kind; thick and velvety and quiet. Her breathing slowed. Night pressed her nose to Wynn's cheek once, then finally let herself rest too.

"Here," Grace handed a token to Kiernan across the bed. "You need rest too. There is a room just down the hall. A bed already made up." Kiernan didn't move.

"Go," Grace commanded softly. "I will make sure nothing harms her."

"Thank you. For everything." He nodded and then paused for a moment, looking at Wynn an extra few seconds before exiting the room.

Grace let out a long breath. She remained beside the bed, holding Wynn's hand in hers. There was something about this girl in her bed. Something weather-worn and wild. Even in rest, she looked forged, like the world had tried to break her and only sharpened her instead. Grace found herself staring, drawn in by the quiet tension that still clung to Wynn's sleeping form. She was like a story told in scars and silence, the kind with chapters torn out, leaving the reader to fill in the blanks. And Grace... Grace felt herself wanting to read every line. Not out of curiosity. Not just for answers or clues. Something deeper had begun to stir, something she couldn't yet name.

~ ~ ~

And at last, she sleeps. The kind of sleep that doesn't wait to be invited. The kind that takes you whole, body and breath and bone, pulling you under like warm water. Her limbs go slack, her thoughts scatter, and she sinks, utterly, into the weight of the moment, into the mattress, into the dark. You can feel it, can't you? That quiet gravity pulling at your own muscles, asking nothing but surrender. It's not the drifting kind of sleep, not gentle or polite; it's solid and swift and earned. So let it take you too. Let the day fall away. Let yourself be held by the bed, swallowed by the hush. There is nothing else to do now. Just sleep. Heavy, still, safe, and well.

CHAPTER FOURTEEN

Wynn woke slowly. Not with the startled jolt she was used to. Not to Dena's voice barking her name, or cold water splashing on her feet, or the sound of carts rattling past the inn before sunrise. Not even to pain. No, this was something else.

Her eyes opened in the hush of stillness. Warmth pressed gently in from all sides. It took her a moment to realize it was coming from beneath her; soft blankets, real ones, and the layered weight of a proper quilt. She lay nestled in a bed that didn't sag or creak or reek of mildew. It cradled her like it wanted her to sleep even longer. She blinked at the ceiling. Wood beams and smooth stone, painted with long green vines that curved and climbed toward an invisible garden. Sunlight spilled in from somewhere, golden and drowsy. She turned her head slightly, carefully, as if afraid this dream might crumble with one wrong breath.

The room smelled of lavender and honey. Of warmth. Of something gentle she couldn't quite name. It took a long minute before it came back to her. Lorkan. The bridge. Avery.

Her throat tightened. She didn't move. Not yet. She didn't know how long she'd slept, but it had been long enough to shift the ache in her bones into something unfamiliar. Relief. Her body, for once, wasn't trembling. Her head didn't pound. Her breath came without effort. It was almost unsettling. She let her eyes wander slowly, soaking it all in.

This was a cold castle room, yes, but it had been softened at every corner. Tapestries hung from the walls, and the painted vines made the room feel more like a forest in bloom than a fortress. There were flowers, fresh ones, set in a glass vase by the window, their petals lazily catching the breeze. A fire danced quietly in the hearth, and near it, nestled on a plush carpet even softer than the bed, was Grace.

She hadn't noticed her yet, so Wynn stayed still and took her in. Her knees tucked beneath her, a stack of books opened in a half-circle at her feet. Her hair, those auburn waves, tumbled over her shoulders like a soft ribbon. She was reading, completely absorbed, her lip caught between her teeth, one hand winding a lock of hair around her finger. Wynn watched her.

There was something ridiculous about it. About how perfect the scene was. Like a painting in an old hall. A princess, draped in firelight and surrounded by books, reading in secret while the world waited.

Of course her room would be like this. Plush, clean, warm. A real bed. A place that smelled like something other than hay and sweat and iron. Wynn resisted the urge to curl deeper into the quilt. Instead, she reached a hand to her own hair and felt the tangles and gritty dust clinging to it. A mess.

A page turned. Wynn kept watching. She wasn't sure why. Maybe because it didn't feel quite real yet. Or maybe because Grace's brow furrowed slightly when she read, and it was... cute. Infuriatingly cute.

Grace looked up, as if she sensed she was being watched. Their eyes met. "Oh!" Her whole face brightened, her smile blooming instantly. "You're awake!" Wynn didn't move, just blinked and gave a small nod. "You've been out *forever*. I didn't know anyone could sleep for that long." Grace tilted her head and grinned. "You snore, by the way."

Wynn's eyes widened. "I what?"

"Loudly. Like a bear. Or like I imagine a bear would."

Wynn groaned softly, half-burying her face in the pillow. "No, I do not."

Grace took a slow sip from a mug beside her. "I'd offer to play you a recording, but sadly we haven't invented those yet."

Wynn squinted at her. "A what?"

Grace's eyes lit up. "Oh! A recording. In some of the books I've read, there are worlds with contraptions that can capture a person's voice, or a song, and play it back later. Music too. Whole orchestras caught in tiny spinning discs. The characters in those books... they love it. They listen to stories and lullabies and—"

Wynn just blinked.

"...You have no idea what I'm talking about, do you?"

Wynn shook her head slowly. "Not even a little."

Grace only smiled wider and set her book gently aside. "Well. That's something we'll have to fix."

Wynn wrinkled her nose. "Fix? I don't need fixing."

Grace immediately flushed, setting her mug down a little harder than she meant to. "No! No, that's not—I didn't mean it like that. I just meant—" She fumbled, then sighed. "You're very... touchy, aren't you?"

Wynn arched a brow. "Only when people say stupid things."

Grace's mouth dropped open, then she let out a huff of laughter, shaking her head. "Alright. Fair enough." She tucked a loose curl behind her ear, her cheeks still pink. "Let's start over."

Before Wynn could say anything, Grace pushed herself up, crossing the stone floor with a skip in her bare feet. She sat down carefully on the edge of the bed, the mattress dipping under her weight, close enough that Wynn could feel the warmth of her. And with it, a faint whiff of her hair. Sweet. Like flowers steeped in water. Roses, maybe, or something even softer Wynn didn't know the name of. She shouldn't have noticed it. She definitely shouldn't have noticed how shiny Grace's hair was, how it matched the firelight.

Irritated with herself, Wynn tucked a ragged scrap of her own hair behind her ear, trying to ignore the dry straw feel of it. She didn't care how she looked. She never had. Survival didn't leave room for vanity.

Grace extended a hand toward her, formal and a little sheepish. "I'm Grace. Princess Grace, of the Tor."

She stared at the hand for a beat too long. She remembered Lorkan's words, *give her a chance, Wynn*. Then, hesitantly, she reached out and shook it.

Grace's skin was soft, absurdly soft, the kind of softness that only came from a life where the toughest task she did all day was turn the page of a book. Wynn couldn't help but feel the contrast, her own hands rough and nicked, calloused from years of scrubbing floors, hauling wood, plucking stubborn chicken feathers, cutting ice from the well in winter. She pulled her hand back a little too quickly.

"Wynn," she said. "Just Wynn." She could give her a chance, but she wasn't ready to trust her.

Grace's hand lingered for a moment in the air before she tucked it neatly into her lap. She tilted her head, studying her with open curiosity.

"You're Tarn born, then? A slave?" The words were light, but Wynn caught the way Grace winced at herself as soon as she said them. "I mean, I guessed," Grace hurried to add. "You needed a sleep token, and... I shouldn't have assumed."

Wynn shrugged, brushing it off. "No, you're right. Tarn born. Slave." She paused, fidgeting with the edge of the quilt between her fingers. "Or, was. Now I'm..." She let the words trail off into nothing.

Before Grace could ask anything more, Wynn lifted her chin and shifted the conversation. "I thought the Dark One's daughter was dead."

Grace rolled her eyes with a dramatic sigh. "Yes, well. That's what my mother wants people to believe. For my safety," she added, her voice tinged with something that wasn't quite anger, or wasn't *just* anger. Her fingers plucked at a loose thread in the quilt, twisting it around and around. "She says she has enemies who would kill me for revenge. So I've grown up here, tucked away like a secret no one wants to know."

Her voice was light, but Wynn caught the edge beneath it. A thread of loneliness, maybe.

She knew that sound.

Grace shifted on the bed, turning slightly to face Wynn, her eyes bright with fresh curiosity. "So, how do you..." she caught herself, "...did, how did you know Lorkan?"

The question hit harder than Wynn expected. She hesitated, smoothing out the blanket and buying herself a second to think. She needed a story, something simple. Believable. "He...he was the Overseer of my village," she said slowly, choosing each word with care. "I worked at the inn most nights. Served him when he came through. He treated me well enough." Wynn shrugged, as if it meant nothing. "One day, he asked if Kiernan and I would accompany him on a trip to the Tor region. Said he needed a few extra hands."

Grace nodded, waiting.

Wynn steeled herself and pressed on. "But we were attacked by bandits. On the road. Lorkan was shot with an arrow... bad." She let the memory twist in her gut. Some of it was true, in its own way. "Before he—" She cleared her throat. "Before he died, he gave me this letter. Told me to deliver it to you." She finished, carefully blank-faced, hoping it would be enough.

Grace stared at her, chewing on a nail. For a long moment, she said nothing. Then, she frowned. "But, his letter said something about *you needing me, and me needing you.*" She shook her head, sending a loose wave of hair slipping across her cheek. "No offense, but...why would *I* need a Tarn slave?"

Wynn barked a dry laugh. "None taken." Her mind scrambled for a way to patch the hole. "Maybe..." she said slowly, "...this trip wasn't just a trip. Maybe it was a quest. Something important Lorkan needed you to do. And he thought Kiernan and I could...help you."

Grace's whole face lit up like someone had thrown open a window. "A quest," she whispered, almost reverently.

But Wynn barely had time to register the look of wonder before Grace sprang from the bed in a flurry of excitement. She crossed the room in a few strides, her bare feet silent on the plush rugs. Around the fireplace, books were scattered everywhere, open, stacked, tumbled over one another like fallen soldiers.

Wynn eased herself off the bed, her legs still a little stiff, and crossed the room toward where Grace knelt among the scattered books. She flipped through *A Study of Storms* with fast, sure fingers, her brow furrowed in concentration.

"I think I've figured this one out," Grace said, not looking up. She tapped the battered spine. "*A Study of Storms.* That was easy."

Wynn crouched beside her, careful not to knock anything over.

Grace pointed to a torn page. "See here? One page ends with *'Where the river...'*" She flipped to the next, "and the next starts *'...splits in two.'* But the edges are ripped, and the way the ink is pressed, this page doesn't belong here. Someone tore out the real ones on purpose."

Wynn nodded, even if she didn't quite follow.

Grace scooted aside a stack of papers and grabbed another book; the well-worn *Hollow Prince.* "This one was harder. The whole story is about a prince cursed into stone by a sorcerer, right? He comes alive only at night, when the moonlight touches him, but during the day, he's just... a statue. And he falls in love with a princess, this lonely girl who finds him in the gardens and talks to him without knowing he can hear her."

Grace's hands moved as she spoke, painting the scene in the air. Her whole face was lit up, animated, like the story was something she could step into at any moment.

"But the prince, he's cursed. If he tells her what he is, if he even speaks the truth to her, she'll be trapped too, turned to stone forever. So he tries to find a way to break the curse without telling her, and it's just... it's so sad because he loves her, and she's right there, but he can't—"

Wynn watched her, a small smile tugging at the corners of her mouth despite herself. There was something almost absurdly charming about how carried away Grace was getting, the way she practically vibrated with passion for a story that, as far as Wynn could tell, had nothing to do with their situation. It was... endearing. Sweet, even. But it was also not getting them anywhere.

Wynn cleared her throat gently. "Grace," she said, as politely as she could manage, "does any of this actually matter?"

Grace blinked, as if being pulled from a dream. Her cheeks flushed pink. "Oh. Sorry. I get carried away sometimes..." She tucked a stray strand of hair behind her ear, still flustered, but there was a brightness to her that hadn't been there before. "Anyway," she said, clearing her throat. "The epilogue... it doesn't match the story at all. It's written in a completely different language, something old. Ancient, maybe. I've checked every book I have, and I can't find a single match to it." She paused, frowning, as if even now it gnawed at her. "It's not Tor, nor Tarn, nor anything from The Vast Region that I know of. It's just... gibberish. Except—"

She turned, excitement sparking again, "—at the very end, there's something I can read in our language. It's signed, *A Bookkeeper.* Which is strange, because you would think it would read *the* Bookkeeper. It seems deliberate."

Grace's voice dropped almost to a whisper, as if saying the name aloud might summon something. "I think maybe... we're not looking for a place. We're supposed to find a person, a *Bookkeeper*, specifically"

Wynn stared at the pile of open books, then at Grace, feeling a ripple of genuine surprise.

"I can't believe how much you figured out," she said, the words coming out before she could think better of them. "How long was I asleep?"

Grace shifted a little, almost sheepish. "It's already midday."

Wynn blinked. *Midday.* She had never slept that long before. And somehow Grace had spent an entire night unraveling a mystery that Wynn hadn't even known existed. "You're... really smart," Wynn said, her voice low, almost cautious, as if the compliment might break something.

She casually tucked another strand of hair behind her ear. "I, um... I stayed up all night," she admitted with a breathless laugh. "I just couldn't sleep, I was far too excited."

Something twisted in Wynn's chest. Spending a whole night awake—by choice—sounded so ignorant, so *Tor*. Like sleep was just another thing you could waste without thinking, like water poured out onto sand.

She swallowed down the sharp reply on her tongue, but Grace must have seen something in her expression, because her smile faltered. "I'm sorry," she said quickly, stumbling over her words. "I shouldn't have said that. About the sleeping."

Wynn hesitated, then offered a small, careful smile. "It's okay. Really." The tension eased, a little. "So..." she continued, eager to steer them back. "What about the last book? The *Mapmaker's Daughters*?"

Grace's whole face lit up again, the excitement flickering back. She grabbed the battered book and clutched it close to her chest. "I'll try to keep it short." She flipped through the pages, her fingers moving like she knew them by heart. "It's a fantasy," she explained. "About three daughters, each with their own tale. The middle daughter was always my favorite. She had the biggest adventure—" Her voice softened, her words taking on that faraway, dreamy reverence only books could inspire. "She gets stolen by fairies as a child and taken to a land that's off all the maps. A land where everything ever imagined or remembered exists, stories, myths, even things people forgot."

Wynn listened despite herself, drawn in by the steady current of Grace's voice.

"The father can't find her because there's no map that shows the way. She has to journey through the land, find her way back..." Suddenly, Grace jumped to her feet. "Wait. *Wait!*"

Wynn scrambled up too, startled. "*What?*"

Grace's eyes were wide, shining with sudden realization. "Beatrix, the middle daughter, needed a ring to cross back into the real world. A ring that allows the person wearing it to move between borders."

Wynn stared at her, uncomprehending. "And?"

Grace spun toward her, breathless. "Maybe it has something to do with the ring around your neck!"

Wynn's hand flew to her chest in shock, feeling the cool press of the hidden ring beneath her shirt.

Grace's face paled slightly. "Oh, sorry," she said quickly. "I checked on you while you were sleeping and... it slipped out. I wasn't trying to pry, I promise." She looked genuinely sheepish, tugging at the sleeve of her tunic. But she pressed on, her voice softening. "It's obsidian, isn't it? I think I've seen it before, on my mother's hand. It replaced the ring my father gave her when they united. When she... changed. Where did you get it?"

Wynn hesitated, heart thudding. She forced herself to meet Grace's wide, earnest eyes.

"Lorkan gave it to me," Wynn said lightly. The words felt strange in her throat, but the instinct to protect herself was stronger. She'd spent her whole life guarding her secrets like bruises. Even now, even here, with Grace making her feel safer than she had in years, she wasn't ready to let them spill out.

Grace looked as if she was waiting for more, her brow furrowed in thought. She could sense it, there was something Wynn wasn't saying, something important resting just behind her lips. But she also saw the way Wynn's shoulders held tight, the way her fingers toyed with the collar of her shirt. She wasn't ready. Not yet.

So Grace softened. She tilted her head, just a little, and let the silence stretch without pressing further. Then, almost to herself, she added with a shrug, "I bet it's that ring. In epic adventures, it always comes down to a ring."

And now, dear reader, I suppose I must interrupt. Because, well, she's not wrong. Yes, yes, I know what you're thinking. *A ring? How very original.* But that's the thing about so-called clichés: they've earned their place. Rings, swords, necklaces, lost scrolls—these little trinkets have a habit of stirring up rather large trouble. A circle, after all, has no beginning and no end. Which makes it an excellent place for a story to spin.

Wynn's stomach let out a loud, unmistakable growl.

They both blinked, and then burst into laughter, the tension crumbling between them.

Wynn wiped at her eyes, still chuckling. "Maybe we should find some food before I start chewing on the books." She glanced around the cozy little room, sudden worry flashing through her. "Wait. Where's Night? And Kiernan?" *How had she not asked until now?* She'd been so drawn in by Grace, so tangled in stories, she hadn't even noticed their absence.

Grace smiled, a little mischievous. "Night's probably in the kitchen with Kiernan. Seraphina's got them working."

"Working?"

"Well... volunteering. Sort of. Kiernan offered to help, and Night..." she shrugged, grinning, "seems very interested in taste-testing."

Wynn snorted. "Of course she is."

Grace tossed the last book onto the bed, and together they headed for the door, leaving the books, and their questions, for later. "There's no rush," she said lightly as they slipped out into the hall. "We've got all the time in the world to figure it out."

Wynn gave a small, uncertain smile, but a prickle of unease stirred at the back of her mind. There's never all the time in the world, she thought. Not really.

~ ~ ~

"All the time in the world." Like Wynn, you and I both know stories rarely offer such luxuries; not to their characters, at least. Still, you have time. Time enough to rest. To set the book aside and leave the adventure dangling just where it is, like a lantern swinging gently in the dark. The tale won't go anywhere, not tonight. So breathe a little deeper, feel the calm press in around you like soft fabric, and let the weight of the world, real or imagined, slide off your shoulders. There's no hurry here. Close your eyes if you'd like. Imagine yourself snuggling down on plush carpet in front of glowing fire... sleep well.

CHAPTER FIFTEEN

The boat rocked gently beneath Avery's feet, its wooden hull creaking in a slow, familiar rhythm. The sun beat down on them, golden and warm, turning the turquoise waters into sheets of rippling glass. Around her, people huddled close together, some clutching bundles of belongings, others simply staring out over the open sea with hollow, anxious eyes. Avery didn't know why they were here, where they had come from or where they were going, but there was a sense of movement, of escape. She leaned over the edge, the breeze tugging at her hair, breathing in the sweet, briny air that seemed too perfect to belong to any real place.

The land they had left behind receded into the distance, a lush and green smudge against the endless blue. It was beautiful, heartbreakingly so, and Avery felt a strange ache behind her ribs as she watched it slip away. At the wheel stood her father, tall and sure, his hands steady on the worn wood. His skin was deepened by the sun to a rich olive tone, and when he turned to glance back at her, his light-green eyes, bright, startling against his darker face, crinkled at the corners with a smile.

Safe. That was the word that floated through her mind. She could stay here forever.

The sky was endless and clear, the air humming with an almost otherworldly calm, when the first shiver ran through her. It was nothing at first, just a subtle wrongness, like a single dissonant note in a perfect song. Avery looked up, squinting against the glare, and saw a ripple on the horizon where the sky met the sea. A low, far-off rumble of thunder vibrated through the air, and the bright turquoise deepened to a more somber teal. Clouds gathered with unnatural speed, rolling in on themselves, thick and black as spilled ink. The wind sharpened, tugging harder at the sails, and the gentle rocking of the boat turned rougher, more uncertain. People stirred uneasily, clutching their belongings tighter, murmuring to each other in voices too soft to make out. Then, emerging from the thick fog like a shadow given form, a ship.

It was massive, black from bow to stern, its sails like heavy funeral shrouds billowing against the rising wind. It made no sound save for the creaking of its ropes and the steady thrum of the sea against its hull. It glided up beside them with an eerie, deliberate grace, close enough that Avery could see the wet gleam of barnacles clinging to its sides, the strange symbols etched along the prow in a language she didn't recognize.

A plank lowered with a thunk, and from the shadow of the other ship, a figure appeared.

The woman moved slowly, deliberately, her long robe the color of crushed violets trailing along the wooden plank as she crossed onto their deck. Her hood was up, casting her face into shadow, but even so, Avery felt the air thicken around her, the hairs on her arms lifting in silent warning. Something inside her, instinctive and primal, tried to scream. *Don't trust her.* She didn't know why. She didn't know how. But every part of her knew it as surely as she knew the sea was salty and the sun was warm.

She tried to call out, tried to warn her father, to shout to the others who had now backed away in wary silence, but her voice caught in her throat, thin and useless. The woman reached the deck fully, and the moment her booted foot touched their wood, the ship seemed to shudder, the boards groaning softly under the weight of something unseen.

No one moved.

Avery stumbled forward a step, desperate to reach her father's side, desperate to say *something*, but the air itself seemed thicker now, heavier, as if every breath she took was weighted with unseen hands.

And the woman—still silent, still hidden by her hood—lifted her face at last. Queen Prima. The Dark One. Avery knew how wrong this was, how she didn't belong here.

Her skin was pale as bone beneath the hood, her sharp cheekbones casting long shadows over her hollowed eyes. The purple robes shimmered faintly in the changing light. The storm winds coiled around her as if obeying her will.

Avery's father stepped forward, his voice steady but with a thread of uncertainty woven through it. "Welcome aboard," he said, with a stiff nod. "What brings you to our ship?"

"No!" Avery cried, scrambling forward, tugging at his sleeve. "Don't! She's dangerous! Please!"

But no one seemed to hear her. Her father's light eyes, so like her own, swept past her without a flicker of recognition. The other passengers stood frozen, their faces slack, their bodies stiff like puppets waiting for their strings to be pulled.

Prima's gaze caught on her.

A brief, flickering glance. Sharp, and knowing.

Avery's blood went cold.

Prima turned her attention back to Avery's father, her voice smooth as silk. "You have something of mine," she said. "Something very valuable."

Avery shook her head wildly. "No! We don't! We don't have anything! Please, leave us alone!"

Shadows detached from the sides of the dark ship, resolving into figures clad in black armor—Dark Knights. They poured onto the deck without a sound, forming a wall around the passengers, around her father, around Avery herself. The wooden boards of the boat groaned under their collective weight.

Her father pushed Avery behind him, shielding her with his body. She clutched at his shirt, her heart hammering so loudly she was sure Prima could hear it.

Prima's voice dropped, silken and deadly. "Give it to me, and your people will be spared. Refuse, and..." She let the threat dangle, unfinished but complete.

From the mist at the edge of the other ship, a figure appeared, moving slowly, almost dreamlike. Avery blinked.

Wynn.

Relief flooded her. "Wynn!" she cried, reaching out. "Help us!"

But something was wrong. Wynn's eyes were glazed, her movements wooden. She looked half-there, as if she were a puppet herself. Her bow was in her hands, the string drawn taut with a black-feathered arrow. Avery's breath caught in her throat.

"No," she whispered.

Wynn let the arrow fly, striking her father squarely in the chest.

Time shattered. Avery screamed, diving to catch him as he fell, his body crumpling into her arms, heavy and limp.

"How could you?" she sobbed, looking up at Wynn, who stood impassively above them.

"How could you do this?"

Prima moved closer, bending low to whisper something in Wynn's ear. Wynn turned without expression, stepping toward Avery.

"Give it to me," Wynn said, her voice low and hollow.

"I don't have anything!" Avery cried. "You have the ring! You took it!" Her voice cracked, fury and hurt tangled in her throat. "You always do this. Keep things from me, use me when it suits you, but never actually let me in. This is your fault!"

The world shivered. The other passengers, Wynn, the knights, the entire ship's crew, faded out of existence as if they had never been there at all. Only Avery, her father bleeding out in her arms, and Prima remained on the battered deck of the ship.

"What is this?" Avery gasped, looking around at the empty, endless sea.

Prima's lips curved into a slow, cold smile. "Your worst nightmare," she said, crouching before her, studying her with the idle curiosity of a cat toying with a cornered mouse.

"Where are you from, girl?" Prima asked, tilting her head. "This ship... this land... it is not of my kingdom. It is not of any kingdom I know."

Avery squeezed her eyes shut, clutching her father's body. "I'll never tell you," she whispered.

Prima laughed softly, low and bitter. "You don't know, do you?"

Avery opened her eyes to find Prima leaning closer, the irises of her eyes swirling. "Interesting," Prima murmured.

And then, without warning, Avery's father vanished from her arms. Prima straightened and, with a final cold smile, dissolved into mist.

Avery was alone. The ship groaned and listed sharply as the storm reached a crescendo. Waves battered the sides, water pouring over the deck in icy streams. The mast cracked with a deafening snap and toppled into the sea. The sky above churned black and silver with jagged veins of lightning. She tried to move, but the deck tilted violently beneath her, tossing her to the boards. She knew now, knew for certain, that this was only a dream. But she could not wake up. She could not swim. The fear was real. The terror was real.

A blinding bolt of lightning tore through the sky, striking the deck and the ship cracked in two with a splintering shriek.

Avery was flung into the churning sea, the icy water closing over her head. She kicked and thrashed, but her limbs were heavy, the current pulling her down into a cold, endless dark.

Wynn... Help me.

The world slipped away into blackness.

Avery jolted awake with a strangled gasp.

It felt real. Too real. Like waking from a place she'd spent years trying to forget. The weight of it clung to her now, thick as the damp stone walls, the memory of warm sun and salt-kissed air flickering at the edge of her mind. She had buried the memory of it so deep she thought it would stay gone. And now that it was back, she couldn't unsee it.

Something had been taken from her in that dream. Or maybe given. Something fragile and unfinished that still trembled inside her. The darkness pressed close, thick and suffocating. The only sound was the slow, merciless drip-drip of water and the rasp of her own breath.

She bit down on a sob. She was alone. Completely alone.

Avery pressed her forehead to the cold floor, letting the tears come now, unguarded and helpless, her body trembling with the force of them. And somewhere, just out of reach, that place still lingered, achingly familiar, and utterly lost.

Prima opened her golden eyes.

The throne room stretched before her, empty but for two knights stationed at the great wooden doors. The dark banners of the Tor hung heavy from the high rafters, their embroidered moons catching the dim light. She flexed her fingers against the cold armrests, her fists curled tight. Anger flared, sharp and hot, through her.

"Send for The Stone," she barked, her voice cracking through the hall like a whip. "NOW."

A knight stumbled to obey, armour clattering as he vanished beyond the doors. Prima stayed seated, the storm of thoughts gathering fast. The girl in her prison, that trembling little foreign creature, had confirmed it. Wynn had the ring. *Her* ring. Well, okay, technically it came from the Fates. But she had no intention of giving it back.

It had to be them, playing their crooked games. Their old, meddling hands at work, whispering riddles and weaving wrinkles into the folds of her destiny. If they thought they could undo her so easily, they had grown arrogant. Forgotten the full reach of her power. Forgotten that she had become the Dark One.

Footsteps echoed down the corridor. The Stone entered swiftly, dropping to one knee before her. His dark cloak swept over the flagstones. "Yes, my Queen."

Prima rose in a slow, measured motion. The train of her gown brushed the floor behind her, a second shadow.

"It is confirmed. The girl has the ring," she said, voice low and venomous. "The Fates laid the pieces. But they do not understand the game they have begun." She stopped before him, her presence pressing down like a physical weight. "You will release the three premonitions," she commanded. "Send word to every village, every outpost in The Vast."

The Stone lowered deeper. "What shall I tell them, my Queen?"

Prima lifted her chin. The torches guttered in their sconces as if leaning closer to hear. "The first: One whose blood flows with water threatens to destroy our lands. She bears the mark of a crescent moon behind her left ear. Any who sees her must capture and report her immediately, or face death for treason."

The Stone nodded, waiting, his body still as marble.

"The second," Prima continued after a beat, pacing again, her voice smoothing into something venomous, "The Fates bless this land with abundance, but remind us that bounty brings imbalance. The Queen shall collect the excess harvest to ensure fair distribution and safe storage. For the good of all."

The Stone's mouth twitched into a grim line.

"And the third," she said, her voice darkening, "The Fates foretell unrest beyond the Northern Mountains. A storm brews beyond the borders, one that may not stay there for long. The Queen has called for new levies and stronger walls. We must be ready." She let the silence stretch, then added with a thin, cold smile, "It is time to call for more Tarn sons and daughters to serve. To remind them where their loyalty must lie."

The Stone stood. "As you command. I will send the fastest messengers riding in all directions."

Prima's gaze sharpened. "And what of my daughter?" she demanded. "Have your men returned with Grace yet?"

The Stone lifted his head slightly. "Not yet, my Queen. We have heard nothing... but—"

The words had barely left his mouth when the hall shifted. From the shadows near the entrance, a figure materialized.

The Hawk entered without a sound.

He wore no armour, only a black leather tunic and a long cloak that fluttered slightly with each step. His face was half-shadowed beneath the hood, but what could be seen was clean-cut and cold, a brutal beauty honed into something merciless. His very presence seemed to suck the heat from the air, drawing a sudden stillness over the hall. He stopped at the firepit and bowed low, one hand pressed against his chest.

"My Queen," he said. "You sent for me."

The Stone stood rigid off to the side, armor stiff and glinting like a warning. He waited for orders, though the stillness of his stance did little to mask the storm beneath it. Prima didn't turn. She merely lifted a hand and flicked her fingers at him. "Send the messengers," she said. "All of them. I want every village, every outpost, every watchtower told of the premonitions by sunrise.

Then you will take a company of knights and bring back my daughter."

The Stone lifted his chin, the movement sharp and stiff. "And if she resists?" he asked.

Prima's eyes flashed, just once, but it was enough to silence the air between them. "Do not return without her."

As the order hung in the air, The Stone shifted, just barely, his eyes flickering toward The Hawk.

The figure, standing silent by the fire, lifted his head and met the gaze full on. The corner of his mouth twitched upward. Not a smile. A challenge. The Stone's jaw tightened. Something passed between them, unsaid but unmistakable. An old fire, banked but not buried.

Oh yes, dear reader, they have history. No love lost between the two. If you sensed something simmering beneath the glares, you were right. The Stone trained The Hawk; not to shape him, but to break him. There were no shortcuts, because there was never meant to be survival. The Stone put the boy through drills until his hands split open, made him spar with dulled blades that bruised ribs and cracked bone, left him standing guard through sleet and storm with no cloak, no fire, and no sleep. But The Hawk endured. He grew faster. Sharper. Meaner. Until one day, with a single, flawless strike, the pupil bested the teacher, and earned the Queen's favor. The Stone has not forgotten. Nor has he forgiven.

The Hawk said nothing, but the weight of his silence spoke volumes. His posture calm, his presence unshaken, he simply looked at The Stone as one might look at a thing long past its use.

Prima's voice cracked through the tension like a whip. "What are you waiting for? Go. NOW."

The Stone gave a clipped bow, every muscle taut with words he dared not speak. And as he turned to leave, he passed The Hawk with deliberate slowness. For the briefest moment, the two stood side by side, one simmering, the other still, but the history between them crackled like lightning in a dry sky. Then he strode from the hall, his footsteps thundering into the distance.

Once the doors had boomed shut, Prima turned fully to him. "And the task that was to be completed at the Eastern Fjords?" she asked.

His voice was low, almost conversational, but carried the lethal edge of a blade. "As you suspected. There was a group of Tor nobles convening. A foolish hope of rebellion."

His lips twisted into something that might have been a smile, though it held no warmth. "They have been dealt with. All of them. Their heads will line the harbor gates by morning. A warning to those who even whisper a word of defiance."

Prima allowed a small, satisfied breath. "Well done," she said. Her eyes gleamed. "I have another task for you."

He inclined his head, silent and waiting.

"There is a girl," Prima said, her voice thick with disdain. "She travels with a fox. She has stolen something from me. Something precious. A dark ring. I want it back and I want *her* broken and before me." She stepped closer, the torchlight casting the sharp bones of her face into harsher relief. "I made the mistake of letting her live once. I will not make it twice."

The Hawk did not flinch, did not blink. His voice, when he spoke, was as sharp as drawn steel. "As you command."

Prima held out her hand, five sleep tokens in her palm. "This should be enough. Use them sparingly."

The Hawk accepted the tokens and gave a short bow. Without another word, he turned and strode from the hall, his cloak coiling behind him like a serpent.

At the top of the worn castle steps, he paused, lifting one gloved arm high into the night air. A shriek ripped through the air and from the shrouded heights, a hawk dove from the castle wall, talons slicing through the gloom. It landed cleanly on his arm, folding its wings with practiced grace. Its eyes, merciless and cold, mirrored his own. Together, man and bird descended the stairs and vanished into the night.

~ ~ ~

It's dark there, isn't it? Not just the kind you see, but the kind that settles; cold, watchful, thick with waiting. The Tor is a place that doesn't let go easily. Fear clings. So does silence. Even now, you might feel it in your own chest, that quiet tremble, that breath you forgot to take. But you're not there. You're here, with blankets to pull close and light that can be easily reached by the flick of a switch or the strike of a match. Let that be enough for now. Let Avery stay where she is, just for a while longer. Let the stone walls hold her while your own walls soften. Breathe slowly. Let the chill stay on the page. You've stepped through enough shadows for one night. Let the gentle warmth find you again, and sleep well.

CHAPTER SIXTEEN

Another night had passed. A day of rest, tucked inside the cradling arms of Grace's castle. Wynn hadn't realized just how badly her body had needed it; real sleep, thick and dreamless, wrapped in cozy quilts that smelled faintly of fresh rain. At Grace's insistence, she'd had a bath. A hot bath. Hot. Something she could hardly remember ever having. Grace had even added bubbles with a kind of ceremonial glee and launched into an enthusiastic explanation about how this was her favorite place to read, how she could spend hours here, tucked away from the world.

She was just beginning to relax, letting the heat unknot the soreness in her body, when Grace burst back in, waving a book excitedly, as if it were perfectly normal to walk in on someone mid-bath. Wynn yelped and sloshed water everywhere, scrambling to cover herself with shaking, indignant hands, while Grace perched on the edge of the tub, oblivious to the chaos she'd caused.

"I may have found something else!" Grace said, flipping open the book. "About the—" She stopped mid-sentence. Her eyes had landed on the still healing wounds crisscrossing Wynn's back, the ones the water couldn't blur or hide. The shift in her expression was sharp and immediate. She stared, stricken, the book drooping forgotten in her hands. In that moment, Wynn saw it all: the horror, the confusion, the deep, aching compassion blooming across Grace's face. And beneath it, something harder to name, the slow, terrible realization that Grace had been spared things Wynn had long ago learned to survive.

Wynn shifted awkwardly in the water, bubbles clinging to her skin, wishing she could disappear beneath the surface. She hated the way Grace was looking at her. Hated that the scars were visible at all, that they made her into something pitiable instead of someone strong.

"I'm sorry," Grace said suddenly, her voice thin, raw with guilt. She turned quickly, nearly stumbling over her own feet in her haste to leave.

Wynn called after her, "It's fine," but the words felt too light, too small in the heavy air.

"No," Grace said through the closed door, her voice muffled but certain. "It's not."

Wynn let herself sink deeper into the bath, the warmth creeping up to her chin. For a long moment she simply floated, staring at the high stone ceiling, trying not to think. But the thoughts came anyway.

It would be so easy to stay here. To let herself sleep on soft mattresses, to bathe in water so hot it chased the chill from her bones and allowed the outside world to fade into nothing but mist and forgotten names. But Avery wasn't here, safe and resting. Avery was likely trapped in Prima's prison, somewhere far beneath the Tor castle, cold and alone and waiting. Waiting for Wynn. The guilt sat heavier on her chest than the scars did on her back. And so, there were things to do, an evil Queen to dethrone.

A soft creak interrupted her thoughts.

The door to the bath nudged open, just a hair, and a sleek black nose poked through the crack. Then a pair of bright eyes. Night padded silently into the room, her white-tipped tail flicking as she crossed the floor and placed two paws up on the edge of the tub.

Wynn blinked at her. "Don't look at me like that," she muttered. "You may not even recognize me. I've never smelled this good in my life."

Night tilted her head, then leaned in to sniff the water, only to pull back with a surprised sneeze as bubbles popped against her nose. Wynn chuckled.

The fox shook her head, gave an exaggerated huff, and turned back toward the door, pausing only to glance over her shoulder with something that looked very much like impatience.

Wynn sighed. "Okay, okay. I guess I've pruned enough."

She stood and reached for the towel, letting the warmth slip from her limbs and cold reality settle back into her bones. Time to go.

Light slanted through the wide kitchen windows, catching the steam rising from a row of fruit pies cooling on the sill. Wynn sat perched on a sturdy stool beside a broad wooden counter, a half-eaten slice of pie balanced precariously on her knee. Her hair, usually tied back or hidden under a hood, now fell loose around her shoulders, clean and silky from the bath; thanks to the strange, sweet-smelling creams Grace had insisted she try. Kiernan had done a double take when he first saw her, like he wasn't quite sure it was really her. Night wasn't sure either. She kept sniffing cautiously at Wynn's leg, then sneezing like the scent had personally offended her. Wynn took another bite, savoring the syrupy tang of cinnamon and sweet apple, her second slice and likely not her last.

She'd spent some of the quiet hours wandering the halls of the Keep, exploring. It was a plain place by royal standards, no golden sconces, no velvet tapestries dripping from the walls, but even so, there were plenty of small treasures tucked here and there. A silver clock shaped like a swan. An ivory comb left on a windowsill. A carved chess set, the pawns worn soft with years of use. Old habits had stirred in her fingers, sly and itching. Wynn had stolen from Tor nobles most of her life, plucking what they wouldn't miss, or what they didn't deserve. Here, in the castle, she fought the same old pull: the flicker of jealousy, the whisper that she could take, and no one would ever know. But she held her hand. Barely.

Grace didn't make it easier. Bubbly as a boiling pot, the girl was. Always talking, always smiling, always bright-eyed with plans and questions. Wynn found herself both admiring and resenting it; the way Grace floated through the world like someone who had never been truly punished by it. It set her teeth a little on edge, though she would never have admitted that aloud.

Wynn stabbed her fork into the soft crust of her pie, sighing through her nose. She supposed it wasn't Grace's fault. And besides, the kitchen was warm. The pie was sweet. And, for the first time in a long while, the company around her felt like something close to home. She let herself lean into the moment, and took another bite.

Across from her, Kiernan stood dutifully at the counter, sleeves rolled to the elbows of an oversized apron, white with flour from chest to boots. His curly locks were dusted with it too, giving him a faintly ridiculous, cherubic look. Seraphina, broad and stern-hearted, guided his hands as he rolled out dough and sprinkled it with herbs and spices. Night sat loyally at his feet, posture perfect, eyes wide, and tail thumping softly against the floor in the desperate hope that another scrap might fall. Beside her, Grace had claimed nearly half the counter with a sprawl of notes, fraying maps, and smudged parchment. She had a pie slice of her own, balanced atop one of the books, naturally, and was scribbling notes with one hand while forking bites into her mouth with the other.

"I think I've found something," Grace said around a mouthful of flaky crust, tapping the map with the back end of her fork. "See here? Where the Still River splits into two branches? There's a small clump of woods, sort of like a V nestled between them. If we head south, it'll take days, but... I think that's where we need to go."

Kiernan leaned over the counter, leaving a handprint of flour across the page. "And you think we'll find a bookkeeper there who knows something about this ring?" he asked skeptically.

"Maybe, it's the best guess I have based on Lorkan's clues," Grace said, chewing and wiping away the flour print. "Kiernan, this pie is delicious. Seraphina has always made tasty pastries but this, the cinnamon and honey... mmm..."

Kiernan's cheeks turned rosy. "It's really her recipe, I just played with some extras."

"Delicious," Grace smiled. "Oh, don't be jealous, you old goat," she pointed her fork at Seraphina, "You know I like everything you cook."

Across the counter, Seraphina watched them all with her usual quiet disapproval, or maybe that was just her face. Either way, Wynn was starting to think the old cook liked their company more than she let on.

Grace licked her fingers and looked up brightly. "Seraphina, you grew up in the south, didn't you? Do you know anything about that region?" A heavy silence answered her. Seraphina kept kneading dough, her gaze stubbornly fixed on her hands.

Grace faltered, glancing at Wynn. "Right," she said flustered. "Wynn, could you...?"

Wynn set her pie aside and slid from the stool, wiping her hands on her tunic. It still made her chest ache, the quiet truth Grace had shared with them the night before: how all her life, the servants had been ordered not to speak with her. How she'd grown up surrounded by warm bodies but starved for simple words. And worse, how she had been forbidden from ever leaving The Keep, her whole world hemmed in by stone walls and locked gates. All that Grace knew of the world came from books, and from the stories Lorkan had told her when he visited. Wynn couldn't imagine a life like that, caged like a bird with clipped wings. It made Grace's endless chatter, her constant questions and eagerness to soak up everything she could from Wynn and Kiernan, make a painful, perfect kind of sense.

"Seraphina," Wynn stepped closer, "do you know anything about the woods where the rivers split?"

Seraphina's hands stilled. For a moment, Wynn thought she might refuse, but then she blew out a breath that stirred the flour dust on the counter.

"Old place," she muttered without looking up. "Mostly empty now. Folk there keep to themselves. Land's heavy with mist. Hard to track, hard to settle. Many a traveller have lost their bearings and gone missing."

Grace, behind her, was scribbling furiously.

"Is it dangerous?" Wynn asked.

Seraphina gave a shrug that could have meant anything.

"Depends on what you're looking for," she said. Her hands kept working the dough, but her voice dipped lower, almost like she was talking more to herself. "Some say the woods have a magic of their own. Long before the Dark One brought it here. Strange things happen there. Always have."

She hesitated, then added, "It's really neither Tor nor Tarn. Folk down there, they don't claim either. Say they're their own."

Wynn thanked her softly and returned to her seat, heart heavier than when she'd left it. They would need to leave soon. The road ahead would not be kind. But for now, the kitchen was warm, and the pie was sweet, and Wynn, knowing what waited, allowed herself one more bite.

Night, who had given up on getting any scraps and had moved, curling up in front of the large hearth, was the first to notice something. Her ears twitched. Then perked. She lifted her head from where she lay, blue eyes locked on the back kitchen door. Wynn noticed it immediately. The quiet alertness. The way the fox held herself, not afraid, but listening. Expectant. Tense.

Wynn's fork hovered mid-air. Then came the sound. Distant, at first. Just a murmur. But growing. Hoofbeats. Fast. Many. The steady thunder of armoured riders tearing across the dirt path toward The Keep.

Her chair scraped loudly against the wood as she stood. Kiernan met her eyes across the counter, recognition and fear passing between them.

Grace looked up from her plate, bemused. "It's probably just some of the caretakers returning," she said, brushing crumbs from her skirt.

"No," Seraphina said, already wiping her hands and moving toward the window. She peeled the curtain back just a finger-width. "It's the Dark Guard. And The Stone."

Wynn felt the blood drain from her body.

Kiernan swore under his breath.

Grace tilted her head, her tone still light but laced now with uncertainty. "Oh, don't worry. They sometimes stop here while on patrols, for lodging, food—"

"They stop in," Seraphina said, her gaze still fixed out the window, "and leave behind a giant mess for me to clean."

Outside, the hoofbeats slowed, grinding to a halt just beyond the gate. Then, *bang.* A heavy fist against the door. Not polite. Not patient. A demand.

Night growled—low, deep, primal.

Wynn's heart was hammering. Her body moved before her mind caught up. She crossed the room, took Grace's wrist with more force than she meant to, and leaned close. Her voice shook. "I need to tell you something," she whispered. "Now." Because this was no patrol. And if The Stone was here, they had no more time.

Bang. Bang!

"All right!" Grace called out. "I'm coming!" Then, under her breath, "Impatient brutes..."

"We have to go. *Now,*" Kiernan snapped, stepping forward.

"What? No," Grace said, confused. "Stay. This is normal. I'll just tell them to leave if you don't want to see them."

"No," Wynn said, more firmly this time, voice low but urgent. "We *have* to go."

A shape passed by the window. A hulking shadow in black armor. Not just a knight, one of *his* knights.

Seraphina moved quickly. She crossed to the center of the kitchen, grabbed hold of the rug by the hearth, and threw it aside. Beneath was a square of rough wood, a hidden cellar door with a thick iron ring set into it. "In," she barked, already pulling it open. Cool air rushed up from the dark below.

Grace stared, startled. "Seraphina—"

"Answer the door. And try to act normal," she said briskly.

Night gave a low whine. Wynn turned, knelt beside her, cupping her face.

"Go," she whispered. "Hide. Forest. I'll find you." Night hesitated, pressed her nose to Wynn's hand, then bolted through the back hall.

Kiernan was already halfway down the stairs. He looked back, hand extended.

"Wynn—come on!"

Wynn hesitated, turning to Grace. "We haven't told you everything," she said, breathless. "I'm sorry."

Seraphina snorted. "Well, *that's* clear." She shoved Wynn gently but firmly toward the opening. "Down you go."

The door slammed shut over their heads, and a second later, the rug whisked back into place. Darkness. Then muffled voices from just above.

The cellar was barely wide enough for the two of them. Wooden shelves lined the walls, holding jars of preserved peaches, pickled onions, dusty bottles of ale, and baskets of root vegetables. Thick cobwebs hung in the corners. The air was cool and smelled of earth, spice, and something slightly sour.

Wynn crouched beside Kiernan, both pressed into the shadows. "It'll be okay."

But Wynn wasn't so sure.

Grace had been kind. She had shared her bath and her stories and her secret books. But she was still Prima's daughter and now everything rested in her hands.

Up above, just beyond the door, Seraphina gripped Grace's shoulders with both hands. "Mistress Grace," she said, her voice low and urgent, "I know that fear when I see it. You can't say a word. Act like yourself. No more, no less."

Grace's throat bobbed with a swallow, but she nodded. "I understand." She turned and straightened her dress, brushed invisible dust from the sleeves, lifted her chin, and stepped to the door.

The heavy wooden latch creaked as she moved it, iron grinding against wood. For half a second, silence. Then—*BOOM.* The door flew inward with such force it slammed into the granite wall. Grace stumbled back with a startled scream as The Stone and four of his knights surged into the kitchen, swords drawn, armour clanking, bootsteps shaking the very beams above Wynn and Kiernan's heads.

"I'm sorry!" Grace stammered, blinking rapidly, backing up a step. "It took me a moment, I—what is the meaning of this?!"

The Stone stepped forward, dark eyes cold beneath his helmet. His voice was quiet, but cutting. "Where are your attendants?"

Grace blinked again. "What?"

"There was no one outside," he said. "Why is it just you... and your cook?" His eyes slid toward Seraphina, who stood at the back of the kitchen, arms folded over her apron. Her gray hair had come loose from its bun, a few stray wisps clinging to her cheek. She looked, for all the world, annoyed.

Grace smoothed her hands down her dress. "Almost everyone's away for the Fates Festivities," she said lightly. "They always go this time of year."

The Stone didn't respond. He reached into his cloak and withdrew a scroll, sealed with the royal black wax of the queen. "By decree of Queen Prima the Dark," he said. "We are to deliver this message and carry out her command." He handed it to her. Grace broke the seal and unrolled the parchment, eyes scanning the words.

The kitchen was so quiet Wynn could hear her heartbeat in her ears.

Then Grace froze. One hand still on the scroll, her voice barely above a breath. "The princess of the Tarn lives?" A pause. A second too long. Grace blinked, snapped the scroll shut, and shoved it back at him. "Well," she said briskly, "what does any of this have to do with *me*?"

The Stone studied her, his eye(s) narrowed. "You are to return to the Dark Castle," he said. Then, his voice deepened, "It is not a request. We ride at dawn."

Grace opened her mouth but he cut her off.

"My knights and I will stay the night. We require food and sleep."

Seraphina dipped her head. "I'll get the stews on," she said quickly, already moving toward the kitchen hearth.

The Stone watched her go. Then he turned back to Grace, his gaze sharp. "You don't mind if we... have a look around, do you?"

Wynn and Kiernan sat in stillness, knees pressed awkwardly together between baskets of root vegetables and shelves of preserves. Above them, the floorboards creaked, then the soft clatter of dishes, the scrape of plates into a washbasin. Seraphina, moving fast, trying to make things look ordinary.

"They're going to find us," she whispered. "They'll check the cellar. They always check the cellar." Kiernan didn't answer right away. He listened. The boots hadn't moved yet. No search. No shouting. Not yet.

Wynn hunched forward, pulling her arms tight around her knees. "We shouldn't have stayed this long," she muttered. "Hot baths and pie... what was I thinking? We were safe for five minutes and I forgot who I was. Who *they* are." She shook her head. "I let my guard down. Like a fool."

Kiernan looked at her through the dim light spilling between the floorboards. "You're not a fool."

She pressed her face into her hands. "Then who am I, K? Who lets themselves pretend, just for a moment, that any of this is normal?"

"You know who," he said gently. "A princess." She flinched at the word, but he didn't take it back.

Her breath caught, rough and bitter. "We're done," she said. "It's over. The Stone's here. Grace is up there playing house with napkins and teacakes and he's going to tear this place apart."

But Kiernan remained steady. "Give Grace some credit. If she were going to turn us in, she would've already."

Wynn looked up at him. "You really believe that?"

"I do."

And then, faint but clear, they heard Grace's voice rise upstairs, loud and indignant. "I don't *care* what my mother wants," she snapped. "You barge in like thugs thinking I'll just roll over and let you act like a bunch of untrained dogs in my castle? No. I want your boots off and your weapons sheathed, or you'll all be sleeping outside."

Wynn pressed her ear closer, listening to the clamor and footfalls of armed men now shifting in surprise, possibly confusion, as they filed out the door.

Kiernan smiled, "She's stalling."

Grace burst into her room and slammed the door behind her, breath catching in her throat. She scanned the room with sharp eyes, Wynn's cloak, hanging near the fire. Her worn boots tucked neatly beneath the chair. She dove forward, grabbing it all and stuffing it under the bed, pressing it deep behind the cedar chest she kept there. Then her eyes landed on the desk, and her heart sank.

The Hollow Prince lay open, face-down beside *The Mapmaker's Daughters*. Lorkan's most recent letter was unfolded beside them. She lunged for the letter, tucking it into The *Hollow Prince* and closing it shut just as heavy boots thundered outside her door. No time. She stood tall, composed, smoothing her skirt as the heavy knock came.

"This is my room," she snapped, throwing the door open before they could barge in. "You don't just walk into a lady's chambers without invitation—"

But The Stone and a knight pushed past her without a glance, already sweeping the room.

Grace followed, furious and poised. "There are rules, you know. Codes. My mother may have conquered The Vast, but she still respects boundaries."

"We're not here for etiquette lessons," The Stone muttered, his eyes already scanning the room. His gaze landed on the desk. On the stack of books. He crossed to it, reaching for the top one. *The Hollow Prince.*

Before he could flip it open, Grace was there. She snatched it from his hands with a sharp tug and tucked it behind her back like a stolen secret. "That's mine, thank you."

"Reading, Princess?" he asked, unimpressed.

She lifted her chin. "I'm the daughter of the Dark One. I can do as I please."

He cocked a brow. "That's not how laws work."

"Oh?" She gave a slow, lazy blink. "Do you want to be the one to explain to her that you tried to lecture *me* over a few books?" She took a step forward, voice cooling to a razor's edge. "Go on, then. Let's see how *that* goes for you."

"Lorkan brought them to you, didn't he?"

Grace tilted her head. "So what if he did?"

"He always did have a soft spot," The Stone murmured. "You know he's committed treason, don't you? Trying to save the Tarn girl." He waited for her reaction.

Grace could play this game. "No, I... hadn't heard."

"No?" The Stone studied her. "You don't seem very upset."

Grace shrugged, casual and cruel. "Should I be? I'm sure my mother will have his traitorous head on a spike by tomorrow. If she hasn't already."

The Stone watched her for a long, cold second. Assessing. Prodding. But her expression was blank perfection. If her heart stuttered in her chest, she didn't let it show.

He turned to her bed. Thinking fast, she stepped past him, slid a book from the shelf titled *Love on the Battlefield*, and thrust it into his hands with a smile that sparkled just a bit too brightly.

"Here," she said. "This one's perfect for you. It's about a cruel, brooding knight who was so cold-hearted the Fates cursed him to forget every name he ever loved." She took a small step back, hands folded sweetly in front of her. "Very tragic. Very moving. Lots of swords."

The younger knight beside him smirked. The Stone said nothing, only stared.

Grace's voice didn't waver. "He wanders the realm, haunted by faces he can't place. And then, one day, he sees her. A peasant girl with dirt on her cheeks and opinions he finds... inconvenient. He doesn't know why, but something about her unravels him." She circled The Stone slowly, like she was delivering a bedtime story instead of standing in front of one of the most dangerous men in the region. "He can't remember her name, of course, he never does. But he remembers her laugh. And the way she talks back. And somehow, she falls for him too. Even after all the horrible things he's done."

She stopped in front of him and tapped the book in his hands. "They battle together. Bleed together. Nearly die for each other. It's all very romantic. Very doomed."

The younger knight had started to laugh, trying, and failing, to hide it behind a cough.

Grace smiled wider. "There's even a scene where she stitches up a wound in his side and tells him she could gut him just as easily. And he thinks he might actually like that." The Stone's jaw twitched. "Anyway," she said, stepping back toward the shelves, voice breezy, "let me know if you'd like to borrow it. I have a whole section featuring cursed men with emotional issues."

She cocked her head, let the silence stretch just long enough, then, "Oh, and I have another one that—"

"ENOUGH!" The Stone threw the book onto the desk. "We're done here." He turned, the knight trailing him out the door.

Grace waited until the footsteps faded down the hall. She stood still for a moment, her heart thudding beneath her ribs like a war drum. Then, slowly, she let out a long breath, turned, and leaned her back against the door. A grin curled at the corner of her mouth. She'd done it. She'd distracted The Stone, lied to his face, and lived to tell the tale. If there'd been an audience, she might've taken a bow. But the smile faded just as quickly as it came. Wynn and Kiernan were still trapped beneath her kitchen. And in the morning, The Stone would come for her. Her mother's orders had been clear: She was to be returned. No excuses. No escape. No freedom.

The thought of that place, the Dark Castle, gripped her heart like a cold, iron fist. Endless stone corridors that stretched on for miles, suffocating in their sameness. The halls felt like they had been carved into the very bones of the earth, dark and unyielding, where light rarely dared to enter. The few windows that existed only let in a bleak, gray light, more shadow than sun, that never warmed the floors or her spirit. There were no soft places there. No cushioned chairs or thick blankets. No flickering candles beside warm fires. No corners to curl up in with a book and lose herself in some world far from her own. And the books? The ones that had been her escape, her secret indulgence? They wouldn't even be allowed past the gates. It didn't matter how much she loved them. Those whispers of other lives, those soft, quiet moments between the pages. No. In the Dark Castle, books were as much a luxury as sunshine or laughter. Forbidden.

She couldn't imagine it. No. She couldn't go back. Not now. Not ever.

And Wynn... Wynn was the first real secret she'd ever kept. The first person who looked at her like she might be more than a daughter of the Dark One. The thought of handing her over was unbearable.

Grace straightened, eyes scanning her room like it might hold the answer. No. She had to think of something. She *would* think of something. She pressed her hands to the door behind her and whispered to herself, "I'm not going back. And neither are they."

~ ~ ~

That was a long one, wasn't it? You've come far. Pages and heartbeats and breath held tight. And here we are now, balanced on the edge of what comes next. Maybe your fingers are still twitching to turn the page. Or maybe, just maybe, your jaw's gone slack with a yawn you didn't mean to let out, and your eyes are doing that slow blink thing, heavy and warm. If so, no one would blame you for closing the book and letting sleep take over. You've earned the pause. Let the story hold its breath a little longer. The next moment can wait until tomorrow night. Whether you turn the page or pop a bookmark here to hold your place, the story will keep. It always does. So breathe. Let the tension slip from your shoulders. Let the quiet settle in. You've done enough for tonight. Sleep well.

CHAPTER SEVENTEEN

The cellar was cool and dim. The excitement above had quieted and they could hear the occasional creak of Seraphina's footsteps, the clink of dishes being washed. Wynn and Kiernan sat on the hard, cold floor, side by side but worlds apart in thought.

Wynn's fingers fidgeted with the fraying edges of her shirt as she leaned back against the stone wall. She hadn't said much since Seraphina had ushered them down here, but her mind wouldn't stop turning. She couldn't shake the silence, couldn't ignore the thudding of her heart as the seconds stretched into minutes, then hours. The knights upstairs were settling in. She could hear them through the floorboards. The sound of a jug slamming into wood. Conversation. Laughter. Laughing as though they weren't here to hunt them. She had to do something. But there was nothing to do here except wait.

"What are you thinking about?" she asked Kiernan, her voice soft but urgent. She couldn't stand the silence anymore.

Kiernan's head tilted slightly, as if considering whether or not to answer. He shook his head slowly. "You don't want to know."

"Tell me," Wynn insisted. "What else do we have to do right now?"

"It's silly."

"I could use silly."

Kiernan hesitated for a moment, then sighed. "I was thinking about making bread. A sweet bread, you know? With pumpkin and spices... The kind that fills the whole kitchen with warmth. I was wondering how to combine the ingredients just right." He gave a soft, absent smile, as though lost in the simple, peaceful thought.

Wynn blinked, taken aback. "That's... not what I thought you were going to say," she admitted, her brow furrowing. "But, that sounds delicious."

There was a pause. She could hear Kiernan breathe out a quiet chuckle. Then he asked, almost hesitantly, "Do you ever wonder what your life would've been like if Prima hadn't attacked? If things were different, if the Fates... hadn't..."

Wynn's teeth clenched, and she shot him a sharp look. "I'm sick of hearing about the Fates," she snapped. "What's 'fated' is just an excuse. People make their own choices, not some... invisible forces." She paused, biting her lip. Then, after a beat, she added more quietly, "I just... can't imagine this being my life. I really can't. Can you see me as some pampered princess? Hot baths, smelly creams, sitting around reading books all day?" Her voice was tinged with disbelief.

"No," Kiernan answered quietly, but there was a faint trace of amusement in his eyes. "That would be boring."

Wynn exhaled sharply, looking away as if lost in thought. "So where do you think you'd be if none of this had happened?" she asked after a moment.

"Oh, probably training to be one of the Blue Knights. Taking my father's place, learning how to fight, how to lead. It's what I was supposed to do." He looked down, fingers brushing over the herbs hanging nearby. "But honestly? It's not me. Not really."

Wynn could feel his words, the heaviness that lingered between them. "I know," she said softly. "I think… It's obvious you belong in the kitchen, Kiernan."

He chuckled softly. "I dream of recipes," he confessed, his voice warming slightly. He reached up and tugged a bundle of dried dill from the rafters, holding it up to his nose. "This dill… I think it'd be so good in a savory pastry, maybe with potato and cheese. Something light and crisp."

Wynn's stomach gave an involuntary growl at the thought, and she grinned despite the circumstances. "Okay, okay. Enough. I'm going to get hungry if we keep talking about food."

Kiernan grinned, but his expression turned serious again. "My father wouldn't have wanted this for me," he said, his voice quiet but firm. "He'd want me out there, following in his footsteps, leading the Blue Knights."

Wynn frowned, sensing the weight behind his words. "But it's where you belong, right? Doing what makes you happy. Not what they wanted."

"When will we ever get that choice?"

The Stone's voice boomed from above, demanding more mead.

"I want to kill him," Kiernan seethed.

Wynn's chest tightened. "Me too," she murmured, feeling a surge of anger that mirrored his. She knew that fire in her own veins. She couldn't let it go, she wouldn't.

Before she could say anything else, the door to the cellar creaked open, and both of them froze. The sudden intrusion made their hearts leap in their throats, but it wasn't The Stone. It was Seraphina.

She stood in the entryway, looking down at them with a hurried but composed expression. She quickly scanned the space, her gaze flicking from them to the shelves, her eyes narrowing. "Hang tight," she whispered quickly, her voice barely audible over the rising tension. "We have a plan. But first—" She turned, gesturing for the dusty black bottle on the top shelf.

"Pass me that."

Wynn's heart was still pounding in her chest as she scrambled to retrieve the bottle.

"Stay quiet," Seraphina added in a low tone before she vanished back up the step, the door closing softly behind her.

Wynn stared at the space where Seraphina had been, then slowly sank back down beside Kiernan, her arms crossed, jaw tight.

"You can't handle it, can you?" Kiernan said after a moment. "Not being able to *do* something."

"Can you?" she shot back. He didn't answer. He didn't need to. Wynn exhaled through her nose, her voice taut with frustration. "I just can't believe our fat—" She stopped herself, jaw clenching at the word. "Our *lives* are in the hands of the Dark One's offspring. A girl who's lived most her life tucked inside a keep, learning the world through books. What does she know of survival? Of real danger?"

Kiernan tilted his head, considering her with a faint, crooked smile. "That book lover's got more steel than she lets on. And I'd say that old cook's smarter than most generals."

Wynn didn't smile back. Not yet. But the corner of her mouth twitched, almost against her will. "Still," she muttered, "this wasn't exactly the rebellion I imagined."

Kiernan leaned back against the wall beside her. "No," he said softly. "But maybe it's the one we need."

And if I may interrupt for just a moment, dear reader... You might be tempted to side with Wynn here. After all, Grace has never swum through a river in the dead of night, or fought for sleep tokens with frozen hands, or stood her ground against the sharp end of a Dark Knight's blade. Not yet, anyway. But I must remind you—I've seen more than a few rebellions in my time. I've been carried into battle tucked beneath arms that trembled. I've dried in the sun after storms, been slept on, bled on, and read in whispers under blankets. And if there's one thing I've learned, it's this: Stories—yes, even me—are perfectly acceptable places to learn about the world and others. Books are where we practice being brave. We can live hundreds of lives without ever having to step outside. We fall in love, we lose, we rage, we forgive. All from the comfort of a soft chair with a cup of something warm. So if you find yourself in a rebellion with nothing but a book lover and an old cook... Well, you too might just have everything you need.

Night had finally fallen. Not the fox, the actual night. The fox had hidden herself in a bush outside and was now impatiently, and somewhat anxiously, watching the castle for any signs of Wynn. She wouldn't have to wait much longer.

The last traces of sunlight had long since faded, leaving only slivers of moonlight seeping through the cracks in the wooden beams above. It painted pale stripes across the dirt floor and Kiernan's boots.

Wynn shifted. "It's way too quiet," she whispered.

Kiernan nodded from where he sat beside a stack of dried roots. "I was just thinking the same thing. You'd expect... something." The silence wasn't peaceful. It was unnerving. Like the hush before a storm hits the trees.

They both looked up when the cellar door creaked open.

Grace's face appeared, her hair tucked beneath a heavy felt hood the color of deep royal plum. She didn't speak, only signaled sharply. *Come up. It's time.* Beside her, Seraphina stood in full traveling garb, a dark cloak thrown over one shoulder, her sleeves rolled and ready. She looked almost amused, like she was preparing to deliver a pie and a lecture in equal measure. Grace held out Wynn's old burlap-green cloak, and a pack of supplies. She nodded once more. Cautiously, Wynn and Kiernan climbed the creaking steps up and out of the cellar.

A large fire still danced in the hearth, its light flickering across pots and ladles and the long wooden table where vegetables had once been chopped and hands had been warmed.

Wynn pulled her cloak on, her fingers fumbling over the frayed ties. "Where is everyone?" she asked in a whisper.

Grace only motioned with her head. Follow.

They stepped through the kitchen door and into the dining hall.

And there they were. The group of dark knights of the Tor, slumped over their trenchers and goblets, heads resting on folded arms, some half-twisted in their chairs. One had a drumstick still clutched in his fingers. Another snored gently into a bowl of stew.

Even The Stone was there, hunched forward at the head of the table.

No one moved. No one stirred.

Wynn's heart began to pound. Not with fear, but something sharper. Hope?

They returned to the kitchen. Seraphina was already at work again, packing food into a satchel with brisk, practiced hands.

Grace set Wynn's pack down. "Seraphina thought," she said lightly, "that they could all use a little rest."

Wynn turned, eyes widening. "You... what did you do?"

Seraphina didn't pause. "Just a little herb," she said. "An extract I keep for stubborn customers. Slips down smooth in stew."

Kiernan was holding the black bottle now, turning it over in his hands. It was dusty, unlabeled, and faintly oily to the touch.

"Does it work like the tokens?" he asked.

Seraphina snorted. "Please. No magic in this. It's an ancient root that comes from the land. But, it only works on those not marked by Prima's power."

"Wait," Grace said softly. "You mean...?"

"It'll knock out the Tor-born," Seraphina confirmed, stuffing a wedge of bread into the bag. "But those born Tarn, under the Dark One. It won't even tickle. I've tried."

Kiernan raised an eyebrow. "Huh," he said. "Interesting."

Wynn went still. Her hand clenched around the strap of her pack. "Wait," she whispered. "If it only affects the Tor-born, then why would The Sto—".

She didn't finish. A wet sound, sudden and horrible, sliced the moment in two.

Seraphina stiffened then gasped, but only once. Her knees buckled first, then the rest of her, as she hit the floor in a heap. An apple she was packing fell from her hand and rolled across the floor.

"Hello, Princess," The Stone said, stepping fully into the hearthlight. It flickered lower, or perhaps the room simply felt colder now. "Or should I say, Princesses?"

Grace screamed. She darted forward, falling to her knees beside Seraphina, but The Stone grabbed her by the back of the neck and hurled her, hard, into the chopping block. There was a sharp crack of wood, the thud of her body, and then she didn't move.

"Grace!" Wynn started forward, but The Stone turned, and one look from him froze her in place.

Wynn's breath quickened. No weapon. No cover. She scanned the room—pots, knives, the iron kettle, the fire.

"You know," The Stone said, eyeing them both like caught deer, blood still dripping from his blade, "I expected Lorkan. Thought I might finally split that thick sanctimonious skull of his."

"He went to get his blade," Kiernan said quickly.

"Oh," The Stone smiled, impervious to Kiernan's lie, "he's dead then. Good riddance." He turned his head slowly, examining them. He looked at Kiernan. "You've grown. Almost didn't recognize you without your father behind you. He used to worry you'd never grow into your bones. Always a little off, weren't you? Not as strong. Not quite as quick. What was it he used to say? 'Like a newborn foal.'"

Kiernan stepped forward. "My father was a better man than you'll ever be."

The Stone smirked. "Not anymore." And then he stepped forward. "You, I don't need to bring back at all," he said to Kiernan. Then his eyes slid to Wynn. "And you... well, I don't need to bring whole." He lunged.

Wynn moved on instinct. Her hand shot out, grabbing the iron pot from the stove, still warm, still full, and flung it hard. It struck The Stone in the chest. He staggered, hissing, and that was enough.

Kiernan grabbed a stool, swung it like a club and the room erupted.

The Stone deflected the stool with his arm, roared, and swung his blade. Wynn ducked, grabbing for a paring knife on the counter. She slashed upward, catching his forearm.

He turned on her. His boot met her stomach and she flew backward, crashing into the shelves. Jars shattered around her. Pain shot through her ribs. She tried to rise but The Stone was already above her. A backhand blow cracked across her cheek and she hit the floor again, ears ringing. But Kiernan was there—roaring now, his face a mask of fury—and he brought the stool down over The Stone's head. Wood splintered. The Stone dropped his blade with a grunt, staggering sideways.

Kiernan didn't hesitate. He kicked The Stone hard in the head, sending him to the floor.

The sword lay between them. Kiernan snatched it up.

The Stone coughed. Blood dripped from his temple. But even on his knees, he laughed. "Maybe your father was wrong," he rasped. "Maybe there's a little iron in you after all."

Kiernan raised the blade. "Don't speak about my father," he snarled. He stepped forward, sword high, ready. But then... he stopped. Breathing hard. Staring. His hands trembled. He didn't move.

Wynn blinked through the haze. "Kiernan—"

"Too soft." The Stone's hand flicked. A knife flew—silent, silver—and buried itself deep in Kiernan's thigh.

He cried out, stumbled, dropping the sword and clutching his leg. Blood poured freely between his fingers.

The Stone rose. Slowly. Grinning.

He stepped over Kiernan, picking up the sword and turned toward Wynn, who was struggling to stand, mouth bloodied. She reached blindly for something to defend herself with, finding nothing.

"Let's finish this," he said.

But, out of his line of sight, Grace slowly came to her feet. Her hair was matted, a streak of blood along her brow, and her cloak hung lopsided from one shoulder. Her eyes were wide and furious.

Kiernan saw her first. He'd fallen sideways, clutching his leg, blinking against the sting of pain. She was moving. Steady. Silent. Towards him.

"Grace?" Kiernan gasped.

The sound made The Stone pause, his head turned, just a fraction too late.

Grace dropped to one knee. Yanked the knife from Kiernan's leg in one brutal pull—he shouted in pain—and before The Stone could even raise his blade, she drove the blade into the side of his neck. His eyes widened in surprise. His mouth opened, trying for something, an order, a curse, a final word, but nothing came. Then his body collapsed with a sickening, final weight.

The firelight caught on the blood now spreading thick across the floor.

And then, stillness.

No one moved.

Not Wynn, still blinking in disbelief.

Not Kiernan, gasping, stunned.

Not Grace, frozen above The Stone's body, hand still in the air, clenching the bloody knife mid-stab.

There was just the fire, crackling softly.

Grace swayed.

"I, um..." she started, eyes dazed. She looked at her hand like it belonged to someone else and then to the body on the floor. "That wasn't... that wasn't supposed to happen." The knife clattered to the floor. And then, so did she.

Wynn rushed forward and caught her before she hit the ground, one arm wrapping around her shoulders, the other brushing hair from Grace's forehead. She looked up at Kiernan, who was pale, sweating, bracing himself against the wall with one hand.

"That was..." she said, breathless, "unexpected."

Kiernan groaned, covering his wound. "I'd like to go back to the part where we were talking about my pumpkin bread."

The fire sparked and hissed again. Blood pooled under The Stone.

CRACK.

The window shutters slammed open with a bang. Both Wynn and Kiernan jumped. A dark shape loomed on the ledge.

Night stood on her hind legs, her front paws on the windowsill, wide eyes peering into the room, ears twitching.

Wynn let out a sharp breath and nervous laugh. "Night! You scared the ever loving stars out of me." The fox blinked slowly, unimpressed, nose twitching at the scent of blood. "You're right, we have to go. Now."

~ ~ ~

That was a lot, wasn't it? Fast and sharp and loud. Heart pounding, fists clenched, breath caught somewhere in your throat. But it's over—for now. The blades are quiet. The dust is settling. And you, dear reader, can rest. Let your pulse slow. Let your breath come easy. And if your thoughts still cling to blood and steel, try this instead: a hidden glen where fireflies drift like floating embers and moss muffles every footstep. Or a tucked-away cottage with a fire crackling low, the scent of tea in the air, and thick quilts pulled up to your chin. Or deeper still, a quiet grove where the trees hum lullabies only the furry forest creatures can understand. Let your mind wander there awhile. Let the weight of the world slide from your shoulders. The next part of this adventure will wait. Sleep well.

CHAPTER EIGHTEEN

Avery sat curled in the corner, arms wrapped tightly around her knees, chin resting on them. She hadn't slept. Not properly. Not since the nightmare. And still, still, she fought it. Her body ached for rest, but her mind wouldn't allow it. Every time she drifted, the dream came clawing back. The feeling of something precious being ripped away.

Where was Wynn now? Safe, she hoped. Free. She had shoved Wynn into that river without hesitation, and though she hadn't had the chance to warn her, she knew she'd done the right thing. Wynn was the one who needed to make it out, who needed to fight. She would hate her for it, but she wasn't here, in this cell, and that was what mattered. And despite all the scowls and eye-rolls, Avery knew she cared. She saw it in the way she always stood between her and danger. Heard it in the silence after an argument, when Wynn didn't say sorry, but stayed close anyway.

Avery bit down hard, forcing herself not to cry. The walls felt tighter than before. The cold deeper.

Footsteps echoed down the passageway. Slow, deliberate, and heeled.

The iron door opened and Prima entered, a shadow with purpose. Her cloak shimmered like oil on water, the deep folds of black velvet whispering with each motion. Her eyes were outlined with a charcoal smoke. But it was her nails Avery couldn't stop staring at; long, lacquered points that clicked softly as she folded her hands in front of her.

"I've heard," Prima said, her voice smooth as she paced the edge of the cell, "that you are fighting sleep." She stopped in front of Avery, tilting her head ever so slightly, the moonlight catching the sharp curve of her cheekbones. "I find that... fascinating."

Avery lifted her gaze but didn't move from her place on the floor, knees drawn to her chest. "I know you were in my dream."

Prima smiled, small and certain. "Yes. That much was obvious."

She crouched then, folding herself down with eerie grace, her long cloak sweeping the damp stone behind her. The tips of her black-glossed nails tapped lightly against her thigh as she considered the girl.

"What I haven't figured out," she continued, her voice softening to something silkier, "is how you knew. No one has ever sensed me before. Not once." Her eyes gleamed like cut glass. Curious. Patient. Dangerous. "Most minds are too pliant. You rs... is not." Then, fingers steepling, she added, "Quid pro quo. I'll tell you how I entered your dreams. You tell me where you're from."

Silence. Avery's eyes narrowed. Her jaw set.

Prima's lips curved again, amused. "No? Very well. I'll tell you anyway."

She rose smoothly. "I used a spell from *a book*. A collection of ancient sleep magic. Most minds, once lulled, are easy enough to enter. But yours..." Her dark gaze fixed on Avery like a pin through cloth. "Yours resists."

Avery shifted, uneasy. But she said nothing.

"You're different," Prima said, now circling the cell like a predator about to strike. "I can feel it. There is something in you. Familiar." She stopped again, eyes flicking downward. "If you fall asleep, I can help you find out what it is. Where you're from. Who you are."

Her voice had grown honey-sweet. Tempting. The words coiled around Avery like vines.

And for a moment, just a moment, Prima saw it. A flicker in Avery's eyes. Longing. Curiosity.

The Dark Queen leaned in, close enough for Avery to smell the crushed rose petals beneath the iron scent of her perfume. "But I won't beg," she whispered.

Then she straightened, sweeping toward the door. She paused just before it, one hand resting on the frame. "You'll fall asleep eventually," she said without looking back. "And when you do... I'll be waiting."

The door closed with a low final thud.

Avery let out a breath she hadn't known she was holding and leaned back against the cold rock wall. Her eyes fluttered shut, just for a moment, and she pictured Wynn. Even when she was terrified, she moved like she wasn't. Avery had always admired that. Envied it, even. Wynn would know what to do in a place like this. She would fight. She would find a way out.

She curled tighter, guilt crawling under her skin. She'd pushed Wynn into the river to save her, but now, now it was hard not to feel like the one left behind.

Prima's words still echoed through her, quiet and cutting. *There's something in you. Familiar.* Avery had brushed it off, but the truth was, she'd felt it too. A flicker. Something she couldn't quite place. She hated it. And, if she was honest, she was afraid of it too.

She opened her eyes again, heart beating fast. Sleep tugged at her, heavy and insistent. She'd lose this battle eventually, but for now, she would hold on. Just a little longer.

~ ~ ~

She's holding on, just a little longer. And you can too, can't you? With such a short chapter, surely there's a little more curiosity left in you, a little more light behind your eyes. So no 'sleep well' from me just yet, not when the fire's still warm and the story's just getting interesting.

CHAPTER NINETEEN

The Hawk slipped through The Keep like nightfall, unannounced and absolute. His cloak, long and black as a raven's wing, barely whispered as he stepped through the open door at the rear of the kitchen. It had been left ajar. Careless. Unwise. His hawk, a sinewy, sharp-eyed thing the color of golden rust, was perched on his shoulder, talons curled into the leather guard stitched into his collar. Its head swiveled silently, mirroring its master's cool, assessing gaze.

The kitchen was still warm, though the fire had guttered low, leaving only a bed of sullen embers. The air stank of burnt stew, spilled mead and blood. A copper pot had been hurled across the room. Chairs were overturned. One lay in splinters.

Just inside the threshold, The Stone lay facedown in a wide pool of blood. His bulk had always seemed immovable in life, an unyielding wall of muscle and barked commands, but now he looked more like a discarded sack. Hollowed out.

The Hawk did not startle. He did not pause. He stepped over the body with measured indifference, barely a flick of the eyes to mark the death. *Finally,* he thought. *How many bones did you break to get here? How many children did you beat into silence and call it strength?* No mourning. No moment of silence. Just a quiet, inward nod to justice—brutal, belated, and richly deserved. But this... this was not the work of time catching up with an old bastard. This had been swift. Recent.

His eyes moved across the room, scanning with a predator's instinct. Blood smeared across the floor in more than one direction. A trail of boot prints and something else disrupted a spill of flour near the pantry. He crouched beside it, studying the marks. Fox tracks. Small, clawed, unmistakable.

He rose and kept moving.

In the middle of the room he found the body of a woman, older, grey-haired, lying facedown in the mess. Not in servant's clothes. She was dressed for weather, travel even. She had been stabbed clean through the back. No signs of struggle. Her fingers still curled slightly, as though she'd meant to reach for something, then simply... stopped.

He glanced back toward the flour, the fox prints trailing out the door before passing through the kitchen and into the main hall. The great dining table stretched before him, lined with knights slumped over bowls of stew, their chests slowly rising and falling in unnatural rhythm. One had a spoon still halfway to his mouth. Another snored gently into his own shoulder.

The Hawk tilted his head, eyes narrowing. "Hm."

He turned away and took the steps two at a time.

Upstairs, in a chamber lined with pillows and scattered candle stubs, he found the remnants of a reader's frenzy; books cracked open, spines bent, pages dog-eared and scribbled upon. A copy of *The Hollow Prince* was folded, spine upon the desk. Another volume lay sprawled beside it: *A Study of Storms.*

He moved through the room with methodical grace, his gloves whispering against parchment. A few pages, notes, perhaps, or copied excerpts, had been pressed between the pages of a dark green ledger. He skimmed, then pocketed them with care.

Downstairs, behind him, the knights stirred.

By the time The Hawk descended, the men were lurching upright, groggy, clutching at weapons or wiping drool from their jaws. Confusion hung thick in the air.

"What—?"

"Where's The Stone?"

The Hawk's voice cut through their babbling like a blade. "Wake up, you fools," he snapped, his tone ice-cold. "While you napped, your commander was murdered, and a princess slipped through your fingers."

They blinked, reeling. One tried to stand at attention and swayed.

"Regroup. Now. Saddle every horse and ride south. Stick to the Tor side of the border. Stay visible. Loud. Let them run from you."

A younger knight, cheeks still soft, eyes still panicked, dared a question. "And you, sir?"

The Hawk turned to him, "I'll ride the Tarn side," he said, already walking toward the door. "If they're smart, that's where they'll be. There are more trees to vanish in." With that, he stalked into the night, his bird loosing a soft, rasping cry as they disappeared together into the dark.

Now, dear reader, some of you may know these kinds of stories well. You feel the pull, the weight, the shape of them and you like to figure things out. And somewhere in your chest, maybe you've already put the pieces together... or maybe not. But you see, The Hawk is Tierney, or was. Wynn's brother. Once a boy of Tarn, now the blade Prima keeps sheathed until he's needed to do her bidding. He was taken, that much we've whispered before. But what you did not yet know, this little revelation I can share with you now, is that Prima went to the Fates. Not with a plea. With a challenge. To *undo* his thread entirely. To unravel it from the tapestry of who he was, and weave it again, not in cotton and memory, but iron and command. They should have refused. They had never done such a thing. But they are older than rules. And they were *curious*, as she knew they would be. So, they took her challenge, just to see if it could be done. And so it was. The boy became The Hawk. She placed him in the hands of The Stone, who believed in forging boys like blades: brutal heat, endless hammering. He beat the "Tarn" out of Tierney with sticks, with fists, with silence. Punished softness. Starved kindness. He turned pain into discipline. Discipline into precision. He remembers nothing of the sister who once looped wildflowers through his hair, or swimming in the lake on warm summer days. He knows only what Prima told him: that he was abandoned. Forgotten. That she found him, named him, forged him. That the pain was a gift. That loyalty is a debt. So no, he does not grieve. But if you look closely, you might still wonder... Is there some memory hidden deep? A glimmer of the truth still there? He holds his emotions and thoughts so tight, he is impossible to read, and I mean that literally. But still, we can hope. This is not a story of easy answers. It is, however, a story of unraveling, and I'm far from finished.

~ ~ ~

Whether it's been one chapter, two, or a handful—who's counting, really?—even the quickest pages can carry weight. And if the day's been long, maybe this is the place to pause. A quiet moment. A breath. Let the book rest on your chest for a while, let your thoughts drift. Of course, in the next bit, we return to our heroines, and I wouldn't blame you if you wanted to go on. But if not, if now feels like the right time, just know the story will be waiting. Sleep well.

CHAPTER TWENTY

Grace blinked awake to the rhythmic sway of a horse beneath her, her cheek pressed against the warm fabric of Wynn's shoulder. They rode doubled up, Wynn steady in front, one hand on the reins, the other resting lightly on Grace's arm to keep her from slipping. The trees arched high above, their leaves whispering secrets in the wind, and somewhere ahead, Night trotted with silent purpose, her slick figure weaving in and around the trunks.

Beside them, Kiernan rode with a slightly hunched posture, muttering something under his breath and occasionally patting his horse's neck as if to keep it calm. He looked unnatural and quite uncomfortable riding the horse.

Grace blinked again, her senses trickling back in. Her legs were soaked. Her head throbbed with a dull, swollen pulse. "How long was I out?" she murmured.

"A few hours," Wynn said, not turning. "You missed the river. Shame. It was the fun part."

Grace stirred. "Why are my legs wet?"

"We crossed the Still," Wynn replied. "Found a low bend where the horses could swim. You stayed mostly dry... ish."

From Kiernan's saddle came a low, grumbled, "We *almost* drowned."

Wynn waved a hand dismissively. "He exaggerates. It wasn't that bad."

Grace lifted her head slightly, taking in the thick canopy, the unfamiliar hush of wild woods. "So... we're in The Tarn?"

Wynn nodded. "It's safer to hide on this side. And I know it better."

Grace looked around again, warily. "I've never been in The Tarn before. I was always told not to come near the forest. That it was... dangerous."

Wynn gave a small shrug. "It can be. But what isn't?"

There was a quiet moment, just the sound of horses trudging through damp undergrowth. "Where did we get the horses?" Grace asked, her voice small.

"Stole them," Wynn said. "Off the knights. Took some of their weapons too." She nodded to the bow and quiver of arrows hanging at the side. Then she patted the horse's neck. "This one belonged to The Stone. You know... the guy you killed."

Grace gave a small whimper and suddenly wrapped her arms tightly around Wynn's waist, hiding her face between Wynn's shoulder blades. "I still can't believe I actually did that," she mumbled. "I don't know what came over me. Part of me keeps hoping it was a dream."

"Nope," Wynn said cheerfully. "You stabbed him in the neck. It was kind of legendary, really. Also slightly terrifying. The mighty Stone, brought down by a book-loving princess. I can't think of a better fate."

"Oh, sure, *now* you like the Fates. My leg is fine, by the way," Kiernan muttered. "Thanks for asking. Only lost a few *jugs* of blood."

"Don't mind him," Wynn said. "He gets dramatic when he's bleeding out."

Grace groaned, her voice muffled against Wynn's back. "My mother is going to *kill* me."

Wynn let out a dry laugh. "Join the club."

The forest was quiet again, save for the sound of a breeze rustling leaves and the soft rhythm of hooves. Grace lay slumped against Wynn's back, the rise and fall of the horse rocking her gently. For a long while, she just listened, to the forest, to the horses, to the slow thud of Kiernan's mount beside them. Then, softly, "So... are we ever going to talk about the fact that you're the Princess of The Tarn?"

Wynn sighed, the kind of sigh that said *I was hoping we wouldn't*. She spoke over her shoulder, "If we must."

"I think we must," Grace countered sarcastically.

And so she told her. Everything. From what she could remember growing up, to the day her parents were killed and her world turned upside down, to the years with Dena at the inn, to Lorkan, to Avery. She kept her voice low, like the trees might lean closer to listen. Grace stayed quiet through it all, save for a soft gasp when Wynn mentioned the lashes, and a stifled curse when she spoke of The Stone and the bridge.

"And that's it," Wynn said at last. "All of it. The Dark Queen, your mother, has Avery, Lorkan gave his life saving mine and then led me to you, and now... here we are."

Grace nodded slowly. "Heading south. To where the river splits."

"It's the only lead we have."

"Kind of exciting," Grace said, trying for a smile over Wynn's shoulder.

"You would say that."

They rode for a bit more, the sky softening to deep purply pink where the rising sun started to peek through the canopy. Then Grace spoke again, quieter this time. "But... why now?

Why would she want you back after all these years? And why order me back too? My mother is nothing if not calculated," she added bitterly. "Unless..."

Wynn turned her head slightly. "Unless what?"

Grace hesitated. "Unless this has something to do with the Fates."

Wynn groaned. "Enough with these fantasy creatures—"

"She doesn't mean that," Kiernan muttered into the air, as if the forest itself might take offense.

"I do," Wynn said.

But Grace lifted her head. "They're not fantasy. She's spoken with them... just before..."

"Before what?" Wynn asked in a tone that signaled she already knew the answer.

Grace's voice dropped. "Before she attacked your family."

Wynn pulled the reigns and then slid off the horse, landing softly on the mossy ground. She turned to Grace, eyes steady. "Tell me everything."

Kiernan shifted in his saddle. "This isn't a good idea. We should keep moving."

"The horses need a rest," Wynn said, already pulling an apple from her bag. "And so do we."

They found a small clearing, hemmed in by trees and morning fog. Grace sat on a half-rotted stump, knees together, fingers knit tight. Wynn and Kiernan leaned against a trunk, boots stretched out. Night crunched on scraps nearby, occasionally glancing up to keep tabs on everyone. The only sound was the soft munching of horses and the hush of wind through the oaks. Then Grace began.

"Everyone knows that after my father died from his sickness, my mother... lost herself. She always said he was her anchor, her other half, and once he was gone, she felt like she lost everything. I tried. I really tried, to comfort her, but I was a child. I was mourning him too. She forgets that, I think. That I lost him too.

And then I lost *her*. She left me behind in her grief. After the funeral, she snapped. She kept wailing—like, *screaming*—and the royal doctors couldn't get her to stop. My nanny tried to keep me away, but I heard everything. She kept saying she had to find the Fates, that they were the only ones who could undo what had been done. It sounded like madness. Everyone tried to stop her, but she just left. Rode out alone. Scaled the mountains herself. And then she... disappeared."

"For exactly one hundred days," Wynn murmured.

Grace nodded. "Everyone thought she was dead, but I didn't. I *knew* she wasn't. I could feel it. And when she came back... she was different. Her hair was gone, yes, but it was more than that. Her voice changed. Her eyes. She stopped laughing, stopped caring. And that's when everything went dark. Literally. She stripped the color from the castle, my dresses, the tapestries, even the flowers. Everything was turned to shades of black, to match the inside of her heart. When I asked her where she'd gone, she denied ever leaving for that long. Said it had only been days. Threw anyone who disagreed with her into the prisons."

"And then... when the next Day of the Fates came around, I watched her climb the mountain again, up into the mist, and when she came back, she summoned every knight into the grand chamber and locked the doors behind her. Locked *me* out. But I knew where to go, I'd found a passage behind the tapestries, a crack in the stone where sound travels, and I heard everything. She spoke of the Fates. Not a metaphor. Not a dream. *Them*. She said that they told her what to do. They had given her the plan, to use the magic from the sleep tokens, to start a war, to take The Vast, to attack *your* family. All of it. And the next morning, I was sent away. To the Keep. I haven't seen her since. But I *know* she's spoken with them again. That's what this is. Why now. Why you. Why *me*. It all connects. The Fates aren't a legend, Wynn. They're real. And whatever they said to her this time... this is all happening because of it."

Wynn was quiet for a moment, thinking about everything Grace had said. Then, with a small sigh, she reached beneath her tunic and pulled out the necklace. She held the ring in her palm for Grace to see.

"I think this has something to do with it too," Wynn said quietly. "Lorkan didn't give it to me. I stole it off the trunk of a passing Tor treasurer." She shrugged, turning the ring slowly between her fingers. "It just looked valuable at the time. But when Lorkan saw it... he got quiet. Said it looked like something Prima used to wear. Something important." She glanced at Grace. "You said the same thing."

Kiernan let out a low, gravelly breath and leaned his head back against the tree trunk. "You see, Wynn. You mock the Fates. You roll your eyes. You scoff. But you never stop to consider how much of your life's been touched by them. That ring showing up now? Grace knowing what she knows? You think it's all just... coincidence?"

Wynn closed her fist around the ring, her jaw clenched tight. "I don't like the idea that my life—*anyone's* life—is being stitched and snipped by some crony old hags with nothing better to do than meddle where they don't belong."

Kiernan didn't reply.

"And if they *do* exist," she went on, voice sharpening like a blade, "and if they had anything to do with what happened to my family—" She looked down at the closed ring in her fist, her voice lowering. "Then I'll find a way to destroy them."

There was a pause. Grace looked at her, eyes wide, uncertain whether to be scared or impressed.

Kiernan raised an eyebrow. "Just to be clear, you're going to do that after you save Avery and then defeat the Dark One and her army of Dark Knights."

Wynn gave a single nod, a grim smile tugging at the corner of her mouth. "Yes. After all that."

"Well," Grace stood brushing off crumbs from her skirt, "This is an adventure. I'm in."

"I guess I am too. Nothing better to do." Kiernan hobbled to stand on his injured leg, "We should get moving."

Wynn gave a small nod, her eyes sweeping the forest ahead. "South, then." They mounted again, the horses stamping softly against the earth, their breath steaming in the cool air of the forest.

As they set off once more, Grace leaned forward over Wynn's shoulder, her voice low and thoughtful. "This reminds me of a story I read once... three brothers, not quite heroes, not quite villains either, who formed a pact to bring down an evil magician. One of them had a wounded leg, I remember that. The youngest carried a stolen relic that turned out to be the key to everything..."

As the forest thickened and the day stretched thin, Grace continued her stories, telling of forgotten mystical lands, magical fairies, a girl who befriended a dreaming dragon. Some stories made Wynn snort. Others pulled a tired smile from Kiernan. The distraction was welcome. But as the sun dipped low and a new darkness pressed in from the east, a gentle rain began to fall, dripping softly onto the leaves overhead, each drop a quiet reminder of the road ahead. The weight of their journey returned, steady and inescapable.

Kiernan's shoulders sagged. The horses dragged their hooves. Grace slipped in and out of naps, drooling on Wynn's back. They were running on embers, and everyone could feel it.

Then came the sound; low voices, the clink of mugs, the distant thump of music. A golden glow bled through the trees ahead, soft and flickering like a hearth's welcome. They slowed.

"Should we go around it?" Wynn asked, half-hoping for a reason to keep moving, half-praying for one to stop.

"We could just sleep under the trees," Kiernan offered, though he looked ready to slide off his horse and never get up.

"No," Grace said, with a quiet finality. "It's obvious, you both need some sleep."

Wynn looked over her shoulder. "We don't have—"

"I know," Grace interrupted. "That's why I packed them."

"You what?" Kiernan blinked. "How many?"

Grace shrugged, utterly casual. "I don't know. Like a dozen or so in my pockets, maybe a hundred in my pack. They were for the servants at The Keep."

Wynn stared at her. "We've been packing a hundred sleep tokens across the kingdom?"

Grace smiled, smug as anything. "You're welcome."

Wynn tied her horse to the nearest post, casting a wary glance at the tavern ahead. Light flickered behind the shuttered windows, accompanied by bursts of laughter, the scrape of chairs, and the clatter of mugs.

Night stood beside Wynn, her dark fur sleek with droplets of rain, ears flattened in disapproval. The fox cast a pointed look toward the tavern door, as if to say, *Really? You're going in there and I'm not?* Wynn knelt beside her, scratching the space between her ears. "I know. I wouldn't want to be out here either," she murmured. "But there'll be music and shouting and someone's going to try and make you into a rug. Find a dry spot, yeah? We won't be long and I promise to bring you some scraps."

Night huffed, clearly unconvinced, but padded off with her usual quiet dignity, tail flicking once like punctuation.

Behind her, Wynn could feel Grace vibrating with excitement. "You've never been in a place like this before, have you?" Wynn asked, mostly to herself.

"No," Grace answered brightly. "I've never been outside the bounds of the Keep since I was sent there."

Wynn turned to her slowly. Kiernan met her eyes with the same unspoken thought: *This is going to go well.*

Wynn sighed and gave Grace a quick once-over. Her clothes were too clean, her hair too brushed, her entire aura too *bright.*

Without a word, Wynn yanked the cloak from Grace's shoulders, flipped it inside out, threw it on the ground, and promptly stomped on it.

Grace recoiled. "What are you doing?!"

"Helping you fit in." Wynn handed the now wet and muddy cloak back to her. "Trust me."

On cue, the tavern doors burst open and a man roughly the size of a boulder sailed out of them, landing with a grunt in the mud. Someone inside shouted something about cheating. Another voice roared a nasty comment back about his mother.

Grace blinked. "Oh."

"Listen," Wynn said, stepping closer. "I know this world. I've worked it, I've lived it. Keep your head down. Don't act like you know everything... in fact, act like you know *nothing*. These are Tarn folk inside. Slaves, servants, miners, people who've worked their bones thin and are looking to forget their lives for a while. Some Tor, maybe, but no one you want to know."

Grace nodded.

"If anyone asks..." Wynn looked at Kiernan.

"You work a farm not far from here," he said without missing a beat.

"Right. Keep it simple."

But Grace was already nodding too enthusiastically. "Ooooh, I've got it. I'll be just like the servant girl in that one book, the one who finds the dusty chest and opens it and a *genie* appears—"

"A what?" Kiernan asked.

"Don't encourage her," Wynn cut in sharply. She turned to Grace. "You know what? It's better if you don't talk at all."

"I got this," Grace said, undeterred. And then, not waiting for them, she snapped the cloak shut with dramatic flair and strode through the door like she'd been doing this her whole life.

"She's going to get us all killed," Kiernan shook his head.

"Probably," Wynn sighed. "Let's go."

The tavern was loud in that particular way of a place trying to forget itself. Laughter tangled with the tuning of instruments, and feet stomped in anticipation of a tune everyone only half-remembered. A jug slammed against a table; someone whooped in celebration. Folk were already drunk on cider and sleeplessness.

Grace was seated dead center in it all, radiant and curious, her chin propped on her hand like she was watching a play unfurl just for her. Wynn groaned.

She pulled her own cloak up and over her head, letting it shadow her face, and stepped inside. Her boots knew how to move in a place like this, heel first, weight steady, step confident.

She scanned the room with quick, quiet precision. Stools, too crowded. Booths, half full. Stage area near the fire, too exposed. The bar, good for watching. And the far back corner, past the reach of the hearthlight and exactly where the ones who didn't want to be seen always sat, a figure. Cloaked in black, posture still, head low, but not too low. His hood concealed most of his face, but Wynn could *feel* his eyes on her. Watching.

Wynn nodded to Grace, and then to Kiernan she said, "keep an eye on her."

"Got it," he quickly went and sat down at the table while Wynn made her way to the bar where a large woman in rolled sleeves and an apron crusted with crumbs and ale leaned over a cask. She didn't look up when Wynn approached.

"Three ales," Wynn said, already pulling coin from her pouch.

The woman glanced at the silver, then froze as Wynn slid a sleep token across the wood. In a blink, the barkeep's hand covered it. Wynn leaned in. "That guy in the back. In black. Is he a regular?"

The woman gave a sidelong glance, just enough to show she'd seen him. Her mouth twisted. "Never. First night tonight. Came in about an hour ago. Ain't ordered a thing."

Wynn dropped another coin beside the first. “We’ll take some potato pie. And send him an ale. Say it’s from the girl at the table in the middle.”

The woman looked over Wynn's shoulder. “The pretty one?”

Wynn turned. Grace was perched at the edge of the table like she owned it, one arm leaning on the surface, the other tucked beneath her chin. Firelight from the hearth played along her shiny hair, catching the glint of auburn and casting a soft glow across her cheeks. She was laughing at something Kiernan had said, her dimples flashing, eyes bright with mischief. There was something effortless about it all, like she belonged here, like the tavern had bent itself slightly to her presence.

Wynn paused, taken aback. “Yes,” she said finally. “That one.”

A few minutes later, Wynn slid into the seat beside Grace, setting down three jugs with practiced ease. Grace beamed. Kiernan was still scanning the room, his hand near his belt. Wynn didn’t drink yet. She looked past them, toward the shadowed corner.

The ale was delivered by a small boy carrying it with two hands. He said something. The figure didn’t move for a long moment. Then, slowly, he lifted his head just enough to look across the tavern. Directly at Wynn. She held his gaze. Didn’t smile. Didn’t blink. She wanted him to know she saw him too.

Grace raised her mug high, eyes alight. “Alright,” she declared. “Everyone together—To the flame that endures!”

Wynn blinked. “What?”

“It’s what they say in *The Kiss of Starlight*,” Grace explained, already too far into the moment to stop herself. “The rebels toast it before every battle.”

Kiernan chuckled and raised his mug. “To the flame that endures.”

Wynn sighed, but tapped her mug against theirs. "To Lorkan."

"To Lorkan," Grace and Kiernan echoed reverently.

They drank.

A burst of laughter rose from the table beside them. Wynn's ears caught on a name—the kind that scraped across her spine like a knife.

"—I'm telling you," one man said, loud and boisterous, "the Dark One's got a bounty so high you could buy your freedom and three more just for turning her in."

"Princess of Tarn," another said with a scoff. "If she's alive."

"She is," a woman cut in. "Word is she's got a crescent moon under her ear. Small, but clear. You see that mark, you don't hesitate."

Wynn went still. Her fingers slipped from the handle of her mug. She looked across at Kiernan, and in the firelit shadows, he was already watching her. Quietly, she pulled her cloak higher and turned her head, angling it away from the crowd.

"—and if you *help* her," the first man went on, voice sharper now, "the Dark One will make sure your whole bloodline dies sleeps in the cells below the castle."

There was a heavy thunk as someone slammed a mug on the table.

"She can rot in her own prison," a new voice growled. "If the Tarnish Princess lives, so does the rebellion."

The table went quiet. One of his friends hissed, "Shut it, Eddric. You want to get us all hanged?"

But Eddric was glaring around the tavern, defiant. He caught Wynn's eyes for just a second, then looked away.

At their own table, Kiernan leaned in and spoke softly, but with something hard behind it.

"Long live the Tarnish Princess."

"Here here," Grace whispered, tapping her mug again.

Kiernan turned back to Wynn, giving her a look that didn't ask anything. It just reminded her: *you're not alone. Not entirely.*

And somewhere in the back corner, the hooded figure had not moved—but Wynn could feel his gaze all the same.

Plates scraped clean and mugs nearly empty, the three of them had sunk deeper into the glow of the tavern. A fiddler had taken up in the corner, joined by a drummer and a woman with a pipe. The space had begun to shift. Tables moved. Boots shuffled. Someone clapped along as the room swelled with music.

Grace bounced in time to the rhythm, cheeks pink, her second mug of ale tilting dangerously in her hand.

"Take it easy," Wynn said, eyeing her. "You ever had ale before?"

"Yes," Grace said brightly. Then, after a pause, "Well. Sort of. Actually, no. Seraphina wouldn't allow it. Rest her soul."

"I'm sorry about her." Wynn rested a consoling hand on Grace's shoulder.

"Me too." She sighed and then took another sip.

Kiernan returned to the table. "Barkeep says we can take the barn down the road. Not much, but it'll keep the rain off." He nodded toward the door. "We should go."

"No," Grace said, just as the tempo picked up and the first couple took the center of the floor. "We should dance a little."

"We're definitely not dancing," Wynn started, but Grace was already on her feet, grabbing her hand.

"Just one," she insisted, eyes sparkling.

Wynn looked back at Kiernan as she was dragged away. "Don't look at me," Kiernan put his arms up. "I'm injured, remember." He pointed down to his bandaged leg.

"Go get the horses ready. I'll get her out."

"And miss this?" He crossed his arms and smiled, far too pleased with this whole scene.

"K!"

He dropped his arms, "Oh, fine." But as he reached the doorway, he couldn't help turning back and catching a quick glimpse.

The music caught Wynn before she could brace for it. Grace twirled once, too fast and with far too much enthusiasm, nearly toppling them both. Then she steadied, arms finding Wynn's like it was something they'd done before.

"I don't do this," Wynn said under her breath, glancing around, shoulders tight.

"You survive," Grace leaned into her, "but you don't *live*."

Wynn's eyes flicked to her, ready to protest, but Grace was already smiling again, pulling her just a little closer, swaying to the beat. It was clumsy at first. Wynn stiff, unsure. But then, something shifted. The warmth of the room, the rhythm, Grace's fingers curling ever so slightly around her hand. And for just a minute, Wynn didn't have the strength or motivation to resist.

As they spun around, Wynn found herself having fun, just a little. Then, Grace laughed, and she felt something unfamiliar and warm under her ribs, her cheeks flushing.

"I told you," Grace said, breathless. "This is the part in the story where they remember they're human."

Wynn studied her then, properly. In the middle of this crowded, half-drunken tavern filled with secrets and danger, Grace looked... bright. Like she belonged here more than Wynn ever had.

The music swelled again. And somewhere behind her, she could still feel the eyes of the hooded man in the corner. But for now, she danced, the tavern erupting with movement as the music continued. In that moment, Wynn's gaze flickered toward the door, where Kiernan stood with his arms crossed, a mischievous glint in his eye as he signaled that he was ready to move on. He seemed to be thoroughly enjoying the scene, though his readiness was clear.

Lost in the swirl of dance and the fleeting comfort of warmth, Wynn hadn't noticed that her hood had slipped down, exposing more than she intended.

A murmur arose from one of the patrons who had been seated beside them. He was staring right at her. The air seemed to still. She reached too late for her hair, trying to hide the mark behind her ear, but his eyes were already wide. A voice, sharp and edged with recognition, rang out in the midst of the revelry: "It's you. The princess."

The words cut through the melody. In that split second, as if a switch had been thrown, the music faltered. Silence fell over the room. Every conversation ceased. Across the room, the hooded figure in the far back slowly stood up, his presence heavy and solemn. For a long, breathless moment, Wynn's heart pounded as she scanned the faces surrounding her. With eyes wide and body tensing, she sensed that the tavern teetered on the edge of chaos, a full-blown brawl waiting to explode.

Then, as if compelled by an invisible force, one by one, the assembled patrons began to kneel. First a solitary figure, then another; soon, every face in the tavern bowed in unison. The pause stretched on, laden with unspoken devotion.

Wynn's voice cracked as she pleaded almost silently beneath her breath, "Stand, please, stand up... don't do this for me. I'm not..." She didn't know how to continue.

But from the midst of the kneeling throng came a rumbling, reassuring proclamation. The large man from the table, Eddric, declared, "Long live the Tarn."

Almost simultaneously, a raucous shout erupted: "Long live the Tarn!" The fiddler, once silent for only an aching moment, struck a chord and launched into the Tarnish Anthem, a melody that Wynn hadn't heard since she was little. One by one, the other musicians joined in and the tavern began to shake with unified song as glasses were raised high, each a small beacon of fervent loyalty directed at her.

Wynn's cheeks burned with a mix of mortification and astonished appreciation as she took in the scene. And then, in the corner of her eye, she saw him, the figure in the back, slipping away quietly through a side door. Whoever he had been, he was gone now, a ghost fading into the night.

The attention weighed on Wynn, every eye fixed on her felt heavy and invasive. In that shared moment, she caught Grace's gaze. The glow that had lit her from within during the dance was gone.

Quietly, Wynn leaned toward her. "Do you have those tokens handy?"

Grace nodded, grabbing the satchel beneath the table.

Wynn took two generous handfuls, letting the weight of them settle in her palm as she stood. "For your silence," she said to the room, voice carrying just enough to draw attention, "I was never here." Then, with a flick of her wrist: "Stolen from the Dark Queen herself." She tossed the tokens high. They caught the light midair, the sheen of obsidian unmistakable, and then chaos erupted.

A gasp. A shout. Chairs screeched across the floor. Bodies lunged for the scattered pieces with greedy hands, boots skidding over the boards. Voices tangled, laughter turning to scrapping and scuffle. Wynn didn't wait. She grabbed Grace's wrist, Kiernan already moving to cover their retreat, and the three of them slipped through the fray, forgotten.

Outside, the rain had picked up, a steady pattering that softened the world into mist and darkness. The horses waited, restless but ready.

As they mounted, they rode past the barn, its windows glowing amber, dry hay likely piled high within. Kiernan cast it a longing look. "Well, there goes the cozy night I was promised."

Wynn offered an apologetic shrug.

From beneath a slanted porch, a flash of charcoal fur emerged. Night shook herself off and trotted toward them, water flying from her soaked coat.

"There you are," Wynn exclaimed. The fox gave her a pointed look, half indignation, half accusation, as if to express her displeasure at being made to wait outside like some untrained mutt. Then came the side-eye. The one Wynn knew all too well.

"Yes, I promised scraps," Wynn sighed, "but I didn't exactly have time to grab them."

Night snuffed, an actual snuff, and then darted ahead, her bushy tail flicking like a banner of protest. She didn't bother to wait, clearly making her opinion known: she was wet, unimpressed, and now also hungry.

Wynn adjusted her cloak, rain soaking in at the collar. "Great. Now she's mad at me."

"No one's thrilled," Kiernan muttered, pulling his hood lower. "Least of all me."

They pressed on, the warm glow and noise of the tavern disappearing behind them, drowned by the relentless rhythm of the rain. As they rode out into the wet darkness, Wynn's mind churned—a maelstrom of revelry, of honor, of a secret she had carried for most of her life, now unburdened at last. Behind her, Grace was unusually quiet, her gaze fixed on some distant point in the trees. There was a stillness in her, not fear exactly, but something Wynn recognized all the same. The tightness in the jaw, the slightly parted lips, the weight behind the eyes. It was the look of someone trying to square the truth of who they were with a world that did not want them in it. Wynn knew that look. She'd worn it herself. And though the night was deep and uncertain, they sped forward into it, the memory of the Tarnish Anthem still playing in their ears.

~ ~ ~

Out there, the rain does not let up. It drips from the tangled branches above, slicks the muddy trail, beads on cloaks and lashes and reins. The horses move slowly, their breath ghosting the air, as they press on into the deep, dripping dark. No end in sight, no comfort waiting but the promise of farther miles. But not for you, dear reader. You are dry. You are still. The world around you is quiet, softened by lamplight and blankets tucked just so. Let the storm stay outside. Let the road stretch on without you. Here, there is warmth. Here, there is rest. Close your eyes, if you're ready, and sleep well.

CHAPTER TWENTY-ONE

The sound came first, ropes slapping against masts, voices shouting in a language not of the Vast, the creak and groan of wood under pressure. Avery stood at a dock, barefoot on sun-bleached boards, surrounded by a flurry of movement. Men hoisted crates, mothers called out to children, someone barked orders in clipped, unfamiliar syllables.The air was thick with salt and warmth; thicker than anything she'd known in the Tarn. The sun felt wider here, lazier, smearing the endless sky with gold. The trees along the shore bent like dancers, their trunks tall and narrow, their leaves feathered, swaying over white dirt where a turquoise ocean lapped gently. She knew this place. The memory of it thrummed in her chest, too deep and certain to be doubted.

There, at the ramp of a long, curved ship, was a man. Her father. He turned toward her, his face shadowed by a broad hat, his expression both urgent and soft. He said something, again, in that same rolling language, and she understood none of it, but somehow she knew what he meant.

Avery stepped closer. "Where's Mother?" she asked. But she already knew. Her father didn't speak. Just shook his head once, slowly, as the boat creaked underfoot.

Then, she was on the ship.

The sun was gone now. The ocean stretched endlessly in every direction, dark and pulsing. Others were huddled low against the deck, cloaks drawn tight, heads bowed. They had been here for days. She knew that. She *remembered* that.

A storm loomed ahead, black clouds churned low over the sea, winds already pulling at the sails. Her stomach dropped. She turned toward the bow, where her father stood steady, unmoved.

"Father," she called, panic rising, "we have to turn. The storm will take us down!"

He didn't answer.

The sky split open.

Rain lashed down like claws, the ship lurching and shrieking. People screamed. Wood cracked. A wave like a mountain rose ahead of them. Avery gripped a mast, wrapping her arms around it, locking her fingers.

Then—hands. Someone, something, pried her grip loose.

"Stop! No. Wait—"

The wave struck and she flew, rolling down the wooden deck and then right off the ship. Saltwater slammed into her, pulled her under, and down she went into darkness. She kicked, reached, but the water took her and swallowed her in a blink. Salt rushed into her nose, her mouth. She kicked and reached for a surface that was vanishing above her.

She could not swim.

She did not scream.

She simply sank.

Then, silence. Not peace. Not stillness, just nothing.

Avery opened her eyes.She was no longer underwater. No longer anywhere at all. Only mist surrounded her. Thick and swirling, lavender and pale silver. It curled in the air as though alive, rising and falling in unseen tides. There was no ground beneath her feet, yet she stood. There was no ceiling, yet the sky pressed down like a weight. The air was neither cold nor warm. It simply *was.* Soundless.

"Where..." her voice broke as it left her lips, almost devoured by the fog. "Where am I?"

No answer. But she knew she had been here before. Not in sleep. Not in waking. *In between.*

A shape took form in the fog, at first just the suggestion of a body, a silhouette, but then more. Tall, regal and cruel, dressed in fabric that moved like spilled ink. Her skin was pale, her head bare. No crown. None needed. Her presence alone bent the space around her.

Avery took a step back.

The Queen tilted her head, as if inspecting a strange looking insect. "So," Prima said softly, "you *have* been here before."

"I... I don't know how I got here," Avery stammered. "I was on a ship. There was a storm, and then—"

"It took you in," Prima mused, almost to herself. "The sea between stories." Her gaze darkened. "But how? And why?"

Avery shook her head. "This is a dream," she whispered. "Just a dream." Then louder, desperate, "*This is a dream!* Get out of my head!"

Prima's eyes flared. She moved and a cold hand seized Avery's wrist with impossible speed. Black nails dug into her skin like talons. The Queen's breath was ice. "*How did you find this place?*" she snarled.

Avery gasped in pain. "Let go!"

"Tell me how you got here."

"I'll never tell you!" Avery shouted, shoving her with both hands.

Mist exploded and Prima vanished like she had never been there. Only fog remained. Her wrist burned where she had been touched. She stood there, shaking, in the heart of a place that wasn't a place, breathing a mist that wasn't air, until...

She woke.

She looked down. The skin was red where Prima's nails had sunk in. She sat up, pressing her back to the wall, chest rising and falling too fast. She didn't sleep again.

In the grand hall, Prima sat upright on her dark throne. Her eyes flew open. The soft gold now full of fire. Her hands flew to her chest, where the girl had shoved her. "How..." she whispered. How had a child pushed her out like that? Dreams were her realm, *hers*.

A cry pierced the sky—a shriek, sharp and spiraling.

She stood and moved to the tall window. A hawk wheeled down from the grey clouds above and streaked into the throne hall. With a beating of wings, it dropped a scroll at Prima's feet, circled once, shrieked again, and vanished into the gloom.

She unrolled the scroll. Her expression did not change, but the flames behind her eyes blazed hotter. *The Princesses both live. The Stone does not. A rebellion rises in the Tarn. I will have them soon.*

She crushed the parchment in one hand. Her knuckles turned white. The veins in her neck pulsed like serpents under skin. "Guard!" she roared. One appeared in an instant. The moment he crossed the threshold, he dropped to one knee. "Your Majesty."

"Send this message to every corner of The Vast," Prima said, her voice flat and cold. "Tor. Tarn. Forest. River. Mountain. All of it."

"Yes, Your Majesty."

"The Tarn will not see sleep," she hissed, her eyes glittering with cruel delight, "until their princess kneels before me."

The guard hesitated. "My Queen—"

Her head snapped toward him like a striking viper. "No sleep," she said again, slower this time, a blade drawn across flesh. "Until she kneels."

He swallowed. "What of the ones who serve you?" he asked carefully. "In the army, I mean. If you withhold tokens from them as well... many serve to earn sleep for their families. They may turn against you."

Prima's expression barely shifted, but the temperature in the chamber dropped a degree. The silence that followed was deliberate, calculated. Finally, she exhaled through her nose, displeased and slightly irritated. "Very well. Those who serve me will get their due. But everyone else—" her lip curled, "—not until she kneels."

The guard bowed his head and turned to leave.

"Wait," Prima said, just as he reached the door. "You."

He stopped. Turned.

"What is your name?"

"Sorn, Your Majesty."

"And you are Tor-born?"

"And raised," he replied, standing a little taller.

Prima walked closer to him with slow deliberate steps. She circled him once, then came to stand directly in front of him. "And what would you do with the Tarn who serve me?" she asked.

He hesitated. Thought. "I would allow them their tokens. But—"

"Go on," she murmured. "Your future depends on your next words."

Sorn met her gaze. Steady. Unflinching. "The Tarn will never be truly loyal to you, My Queen. Fear does not grow loyalty. It grows rot. You've had the power to crush them for years. Why not simply do it?"

Ah. Now here, dear reader, is where things get interesting. Characters like Sorn often drift unnoticed through the halls of stories. Background men in background armor, made of obedience and mediocrity. Until the story tilts, and a vacancy opens, and suddenly, there they are. Promoted. Prominent. Dangerous. But make no mistake: Sorn has been waiting for this. He was overlooked for years, especially by The Stone, who dismissed him as a dull, self-important footnote. And perhaps he was. But there's a special kind of cruelty that forms in the hearts of those always underestimated. Sorn has it. A mean, petty sort of venom that thinks less of everyone else and too much of itself. Not brilliant. Not wise. But sharp enough to cut something if pointed in the right direction. And Prima? Well, she does enjoy wielding sharp things.

She stepped in close, her voice low. "I do not do what you suggest because I already *have* the power. And that power has allowed the Tor to prosper while the Tarn break in the mines and blister in the fields. Who do you think dies for our comfort? If I crush them entirely, who will suffer in their place?"

Sorn bowed his head. "Forgive me, Dark One. As always, you are right."

"But," she said, her voice cutting the air like glass, "I like how you think."

He looked up.

"I've just received word that The Stone is dead. You, Sorn of The Tor, have just been promoted to General of the Dark Knights. Congratulations."

His eyes widened, but he managed a low, reverent bow. "I am honored, my Queen."

"Good. Spread the message. Prepare your knights. There is rebellion kindling in the Tarn. I want it smothered before it burns. And as for the ones who fight for me..."

He nodded. "I will threaten their families at the first sign of betrayal."

A slow smile curved at her lips. "I'm glad we understand each other. Go," she said, turning back toward her throne. "The Vast doesn't wait. And neither do I."

He bowed once more. "As you wish, my Queen."

And with that, dear reader, a pawn became a piece worth watching. Not because he is noble. Not because he is smart. But because he found himself in the right place at the right time.

~ ~ ~

So much going on, isn't there? So much to think about. Hopefully a distraction from your own life, or at least a chance to shut out your world for a while. Because thoughts, as you know, have a way of clinging tight when the lights go out—spinning, pacing, refusing to sleep even when you wish they would. In those moments, remember this: you're allowed to set them down. Let them wait on the windowsill. Let them drift like leaves on a stream, slow and quiet and far away. You've done enough for today. Sleep well.

CHAPTER TWENTY-TWO

The world had gone quiet again. No river, no chase, no mystery men in black. Just a soft hill, cradled in a ring of trees like the cupped hand of the forest. The grass beneath them was damp but gentle, dotted with fallen leaves and the odd acorn. Overhead, light filtered down, the kind of light that did not scream *morning* but rather nudged it gently into being.

Wynn was the first to stir, woken by the warm, wet sensation of something dragging across her face, slowly, insistently. "Night," she mumbled. The fox, tucked like a curled scarf in the crook of her arm, gave her one final lick and then sneezed. She blinked blearily, stretching one leg, then paused. Her other hand was resting gently across something solid yet soft. Grace. More specifically, Grace's hip.

Wynn's breath caught. She froze, unsure whether to move it quickly or slowly or not at all.

Then Grace shifted, curling inward with a little moan, and Wynn pulled her hand back quickly. She sat up, ruffling Night's fur to cover her fluster.

A few feet away, Kiernan groaned and stretched. He sat up, rubbed the back of his neck, and blinked at the trees overhead.

"Well," he said, voice rough with sleep, "did the princesses sleep well?"

Wynn shot him a look. "Don't."

Grace made a soft, pitiful sound behind her and rolled onto her back, one hand pressed to her forehead, the other draped dramatically across her chest.

"I feel *awful,*" she moaned.

Kiernan couldn't stifle a laugh, "Did someone drink one too many ales last night?"

"Everything hurts." She continued complaining.

Wynn raised an eyebrow, entirely unsympathetic. "What, miss your plush pillows and warm blanket?"

Grace cracked one eye open. "Yes," she said flatly. "Yes, I do. No one should have to sleep like this. It's uncivilized."

"I slept quite well," Kiernan offered, standing slowly and brushing off the leaves.

"Me too," Wynn agreed, tugging on her boots. "Survival has a way of making a grass bed feel like luxury, even if it is soggy."

Grace sat up slowly, wincing as she did. Her hair was a mess of tangled waves, and her tunic had wrinkled in enough directions to look intentional. "Can't we stay just a little longer? Five minutes? Ten?"

"What," Wynn said, slinging her pack over one shoulder, "you're all for adventure until it gets uncomfortable?"

Grace pouted. "I didn't say that."

"This *is* adventuring," Wynn replied. "Welcome to it."

Then Night growled. Low and quiet. Ears laid flat against her head. Body stiff. Wynn turned instantly. "What is it?" Night stood tense as a bowstring. Her tail flicked once. She was looking up, above them.

Wynn followed her gaze.

Perched high in the upper branches of the tallest tree, mostly still but watching—*a hawk.*

Not just any hawk. Its feathers shimmered with a copper sheen, head tilted as if it *knew* it had been seen. Then—*shriek.* With a burst of wings, it launched into the sky and vanished into the canopy, leaving the air disturbingly empty.

"What was *that* about?" Kiernan asked, already reaching for his sword out of habit.

"I don't know," Wynn said, her voice tight. "But we need to go. Now."

She turned to Grace. "Up, princess. Enough with the beauty sleep."

Grace groaned again. "You're enjoying this."

"Maybe," Wynn said. "But we really need to make a move." Because something had seen them. Something had been watching. And in The Vast, nothing watched without a reason.

They rode in silence for some time. The forest had begun to thin, trees spacing wider apart as the terrain sloped gently downward, flowing into a lowland valley. Morning light dappled the path in broken patches, softened now by cloud and distance. The farther they rode, the more the air changed, growing stiller, heavier, touched by a damp chill that clung to their cloaks and curled beneath collars.Then the fog began.

It wasn't sudden, not all at once, but a slow, rising breath from the earth itself. It crept across the ground in ghostly tendrils, licking the horses' hooves and climbing up their legs. With each step, it thickened, until the land ahead was no longer a path but a pale sea, rolling and edgeless.

The horses slowed. Wynn raised a hand, signaling the others to stop. Her mare pawed the ground nervously, huffing a soft whine through her nostrils.

Grace pulled her notes from her satchel, eyes scanning the ink-stained parchment as she traced a trembling finger along the drawn lines. "I think..." she murmured, "I think whatever we're trying to find is down there. See," she turned the page toward them, "we follow the river until it splits. There should be a crossing near the divide. And between the rivers... that's where whatever we're looking for will be."

Wynn looked out over the descending valley, now half-swallowed in mist. "Alright," she said quietly. "Stay close. Don't drift too far from the path. Seraphina said folk get lost in this fog."

Kiernan grunted his agreement, but even he looked uneasy. The fog was rising fast now, curling around tree trunks and swallowing low branches. Each breath drew in air that was colder than the last, sharp and damp, with the faint mineral tang of stone and river.

"Night..." Wynn clicked and the fox looked up at her name. "Up." She patted the saddle in front of her and Night obeyed, leaping with ease and settling in front of Wynn. As they continued, she welcomed Night's warmth in front and Grace's in the back. The forest sounds faded, one by one. First the rustling birdsong, then the insect hums. Then, even the wind seemed to fall away. All that remained was the soft, rhythmic sound of hooves over loamy earth. One step at a time.

Wynn felt Night shift in front of her.

"I don't like this," Grace whispered, drawing her cloak tighter. Her voice sounded far too loud in the hush.

"Neither do the horses," Kiernan said, patting his mare's neck.

The path narrowed. Mist beaded on their eyelashes. Ahead, faint and constant, came the sound of rushing water, not thunderous, but steady, like a spill from a low stone lip. A waterfall.

Wynn nudged her horse forward, Kiernan stayed close behind. The trees opened slightly, and there it was: a broad rock face like a cleaved mountain, rising out of the fog, old and worn by years of water rushing into it. The river tumbled towards it, breaking over the stone with quiet insistence and dividing below—split cleanly in two, as if the land had parted it by blade.

"How are we supposed to get on that?" Kiernan asked, squinting toward the massive divide.

Wynn didn't answer right away. She studied the flow, the land, the shape of the river's winding arms. Then, simply, she said: "We go farther down."

They turned to follow the river on the right, its voice the only sound in an otherwise breathless world. The water here was no longer the wild, thrashing torrent they had once crossed under pursuit, here it had calmed, meandering wide and quiet through the tall grass valley.

For another hour, they pressed on, the sun barely visible above as a pale disk in the sky. The mist clung to them, draping the world in a fuzzy white. Sometimes they glimpsed a shape in the distance; a tree, a boulder, a trick of light, but mostly they saw nothing at all.

Then, at last, Wynn raised her hand. "There," she said.

They rounded a bend, and the river opened wider beside them; broad, shallow, glimmering faintly in the dull light. The stones beneath were visible, smooth and flat, and the water here barely reached their knees.

They dismounted briefly, letting the horses drink, stretching their legs and scanning the shore opposite. Wynn knelt by the water's edge, dipping her fingers in. Cold, but not too swift. Crossable.

"This will do," she said. "Once we're over, we'll be on the land between the rivers."

She looked to Grace, then Kiernan. "From here on," she added softly, "we watch every step."

Because there were stories about this place, Seraphina had said. The kind that didn't end with a cozy fire and a warm tea. And now... they were in it.

Wynn moved slowly, guiding the horse with Grace still mounted on it, across the river and to the other side. When they reached the shore the land tilted sharply upward, the beginnings of the rise that cut clean into the heart of the land between rivers. The fog was even thicker here. Not like before. This was no mere veil, it was a wall.

Grace dismounted and walked closer to the front now, studying her notes with quiet intensity, though the paper had gone soft with the damp air. Kiernan flanked the rear. Night padded silently beside Wynn, ears twitching, nose raised as if scenting something Wynn could not. The terrain steepened with each careful step. Slick grass and loose stone made the climb slower than expected.

"Can anyone hear the river?" Grace asked softly, her voice wrapped in fog.

"No," Wynn murmured. "Just keep going."

And then, Kiernan stopped.

Wynn turned, nearly colliding with his chest. "Why'd you—"

"Shhh," he hissed. His eyes flicked left, right. Then: "Did you hear that?"

"What?" Wynn snapped, one hand clutching her chest. "Kiernan! You scared the spirits out of me. Don't do that!"

"Sorry," he said quickly, eyes still scanning. "But I swear, I hear something... humming?"

The three of them stood in still silence, fog eddying gently between them.

Then Grace spoke, slow and breathy: "I hear it too."

The sound came thin and strange, it had no direction, no shape. Only a persistent presence. Eerie. The horses reared suddenly, hooves clattering against stone, reins jerking. One let out a sharp cry and tried to bolt back down the trail. Only Kiernan's strong grip on the reins kept it from fleeing.

"They won't go farther," he said, breath short. "They're too spooked."

Wynn rubbed her mare's nose gently, trying to soothe her. The creature trembled beneath her touch. "Then we go without them," she said at last. "Tie them here. We'll find them again once we're down."

Kiernan nodded and began tethering his horse to a bare knot of stone. Grace moved slowly, eyes still scanning the fog as if she half expected the mist to take shape and speak.

Wynn bent to knot her own reins and as she stood her cloak shifted with the motion. Grace's eyes caught something in the pale light. A glow.

"Wynn," she whispered. "Your shirt..."

From beneath her collar, a soft purple light pulsed faintly, slow as a heartbeat. It shimmered softly through the linen. Wynn pulled the fabric aside. The obsidian ring was giving off a soft purple hue.

They locked eyes. "We must be close to something," Grace whispered.

Night jumped up, placing her two front paws on Wynn's waist and leaning in to smell the ring. She sniffed, then huffed and dropped back down shaking her head in disapproval.

Wynn tucked the ring back against her skin, her fingers lingering there for a moment, then nodded. "Let's go."

They turned to face the climb. The path now was nothing but loose shale, slick, broken, and narrow. One misstep would mean a fall. The fog clung tighter here, until the edges of their own bodies seemed to fade.

Kiernan squinted into the white and swallowed. "I think..." he started, then cleared his throat. "I think we should hold hands."

Wynn turned her head slowly, eyebrows raised. "Really?"

"So we don't lose one another," he said quickly. "Just in case."

"I agree," Grace said, her voice quiet but firm.

Wynn rolled her eyes, but the wisp of a smile curled at her lips. "Fine. But if either of you gets sentimental about it, I'm letting go."

Grace reached out first, her hand finding Wynn's with a gentle squeeze. Warmth passed between them, not just skin, but something steadier. Wynn's fingers curled around hers without thinking. Kiernan took Grace's other hand, and together, they climbed.

The fog stayed dense, a world of gray and silver. It was disorienting, making it impossible to see how far they had come or how far they had to go. Night stayed close to Wynn's side. One step. Then another. And then—

Finally, the fog broke. Not all at once, but in a sudden thinning. Air rushed upward and the edge of the cliff arrived too fast. Wynn's foot landed on nothing. She gasped, her body pitching forward.

But Grace's hand was still in hers, tight. She yanked her back with a cry, arm wrapping around Wynn's waist just in time. Wynn stumbled, heart hammering, and landed hard against Grace's chest. For a moment they were face-to-face, breathing fast and deep. Too close, and too shaken to speak.

"I—" Wynn started, but couldn't find the rest.

Grace held her a beat longer before huffing, "You were about to step off the damned cliff."

"I noticed," Wynn said dryly, voice tight with adrenaline. "Thanks."

Kiernan crouched low near the edge, he and Night peering over together. The fog was lifting just enough to reveal what lay far below. "It's like we're on the tip of a slice of pie," he said looking down. A sharp, sheer drop... and a glimmer of water carving through stone.

They had reached the end but there was nothing. No structure. No path. No shrine or monument or hidden temple like Grace had promised in her notes and mutterings. Only the river below.

Wynn frowned. "This... can't be it."

Grace didn't answer. She had already stepped back, pacing in a tight line. Her fingers gripped the leather binding of her notes. She flipped a page, then another, brows furrowed.

"I don't understand," she muttered. "I was *sure.* The river forked, the land cut in... this is the point. It *has* to be. I checked and rechecked Lorkan's clues. After all that? After how far we've come and... NOTHING!" She kicked a stone that clattered over the cliff's edge and disappeared.

Wynn watched, uncertain. She'd seen Grace confused before. Tired. Teasing. Even scared. But this... this was new. A frustrated, furious Grace. And for all her sharp wit and stubborn pride, there was something unexpectedly endearing about it. She looked like she wanted to shout at the sky and stamp on the earth.

"You know," Wynn said, just to say something, "you're kinda cute when you're—"

"That *doesn't help,*" Grace snapped, not unkindly, but sharp enough to shut Wynn's mouth with a twitch of a grin.

Wynn sighed and turned back to the drop. She crouched, brushing her fingers along the stone, as if the answers might be hiding in the cracks. "Maybe we missed something," she murmured. "Something smaller..." She looked up, sensing something off. "K?"

Silence.

She stood. Looked left. Right.

"Kiernan?" Louder now. "Night? NIGHT!?" The fog gave no answer, only swallowing her voice. Her chest squeezed tight. She stepped forward, eyes scanning the gray. "Kiernan? Night?" Nothing. "Grace!"

"What", Grace looked up from her notes. Clearly annoyed that her train of thought had been interrupted.

Wynn was about to answer when Night appeared and circled her legs. She let out a sigh of relief. Then she heard her name and

"Over here!" It was Kiernan's voice coming from the left. Night nudged her towards the voice.

"Wynn! Grace!"

They both turned, fumbling across the uneven stone, following his voice. When they reached him, he was crouched beside a jagged crease in the earth, a hollow tucked between two outcrops of stone, half-hidden by a curtain of vine and root.

He looked up at them, eyes wide with wonder. "You're not going to believe this," he said.

Wynn crouched beside him, brushing the moss aside. Her breath caught. Beneath the veil of roots and leaves, slick with mist, was an opening. Worn steps, ancient, carved into the rock, spiraled downward into the dark.

Grace knelt beside her. "Is that..." she whispered, blinking as if afraid the sight would vanish, "are those *stairs*?"

Wynn nodded once. They had found something. And whatever it was waited below.

~ ~ ~

Not every step leads somewhere quickly. Some chapters drift, the way mist curls through trees, soft, slow, and full of quiet wondering. You wandered with them through the hush, through the not-knowing, and maybe your eyes grew heavy along the way. Good. That's how it should be. Stories, like journeys, need their pauses. Their breath between beats. So if the fog blurred the edges a bit tonight, let it. Let it carry you gently toward sleep, where nothing needs finding, and everything can wait. Sleep well.

CHAPTER TWENTY-THREE

The mist whispered behind them, thick as wool, pressing at their backs as they stood at this passageway into the earth. No one spoke at first. Wynn examined the stairs vanishing into darkness, a slimy film clinging to their edges, the air below breathing cool and steady like something ancient that had never quite fallen asleep.

Then Kiernan cleared his throat. "I think I should stay and keep watch," he said quietly, as if louder words might wake something from below. "This feels like it's meant for you two. Didn't Lorkan say something like that?"

Wynn turned to him, half a protest on her lips, but something in his expression stopped her. He wasn't scared or sulking. He simply looked resolute, the way he always did before being difficult.

"If we don't come back—" she began.

He raised a hand, cutting her off with a crooked grin. "Start a rebellion. Rescue Avery. Defeat the Queen. Yeah, yeah. I got it."

Wynn chuckled, low and warm, but it didn't quite hide the worry in her eyes. Still, she nodded once. "Night. You should st—," but before she could finish, the fox had darted past and was already down some stairs. She paused, not turning around to acknowledge Wynn's comment, just waiting for her to follow. "I guess you're coming too."

"Be careful," Kiernan said as Wynn and Grace turned toward the dark.

They descended slowly, hands brushing the rough, damp walls on either side. Each step echoed, their footsteps overlapping. The deeper they went, the cooler the air grew, rich with the scent of damp earth and something stronger, incense maybe, a woody smell Wynn couldn't quite place.

Then, just as the dark began to press too close, a torch flickered to life along the wall. Then another. And another. The flames sparked awake as they passed, one by one, bathing the stairwell in warm gold. The shadows retreated as if in welcome. Wynn glanced back at Grace, who stared wide-eyed at the glow.

"Magic torches," she whispered, her voice small and awed.

"Just your usual cave decor," Wynn said, trying to keep it light, though the timbre of her voice betrayed her.

"Naturally," Grace agreed with a nervous laugh.

After descending another couple of minutes, the last step leveled out, and the world unfolded into a chamber—no, a cathedral of stone. A cavern so vast it had no end in sight. High above, the ceiling disappeared into shadow, crisscrossed with roots and hanging lanterns. All around them were shelves. Shelves upon shelves of books, ancient and leather-bound, others gilded and threadbare and hand-stitched. They stretched higher than a person could reach, stacked into the curves and crannies of the rock. Ladders leaned against the walls and narrow spiraled staircases led to the highest levels. There were reading nooks carved into the walls, alcoves glowing softly with enchanted lanterns, tables piled high with scrolls, scattered pages and dried inkpots.

A wide hearth blazed to their right. A giant fireplace set in a mantle of smooth riverstone. The flames crackled cheerfully, casting orange light across the polished flagstone floor, where woven rugs softened the rock beneath their feet. Somewhere, far off, a bell chimed. Faint and melodic. As if time passed differently here.

Wynn blinked. "What is this place?"

Grace didn't answer. She couldn't. She had pressed one hand to her chest, lips parted in wonder, and Wynn swore she saw her eyes shimmer.

Slowly, Grace stepped forward, drawn to the shelves like a moth to flame.

"Grace," Wynn warned, "you're going to have to contain yourself."

Grace only laughed, breathless, bright. "This is my *everything*," she said. "I think I need to live here."

She reached out, fingers trembling slightly, and brushed the spine of a thick green volume embossed with gold.

And then—

"Please," said a voice. Smooth. Calm. Firm. "Don't touch my books."

Grace flinched back instinctively, hand recoiling as if stung.

From the distance a figure slowly emerged. Tall and slender, they moved with the kind of poise that didn't ask for attention, they simply *had* it. Their short pale hair curled slightly around pointed ears, and their skin held the shimmer of moonlight caught on fresh snow. A velvet tunic of deep red hugged their slender frame, cinched at the waist by a golden belt that glinted with quiet elegance. Simple glasses perched on the bridge of their nose.

They closed the book they'd been holding with one hand, tucking it under their arm. The other hand reached up, removing their glasses slowly, deliberately. Their gaze found Wynn's. Then Grace's. And they smiled. "Lorkan said you would come."

"Are you an elf?" Grace asked in awe. "Like, a real one?"

"Please," the elf responded, motioning with one long-fingered hand toward a couch of such size and softness it seemed conjured from a dream. Upholstered in deep green velvet and tufted like the clouds over the northern hills, it could have fit ten men across, or two very confused girls and a fox who didn't know how to respect the rules regarding furniture.

Wynn and Grace obeyed without a word. Night jumped up, sniffed a cushion, then, tail flickering, circled once and curled up like she belonged here.

The elf placed the book gently on the table behind them, then sat, not in a chair, but on the edge of a long, low writing desk carved from the base of a large oak. They leaned forward slightly, elbows on their knees, expression unreadable. There was something strangely captivating about them. Not beautiful, exactly, something beyond that. And their voice, when they spoke again, was ageless and smooth—neither male nor female, yet both, wrapped in velour and hush.

"My name is Illen," they said. "I am a Bookkeeper, a protector of the stories. And this," they motioned to the walls of books, "is my library."

Grace blinked, leaning forward. "Is this where Lorkan got all his books?"

"Yes," Illen said, tilting their head. "Many of them. Some he copied, or borrowed, or stole. So he thought. But I always know when a book leaves my collection."

"And how did you know him?" Wynn asked, more wary.

Illen's smile faded, just a flicker. "*Did,*" they confirmed softly. "Then, he is no longer of this story... as I suspected, with you two here." They rose, dusting their tunic with a practiced hand. "Would you like some tea?"

Grace brightened immediately. "Yes, please!"

Wynn narrowed her eyes. "Is it going to knock us out or make us reveal our secrets or something?"

"I assure you," Illen said, with the tiniest crinkle of amusement at the corners of their eyes, "it is not poisoned. And, you have no secrets from me. It is simply tea. And I've been told, it's rather good."

A moment later, steaming porcelain cups appeared on a table before them, as if summoned by thought. Grace inhaled and sighed, cradling hers reverently. "It smells like apricots," she whispered. "And cream."

Wynn gave hers a cautious sniff, then sipped. Her eyebrows lifted despite herself. "Okay. That's pretty tasty."

They sat like that for a while, three figures and a sleeping fox in a cavern of books, flames crackling low in the hearth, the light from the torches golden and steady. The library had a coziness to it; the sound of turning pages somewhere beyond, a faint scratch of quill on parchment, the murmur of stories being read.

Illen spoke again. "Years ago, a dark presence moved through the land. It ordered the destruction of books, scrolls, any written memory. The death of history. A forgetting."

Grace sipped her tea and said with casual dryness, "Yes, that would be my mother."

Wynn gave Grace a glance. "They're nothing alike."

"Oh, no," Grace said, waving her hand vaguely toward the towering shelves. "She's all fire and fear, *rah rah I will rule this land.* I'm more... this." She let her hand fall gently onto a nearby cushion, brushing the soft velvet back and forth.

Illen nodded thoughtfully. "Good to know." They took a slow sip of their own tea, eyes distant, as if consulting some chapter only they could see. "Lorkan found this place because—well, as he put it—he tortured a few people. Someone finally relented and told him about this place, hidden beneath the twin rivers. One of the Fundamentals."

"Fundamentals?" Grace asked.

"Ancient libraries. There were once eight," Illen said. "This is one of only three that remain." They did not elaborate.

"Lorkan came to destroy it. He was not the first, nor will he be the last. But when he stepped into this room and saw the shelves, the fire, the peace of it all... he simply couldn't. He stood at the base of the stairs, dropped his sword, and said he was tired. I believed him."

Wynn leaned forward, setting her cup down. "And you just invited him in?"

"I gave him tea," Illen said with a wry smile. "And welcomed him. Because you see... I was expecting him. Just as I was expecting you. It is all a part of the same story."

Wynn groaned and flopped back on the couch. "Please don't start talking about the Fates."

"Oh," Illen said quickly, raising a hand. "We Bookkeepers detest the Fates."

That made Wynn sit back up.

Illen's face darkened with something sharp and ancient. "They meddle. They twist. They write endings into beginnings and call it destiny. They do not believe in choice. I, on the other hand..." They looked at Grace, then Wynn. "I very much do."

Wynn set her teacup down, though the warmth still lingered in her hands. "As good as this is," she said, "why did Lorkan direct us here?"

Illen leaned back slightly on the edge of the desk, the firelight catching the gold of their belt. They didn't answer right away. Their eyes, the color of turquoise riverglass, fixed on the ring glowing softly at Wynn's chest.

"Because," they said at last, "I am the only one who can tell you what you need to know. And," they lifted a finger, pointing at the circle of light beneath her cloak. "And... I know what that does. And where it can lead you."

Wynn's hand instinctively rose to the ring.

Illen's gaze grew distant as if they were looking into another room, or another time entirely. "Years ago," they began, "your queen disappeared from the Tor for a time. You know this. But what most do not know is where she went. She sought out the Fates, begging them to end her suffering."

Wynn rolled her eyes. Grace, though, leaned forward, caught up in the words.

"They gave her that ring," Illen continued. "A ring forged in a realm that bore the Fates. And with it, they guided her toward a place of... power. Not of this world exactly, but beside it. Beneath it. Between." They stepped away from the desk now, pacing slowly as they spoke, trailing one hand along the spines of books that looked older than kingdoms. "They sent her to The *Margins.*"

Grace echoed the word under her breath while Wynn spoke up, "Where?"

"It is not a place you can find on a map," Illen said. "The Margins exist in and between all stories. It is where stories are drawn from—the raw, restless ink of possibility. Time, as we know it, doesn't run in the same way. Not really. Things exist and un-exist. It is chaos, and it is clarity. Many have gone in seeking answers, but few have come out."

Illen turned to them now, voice low. "And none return unchanged."

"Why would the Fates do that?" Grace asked.

Illen shrugged, "Because, that's what they do. They manipulate, they test, they push boundaries and lives. They do it, simply because they're amused by it." They took a breath before continuing. "Prima went in. And what she found changed everything. She found a book."

Wynn's brows pulled together. "What kind of book?"

Illen's smile was faint. "*The Book That Will Put You to Sleep.*"

"That's... actually what it's called?" Wynn asked.

Illen gave a single nod. "The Originals are... literal. Their titles are not meant to dazzle. They are meant to tell you their purpose."

"There are others?" Grace asked, eyes wide.

"Oh yes," Illen said. "There are others like it. Original books. Spells so old they shape the very worlds we live inside. Some say the stars are written in them. Some say the stars are written *by* them."

"And my mother took one," Grace said quietly.

"No," Illen replied. "Nothing can take an Original out of The Margins. Not anymore. We made sure of that. The books stay where they are. But one can... *borrow* from them. One can take a spell—if The Margins allow it."

They paused, eyes catching the firelight. "This is why Prima fears what books can offer. Why she destroys them. Outlaws them. Censors anything that might teach, or awaken, or stir the wrong kind of question in the wrong kind of mind. She is not the first."

"Books are power," Grace chimed in.

"Yes," Illen's voice was almost tender. "Books frighten those who want the world to remain exactly as they command it. I have witnessed the burning of shelves more times than I can count—by kings, queens, and frightened villagers alike. People say it is stories they fear. But it's never the stories, not really." They looked toward Wynn and Grace. "It's the thinking that comes after."

"So," Wynn swallowed. "This is how she made the sleep tokens?"

Illen nodded slowly, their face lit by firelight. "Yes. At first, she used the ring for what it was meant to do. What the Fates allowed. She entered The Margins and took a spell to control sleep. Hold it back and bind it. She used it to create the tokens. To commodify rest. That alone was bold. Unforgivable, some might say."

Grace's brow furrowed. "But she didn't stop there, did she?"

"No," Illen said. "She's gone back. Used the ring to enter The Margins a second time, to take another spell, one that lets her reach into dreams. She can shape them and twist them so the boundary between what is imagined and what is real blurs around the dreamer."

Wynn leaned forward. "And the ring lets her just... *take* spells?"

"It allows her to enter The Margins. It is she who chooses to take from the Original books. And now," Illen paused, "she craves more, searching for a spell that would let her control the Fates themselves, shield herself from their grip, or perhaps even take their power."

Wynn blinked, unsettled. "Why? Is she afraid of them?"

Illen tilted their head. "Perhaps. Or perhaps she simply cannot abide anything she cannot command. The Fates do not answer to queens. And that... gnaws at her. But she has interfered with them before. Twisted the loom when it suited her."

"What do you mean?" Wynn asked, voice sharp with suspicion.

There was a beat of silence. The fire snapped in the hearth.

"She went to the Fates," Illen said, voice low and deliberate. "Not with a plea—but a dare. She challenged them to rethread a life."

Grace frowned. "That's not possible. You can't undo a thread once it's woven—"

"You *shouldn't*," Illen agreed. "But your mother can be very convincing. She wanted to see if the boy could be removed from the tapestry of his own life and woven again. And the Fates took the bait."

"Who?" Wynn asked warily, already knowing the answer, "Who would she do that to?"

There was a long, quiet breath. "Your brother."

"No," she said, shaking her head as if that could push the truth away. "He doesn't remember anything? He doesn't remember me?"

"He remembers nothing," Illen said softly. "They rewove that thread."

Wynn turned toward the fire, but not to warm herself. She needed to look away, needed something to hold her together while her chest fell open. She had mourned his loss once already. But some small thread of hope had always remained, buried deep, a fragile tether she refused to cut. Now, it snapped. There was a silence. Even the flames seemed to quiet.

"And now," Illen continued, "Prima seeks that kind of power for herself. Not just to change the thread of lives... but to control them."

Grace reached out and put her hand on Wynn's leg. She turned to the elf. "Is a spell like that even possible?"

"She hasn't found it yet," Illen said. "And she won't. While the ring stays off her hand, she has no way into The Margins."

The fire cracked sharply behind them. Wynn flinched. It sounded like something splitting in two. "To have the power of the Fates would give her ultimate control. Over everyone." The immensity of it hit Wynn hard—the ultimate cost of failing to defeat her. "And she can enter people's dreams?"

"Only if she's touched them," Illen replied. "Her reach is long, but not endless."

Wynn turned to Grace. "Does she come into yours?"

Grace gave a short, breathless laugh. "No. I don't think so. She hasn't touched me once since I was sent to live away. I used to hate her for that. Now?" She looked down. "Now I think I should be grateful."

Wynn looked down at the ring glowing softly against her chest, then up again. "Can any of this be undone?"

Illen stepped forward again, solemn. "Yes, I believe so." They looked at each of them in turn. "That is why Lorkan sent you here." They glided across the worn slate floor, long fingers trailing along a shelf as if considering a particular volume, though they plucked none. "You'll need to go north," they said, "to the mountains above the Tor. Not the lower ridges where the snow melts into rivers—you must climb. Near the top, there's an opening. An opening in the rock, like a mouth, sharp and wide. You'll know it when you see it."

Wynn crossed her arms. "That's... not vague at all."

Illen only smiled. "Inside, you'll find the thrones of the Fates. But they will not be there. They only appear on the Day of the Fates, when the harvest moon is full."

"They have thrones?" Grace asked, eyes wide.

"Of course they do," Illen said. "Those cronies are nothing if not dramatic. Past their thrones you'll find a narrow tunnel. Follow it into the mountain. At the end, you'll find a door. The ring will provide you entrance."

Wynn's hand went instinctively to the glowing circle at her chest.

Illen's expression grew serious. "Be careful in The Margins. There are things there... old things. Creatures from ancient stories. They guard the Originals. They don't like visitors."

"Great," Wynn muttered. "Sounds like fun."

"Sounds like an adventure," Grace said softly, trying to sound braver than she felt.

"If you know all this, why don't you fix it?" Wynn's tone was sharp. "Why don't you go to The Margins and undo all this?"

Illen turned. Their face softened. "Bookkeepers are rarely allowed to leave their libraries. We are here for... information, guidance. Lorkan believed in you both, prepared you both to defeat The Dark One." They stepped closer to the firelight, their presence flickering with the flames. "When you find *The Book That Will Put You to Sleep,*" they said, "you must look for the undoing spell. If the book allows you to see the spell, it should make things right. But Wynn," Illen paused, "the spell will only undo what Prima has done. It can not undo what the Fates have done to your brother. I know of nothing that can undo that. I'm sorry."

Wynn swallowed, deflated.

Grace wanted to console Wynn but didn't know how. Instead she tried to keep the focus. "You said, *should*. The spell *should* make things right."

Illen's gaze didn't waver. "The Originals offer no guarantees. Stories... don't always end the way we want them to." There was a long pause. Night yawned and stretched her body out on the plush sofa, comfortable to stay in this space forever.

"You need to know this," they said, voice quieter now, "The Margins will take something from you. They require something in return. A trade. It consumes so it can continue to allow for further creation. Sometimes, an offer can be made, and sometimes, it takes what it wants."

"My mother's hair," Grace interrupted. "It took that, didn't it?"

Illen nodded in confirmation. "It has also taken away her ability to love."

"Ha!" A laugh Wynn could not contain erupted. "Did she ever have any?"

"Yes." Grace turned, looking slightly defensive. "You didn't know her before... she wasn't always like this." There was an awkward moment between the two. Grace looked back at Illen, "Are you saying she can't love anyone or anything?"

"To be honest, I don't know the particulars. The Margins can be a mystery. But I do know," they hesitated with their next words, "that she asked to trade for it. She gave it up willingly, not wanting the pain of losing someone she loved ever again."

Grace looked down at her lap. Processing. Her expression didn't even change at first, as if the words needed a moment to settle. But Wynn watched her closely, saw the exact second it all sank in. How her fingers curled just slightly at her side, how her lips pursed, just a little.

"No," Grace whispered at last, not like a protest, but like a realization breaking open. "I mean, I always thought my mother didn't love me. But not really. Just, in a, *she's busy taking over The Vast, so I feel neglected,* kind of way." Her voice trembled, more hollow than angry. "But she really can't. And she never wanted to."

Wynn wanted to say something. Anything. But what comfort could she offer? This was a kind of rejection so deep and final it cut at the roots. It was worse than cruelty, it was indifference. Grace's mother did not just choose *not* to love her. She made sure she couldn't. And that, Wynn realized, was a grief all its own. She had lost her mother too, but not like this. Her mother had held her, sung to her, whispered stories into her dreams. Her mother had loved her until the end. Grace may have had that for a moment, but now it was stripped from her. Quite possibly forever. How do you grieve something like that?

Wynn placed a hand gently on Grace's shoulder. Not in an attempt to fix anything, but just so she wouldn't have to feel it alone.

Illen broke the tension. "There's one more thing."

"Why does that sound like something else I don't want to hear?" Wynn groaned.

"There is someone you know," Illen said, "who has been to The Margins before. Someone who came into this story from there—and does not belong to it."

Wynn blinked, her breath catching in her throat. "Avery," she said quietly.

Illen nodded. "Yes."

Grace turned to Wynn, startled. "How do you know that?"

Wynn shook her head, slowly. "I just... do. It makes a little more sense now."

The elf stepped forward, folding their hands. "When Prima entered The Margins all those years ago, she did so recklessly. She sought power without understanding the cost. And in doing so, she disrupted more than just her own path—she stirred other stories. Unfinished endings, half-written characters, entire arcs that collapsed or collided." They sighed, almost apologetically. "It's been... messy. We Bookkeepers have spent some time trying to put things back in order. To reshelve, in a sense. But unfortunately, some things can't be returned to where they came from."

Grace's brow furrowed. "So Avery's from another story? Like a different book?"

"Kind of. She is what we call an orphaned character," Illen said. "Unmoored from her tale, pulled through The Margins into this one. Her presence here causes a narrative imbalance."

"That explains... a lot," Wynn said. Her voice was low, almost mournful. "Her eyes, her skin. She didn't speak when I first met her. Does she know?"

"I don't know," Illen said gently. "But what matters is that The Margins will welcome her. She's part of it in a way none of you are. She may even be able to guide you."

Grace leaned back into the cushions. "Oh, I love it when a side character becomes someone important. When they..."

"Avery is not a *side* character," Wynn snapped and stood up. "She's a person."

"Right," Grace reached out but Wynn pulled away. "I'm sorry, I didn't mean it like that."

Accepting her apology, Wynn sat back down. "Does Prima know about her?"

Illen shrugged. "I don't know."

Wynn huffed, "This just got far more complicated."

Illen only smiled. "You're in a story. Complicated is what makes it good."

Grace nodded in agreement.

Wynn looked skeptical. "If you know so much about this story, why can't you just tell us how it ends?"

Illen's face softened. "No one can know how a story ends, until it does. Not even a Bookkeeper. We can assume, but we can't really know."

Wynn exhaled slowly. "Well," she said, her voice dry, "this has been informative. And also... deeply depressing." She looked down at her hands, then toward the fire, the weight of what lay ahead pressing in at the edges of her expression. "We should go."

They stood, collecting themselves. Night, who had clearly grown fond of the warm cushions, stretched with a grumble but padded loyally to Wynn's side, tail low and eyes sharp.

Just before they reached the steps, Grace turned back, hesitant. "Umm... can I come back here? I mean, can I learn to do what you do?"

Illen laughed, genuinely, for the first time. "Well, I am over a thousand years old, born to a line of elves trained for bookkeeping since before your lands had names..."

"So... no, then." Grace sulked.

Still smiling, Illen inclined their head. "If you succeed, you may return as often as you like. So can you," they added, turning to Wynn.

Wynn shook her head. "Oh, this place is great and all. But it's all her."

Illen nodded. "And, girls..."

They turned back.

"In my experience, darkness always overreaches. It forgets that what it cannot see—loyalty, sacrifice, love—is what undoes it in the end. Remember that, both of you."

Grace and Wynn looked at one another, letting the weight of the words settle. And as they turned to leave, the lights in the library dimmed just a little, like the end of a chapter.

~ ~ ~

Somewhere, deep beneath the mountains, there are libraries carved into stone. Endless chambers lined with ancient books, their pages breathing magic and memory. The air is warm there, humming faintly with firelight. Plush chairs wait in quiet corners. Wool blankets are folded just so. No one speaks above a whisper.

And if you listen closely, you can hear the turning of pages, slow and steady, like a heartbeat at rest. Even if places like that only exist in our imaginations—well, that's where you are now, isn't it? Tucked beneath a velvet throw, eyes growing heavy as the story fades. Let the cave hold your dreams tonight. Sleep well.

CHAPTER TWENTY-FOUR

They climbed in silence for a while, Wynn in front, Grace just behind, and Night bringing up the rear, her paws soft against the carved stone steps.

"So," Grace said, her voice echoing up the stairwell. "All we have to do is get Avery—"

"From the Dark Castle cells," Wynn muttered over her shoulder. "No problem."

"Right," Grace said, undeterred. "Then, find the hidden entrance in the Northern Mountains. Navigate a tunnel. Enter The Margins. Slip past ancient story monsters. Find a book that might not want to be found. Get the undoing spell."

"Then somehow get back here," Wynn added, "and say the spell in front of your mother." She glanced back with a half-smile. "Really, piece of cake."

Grace shrugged. "I don't know. I've read crazier things."

"This isn't a story, Grace," Wynn said quietly. "There's no one writing a happy ending for us."

But Grace only smiled, placing her palm on the stone wall as they climbed. "Sounds like everything is a story to me."

Ah, dear reader, as we both know, she's not entirely wrong. But I can't be giving away endings, can I? That would spoil the unfolding. Stories, like spells, must be cast in the right order. And happy endings? Well, those are never quite as simple as they seem. Endings, especially the happy sort, are slippery little things. Happy for whom, after all? So, let's not rush. We've pages yet to turn.

They were nearly to the top now, the fog-covered air beginning to glow through the opening above. Grace kept talking, as if to fill the space with something lighter. "And if I were reading this story, I'd say something else is about to—" They stepped into the hazy light. And froze.

Kiernan stood less than a foot away, his wrists bound, a hand covering his mouth, eyes wide with warning, and a knife pressed to his throat.

"—happen," Grace finished her thought.

Behind Kiernan stood a tall, hooded figure draped in dark robes, a hawk perched watchfully on their shoulder. The figure's face was mostly shadowed beneath the cowl, but the glint of a blade and the hawk's sharp gaze made everything else irrelevant.

Wynn didn't move. Grace didn't breathe. Night growled low, her hackles rising.

"Well," Wynn said, exasperated, "I'm starting to hate this story."

The hooded figure didn't so much as blink. "Put all of your weapons on the ground." His voice lacked emotion.

Wynn didn't move.

"If you question whether I will gut your friend—" The knife pressed in harder. Kiernan's eyes screwed shut. A thin thread of blood slipped down his neck.

Wynn's hand drifted to her side. Slowly. Deliberately. She unhooked the dagger at her hip and dropped it. It hit the slick rock with a sharp clatter and slid to a stop at Night's feet.

She studied the figure's stance. Too confident, too calm. He wasn't just willing to kill. He'd done it before.

Grace lifted her hands delicately into the air, fingers splayed like a dancer pausing mid-performance. "I haven't got a thing," she said with a sigh, her voice suddenly light and clipped. "In fact, thank the Fates you've come. I thought I was going to have to keep this pretense up forever."

Wynn whipped her head toward her, startled. Grace's voice had shifted, aloof now, haughty, like silk stretched over steel.

"I am Grace," she declared, chin high, "daughter of the Dark Queen and princess of the Tor. I demand that you apprehend these two and take me to my mother at once." She sounded like a spoiled child in the middle of a tantrum.

Wynn stared at her, stunned. Whether it was true or just a trick, Grace gave nothing away. No fear. No flicker of regret. Just imperial detachment and perfect posture.

The Hawk tilted his head. "You think I buy that, princess?" he said, not lowering the blade. "I've been watching all of you. Waiting for this moment. I saw you dancing in the tavern last eve."

Grace didn't miss a beat. "Then you saw me trying to stay alive. I've been deceiving these two ever since they showed up at the Keep. They killed my beloved cook and The Stone in front of me and then threatened to kill me. What choice did I have?"

Silence followed. No one moved. All unsure what to believe, or what might happen next. Wynn shook her head slowly, disbelief knitting her brow. Her eyes went from Grace to the face beneath the hood.

"There's something—" she began, and took a single step forward.

"Stay where you are," The Hawk growled. Kiernan stiffened, breath catching behind the hand still clamped over his mouth. But Wynn didn't stop.

She walked forward, slowly, defiantly, step by step until she was inches away. Night prowled close behind, hackles still raised. And then, in one swift motion, she reached out and yanked the hood back. She froze.

The face beneath was older. Sharper. The boy she remembered had been scraped away by time and hard living, but those eyes, his eyes, they were the same. That impossible turquoise, the color of the lake that shimmered just past the cliffs where they used to swim in the summer.

Her breath caught. Her heart, traitorous, leapt with recognition.

But there was no warmth in his gaze. No flicker of memory. His hair was darker now. His frame broader, like he had been honed as a weapon, all precision and muscle.

"Tierney," Wynn breathed, staggering back like the word itself had struck her. "I knew it."

The Hawk didn't blink. Didn't lower the knife. "I don't know who you speak of," he said coldly. "But I assure you, I will kill this man where he stands. Now get back."

She stared at him, her chest burning. No. No. Not like this. *Not like this.* Of course he didn't remember. That's what they'd done to him. The knowledge of it all still felt raw. And now here he was, weapon drawn against her friend, standing like the very symbol of all she'd lost. *This seemed cruel*. Even for the Fates. Or whoever was playing games with their lives.

"Of course," Wynn said, more to herself than him, her voice cracking. "Of course it's you. Why not twist the knife a little deeper?"

The hawk on his shoulder screeched—sharp, wild. But Wynn didn't flinch. The words came out trembling, gathering weight as they left her mouth, rising like a storm surge. "You are Tierney of the Tarn. Son of King Oren and Queen Elowen."

She hadn't spoken their names in over a decade. They struck the air like stones flung at stained glass. "And," she added, voice low, *furious*, "you are my brother." She pulled her hair to the side revealing the crescent tattoo. A twin to the mark beneath his left ear. "Why do you think you bear that mark?"

Grace, still standing with her hands aloft in mock surrender, sighed. "Well. This is a twist. I'd like to say I didn't see it coming but—"

"Shut up," said both The Hawk and Wynn, in perfect unison.

The Hawk's eyes flicked to Grace. He nodded toward a coil of rope slung at his side.

"If you speak the truth," he said, tone curt, "then bind her hands."

Wynn narrowed her eyes.

Grace hesitated only for a heartbeat, then stepped forward. The rope was scratchy, and covered in stains of old blood. She began wrapping it around Wynn's wrists, keeping her movements slow and performative. When their faces were close, Grace murmured under her breath, so soft only Wynn could hear: "Trust me."

Wynn wasn't sure that was something she could do. Not anymore. Not with everything hanging in this balance. Grace finished the knot, and as she drew back, she slapped Wynn clean across the face. The sound cracked through the air like a whip. Wynn's head snapped to the side, her cheek already stinging.

"That," Grace said, her voice bright with venom, "is for taking me away from my books. I'll be happy to watch my mother kill you."

The Hawk, apparently satisfied, stepped back from Kiernan and shoved him toward Wynn. Kiernan stumbled forward.

"I knew it too," he said quietly, eyes flicking to Tierney.

The Hawk turned now to Grace. He withdrew another rope from the folds of his cloak. The hawk on his shoulder shifted, adjusting its talons. "Your mother demands your return," he said, matter-of-fact. "She did not say safe. So if you don't mind—"

Grace raised her chin in perfect indifference, wrists extended as if she were offering her hands for a manicure, not manacles. "Oh, if you must," she said, exhaling with exaggerated boredom. "I really don't see the point. Do I look like a threat to you?"

In response, The Hawk pulled the rope tight. Too tight.

Then, with practiced efficiency, he tied them together—Wynn in front, Grace behind her, Kiernan last. "If you don't mind," The Hawk said as he fastened the final knot, "I don't need any of you disappearing into this fog." Which was precisely what Wynn had been thinking about doing.

Before The Hawk could move on, his eyes landed on Night. The fox crouched low beside a boulder, ears pinned, teeth bared. The Hawk reached into his cloak and began to uncoil another length of cord, but Wynn clicked her tongue. Just once.

Night's ears twitched and in a flash of fur, she turned and bolted into the mist, vanishing quietly as if she had never been there at all.

"If she returns," The Hawk growled, voice suddenly sharp, "I'll put an arrow in her side."

Wynn didn't answer.

"Move," The Hawk ordered.

Bound together, they began their descent down the uneven path. The mist swallowed them one by one, until the only sound left was the shuffle of boots, the occasional slip on rock, and the slow, deliberate beat of wings overhead.

They descended slowly through the fog-drenched path. The Hawk led the way, his long strides precise and relentless. Wynn, in the front of the prisoner line, kept her gaze fixed on his back. She didn't want to look at him. Truly, she didn't. But her eyes betrayed her. The more she watched, the more she saw her father.

The same broad shoulders. The same tilt of the head when he was thinking. Even the way he adjusted his stance before climbing down a steep step—it was all Oren, King of the Tarn. She clenched her jaw.

But that was where the resemblance ended.

Whatever the Fates had done, it had carved something essential out of him. The boy she knew, the brother who used to sneak her sweets from the kitchen, who had her back when the world pressed too hard, that version was gone. And in its place, this one, this man wore their father's face, but not his heart. He seemed hollow.

The Tierney she remembered had been stubborn, sure, but never cruel. Never detached like this shadow. The real Tierney would have found her. Would have run into the ruins if he had to, scaled the cliffs, burned the empire down to reach her. Not stood ahead of her with cold eyes and a blade drawn. But now, it all made sense. All those years she'd wondered why he hadn't come. Why he hadn't escaped and searched for her. Why he'd let the silence stretch so long between them.

He hadn't.

He couldn't.

He'd forgotten her completely.

A sharp tug on the rope snapped her from her thoughts.

"Keep moving," The Hawk barked over his shoulder.

Wynn stumbled but caught herself. Behind her, Grace gave a dramatic little grunt of annoyance as the toe of her boot stubbed on rock.

What *was* going on with Grace? Was this still a performance, or had that line blurred? *Trust me,* she'd said.

Almost as if in response to the thought, Grace cleared her throat. "So. Hawk? Or should I call you *The* Hawk?" Her voice had taken on that lilting, maddeningly pleasant tone Wynn recognized from the Keep. She was about to cause trouble in the most civilized way possible.

The Hawk kept walking.

"Have you always gone by *The Hawk*? I mean, I assume that's not your birth name. Or maybe it is, in which case, how dramatic. Also, how long have you been doing dirty deeds for my mother?"

He halted just long enough to shoot her a look that could've frozen molten iron. "Silence."

Wynn couldn't help it. She let out a short laugh. "Good luck with that."

Grace grinned like someone had just handed her a second slice of cake. "Anyway," she continued breezily, "do you get dental? Bonus gold? Does she pay you in, I don't know, sleep tokens?"

"*Enough,*" The Hawk growled.

But Grace, as usual, took it as a suggestion rather than a command. She kept on, lobbing questions like a noblewoman tossing breadcrumbs to ducks. By the time they reached the bottom of the trail and the fog began to thin slightly, The Hawk's ears were surely bleeding.

The horses were waiting, tethered where they had left them. But, there were three of them now. The Hawk's horse stood apart, tall and midnight-black, muscles bulging beneath a coat that shimmered blue in the mist. Its eyes rolled slightly when the group approached, nostrils flaring.

The Hawk began tying the horses into a line, just as he had the prisoners. His movements were curt, efficient, and not gentle. He kept the end of their rope looped around his fist, ready to yank it tight if anyone made a move.

He was halfway into his saddle when Grace's voice piped up again, this time with the full energy of someone throwing a royal tantrum. "You can't possibly expect us to *walk,* can you?" she said, aghast.

The Hawk froze, mid-mount.

"I mean—" she gestured disdainfully at the path ahead "—make the Tarn vermin walk." She nodded primly at Wynn and Kiernan. "But I simply can't. I've been in a castle my *whole* life. My feet are *already* sore from all this uneven terrain. If I fall and hurt myself, my mother will..."

"Alright!" The Hawk snapped, the snarl in his voice sharp enough to echo. "If I let you on the horse, will you silence yourself?"

Grace shrugged.

He turned sharply toward her, clearly at the edge of his patience. "*You* will ride. *You two* will walk."

Grace beamed. "That's better," she said, all sunshine and smugness.

Wynn gave her a sidelong look. Despite everything, ropes, fog, treachery, she felt the faintest flicker of amusement. Watching Tierney—*The Hawk*—be driven to the edge by Grace of all people was a strange kind of balm.

Kiernan muttered something that sounded like, "unbelievable."

Grace was hoisted into the saddle, and her hands were bound to the front strap so she couldn't steer. Not that she seemed to care. She adjusted herself with the flair of someone preparing for a royal parade.

The Hawk mounted his own horse without a word, took hold of the rope attaching them, and gave the signal to move. Wynn looked back one last time, searching the tree line. Fog curled and folded through the branches like breath through a veil. She clicked her tongue softly. No response. Night had vanished into the mist like a spirit.

She faced forward and they began the march.

It didn't take long. They had barely trudged a half mile, boots tripping over wet roots, before Grace broke the silence once more. "Can't you see the man is injured?" Her voice, though laced with concern, carried that unmistakable tone of dramatic offense, as if *she* were the one being made to limp through the mist with a bloodied leg.

Wynn turned her head just enough to glance back at Kiernan. He was trying to hide it, but his limp had worsened with every step. The bandages around his thigh were soaked through now, seeping crimson like ink bleeding through parchment.

"I'm fine," Kiernan said, too quickly.

Grace sniffed. "You know," she said, adjusting her posture on her horse, "we'd go much faster if he were riding too. This seems wholly inefficient. I mean, *you're* The Hawk, you must know better than me, but I would think my mother might prefer we arrive *before* the next moon."

The Hawk pulled his horse to a halt with such force the reins snapped taut. He dismounted in a single, fluid motion. Every step he took toward them seemed measured, dangerous. His blue eyes cut like twin blades of ice.

Wynn instinctively braced, thinking, hoping, he'd go for Grace first. For a moment, it seemed like he might.

But he stopped beside Kiernan instead, yanked at the knots around his wrists, and without a word, pulled him forward by the arm. At the last horse, The Hawk paused, fished out a strip of black cloth, and blindfolded Kiernan before lifting him into the saddle.

Then he tied his hands tightly to the saddle horn and walked away in a stormy silence. The whole process took less than a minute. When The Hawk turned back, Grace gave Wynn a smug little wink.

Wynn didn't respond, at least, not outwardly. Internally? She felt something shift. Not trust, not yet. But maybe a hint of it. A kind of wary appreciation, reluctant and inconvenient. She didn't know what Grace's game was, or who she was playing for, but there was something in her defiance, in the way she used her voice like a weapon that Wynn found... attractive. Wynn tore her gaze forward again. *Not now. Don't be stupid.*

The Hawk passed Grace on his way back to his own horse. He stopped just long enough to throw a glare up at her. "Happy now, Princess?"

Grace tilted her head thoughtfully. "I mean, it's better. But really, we *all* ought to be on horses if we're to—"

"No more!" His words were final. Then he turned to Wynn. His glare sharpened. "She walks."

He stomped back to his mount, boot heels grinding into the mud. The rope tugged again as he remounted and gave the signal to move.

The group started forward once more, now with one of them blindfolded, two of them bound, and one of them quietly wondering why, exactly, her heart had started to beat faster when Grace winked at her. Must've been the adrenaline. Or all this strange fog. Definitely the fog.

~ ~ ~

There are moments, even in the tightest situations, when something stirs, quiet and unwelcome, like emotion slipping in at the most inopportune time. A glance too long. A truth too close. A thought no one dares to name, lingers, waiting. Emotions have a way of doing that; of showing up when we least expect them, especially when there's no room for them. But we don't need to sort this all out tonight. Let them have their silence. Let the cold fog hold the weight for now. As for you, tuck in, breathe deep, let go, and rest while you can. There are miles still to travel. Sleep well.

CHAPTER TWENTY-FIVE

The moment they stepped beyond the southern mists, the sun disappeared behind the Western range. The air cleared, cool and sharp in Wynn's lungs. Overhead, the moon started to rise and stars blinked awake between the swaying silhouettes of Tarn trees. It felt strange to be in familiar terrain again, these ridges and groves belonged to *home*, not this nightmare march toward the Dark Queen.

Wynn walked slower now, not enough to draw attention, just enough to shift to the side. And there, just to her left, slipping in and out of shadows, she saw Night. Her black fur glinted faintly under moonlight as she darted through the underbrush, keeping pace. Wynn didn't dare smile, but the sharp ache in her chest eased just slightly. *She's here. She's still here.* But the comfort barely settled before danger flared.

The Hawk's horse stopped abruptly.

Wynn froze.

Still astride his great midnight steed, The Hawk reached over his shoulder and drew his bow in one clean motion. The arrow was already notched and aimed, pointed directly into the trees.

"No," Wynn whispered. Her breath caught. Her shoulders locked. Her voice, when it rose, was low and cold and lethal. "If you shoot that fox," she said, "I swear to the Fates, I *will* kill and roast your hawk."

He turned slowly in the saddle, eyes narrowing, bow still taut.

From behind, Kiernan spoke, his blindfold shifting slightly with each word. "You know," he said, "she hates the Fates. So if she's swearing to them right now... I wouldn't test her."

The Hawk held still a moment longer. Then, grudgingly, with a sneer, he lowered the bow. "He better keep his distance," he muttered.

"She," Wynn said, eyes hard. "And she'll do as she pleases."

They moved on.

A little while later, Kiernan lifted his head, sniffing. "Something's burning," he muttered through the blindfold. "Charred wood... smoke."

" I smell it too." Wynn's stomach turned before she saw the first plume of it, thin, pale gray rising from the trees ahead. They stepped into a clearing.

The tavern they had stopped at the evening before stood blackened and hollow. Or rather, the outline of it did. The roof had caved in. The barn behind it was little more than skeletal beams collapsed in on themselves. Nothing was left but smoldering piles and scorched dirt.

The Hawk's horse reared up, startled by something hanging from a large oak tree, and the group came to a sudden halt. Strung up in a tree nearby were four bodies, limp and lifeless, suspended like warnings. Wynn's breath caught—the barkeep. And next to her, the large man who had identified her by her tattoo.

"What?" Kiernan questioned. "What are you seeing?"

"The tavern from last night. It's... gone. Burnt to the ground," Wynn responded breathlessly. "And, bodies. Tarn.

Hanging." She stood rooted, cold seeping through her limbs. "Is this your doing?" she turned to The Hawk, her jaw clenched.

He turned to her, eyes flashing, offended. "No," he said. "It wasn't. I had nothing to do with this."

Wynn searched his face, saw no deceit there. Just confusion.

"We keep moving," he kicked at his horse and they moved on again, the ash clinging to their boots.

"This has your mother written all over it," Wynn said callously over her shoulder to Grace. Grace didn't respond. She didn't look away either. Her gaze stayed fixed on the hanging bodies until the path curved and the smoke disappeared behind them.

The forest thinned and the underbrush gave way to mossy clearings and dark pine. The rope between them tugged with each uneven step, and Kiernan's horse plodded along quietly at the rear. Grace shifted on her mount. Wynn wondered if she'd fall asleep.

Then, ahead, a light. It started small, flickering in the distance. Then another. And voices, low and muffled, carried on the breeze. Hope bloomed for a heartbeat.

But as they neared the source, the shape of the camp came into view—black tabards, gleaming pauldrons, swords resting too comfortably on laps. The Dark Guard. Fifty, at least, scattered throughout. Their armor caught the firelight in cruel angles, and when they saw who approached, led by The Hawk, they snapped to attention. The Hawk didn't dismount. He didn't need to.

The way they moved, scrambling to stand, some half-bowing, others backing away, told Wynn everything she needed to know. They feared him. *Good.*

But they didn't fear her.

No. When *she* passed through their firelight, every face turned. Not with awe. With hatred.

Hungry, bitter eyes followed her, waiting. A few of the Dark Knights muttered under their breath. One spat on the ground as she walked by. Another let her hand rest too long on her sword hilt, her gaze locked on Wynn's face like she was already imagining what it would feel like to strike her down.

Wynn stiffened, fighting the impulse to shrink. She wouldn't give them that. But her heart raced. She was bound, exhausted, and outnumbered.

Out of the tent slithered a lanky knight with limbs like crooked branches and a nose so long and hooked it seemed better suited to sniffing out secrets than leading men. His armor was polished to a vain shine, though it hung awkwardly on his bony frame, like a costume. The others stiffened as he appeared, not with respect, but with the wary stillness of people hoping not to be noticed.

"Didn't know we were keeping pets now," he sneered, voice dripping with mockery, low and serpentine. His lips curled in a smile far too pleased with itself. "Want me to—?"

"*She's* not yours to touch," The Hawk said sharply. The words were quiet. But they snapped like a whip. The knight froze. The Hawk's gaze burned into him. "Not a hair," he said. "On *any* of them. Do you understand me?"

The knight smirked. "I think it is you who may not understand. I am..."

"I know who you are, Sorn," The Hawk interrupted. "What I do not know is why you are here and not groveling at Prima's boots?"

The other knights stifled their laughter as Sorn stepped forward, embarrassment and malice set in his jaw. "You haven't heard?" His lip curled. "With The Stone dead, I have been made general of the Dark Guard. You answer to me now, you Tarnish Dog."

"I answer to no one but the Dark One." His voice was definitive.

The other knights in the group stood looking from one to other, wondering whose lead to follow.

"My, my," Grace broke the tension, "this is quite dramatic. Are you two going to compare the length of your… *swords* next?"

Kiernan, still blindfolded on his horse, choked on a laugh.

"Silence!" Sorn snapped. "And who are you?"

As worried as Wynn was to be surrounded by so many eyes who hated her, and some Tarnish ones, who looked at her more with awe, she could not help but be amused at the prospect of anyone trying to challenge Grace.

"You don't see the resemblance?" Grace acted affronted, "I am the princess of The Tor. Your princess. Which, I think, means that *you* answer to *me*."

Sorn seemed surprised and not quite sure how to respond. He looked at Wynn, realization taking over, and then stepped towards her, "You're…"

The Hawk moved his horse between them. "She is none of your business, Sorn. They are my prisoners. I was tasked with bringing them back."

It was obvious that Sorn was a man who did not like being challenged. He collected himself. "Since you are on official duty for the Dark One, I will allow you to stay at the camp for tonight. Tomorrow, *my* Guard and I will move on to Glenshire, before going to the northern villages. The Dark One has charged me with stifling all rebel activity. And," he puffed his chest out, "it is no longer Sorn, you may refer to me as The Blade now."

"What?" The Hawk asked with a mixture of annoyance and amusement.

"Oooh," Grace chimed in, "are we doing this now? Is this a thing? Because I would like to be called The Spine Breaker or The Annotated One, or even…"

"Enough!" Barked Sorn.

As entertaining as all this was, Wynn needed to get something off her chest. She stepped around the Hawk's horse, trying to contain her anger. "Was it you and your Guard that burned that tavern? Killed those people?"

Sorn looked at Wynn with disdain. "We've burned many things. Killed many Tarn rebels. And that was just today. You'll have to be more specific." He was goading her, and she took the bait.

"You son of a..."

The Hawk dismounted, landing with a heavy *thud* between the two. The fire flickered across the sharp lines of his face. "I've had enough of this." Sorn took a step back. He was at least a foot shorter than The Hawk. "You will give me a dozen of your knights to protect our journey into the Tor and to the Dark Castle. We will set up here for the night and be on our way in the morning."

Sorn thought about it. "I will give you half a dozen. All Tor born and loyal to the Dark One, to keep an eye on them, and you."

About two minutes later six knights moved forward to stand in front of The Hawk. He did not waste time letting them know who was in charge. "Secure the prisoners," he ordered, voice slicing clean through the crackle of the fire. "Tie them to those trees. I want a perimeter set." There was a pause, small, but telling. One of the knights muttered something too low to catch, and another laughed under her breath. Still, they moved. They obeyed. But they did it slowly. Begrudgingly.

Wynn's back hit bark a moment later. A rope tightened around her wrists, rough against the skin already rubbed raw. She winced but didn't make a sound. Grace was tied a few feet away, looking infuriatingly serene. She leaned like it was just another tree in a royal orchard, ankles crossed daintily, as if someone might soon arrive with tea.

Kiernan was eased off his horse and propped up nearby, his blindfold removed. He made no sound, but his hands went up to his chest, trying to loosen the tightness of the ropes.

As one of the knights stepped back, The Hawk spoke again. "I'll take first watch."

There was no argument. But there was no respect, either.

A few knights exchanged glances. One scoffed. Another adjusted his sword with just a bit too much force, like he wished he could say something but knew better. None of them met The Hawk's eye. A few nodded. Most simply went back to pretending they weren't afraid of him.

The firelight danced. Wynn couldn't see her, but she knew Night circled far enough away not to be seen.

Wynn stared at the flames, feeling the weight of rope, exhaustion, and memory press down on her all at once. She was captured, surrounded, and watched by the brother she once trusted more than anyone. And yet, when she glanced sideways at Grace, who caught her eye and gave a little smirk, Wynn felt a flutter of something stirring.

"The Spine Breaker?" Wynn couldn't help herself.

Grace shrugged, "Get it? Books? Spines?"

Wynn shook her head. "Oh, I got it."

The smell of roasting meat made her stomach fold in on itself. She couldn't remember the last thing she ate.

Grace sniffed the air delicately. "You know," she said, loud enough to be heard, "it's only polite to feed your guests."

A few knights glanced over. One barked a laugh. The Hawk didn't react.

Grace went on, undeterred. "I don't think my mother will want me returned half starved, after all. She's a monster, yes, but she's a *refined* monster. She'll expect I've been... properly treated."

The Hawk looked up from where he was checking his saddlebag. His eyes narrowed. He stared at Grace like he was deciding whether to gag her or let her keep talking just to see how far she'd go. Then he rolled his eyes and jerked his chin at two knights by the fire. "Fine," he muttered. "Give them something. At least with food in your mouth, you'll shut up."

Grace stuck her tongue out at him.

"Very princess-like." Kiernan commented.

A few moments later, scraps were brought over, tough meat, half a heel of bread, and a tin cup of water each. Wynn wriggled awkwardly, managing to lift the food with her hands still bound. Kiernan, made do with stiff fingers and quiet curses. Grace, naturally, had no trouble at all. She even chewed like it was roast duck instead of burnt rabbit.

Time passed. The fire settled into quiet coals, low and glowing. The mist was no more, but a fall chill clung to the ground, curling around their ankles and seeping into their bones. The silence was starting to feel permanent when Grace, eyes bright, broke it. "Have you ever heard of *The Adventures of Threshwick*?" she asked, looking directly at The Hawk.

Wynn groaned softly and tipped her head back against the tree. Here we go.

The Hawk didn't answer.

"No?" Grace smiled. "I think you'd like it. It's about this handsome but *brooding* knight who travels the lands getting into all sorts of mischief. Mostly helping people, though he doesn't *want* to, of course. He's kind of grumpy. Like you."

Wynn scoffed loudly.

Grace, unbothered, continued. "The best part is when he meets this girl. At first he thinks she's some helpless little thing, crying outside a cave. But really, she's trying to lure a bear out to steal its honey. Nearly gets them both killed." She laughed, light and real. "It's quite funny, but I won't ruin it. You'd like it."

The Hawk didn't respond. He just stared into the trees, jaw tight, like he was trying to pretend the conversation, and Grace, weren't happening.

Wynn stole a glance at her. She was smirking slightly, eyes still on The Hawk. Had she just called him *handsome*? Wynn frowned. That was, he was, her *brother*. She wasn't sure what bothered her more: the fact that Grace might have meant it... or the sudden, utterly irrational heat that crawled up her own neck at the idea of the two of them together.

It was silent for a long time.

Grace, despite the ropes and circumstances, was undeterred. "So, *Hawk*," she said, chipper as anything. "Have you always gone by that? Or is it one of those names you get *after* something dramatic? Like after you got *that* hawk?"

The bird let out a shrill cry from a nearby branch, as if responding on cue.

Grace tilted her head. "Is it trained? Can it fetch things? Hunt? Or is it just for the brooding aesthetic?"

The Hawk turned slowly. Then, without a word, he crossed the space between them and tied a strip of cloth over her mouth. "Much better," he said, stepping back.

Grace blinked wide eyes at him and, impressively, managed to look both affronted and amused while gagged.

The Hawk turned to the knights still loitering near the fire. "Rounds of two. Rotate every three hours. Rest while you can." Some grumbled, but none disobeyed. A few retreated toward tents pitched under the trees.

The Hawk returned to his satchel and pulled something from it. Sleep tokens. Wynn watched, her body tensing before she even knew why. He moved toward her and Kiernan, but before he could take a step closer, one of the knights near the fire muttered, just loud enough to be heard: "Pretty sure the order was *no one of Tarnish blood* sleeps. Not 'til *she* kneels before the Dark One." The knight's eyes landed on Wynn. He didn't even bother to hide his sneer.

The Hawk paused. He didn't respond. Didn't argue. But there was a flicker of something—irritation? across his face as he turned away from the knight and kept walking. He stopped in front of Wynn, holding out the token. "Take it."

Wynn looked at it. Then at him. Her hands didn't move. "If my people can't sleep," she said, voice quiet but steady, "neither will I."

The Hawk exhaled sharply through his nose. "Be that way." He returned the tokens to his bag.

One tree over, Kiernan chuckled, low and hoarse. "*Your* people, huh?" Wynn turned to him, confused. He shrugged against the rope. "Nothing. Just, haven't heard you say that before."

She leaned her head back against the tree, the bark rough against her scalp, her muscles aching with weariness and cold. And Wynn thought, not for the first time, about the thousands of Tarnish who still lived under Prima's rule. Sleepless. Watched. Owned. Were all Tarn-born suffering because of her?

"K?" Wynn whispered.

"Yeah?"

"The village north of Glenshire is..."

"I know."

They didn't continue, but their eyes expressed the danger they knew their home was in.

The camp had gone quiet. The fire was little more than embers now, pulsing orange with the occasional sigh of a spark lifting into the night. The trees stood tall around them, a circle of dark sentinels. Grace was slumped against her rope, head drooping to the side, hair tousled over her face.

Besides the knights standing on the perimeter, only The Hawk, Wynn, and Kiernan remained awake. All Tarn-born. All silent.

The Hawk sat opposite Wynn, arms crossed over his chest, leaning against a tree. Watching. The quiet pressed in. Wynn's wrists throbbed where rope met skin.

"So, that guy," Wynn nodded towards the main camp. "What's his deal?"

The Hawk sat with his arms folded over his chest. At first it didn't seem like he would respond, then, "Sorn's an idiot. Worse actually. He is an idiot with something to prove."

She couldn't help asking the question she really wanted answered. "You really don't know who you are? I mean... where do you think you come from?"

For a moment, she thought maybe she overstepped.

"I was thrown out," he said finally. Voice flat. "By my parents. Or someone. I don't know. I was small. I wandered into the Dark Castle grounds."

Wynn stared. Her throat was dry.

"The Stone nearly killed me," he went on, eyes trained on the dying fire. "But the Dark One stopped him. Said she saw potential. Said I could be useful." A beat. "She ordered The Stone to train me." That pause lingered in the air. Something unsaid hanging heavy beneath it. Wynn didn't need him to explain what kind of training that meant. The tension in his shoulders, the way his jaw clicked when he mentioned The Stone, it said enough. "I owe the Dark Queen my life."

It made Wynn sick to hear him say that but she knew arguing with him, trying to convince him otherwise, would do nothing. She looked at him, examining his features. And all she could see was Tierney, her brother. Leaner now, older, changed, but the shape of him still echoed the boy who used to make her laugh so hard she couldn't breathe. The boy who taught her to swim. Who'd made up silly songs about the fish in the lake. But now?

"And the crescent moon?" she asked, quieter still. "Behind your ear. Like mine. How do you explain that?"

The Hawk didn't answer. But something flickered behind his eyes. Confusion. Like the question hit somewhere he hadn't let himself look. Wynn saw it. And he knew it. "Keep your mouth shut, or I'll shut it for you," he snapped, sharper than before. Then he stood and turned, stalking toward the darkness without another word.

Wynn leaned her head back again. Was Tierney still there somewhere? Could he be? She watched him disappear into the dark, swallowed by the night. Then the thought she'd been holding off all night slithered in. *Kneel before the Dark One.* That was the order. That was the cost. The Tarn kept from sleep, kept from peace, kept on the edge of collapse until the haze would settle in and then—death. All of it, until she knelt. Until she gave herself over to the very monster who had slaughtered her family and smiled as she did it.

Her fingers curled into tight fists.

What was one moment of surrender to spare them? If Prima kept her word. She could hear Lorkan's voice in her mind, quiet and clear: *"Do what needs to be done. But, be careful what you trade."* Wynn could be prideful, stubborn even. But this—this wasn't about pride. Not anymore. To kneel wasn't just to bend. It was to break something ancient. Something rooted in the bones of the Tarn. To kneel was to say the Dark One had won. That all Tarn were hers to rule. And that was a price too steep to pay.

~ ~ ~

The fire is almost out now. Our heroine is not where she wants to be, captive, cold, too many eyes watching; but the stars are still above her, and somewhere, not so far off, a fox stirs. You may worry for her. That's allowed. But worry has a way of creeping into the quiet, stealing hours that would be better spent dreaming. When there's nothing to be done in the moment, sometimes the best thing, the bravest thing, is to sleep anyway. So lie back. Let the sheets hug you a little tighter. Let the night do what it does best. The answers will come. Sleep well.

CHAPTER TWENTY-SIX

Even though she hadn't slept, Wynn felt the morning light come too soon and The Hawk wasted no time commanding everyone to pack up and get on the road. As they left, the main group, led by Sorn, was just starting to stir awake. Wynn heard a soldier grumbling loudly about an animal having defiled the ground just outside Sorn's tent. Another cursed, sniffing his boot and accusing someone of relieving themselves in the night. Wynn didn't glance back, but a small, secret smile tugged at her mouth. She couldn't have been prouder of that sassy little fox.

Three of the Dark Guard rode silent at the front and end of their line. Grace, somehow, was back on a horse. She had insisted on it, something about a lady's dignity and a sore hip, and no one had argued. She sat tall in the saddle now, hands bound but chin lifted, as if she were simply out for a reluctant autumn ride.

Wynn and Kiernan were not afforded the same courtesy. They walked.

The Tarn forest was beautiful in the early morning light, achingly so. The rays burning off the morning mist made for a mystical feel. Wynn wished she could be invisible in it, rather than dragged along like a prize. The chill had deepened overnight. Frost clung to the low ferns, and the horses' breath came out in clouds. Leaves, now fully changed, blanketed the path in soft rustling reds and oranges and ochres. Some still clung to the trees like they weren't quite ready to fall. Others drifted down gently as they passed, landing on shoulders, heads, caught for a moment in Grace's hair before she flicked them away.

It smelled like woodsmoke, musky earth, and the fading sweetness of apples, like every memory of fall Wynn had ever loved. She used to think this was her favorite season. Not for harvest or festivals or even the colors, but because it meant all the interior hearths would be lit again. That fire meant warmth. That fire meant gathering. That fire meant the Inn would start to smell like spice bread and burning cedar. She hated the hundreds of hours she had to spend chopping wood, but she loved the initial crackle it made once set alight.

She walked now with her wrists raw from the rope and legs sore from the relentless pace, thinking about those fires. Thinking about the woodpile behind the Inn and the way the air changed just before the first frost. Thinking about how, if this were a different kind of day, a different kind of life, she might be curled under a wool blanket with Night's head on her lap, watching the light flicker on the ceiling. She clicked her tongue softly, hoping to catch a glimpse of the fox somewhere in the trees, but there was nothing. It was probably better she was staying out of sight. Safer that way. The fox knew how to take care of herself. She always had. Still, Wynn selfishly hoped for a glance, just to know she was there. A flicker of dark-silver fur between the branches. A glint of eyes in the distance. But the trees gave nothing back.

A leaf landed on her sleeve, curled at the edges, gold as a coin. She didn't brush it away.

Almost as if she could read Wynn's mind, Grace gave a sudden, dramatic sigh from atop her horse. "Oh, I *just* love the fall," she announced loudly, as if everyone around wanted her opinion on the matter. "Don't you all just *love* it? The colors, the crunching, the coziness of it all. It's practically poetic!"

Silence.

"Anyone?" Grace asked, turning to look at the knights. "Some of you must like a sweet hot drink in front of a fire when you're not off taking over villages or shedding blood for my mother." She waited. "No? Just me then."

"Don't make me gag you again, princess," The Hawk yelled over his shoulder.

Grace rolled her eyes and mumbled under breath, "You wish."

Wynn looked up, just in time to catch Kiernan smirking beside her. He leaned in slightly, voice low. "Do you think Grace is a little... crazy?"

Wynn let out a laugh, sharper and louder than she intended. All the heads turned in her direction. "Maybe," she replied, quieter now, the smile still curling at her mouth. But privately, she thought: *I kind of like it.*

Grace wasn't like anyone else she'd met in The Tarn or The Tor. She seemed entirely unbothered by others and blissfully ignorant as to how out of place she was; always asking relentless questions, speaking aloud things most people would never admit to thinking. Wynn didn't understand her, but maybe that was the point. She had a kind of unshakable optimism, disarming and infuriating all at once. Grace greeted others with easy smiles and open hands; she met them with silence and a hand on her blade. Grace was air, curious, bright, untethered. She was earth, steady, rooted, slow to trust and slower to forgive. And yet, here they were, two princesses shaped by ruin in opposite ways, walking the same path toward something neither could name.

It was a while before Kiernan spoke again, breath starting to hitch slightly with each limp-stepped stride. "Are we..." he started.

"Yes," Wynn said without turning. "We're on the road to Wickmere."

Wickmere. Her village. She didn't know how far they'd come exactly, but a few kilometers to the north, if she wasn't mistaken, the old castle ruins should be rising in the trees.

She glanced sideways, past the line of Knights, to The Hawk. He gave nothing away. Not a flicker of memory in his sharp eyes. But surely he remembered this land. There must be *something* that stirred in him here.

If it did, he didn't let on.

The road widened. The trees thinned. And then, without fanfare, they were there.

Wynn could feel it in the dirt underfoot, in the change of light between branches. In the shape of the stones, the bend of the road. The same crooked fenceposts, the same low barns and soot-streaked chimneys; smoke rising up from a few. Someone's laundry was freshly hanging, blue and cream linen, snapping softly in the breeze. And here she was, walking through it bound with rope.

The road through the village felt narrower than she remembered. Or maybe that was just the press of eyes. At first, it was just the sound of boots on dirt and hooves clipping beside them. But then doors creaked open, one, then another. Faces emerged. Most were Tarn. She could tell by the tiredness in their eyes. There was Mirell, the candle-maker, her hands still wax-stained from her craft. Eddin the cobbler, who had made Wynn's boots when her feet were still growing, one slightly larger than the other. Salla, the seamstress who used to hum lullabies even when no children were around. Wynn's chest tightened.

And then she saw Hans, the butcher, arms crossed now like a judge at a hanging. He looked smug. At that moment, everything came back. The boy, the scrap of dried meat, the sharp crack of the lash. Her knees in the dirt. Lorkan. The ache in her back returned as if summoned by the memory. *Was that only a week ago?* It felt like a lifetime had been folded into those days. She'd lived a dozen versions of herself since then.

The Knights slowed as they reached the center of the village, halting beside the old fountain well. The horses drank noisily, disrupting the silence.

Grace leaned forward in her saddle, glancing around. "Why is everyone staring?"

Wynn didn't answer. She just shook her head.

And then someone shouted. "It's the princess!"

Grace straightened immediately, it was obvious she thought the comment was directed at her.

But all heads turned to Wynn. She froze, throat tight.

She waited for the anger to come. For curses. For spittle. For someone to point and scream, *She's why we can't sleep. She's why our children cry through the night.* Instead, the man shouted again, louder this time. "Don't kneel!"

A beat.

Then another voice, this one cracked with age: "Never kneel before the Dark One!"

"The Tarn rise!"

Wynn blinked. A stirring moved through the crowd. Not fear. Not submission. But something heavier. Hungrier. Tired and angry and still standing. She looked at them, really looked. And beneath their exhausted features, a quiet fury of a people not yet broken.

The Knights began to shift uneasily. One barked, "Back! Get back!"

But the villagers weren't moving.

A woman in an apron stood firm beside her child. A man with a limp refused to lower his eyes. And further back, Tor shopkeepers grabbed at their servants, pulling them away. Some obeyed. Some didn't.

The horses snorted, hooves striking the ground nervously. One Knight reached for his sword. The air tightened. Something was waking in Wickmere.

"Stand down," The Hawk growled. "Stand down!"

The Knights started to back up but their swords stayed at the ready. Wynn looked around. One wrong word, one spark, and blood would spill in her name. The thought made her stomach turn. She couldn't let that happen.

"Stop!" she shouted, her voice raw and louder than she meant it to be.

And somehow, everyone did. The Knights froze. The villagers stilled. Even the horses seemed to steady. Dozens of eyes turned to her, waiting.

She didn't know what to say.

Her heart pounded so loudly she could hardly think. *I'm no leader. I'm just—* "I may be the Tarn Princess..." she said, surprising even herself. Her gaze found The Hawk, holding there for a moment, "...the last of my family."

A murmur rippled through the crowd.

"But whatever happens to me... whatever I do, the Tarn spirit doesn't end here." She turned, trying to look at all of them. So many faces. So many worn-out eyes. "It lives in all of you. In how you're still standing. Still rising. Even now."

She let out a breath, steadying herself. "I grew up among you. I know how strong you are. How stubborn. How the Tarn survives things no one else could. You don't fall. You bend, maybe, but you don't break." Her voice dropped, quieter but stronger somehow. "I've spent a long time hiding who I was. Thinking I had to carry this on my own. That the truth of who I am, and what I've lost, was mine to bear." She paused, her gaze flicking sideways to Kiernan and, just briefly, to Grace. "I was wrong."

Her words settled. "We're stronger together. And we'll need to be, if we're going to survive the Dark Queen."

The silence that followed was thick. It was holding something. Respect, maybe. Or the first, smallest breath of hope. And then a voice broke through it, sharp and furious.

"Kiernan!"

An older man pushed through the crowd, red-faced and shouting. "Where have you been, boy?" Kiernan stiffened beside her.

The man marched straight up, grabbing him hard by the arm. "This is my Tarn! My slave! I demand him returned. I've got a harvest going to rot without him, and—"

The Hawk moved before the man could finish. He swung down from his horse, landing with practiced silence. The crowd parted as he walked forward.

The farmer, Friedrickson, took one look at the masked figure and backed up a step, hand slipping from Kiernan's arm. No one breathed.

The Hawk reached out. His knife flashed, not in threat, but with purpose. In one clean stroke, he sliced through the rope binding Kiernan's hands. Then, with a sharp shove to the back, he pushed him into the crowd.

"The Dark One never asked for this one," The Hawk said to the Guard. "We continue." He didn't wait for an argument. He turned, mounted again, and snapped, "Move out."

The Knights obeyed. Anything to keep the tension from boiling over.

Wynn felt herself tugged forward by the rope at her wrists. No time for farewells. But as she passed Kiernan, she turned just enough to whisper, "Help them, K. Prepare them for Sorn and his knights."

Kiernan's face was still stunned, but then something in it hardened into purpose. He nodded. "I will. I promise." And then he was gone behind her, swallowed by the people.

The procession moved on.

They passed the Inn before the edge of town. Or what was left of it. The scorched beams jutted out like blackened bones from the foundation. The sign had burned through, but she could still see half the lettering etched into the wood. She didn't stop walking. But something in her slowed. Even now, after everything, a part of her ached at the sight.

Grace's voice broke the silence, soft but curious. "What was this?"

And maybe it was the ash, or the wind, or just the ache of memory, but her throat burned. She thought of Avery. Of quiet laughter in the kitchen. Of muddy boots on newly washed floors. It wasn't much, but it was... "My home," Wynn said, low, and kept her eyes ahead. And then, ahead, in the trees beyond the road, she saw her. Night.

The little fox stood at the edge of the woods, tail twitching, eyes locked on Wynn's like she'd never left. Just watching. Waiting. She may have lost Keirnan but with Night out there, Wynn didn't feel quite so alone.

They'd only just left the village behind when Grace shifted on her saddle with an exaggerated sigh. "I want to walk now," she announced.

No one responded.

"I said," she raised her voice, "I want to walk."

A knight near the front muttered without turning, "No one cares what you want."

Grace looked thoroughly scandalized. "Excuse me? I am the Daughter of the Dark One and your princess, and I want to walk." When no one made a move she looked around and then promptly swung a leg over her horse with a bit too much flourish, tumbling to the ground like a sack of root vegetables.

There was a dull *thump* as she hit the dirt, landing in a cloud of dust. The procession halted. Even the horses seemed to blink in surprise.

Grace, unbothered, stood, brushed herself off with bound hands, lifted her chin, and took her place beside Wynn without a word.

One of the Knights looked to The Hawk. "What do we do?"

The Hawk didn't even glance back. "We move on."

And so they did.

Having gotten exactly what she wanted, albeit with a few bruises, Grace walked on beside Wynn.

Wynn, meanwhile, couldn't help the smirk tugging at her lips. "You're ridiculous," she said under her breath.

Grace didn't respond to that. She just kept walking and then asked casually, "So, that burnt pile of rubble back there, that's where you and... Able?"

"Avery," Wynn corrected.

"Right. Avery. Sorry. That's where you two worked?"

"*Worked* is a very nice term for what others call slavery," Wynn said.

Grace glanced over, brow furrowing thoughtfully. "Huh."

"What?" Wynn asked.

"I'm just starting to picture the life you've led."

"Don't," Wynn said flatly. "I don't need your pity."

Grace looked confused. "I wasn't going to say that." She paused. "I was going to say, all those people... that town... it just seemed kind of... nice."

Wynn blinked. She hadn't expected that. But then she remembered. Grace hadn't grown up with anyone. No friends. No chores, no neighbors, no markets. Just silence. Surveillance. Loneliness.

Wynn softened, just a little. "I don't know what to make of you," she muttered.

"What do you mean?"

"I just don't know which version of you is the act."

Grace didn't answer right away. When she did, her voice was quieter. "You're the only one who might know exactly who I am. Who gets me."

"We've only known each other for a few days."

"That's longer than I've known anybody." She turned quickly, "And my servants at the Keep don't count."

Wynn didn't respond. Not right away. She just walked beside her, feeling the weight and warmth of the moment settle between them.

And then: "No more talking," The Hawk barked from ahead. "Or, I'll gag the both of you and drag you back to the castle."

There was a pause. Then Grace leaned in and whispered, "Your brother is kind of—"

"A giant horse's ass," Wynn finished.

They both tried to stifle a giggle but the more they tried to contain it, the harder it was. It felt a little dangerous. It felt a little wonderful.

The Hawk turned, shot them a look that could curdle milk, and they went silent again. But the laughter lingered like a secret between them, one neither of them could shake.

A few hours later, the sky had faded from gold to hues of deep violet. The wind bit colder. And the path sloped toward a massive stone bridge arcing over the roaring Still River below.

The Hawk dismounted.

Without a word, he strode back toward Wynn, a coil of rope in hand. He looped it around her neck and clipped the other end to a metal ring on his harness.

"I heard about your little stunt the last time," he muttered. "This time, if you try to jump..." He gave the rope a tug and the noose tightened against her throat.

Wynn didn't flinch. She looked him dead in the eye. "It was you who taught me to swim, you know."

Surprise flickered in his face. But he said nothing. Just turned, mounted his horse again, and led them forward. The procession crossed onto the bridge, hooves and boots echoing against the stone. Below, the Still River roared.

Grace stared over the edge, wide-eyed. "You jumped?"

Wynn glanced down. The spot where Avery had shoved her, it wasn't far now. She could still picture Avery's face, wild with fear, fierce with love. "Not exactly," she murmured.

This time, there would be no daring escape. No river to save her.

The bridge gave way to the Tor lands, colder, harder, the air thinner somehow. The trees started to disappear, replaced by rocks and low, scraggly brush. Light drops of rain came down and, in the distance, the Tor Mountains rose, jagged and ominous.

The Hawk turned in his saddle. "We don't stop until morning. We ride until we reach the castle."

Wynn's heart sank.

"I'd like to ride now," Grace piped up, her voice bright. No one responded. She shrugged. "It was worth a try."

She smiled sideways at Wynn, clearly trying to keep things light.

But Wynn couldn't smile back. All she could feel was the rope around her neck, the ache in her legs, the curling dread of what was to come. She had no idea how to get out of this. And morning was still a long way off.

Out there, she still walks, each step slower than the last, her boots soaked through, the night air sharp enough to sting. Her fingers have gone stiff, her nose red with cold, and every part of her aches for something simple: dry socks, a bowl of stew, the weight of a warm blanket pulled to the chin. But that's not hers tonight. That's yours. You have the quiet hush of the room, the soft pillow cradling your head, and the perfect shape your body makes in the mattress. The kind of warmth that pools slowly, from toes to shoulders. So breathe it in. Let yourself sink deeper. Be grateful for the soft things, sheets, pillows, stillness, and let that gratitude be your last thought as you close this book and your eyes. Sleep well.

CHAPTER TWENTY-SEVEN

True to the Hawk's command, they did not stop through the night. The rope stayed tight around Wynn's neck, tugging at her throat each time The Hawk shifted in his saddle. By morning, if it could even be called that, Wynn struggled with each step. Her toes and the soles of her feet felt rubbed raw and her wet cloak offered no reprieve from the bite in the air. Each breath she exhaled turned to mist and vanished before her face, as if the air was trying to leave this place. The sun had risen, allegedly, but it brought no light, no warmth. Only a greying sky that pressed lower the closer they drew to the castle. Even Grace, still walking beside her with a torn hem and wind-bitten cheeks, had gone quiet.

They had passed through several villages on the road, all abandoned in spirit if not in flesh. No windows opened. No doors creaked. Once, a child's eyes peered through an open slit in a shutter, but the moment they saw the procession, the opening closed shut. The Hawk never once glanced at the villages. Neither did the knights. Wynn did. She saw what was left behind. She felt it.

Then came the castle.

She had first glimpsed it an hour ago, a dark spire rising in the distance like a fang. Now, it towered above them. Its walls were built from stone blacker than night, veined with something deep purple that glinted in the dull morning haze. Tattered banners made noise in the wind, and the main gate, a monstrous iron maw, stood open, waiting.

"Home sweet home," Grace muttered, her voice thin with sarcasm and exhaustion.

As they crossed into the outer ward, where the castle town lay, people began to appear from doorways and alleys, their faces pale and gaunt. Some watched in silence. Others whispered. A few spat as Wynn passed. "Tarn garbage," someone hissed.

A stone whistled past her ear, missing by inches. Grace flinched. The knights didn't react. Wynn pulled her hood over head.

Then she saw them, Tarn slaves, tucked into doorways, with a withered sleepless expression Wynn knew too well. They clambered to get a glimpse of her. One man, older, with a twisted back and a milky eye, held her gaze and whispered as she passed: "Don't yield."

The procession entered the inner gates. Now the castle loomed directly above them, blotting out what little light filtered through the overcast sky. Wynn's chest tightened. Her nightmares had always started like this.

The Hawk dismounted.

Behind her, Grace leaned close and murmured, "No matter what, do not kneel before her. Trust me."

Wynn turned slightly, her eyes searching Grace's face. "Trust you?" she whispered. But The Hawk gave the rope a sharp pull and she choked back a cry before stumbling up the stairs. No more questions. No more chances. Only what waited inside.

The iron doors groaned open, revealing the hollow and terrible heart of the castle. For such an immense space, it was shockingly empty. The towering ceiling arched like the ribcage of a long-dead beast, and everything echoed, their steps, the rustle of cloaks, the faint crackle of fire in a massive circular pit at the room's center. The blaze gave off no heat. It was as though the flames themselves had learned to obey their queen: look powerful, offer nothing.

The Dark Guard lined the hall, unmoving, a silent forest of iron and shadow. At the far end, atop the obsidian throne, sat Queen Prima. Her bald head, rimmed with a black crown, gleamed in the firelight. Her eyes were painted with kohl so dark they seemed bottomless, and her fingers draped over the throne's arms, black nails glinting like knives. Wynn had seen her only once before—when she stood over the broken bodies of her parents, sword still dripping.

That memory came rushing back with such force that Wynn nearly stumbled. Her breath hitched. Fear, ancient and electric, flooded her veins.

And then the silence shattered.

"Mommy!" Grace's voice rang through the hall like a child's cry at a masquerade ball.

Wynn turned, stunned, as Grace pulled free from the knight beside her and darted forward, wrists still bound.

"Oh, Mommy, it was awful!" Grace wailed. "She was awful! They tied me up, made me walk miles, my shins are bruised, my hair... look at my hair!"

No one moved. Not the knights. Not the queen. Even The Hawk tilted his head slightly. Wynn stood frozen at the threshold, rope still in The Hawk's grip.

Grace reached the throne, thrusting out her hands dramatically. "Do you see this? Rope burn! Honestly, Mother, I'm half-starved!"

Prima blinked once. If she was capable of being taken aback, it showed in the faintest twitch at the corner of her lip. She looked her daughter up and down, assessing... "Cut her loose," she finally said with a wave of her hand. A knight stepped forward to sever Grace's bindings. Grace threw her arms around her mother, who sat as motionless as a statue.

Wynn watched, aghast. Who hugged the Dark Queen? Maybe Kiernan was right. Maybe this girl *was* actually unhinged.

Grace let go and took her place beside the throne, straightening her dress, chin high. "She is absolutely dreadful, Mother," she said, pointing to Wynn. "She killed Lorkan and my beloved Seraphina. Right in front of me."

Wynn's head jerked up. *What?*

Grace sniffed. "Make her suffer, Mommy."

The chill in the room sharpened. Prima's gaze, once resting on her daughter, now locked onto Wynn.

The Hawk tugged the rope and Wynn stumbled forward, her hood still up. When they reached the center of the hall, The Hawk dropped to one knee, bowing his head. Wynn did not.

She stood, rope around her neck, eyes hidden beneath her hood.

Prima descended from her throne like a vulture from a cliff. She moved with slow, deliberate steps, the train of her dress whispering over the floor. When she reached Wynn, she stood before her. Even with her heeled boots, Wynn matched her height. In one fluid motion, she brushed back the hood.

Wynn flinched.

Prima cupped her chin. "You look just like your mother," she murmured, nails skating lightly across Wynn's cheek.

Wynn clenched her jaw. Her heart thundered as she remembered Illen's words: *if she touches you, she can enter your dreams.*

Prima let her go and stepped back. "Remove the rope."

The Hawk obeyed, finally releasing the hold on Wynn's neck.

Prima stood, one eyebrow raised, waiting. "Kneel," she commanded. Her voice echoed in the empty hall.

Wynn swallowed nervously. She didn't move.

"Kneel before me," the queen said again, this time a little sweeter, "and I will spare your people."

Wynn hesitated. Her body betrayed her, a small shake in her knees. She glanced at Grace. Was that the barest shake of her head? Wynn looked back to Prima. She bent... just slightly. Just enough. Then stopped. A slow, defiant smile crept across her lips. "You know," she said, "I've never been good at following orders." She rose and stood tall.

Fire lit behind Prima's eyes. The Hawk moved as if to force her down again, but Prima snapped. "No! It has to be her choice."

"I will never," Wynn said. Her voice trembled, but it did not break. "The Tarn will never bow before you." Her eyes flicked to The Hawk. "Even if he already has."

Prima let out a disappointed sigh. "We'll see. Take her to the cells," she said, waving a hand. "Let her think about it a little more."

Two knights stepped forward, seizing Wynn by either arm. She twisted in their grip as they began to drag her backward, boots scraping against stone. Her voice rang out across the throne room, "The Tarn will never yield!"

But she had barely passed the edge of the fire pit when Prima's voice sliced through the air. "Wait."

The knights halted. Wynn was yanked back around to face the throne. Prima's eyes were sharper now, focused, narrowing to flints. "I believe you have something of mine," she said coldly. "A ring."

Wynn stiffened, she could feel the ring against her chest. "I don't know what you're talking about," she said, teeth clenched.

"Search her."

But before the knights could move, Grace burst forward. "You *liar!*" she screamed, hurling herself at Wynn. "You took it, I know you did! You took my mother's ring! How *dare* you!"

Wynn barely had time to brace before Grace slammed into her, knocking them both to the ground. She attacked Wynn, grabbing, clawing, making a show of fury. The guards leapt in, pulling her off with effort, others hauling Wynn back to her feet.

"Grace!" Prima barked. "What are you doing?"

Wynn knew that move. She'd used it herself, dozens of times. A scuffle, a cry, a distraction. And she saw it then: Grace's hand slipping low, palming the ring and tucking it into the folds of her skirt as the guards pulled her back.

Grace shook free of the guards. "I've had enough of her," she said, biting out the words. "I hate her."

Wynn locked eyes on Prima.

"Your daughter is as crazy as you." She could see that the comment hit Grace hard but she continued. "I'll never tell you where that ring is," she spat, defiance rising like a flame in her chest. "I hid it. You'll never see it again."

Prima's gaze snapped back to her. There was no smirk now. No victory. Only a flicker of something colder. More calculating. "We'll see what some torture and another sleepless night can loosen from your tongue," she said quietly. Then, to the knights: "Take her."

The guards resumed their march, dragging Wynn away. "The Tarn will never yield!" she shouted once more, her voice echoing across the high, vaulted room, louder this time. Stronger.

The great doors groaned shut behind her.

For a breath, the throne room was silent again, like something terrible had just passed through and left a residue behind. Grace allowed herself the faintest smile. It vanished the moment Prima turned back toward her.

"Good," Grace said quickly, her voice sharp, dismissive. "Keep her down there. It's what she deserves."

Prima's golden eyes lingered on her daughter, evaluating. "You've grown up," Prima said, voice flat but curious.

Grace dipped into a practiced curtsy, her tattered skirt fanning out like a stage curtain. As she looked at the woman before her, Illen's words echoed in her head. *She gave up her ability to love.* She swallowed and smiled, "I've missed you, Mother."

Prima's lips twitched at the word *missed*, but she said nothing.

Grace rose. "Why have you summoned me back to the Dark Castle now?"

For a moment, Prima didn't answer. Her gaze wandered past her daughter, beyond the walls of the room, beyond the present. Her mind turned back to the Fates, to their maddening whispers: *a princess will be your undoing.* She had thought of Wynn, of course. The cursed child. The spark in the dark. But Grace? This spoiled, pretty thing? No. Clearly, she posed no threat. Or, did she?

"It is time," Prima said finally, her voice returning to steel, "to train you to one day become the next ruler of these lands."

Grace stiffened. "Me?"

Prima nodded once, turning to The Hawk. "You two will be united." A beat passed. The words dropped like iron into water.

Grace and The Hawk exchanged a look. Eyes wide. Breath caught.

Prima ignored them. She turned her sharp gaze on The Hawk. "I assume your sister told you who you are. Your bloodline?"

The Hawk didn't answer, but he didn't have to. The answer was in his face, the hard line of his jaw, the confusion in his eyes.

"Good," Prima said. "Then this will make sense to you. To quell whatever little rebellion the Tarn are playing at... you two will unite. Officially. Publicly. A royal union between the Tor and the last of the Tarn."

If she cared what either of them thought, about being pawns, about being bound together in something neither chose, she didn't show it. She sniffed. A faint wrinkle curled her nose.

"You both smell of wild animals," she said coolly. "Clean yourselves. We will celebrate with a ceremony tonight."

Staring at one another, neither Grace nor The Hawk spoke. There was nothing to say. The command had been given. They only nodded, stiff and silent, then turned. The Hawk strode through the front hall, his boots echoing. Grace lingered half a second longer until a nursemaid in gray slipped in through a side door and gently motioned for her to follow. Grace didn't look back. She curtsied again, turned, and let herself be led out of the hall like the obedient daughter she wanted her mother to believe her to be.

The throne room was quiet again. Prima stood for a long moment in the firelight. She stepped slowly back toward her throne, trailing her black fingers across the arm as she sat. Her eyes flicked toward the doors where Wynn had been taken. A soft breath escaped her. Almost a sigh. "If she won't kneel," Prima murmured, voice like silk over steel, "I'll improvise."

Wynn was dragged down into the castle's underbelly, through damp corridors that twisted into darkness. At the bottom of a stone stair, the guards shoved her into a cell. The iron bars slammed shut behind her. Without a word, they left.

She stood for a moment, chest rising and falling, trying to see through the dimness. Searching...

Then she saw it. The small shape curled in the neighboring cell, motionless beneath a thin blanket. "Avery?"

The lump shifted. A face emerged, blinking. "Wynn?"

They rushed to the bars between them, gripping the cold iron as they pressed close, trying to hold each other through the metal. For a heartbeat, there was only relief.

Then Avery pulled back slightly. "Please don't tell me you came here for me."

Wynn gave a crooked smile. "Well... it's part of the plan."

Avery began to pace. "Wynn, she's evil. She's going to kill you."

"Oh, she's *definitely* evil. And she'll probably *try* to kill me. But..." Wynn softened, "it's good to see you."

"You too," Avery said quietly. "I missed you."

Wynn looked at her properly now, how her fine-boned features seemed even thinner, her darker skin pale with exhaustion. And suddenly it seemed so obvious: she didn't look at all like Tarn or Tor. She didn't belong here. She never had. "Avery..." Wynn began, but Avery cut in.

"I'm sorry I pushed you," she said. "Off the bridge."

"Oh, *that*," Wynn waved it off. "You're forgiven."

Avery leaned in, whispering, "Wynn, Prima can enter dreams. She manipulates... she does something to them."

"I know," Wynn said. Her eyes darkened.

Avery blinked. "You do? How?"

"We've got a lot to talk about, because I learned something else." She looked at her, "Something about you."

Avery's eyes started to widen, but Wynn could tell she was only confirming something Avery already sensed. They both sank to the stone floor, sitting cross-legged in front of the bars, mirroring each other in the flickering torchlight. The conversation that followed doesn't need to be told again, not to us, dear reader. We already know the pieces: Lorkan, the Keep, Grace, Illen, Tierney...

"And just before we were caught," Wynn said, "that book elf told us about The Margins. The spellbook. *The Book That Will Put You to Sleep,* and the undoing spell."

Avery's eyes sharpened. "The Margins," she whispered. "That's what they feel like."

"You remember them?" Wynn asked, leaning in.

"I do now. Prima's been invading my dreams, trying to force me to show her. But I can usually fight her off." She met Wynn's gaze. "I *have* been there. I think I can help."

Wynn reached through the bars and took her hand. "That's what the elf thought, too."

"And your brother doesn't know who he is at all?"

Wynn shook her head. "I don't know if he ever will."

"That's... a lot, Wynn." Avery slowly looked up and then she smiled, "looks like somebody else wants to save the day." She nodded at Wynn to turn around.

Wynn glanced at the narrow, barred window high up on the far wall. She rose, stretched on her toes, and peered out, just as a little pointed face emerged between the slats. A wet fox nose twitched. Two bright, clever eyes blinked. "Night!" Wynn exhaled, warmth catching in her chest. The little fox gave a quiet whine and pressed her nose between the bars. Wynn reached through and scratched her fur gently. Night licked her fingers, brisk and impatient, like she was scolding her for ending up in a cell.

Avery laughed softly. "I never thought I'd say this, but... I missed that darn fox."

Wynn grinned, despite everything.

"What about Kiernan?" Avery asked. "Is he...?" Her breath caught and she couldn't finish the sentence.

"Oh, no," Wynn shook her head quickly. "He's alive. He's back in the village. Safe. I hope."

"Really?" Avery blinked. "That doesn't seem very much like him."

Wynn tilted her head. "What do you mean?"

Avery gave her a look. "Staying out of trouble? That's never been Kiernan's style. He loves you, Wynn. He can't stay away."

Wynn blinked, caught off guard.

"Loves me?" she repeated. Not like *that*, surely. Could he? No. Kiernan was more like a clumsy, goofy brother. Loyal, stubborn, protective. She pictured him tripping over his own sword, shouting too loudly, always one step behind. Still... the way Avery said it lingered.

"There has to be a plan," Avery said, more urgently now. "Is there a plan?"

Wynn hesitated. "I don't know," she admitted. "I've pretty much been winging it until now. I just... I needed to get to you. That's the only thing that felt clear."

"That doesn't sound like the Wynn I know."

"I know," she said softly, exhaling. The truth was, she hadn't really felt like herself since Lorkan died. He had always helped her see the path forward, even when she didn't want to. Without him, everything had felt blurred. Heavy. She'd told herself she was doing this for the Tarn, for her people, but really... it was about Avery. About keeping just one more piece of her world from disappearing.

She had never been good at trusting others. Plans were safer when she made them alone. And yet, here she was, putting her trust in Grace, a girl she barely knew. A strange, impulsive princess who talked way too much. Grace, who confused her, infuriated her, and for reasons she still didn't understand... gave her hope.

Wynn let out a breath and leaned her forehead against the cool stone wall. Night huffed softly, still just beyond the bars. Grace was their *only* hope now.

~ ~ ~

The walls are damp, the light thin and flickering, and hope, for now, feels distant. Still, the story presses on, even through shadowed corridors and damp stone. But you don't have to. Not tonight. You can leave the cold behind on the page, draw the blankets a little tighter, and let your breath slow in the safety of your own quiet room. You're not the one locked in that cell. Not the one with aching bones and fading strength. You are warm, and dry, and safe tonight. So if sleep is calling, let it come. And if not—if the ending tugs just a bit too hard—well, you're almost there, and I'll turn the next page with you. Either way, rest easy. Sleep well.

CHAPTER TWENTY-EIGHT

It was hard to tell how much time had passed. The barred window at the top of the stone wall had gone from a light gray to dark gray. Evening was coming. But then, everything in the Tor seemed dull and gray, the color completely drained from the world, leaving only ash behind.

Wynn sat cross-legged on the cold floor of her cell, elbow resting on one knee, head tilted toward the light. The hunger gnawing at her stomach was second only to the exhaustion pressing on every inch of her body. Still, she hadn't touched the tray of food the guard brought earlier, not after Avery leaned over and whispered, "Don't eat it. They've been putting something in mine. Sleep in this place is dangerous."

Wynn was sure that even laced food wouldn't work without the token, but here, in the Dark Castle, she wasn't so sure. The thought of Prima entering her dreams terrified her. She needed sleep, but she was more stubborn than tired.

"Night left," Avery said from the next cell over, her voice hushed. "Probably went to get herself a rabbit, or three."

"Lucky her," Wynn murmured, side-eyeing the untouched bread like it might leap up and betray her at any second.

They hadn't spoken much in the last hour. Just the occasional comment, the comfort of knowing someone was near.

"Do you remember your home at all?" Wynn asked.

Avery nodded. "I remember, it was hot. Like the heat of one of our summer days, but all the time. And a lot of sun, endless warm-salty-water, and fish."

"Fish?"

"Colorful ones."

"It sounds nice."

"I think it was."

The door at the end of the corridor creaked open. Footsteps. They were too even, too measured to belong to a guard.

Wynn stood. She was already at the bars when the figure appeared—Tierney. He looked... not like himself. Not entirely. He wore formal attire, black leather trousers and a matching vest. A deep violet silk shirt hugged his frame beneath it, the sleeves pushed up just enough to show the edges of bracers. A sword was belted at his side, and his dark hair had been brushed and styled, though it refused to behave fully. His blue eyes, so much like hers, seemed sharper in contrast to his outfit. He looked like their father, except... more severe. Her father had been all warm hands and soft smiles. Tierney had those same bones, but none of the light. Not anymore.

He stopped in front of her cell.

"Nice outfit," Wynn said. "Very villian-esque."

Tierney huffed something that might've been amusement. His face settled again. Too blank. Too guarded. He didn't speak. He just stood there, looking her over like she was some kind of puzzle with a missing piece.

It made Wynn squirm. "Right," she said, clearing her throat. "Well. This is Avery. Avery, this is... my brother."

Avery blinked, "Your what?"

"Tierney of the Tarn," Wynn said, gesturing at him. "Though I used to call him Turkey." There was the faintest twitch in his brow, just for a second. Wynn caught it, like a ripple over still water, and then it was gone.

Avery leaned forward slightly, squinting at them both. "Huh. I can see it."

Tierney didn't smile. Instead, he turned to the end of the corridor and gave a curt nod. A guard who had been lurking in the shadows straightened, then disappeared without a word. The door creaked closed behind him.

Silence.

Tierney turned back to Wynn. "I'm to torture you later tonight."

Wynn blinked. "Are you planning on wearing *that*?"

"I'm to find out where you've hidden the ring," he said flatly. "My methods are... effective."

Avery bristled behind her. Wynn felt her stomach tighten. She wanted to say something clever, something sharp and untouchable, but her mouth was suddenly dry.

"Well," she managed, "don't expect me to make it easy. I was always the more stubborn one."

He didn't argue. He didn't have to. Something was wrong. Off-kilter. His eyes weren't cold the way she remembered when first seeing him. They were conflicted.

He drew a breath. "The Dark One has... ordered me to unite with Princess Grace tonight. In ceremony. To officially connect The Vast."

Wynn stared. Trying to reconcile what he had just said. "What?"

He looked down at his boots, then back up again, his expression unreadable.

Wynn felt it all at once: the sharp twist of shock, then confusion, then something white-hot and splintering. It lodged behind her ribs. Grace. Grace and Tierney. In ceremony. She tried to breathe. Tried to think. Tried not to imagine the two of them standing, palms pressed together, united. *Had that been the plan all along? Had Grace been playing her?*

Her voice came out rough. "Of course. Why not? Grace has a taste for the dramatic."

Tierney looked away, jaw flexing.

She wanted to punch the wall. Or scream. Or curl up and disappear. But all she did was cross her arms and glare. "And what," she asked, "you're just going along with it? After everything? You finally learn the truth, that you're prince of The Tarn, and you just fall in line?"

He flinched. It was subtle, but it was there. The only crack in his otherwise frozen face.

"I..." he started, then stopped. The words wouldn't come. "The Dark One confirmed what you, what I..."

"That you're my brother," Wynn finished for him.

He nodded. "That I am of royal lineage."

"Unbelievable. She shares all of this with you now because it benefits her. Or maybe it's a test. And you, you just go along with it because what? Because she believes you to be loyal? Because you feel you owe her your life?"

Tierney's face didn't change.

But Wynn saw it, just behind his eyes, the war he was waging with himself. And maybe, just maybe, he was losing. Wynn narrowed her eyes at him. "Why are you even telling me all of this?"

He hesitated. His mouth opened, but nothing came out. Whatever answer he had, it didn't seem to want to leave the safety of his thoughts.

Wynn tilted her head. "You don't even know, do you?" Still, he said nothing. She leaned forward, voice low and deliberate. "Our parents would be so disappointed in you right now."

It landed like a slap. Exactly as she'd meant it. She wanted to cut through whatever mask he was wearing. Wanted to find something, *someone,* underneath. But his jaw only tightened.

Slowly, The Hawk returned to his face, like armor being refitted piece by piece.

"Tell me where the ring is," he said.

"No," Wynn snapped, immediately.

He didn't flinch this time. Just gave a cold nod. "Then I'll be back tonight. And, Wynn, you *will* tell me."

Her breath caught. It was the first time she had heard him say her name. It hit harder than she expected. Something cracked open in her chest.

But before she could respond there was a blur of movement behind him, a sharp thud, and he dropped like a sack of grain.

Standing in his place, panting and holding a stone in her hand, was Grace. She tossed the rock aside with a clatter. She was flushed, eyes wide, breath short, and entirely too calm for someone who had just knocked out The Hawk.

"I... don't think I killed him," she added, looking down at the body.

Grace looked beautiful. Unfairly beautiful. A shiny onyx gown hugging her figure and her hair pinned in an intricate updo with a pair of auburn curls framing her face. She looked less like the girl Wynn had first met at the Keep and more like a real, regal princess in every sense.

Wynn blinked. "You look... nice."

Grace looked up, startled, and then blushed, tucking a loose curl behind her ear. "Well," she said, lifting her skirt and stepping daintily over Tierney's unconscious body, "thank you."

There was a glint of dull metal in her hand, a key, and with barely a pause she began working the lock on the cell door.

"I stole this off the main guard's belt. He was easily distracted." She pushed up her cleavage.

"I can see why." The compliment was out before Wynn could stop it.

Grace smiled, "You wouldn't believe how many keys he carries around. I had to guess."

Wynn was still staring at her. “You knocked out my brother.”

Grace, standing there with one slippered foot next to Tierney’s unconscious head, gave a breezy shrug. “Yes.”

“The one who was about to torture me?”

“Yes, well…” She stepped through the open cell door, poised even in the dim, damp space. “We can’t have that, can we?”

Wynn instinctively stepped back, suddenly very self-aware. The cell she’d been sitting in for hours smelled like mold, sweat, and urine. She probably did too. Meanwhile, Grace smelled like roses. The kind that bloomed in protected gardens and never had to fight for their place among thorns. Their eyes locked. For a moment, the room held its breath.

“Umm, hello?” came Avery’s voice, flat and unimpressed. “Anyone want to fill me in?”

Wynn shook herself. “Grace, this is Avery. Avery, Grace… Princess of The Tor.”

“Yes,” Grace added lightly, “The Dark One’s daughter, but don’t hold that against me.”

Avery raised an eyebrow. “Noted.”

“I’ve come to rescue you.” Grace flashed a wink, already crossing to the next cell. “Wynn told me a lot about you.”

“Funny,” Avery said suspiciously. “She hasn’t said too much about you.”

Wynn shrugged.

“We don’t have much time.” Grace began fiddling with the iron lock. It clicked open a moment later. “Follow me,” she said, rising and instinctively grabbing Wynn’s hand.

“Where are we—?”

“I used to play down here as a child,” Grace said over her shoulder, already leading them out of the cellblock and into a narrow, half-forgotten passageway. The stone walls around them were sweating with the cold.

“*Down here?*” Wynn asked, bewildered.

"Yes, well, I was a weird kid," Grace replied, voice echoing faintly. She plucked a torch from the wall, casting golden light over the damp walls and her pale, composed face. "Anyway. I know this place like the back of my hand."

Avery muttered, "Remind me to worry about you later."

As they followed the winding corridor, the smell of prison gave way to earth and old stone. Wynn's thoughts refused to quiet. "That little scene up in the throne room was..." she began.

"Yes, sorry about that," Grace said quickly. "I didn't know what else to do. I knew my mother would buy it—me, all weepy and obedient. That's how she's always seen me. So I gave her exactly what she wanted."

"It was great," Wynn said, surprised by how much she meant it. "You were great."

Grace glanced back, a pleased little grin tugging at her lips. "Why thank you. I do love a bit of theatre." They rounded a bend and came to a small iron door. "Here," she said, then paused. "Oh, right. Almost forgot." She reached down into the bodice of her dress and retrieved the small obsidian ring. "I had to keep it where no one would look," she said with a smirk, offering it to Wynn.

Wynn took it, her fingers brushing Grace's for a moment too long. The ring was warm from her skin. Before she could speak, Grace turned back to the door and gave it a hard push, grunting as it popped open. The hinges protested, but the iron groaned—and there, perfectly seated on her hind legs was Night, looking slightly annoyed at having to wait in the dark.

"Night," Wynn breathed, dropping to her knees.

The fox bounded forward. She licked Wynn's face and Wynn buried her fingers in Night's dark fur. She felt the ache in her chest loosen, just slightly.

"I only needed to call her once and she came running," Grace said, crouching beside them. "Smart girl. She'll lead you the rest of the way out. Once you're free of the tunnel, you'll find a pack, with warmer clothes, food, and a map. You'll need to head for the northern mountains."

Wynn looked up sharply. "Wait... *you're not coming?*"

Grace's smile was faint. "No."

"But—"

"Wynn," Grace said softly, a small, wistful smile playing on her lips. "As much as I want to step into this mystical land of story with you, I think this is something for you and Avery to do."

Wynn furrowed her brow. "What do you mean?"

Grace met her gaze, steady and sure. "Reclaiming your land. Breaking the spell on your people. Facing the woman who took your family from you. Wynn, this is your story. Can't you see that?"

Wynn looked at her, heart thudding. She didn't answer right away. Then, quietly, "What if it's *our* story?"

Grace's smile deepened, sad and brave all at once. "Then, if it is... I'll stay here and play my part. If you don't come back, someone else has to stop my mother. Besides, I plan on making a bit of a mess here. Buy you some time." She stood, pulled a pin from her hair, and with a shake of her head, auburn tendrils tumbled around her face. Then, gripping the hem of her gown, she ripped a long tear through the fabric, exposing one leg.

"Hit me," she said.

Wynn blinked. "What?"

"I said *hit me.* Hard. It needs to look like you overpowered me."

"I'm not going to—"

"Yes, you are. I'll say I came down here looking for my betrothed, but saw a figure helping you escape. You attacked me. I was no match for your wild strength. The drama writes itself. Just do it." She pulled back and closed her eyes, bracing for the hit.

Wynn hesitated. Then, with a grimace and a small apology already forming on her lips, she readied her fist and swung. It connected with a sickening crack. Grace's head snapped sideways. Blood sprang from her lower lip.

"I'm sorry!"

But Grace straightened with a small laugh and pressed two fingers to her split lip, pulling back to look at the blood. "Ow. That hurt, a lot more than I thought it would. But, this is *perfect.* Now *go.* We don't have much time."

She turned quickly, shoved the small iron door open wider and began herding Avery and Wynn through.

Avery stumbled, then muttered, "Is she always like this?"

"Most of the time," Wynn replied.

But just before she stepped through, Wynn paused and turned back. "You're not going to... unite with my brother, are you?"

Grace stared at her like she'd lost her mind. "What!? Fates, no. I'm going to make a whole *scene* about this escape. I'll cry, I'll scream, I'll faint. I'll obviously be far too overwhelmed to go through with the ceremony tonight. Besides, your brother's probably going to hunt after you now, which is exactly why *you need to go.*" She grabbed Wynn's arm, pulled her close. "And Wynn?"

Wynn looked up just as Grace kissed her. Her lips were warm, soft, tinged with honey and a hint of blood.

Grace pulled back, "Be careful."

Wynn couldn't think. Could barely breathe. "You too," she managed.

And then the door slammed shut behind them, cutting off the torchlight, the smell of roses, the taste of something unexpected. They were in darkness again.

Avery raised her brows. "Umm. What was *that?*"

"Nothing," Wynn said too quickly.

"Looked like *something* to me."

Wynn didn't respond, but she felt it too. Not nothing. *Something.*

~ ~ ~

Ah, young love. So hopeful. A promise, or perhaps just a breath shared in the stillness before the storm. It lingers, doesn't it? Like the memory of warmth against a cold night, soft as a sigh. But kisses won't shield against duty, and the road ahead won't wait forever. Still, for now, all is calm. The fire crackles low. The night air presses outside, but you are hopefully wrapped in stillness and story, tucked deep beneath your blankets where no chill can reach. Let the tension in your shoulders loosen. Let your thoughts grow slow and quiet. You've earned the comfort of this moment. Drift, if you wish. Or turn the page, if your thoughts won't let go of Wynn just yet. Sleep well.

CHAPTER TWENTY-NINE

With full stomachs, gear strapped to her back, including a quiver full of arrows, a bow, and thick smoky-gray wool cloaks draped over their shoulders, Wynn, Avery, and Night slipped into the encroaching dusk. The back wall of the castle loomed behind them, its stones dark and silent. Thanks to Lorkan, and every stealthy, rule-breaking lesson he had ever passed on, there were no shouts, no alarms, no eyes on them as they disappeared into the trees. Night led them with quiet assurance. Her white-tipped tail flicked ahead of them like a living compass, always one step ahead, pausing only to glance back as if to say, *Keep up.*

Evening deepened quickly, and with it came a sharp bite to the air. What had started as a whisper of chill had turned into a creeping, gnawing cold. The deeper they moved into the lowlands at the base of the mountains, the more the wind began to howl. Not loud, but constant, threading through the thin trees and tugging at their cloaks with invisible hands.

Three hours later, the moon had risen in full, round and brilliant and watching. It cast silver light across the rocky spines of the Northern Range, turning every crag into a shadowed monster. They stopped at the base of a jagged wall, no trail, no path, only the steep face of the mountain looming above them.

Avery stared up, her breath visible in the cold. "I don't know if I can do this," she whispered.

Wynn, truthfully, was having her own doubts. Her legs already ached, her fingers stiff in the chill, but she pushed the fear down. "Sure you can."

Avery looked at her and shivered. Wynn stepped in close, placed her hands gently but firmly on Avery's shoulders; the way Lorkan used to do with her. "Listen, A," she said. "You've done a hundred dangerous things with me. Think about all the Torn nobles we've robbed together. You faced Dena every day. And that bridge? You pushed me off that thing with barely a second thought. And honestly, that might be the most daring thing I've ever seen."

Avery gave a shaky laugh. "That was a little crazy, wasn't it?"

"Crazy in the best way. And don't forget, you came here from another land entirely. That's not nothing. You're made of tougher stuff than you think."

She reached into the pack and pulled out a coil of fibrous rope. Without hesitation, she looped it around her own waist and tied a sturdy knot. Then she stepped forward and did the same for Avery. "I won't let you fall," she said, quiet and steady. "I promise." Just then, a soft scrabble echoed above them, stone shifting under small paws. They looked up.

Night was already halfway up the first ledge, a perfect fox silhouette against the moonlight. She turned, poised on a narrow shelf, and gave a sharp little yap. Her eyes gleamed with certainty, as if to say, *Come on. This way.*

"Night!" Wynn called to her. "Come down. This is too steep." In answer, Night stubbornly sat on her haunches. "Night. It's too dangerous. You need to stay." Night turned and jumped up to the next ledge, looking back defiantly. Wynn let out a gruff of frustration. "Fine, you stubborn... you better not get yourself killed."

Avery blew into her hands for warmth and squared her shoulders. "Alright. Let's do this before I lose my nerve." And together, under the light of the moon, they began to climb.

The wind bit at them, cold enough to sting through even their thick cloaks. It came in gusts, unpredictable and snarling, and more than once Wynn had to throw herself against the wall of stone just to stay upright. Avery slipped twice, sharp gasps, a scramble of boots on rock, and both times Wynn braced hard, the rope between them snapping taut, holding Avery's weight with trembling arms.

They didn't speak much, the climb taking all their strength and breath.

Wynn's hands were raw from gripping stone and rope. Her legs burned with every upward push. The rope cinched around her waist like a reminder: *You're not alone. You're responsible for more than yourself.* She tried not to look down, though the temptation clawed at her. The ledges behind them were shrinking, swallowed by the darkness below.

Only Night seemed immune to it all. The fox darted ahead, sure-footed and swift, her dark shape flickering from ledge to ledge making it look easy.

After what felt like a lifetime of ascending, they reached a narrow ledge with just enough space to stand without clinging to the wall. They collapsed against the rock, panting, faces wind burnt and muscles screaming. For a few long seconds, they simply tried to collect their breath, then Avery fumbled with the pack and pulled out a canteen.

"Here," she said, her voice hoarse.

They shared small sips of water. Wynn tilted her head back, eyes closing for a moment of rest. But when she opened them, what she saw took all the air from her lungs.

The Vast stretched out beneath them in silence and silver moonlight, spilling across the land like milk. The Still River carved its way through the terrain below, a silver thread that shimmered between the hills. Tiny lights glittered on either side, villages and homes, Tor and Tarn alike. Prima's rule, the fear, the cruelty, it all looked impossibly far away from up here. Small. Almost peaceful.

In the distance, the Dark Castle punctuated the landscape.

"It's all so beautiful from up here," Avery whispered beside her.

"It is," Wynn agreed. And it was worth fighting for.

But just as they let themselves lean into that moment, a gust of wind slammed into them with enough force to make them stagger. They both pressed their backs to the wall, gripping the rock face with cold-numbed fingers.

"I wish it would stop doing that," Avery groaned.

"Me too," Wynn muttered, heart pounding in her chest. The wind eased, briefly, and Wynn slowly straightened. She stepped forward a little, too close to the edge, peering down. Her eyes narrowed.

"What are you doing?" Avery hissed, pulling her cloak tighter. "It's not funny. You're too close."

But Wynn didn't answer right away. She was squinting into the dark, something catching her eye, something moving. A thread of light snaked its way along the ground far below, barely visible. Lanterns. And behind that light, shapes. Figures.

Her breath caught."I can see them," she whispered.

"Who?" Avery leaned forward, careful but alarmed.

"The Dark Guard. There's a line of them making their way to the base. And..." Wynn's voice dropped. "My brother. He's already climbing."

As if summoned by her words, a sharp *screech* split the air. Wynn ducked instinctively as a massive hawk swept past her, its wings slicing the moonlight, feathers nearly brushing her head.

The bird climbed fast into the sky again, vanishing toward the crags.

Wynn turned back, her face suddenly pale, breath shallow. "He's not far." She tightened the straps on her pack. "We have to move. Now."

They shoved off the wall and continued upward, limbs shaking with fatigue and urgency. Every few ledges, Wynn risked a glance downward, and every time, the flicker of motion was closer. He was gaining.

The fox's silhouette reappeared high above them, waiting. Night yipped once, sharp and urgent. Wynn gritted her teeth and pressed on, whispering under her breath, "Just a little farther."

The mountain was changing around them. Patches of snow had begun to appear, dustings at first, then clusters, clinging to ledges and caught in crevices. Above them, the sky had deepened into a sheet of black velvet pricked with stars and from that the hawk returned, screaming down from the heights in a streak of feathers and fury, slicing the air above their heads. Night snarled and leapt, jaws snapping at the bird as it looped back and forth, circling closer with each dive.

"It's trying to lure her," Wynn realized aloud, heart hammering.

The hawk made another pass, closer this time. "No!" Wynn shouted. "Night! Leave it!"

But the fox crouched, hackles raised, ready to spring again.

"Night!" Wynn barked, louder now. "Stay!"

The fox paused, trembling with restraint, then slowly lowered herself back to the rock with a reluctant growl. But the wind shifted, and so did everything.

A patch of snow beneath Night gave way. With a sudden yelp, she slid toward the edge, claws scrambling.

"Night!" Wynn lunged, just catching the fox by the scruff before she could disappear over the side. She dropped flat, belly scraping stone, legs kicking for purchase. Night dangled in the open air, front paws scrabbling helplessly, whimpering. "I've got you," Wynn hissed through clenched teeth, arm straining. "I've got you. Hang on—"

She didn't see the shadow coming until it was too late.

A whoosh of air. A flash of wings. The hawk dove from above, this time not at Night, but at Wynn. She felt the claws rake past her collarbone, sharp, slicing, and then a violent tug as something tore from her neck. The leather strap snapped.

"No—" Wynn gasped, twisting just in time to see the hawk climbing back into the air, the ring clenched in its talons. Gone. She wanted to scream after it. To throw something. To run. But Night was still in her grip, still slipping. Grunting, Wynn pulled her fox up in one desperate heave and collapsed backward against the rock.

She clutched Night to her chest. Above them, the hawk let out a long, echoing cry and vanished into the dark. Wynn's chest heaved. She looked down at Night and hugged her. The fox, either grateful or oblivious to the danger, licked at her face. The mountain groaned around them as another gust of wind surged past.

"We need to keep moving," Wynn said at last, standing and securing Night against her chest in the sling she'd knotted from her cloak. She offered Avery a hand, and together they pressed on, climbing carefully now, each foothold checked, each breath visible in the air.

Save for the wind and their steady exhales, they climbed in silence, until the rope between them snapped tight. Wynn turned back, finding herself suddenly off balance. Avery hadn't moved. She was pressed flat against the rock on a narrow ledge, fingers white on the stone, tears freezing on her cheeks. "I can't," she said, voice raw, shaking. "Wynn, I can't. I just can't."

They didn't have time for this. Wynn could feel it; Tierney was close. *Too close.* "Avery," she snapped, her voice hard and cutting, "yes, you can. We don't have a choice."

Avery didn't respond.

Wynn tugged sharply on the rope between them. "Now move. Or I'll untie this rope and leave you here."

Avery's eyes shot to hers, full of disbelief. "You wouldn't."

Wynn's gaze was steel. "To save my land? You *know* I would."

Below, the sound of boots on rock echoed faintly upward.

"Avery," Wynn growled, her voice low and urgent, "move your ass. Now."

Something shifted in Avery's eyes. Not calm. Not courage. Just *resolve*. She took a breath, and reached for the next handhold.

They climbed in frantic silence, fingers bleeding, hearts thundering. The hawk screeched again somewhere above.

Wynn spotted the ledge first. And there, just beyond it, a gaping mouth in the rock wall.

She recognized it instantly. *Illen had been right*. She hauled herself up then turned back, grabbing Avery's arm and pulling her over the lip. They both collapsed at the mouth of the cave.

Night scrambled out from Wynn's makeshift pouch and shook herself off.

Avery looked over, pale and shaking. "You wouldn't have left. Not really."

Wynn met her eyes. "No," she said softly. "Never."

"What are we going to do without that ring?" Avery asked.

Wynn grabbed for her neck. There was a long scratch where the hawk's talons scraped over her skin. "I don't know. But, we have you, and if Illen was right, you should be able to enter."

They heard a grunt and a hand slapped against the rock. Fingers clawed at the ledge. Wynn and Avery scrambled to their feet just as Tierney hauled himself up, gasping. His cloak flapped behind him, hair wild with sweat and wind; he looked more hawk than human, his eyes sharp and burning.

But Wynn was already moving. Her bow was in her hand, arrow notched and drawn, her stance set. "Take one more step," she warned, "and I'll put this through your chest."

Tierney froze, chest heaving. "Wynn—"

"I mean it."

He stared at her, then slowly reached for his sword. "I don't think you would," he said, voice low.

"You're right. I wouldn't put it in your chest," she lowered her aim and let the arrow fly. It struck his thigh with a thud of finality. He cried out, staggering back, his foot slipping on the frost-slick rock. Tierney dropped his sword and tumbled from view, his body disappearing over the edge. The hawk shrieked and dove from above.

"No!" Wynn cried, reaching out instinctively, she only meant to wound him. She raced to the ledge and looked down. About ten meters below, his body had landed on a narrow outcrop.

She held her breath, then saw him stir.

Avery had crept forward, eyes wide. "Is he..."

"He'll live," Wynn said, already turning back to the entrance in the mountain. "Let's go."

Below, Tierney groaned and rolled onto his side, his breath hissing through clenched teeth. The arrow in his thigh was lodged deep. Gritting his jaw, he grabbed hold of it and yanked it out with a guttural cry, flinging it over the edge. Blood seeped out and he tore his sleeve off, tying it tightly around the wound. Panting, he glanced at the ledge above. Empty now. She was gone.

A flapping sound drew his attention. The hawk landed near him, clicking its talons against the stone. In its grasp: the leather cord and ring that had once hung from Wynn's neck. The hawk dropped it beside him. Tierney stared at it for a beat. Then he picked it up, turning the ring over in his hand. "Good girl," he muttered, slipping it into his pocket. He propped himself up with a grunt. This wasn't over. Not yet.

The hawk took off again, wings slicing through the air as it dove down the mountain, past icy crags and outcroppings, soaring over a gathering of knights just arriving at the base. It flew onward, over trees, rivers, the outskirts of villages, until the looming walls of the castle came into view. The hawk swooped past stone turrets and battlements, curling around to pass by the open windows of the throne room. Inside, Grace stood in front of her mother.

Her dress for the union was torn. Her hair had come loose, falling in a tangle around her shoulders. Her arms were crossed as Queen Prima's voice cut through the cold air like a blade.

"You think me an imbecile?" Prima said, her voice low and venomous. "You expect me to believe someone crept into this castle, knocked out The Hawk, unlocked the prison doors, freed the prisoners, and then you, my daughter, just happened to find them and heroically failed to stop their escape?"

Grace tilted her head. "I think you stopped caring about the truth a long time ago."

Prima's eyes narrowed. "I stopped believing in excuses a long time ago." Before Prima could continue, a knight rushed into the room and dropped to one knee. Grace recognized him from the forest camp.

"Your Majesty," Sorn said, bowing low, sweat shining on his brow. "We did as you commanded. We quelled the uprisings in many outlying villages." He hesitated. "But when we marched on Wickmere... we were too late. The Tarn... they were waiting for us. They were organized." His jaw tensed. "We were outnumbered. My knights fell back to the bridge to hold the line, but they didn't stop. The Tarn kept coming." He looked up, as if still unable to believe it. "They've taken the bridge, Your Majesty. They're crossing into the Tor."

Prima rose from the throne slowly, her expression like an oncoming storm. "What are you waiting for? Take an army to the bridge. Stop them! Order the arrest of every Tarn servant in our cities, kill them if they resist."

"Yes, my Queen."

"And Sorn," she stopped him as he turned to rush out, "do not fail me." Then she turned to Grace. "And you. You'll unite with The Hawk the moment he returns."

"Can't wait," Grace quipped.

"But until then," Prima said sharply, gesturing to the guards, "take her to the cells. She could use a timeout."

The guards stepped forward. Grace rolled her eyes.

"Ugh. The prisons are cold," she whined, "and they smell." The guards grabbed her by the arms. Grace didn't resist.

They dragged her down the narrow stone stairwell and through the winding corridors beneath the castle. The torches flickered as they passed, their light casting shadows that danced across the walls. When they reached the cell, the guards forcefully shoved her inside. She stumbled forward and turned around with an overly dramatic sigh as the door clanged shut.

"Ouch. Careful," she said. "That's my royal elbow."

They ignored her.

When their footsteps had faded, Grace let the silence sit for a moment. Then she reached down into the bodice of her dress and pulled out a small iron key. With a grin, she twirled it once between her fingers. "Imbecile? No," she whispered. "Gullible? Yes."

As soon as Wynn and Avery stepped into the passage, the wind vanished. The air was still, ancient, and close. Darkness wrapped around them. Absolute. Not the kind you get used to after a moment, not moonless or overcast, but *total*.

"I can't see anything," Avery whispered, close to panic.

"Me either," Wynn replied, heart thudding a little faster now. She hadn't thought this far ahead. She had no lantern, no matches, just a stomach full of cold nerves and a rope still tied around her waist. That's when Night growled. Wynn knew her growls well. This was not a growl of fear or protection, this was the growl she used when she wanted attention. Wynn felt the tug at her cloak, then a steady pull.

"She's trying to lead us." She crouched, fingers fumbling for the fur at Night's neck. With careful hands, she untied the rope from her own waist and looped it gently around the fox's shoulders like a harness. "Can you lead the way?" she murmured. A warm tongue licked her cheek. Wynn straightened. One hand on the rope like a leash, the other reaching back to find Avery's fingers. "Stay with me," Wynn said.

Together, they moved forward with slow, hesitant steps. Water dripped steadily from somewhere above, each drop echoing like a distant drumbeat. The walls, Wynn could feel, were smooth in places, jagged in others. The tunnel felt long, but they couldn't see more than the black pressing in from all sides. The rope tugged gently with Night's movements, guiding them left, then right, winding deeper into the dark.

After what felt like ten minutes, but could've been five or fifty, Wynn noticed the echoes shift and the air open up as they stepped into a much larger space.

"We're in a cavern," Wynn murmured, awed. "I think... a big one." It was cooler. The silence, wider. "How are we supposed to do this if we can't see—" But the sentence died in her throat. Just then, with a low *fwoosh*, a torch along the far wall burst into flame.

Then another.

Then another.

One by one, in slow succession, the stone walls began to glow, revealing themselves in flickering amber light. Shadows danced across the carved stone as torch after torch lit of its own accord, like some invisible hand was walking ahead of them.

The cavern was massive, almost perfectly circular, its ceiling lost in shadow. Carvings lined the walls, swirls and sigils, stars and eyes and curling threads of fate chiseled into the rock. At the far end, three empty thrones cut from the stone itself, impossibly tall, as if the mountain had grown them.

"What is this place?" Avery breathed.

Wynn didn't answer right away. Her heart beat differently now, deeper, like something old inside her had awakened. She stared at the thrones, felt the hush of the air change. "It's where the Fates come," she whispered.

"I thought you didn't believe in the Fates?" Avery said with awe.

"I don't."

Avery stepped carefully across the floor, eyes wide as she stared at the cavern around them, the flickering torchlight, the three carved thrones, and the impossible hush that had settled like a held breath. "Where are they?"

Wynn approached the thrones, scanning them with reverence and curiosity. "Illen told us they only come here on the Day of the Fates. One day, once a year." She moved past the center throne and crouched beside the one on the left, fingers brushing the stone, searching. "They also said..." she trailed off, then stopped. "Here."

Behind the left throne, nearly invisible, was a narrow crack in the wall, barely wide enough for a person to slip through. "Come on," Wynn said. "We keep going."

She pulled a torch from its sconce and used it to light their path, the flame wavering but strong. The space beyond the crack swallowed them in darkness. The walls pressed close on either side, their footsteps echoed faintly as they moved deeper into the mountain's belly.

Night trotted ahead. Then suddenly, she stopped, ears up, body rigid, and let out a low, guttural growl.

Wynn froze. "What is it?" She turned, listening. Nothing. Just silence. Night growled again, a warning sound that prickled Wynn's spine. "Night, stop it," Wynn said, voice hushed but firm. "You're scaring us. Let's go."

The tunnel narrowed again. Avery moved closer behind Wynn, close enough that their shoulders brushed. Then, the passage ended abruptly, a flat stone wall in front of them. Wynn raised the torch and stepped closer. At first, it looked like just another stretch of stone, rough, unremarkable. But as the torchlight flickered across its surface, something emerged.

Not a door. A shape. Subtle, almost invisible unless you were looking for it. The outline of a book. Tall, rectangular, carved so finely into the wall it might have been mistaken for a natural groove. But it wasn't. Wynn could see the delicate indentations of pages, the curve of a spine etched in the rock. She reached out and traced it with her fingers. No handle. No hinge. No mechanism. Just the shape of a book, ancient and waiting.

Night stood guard behind them, facing the darkness and on high alert.

Wynn looked to Avery and stepped aside. "You're on."

Avery hesitated, then reached out and pressed her palm flat to the stone. The rock gave a low, shuddering sigh, like the exhale of something old and long asleep. Then, a thin seam split down the right side, and slowly, the stone began to part, not like a door, but like the turning of a page. A soft pink mist spilled through the crack.

Avery pulled her hand away, breath catching in her throat, as the stone continued to open, revealing not a room, but a wall of cloud. It curled and rippled, glowing gently.

Wynn stared at it, "You ready?"

Avery's eyes were wide, but her voice steady. "I've been here before," she whispered. Then she looked at Wynn. "Are you?"

Before either could answer, Night darted forward, and her tail vanished into the haze, leaving behind a swirl of mist.

Wynn didn't hesitate. She grabbed Avery's hand. "Let's go." They stepped into the unknown.

~ ~ ~

So they've stepped into it now; the space between the stories, the place where beginnings begin. We won't follow them just yet. For now, let the door stay cracked, the air humming with a kind of quiet magic. And you? When you close your eyes tonight, picture what might wait in that place. Towering shelves of forgotten tales? Rivers made of ink? Shadows that whisper and creatures of all shapes and sizes? It's your dream, after all. Let it be strange. Let it be beautiful. Let it be yours. Sleep well.

CHAPTER THIRTY

There was no need for torchlight now. They were surrounded by a strange, soft pink glow that seemed to hum from within the fog itself, alive, somehow, and listening. It reminded Wynn of the veil of fog in the southern lands, a different color but it felt like it came from the same place. Wynn took one cautious step, then another, and the ground gave just enough to feel like earth but not enough to be sure. It felt, Wynn thought, like walking on kneaded bread dough. Night pressed close to her leg. Avery stood just ahead, head tilted like she was hearing something Wynn could not.

The air pulsed with possibility, with chaos, with untold beginnings and unraveled endings. *Grace would love it here*, Wynn thought. She opened her mouth to speak, but the mist shifted, interrupting her.

Somewhere to the left, a battle screamed into being, swords clashing, horses rearing, voices howling in languages no one had spoken in a thousand years. A second later, it vanished, leaving nothing behind. Shapes loomed in the distance. Some looked like mountains. Others... didn't. Then came laughter, joyful, cruel, full of heartbreak, and it, too, dissolved. Emotions drifted over them. Fury brushed her cheek and was gone. Love curled around her wrist. Revenge wrapped itself like a scarf across her shoulders. She staggered slightly as she felt it all.

"Do you feel that?" Wynn asked.

Avery nodded. "It tingles."

"I feel like I could touch something," Wynn murmured, stretching out a hand into the fog, but there was nothing to grasp. Just mist and the echo of stories not meant for her. Beside her, Night growled low and looked up at Wynn. She didn't like it here.

"Avery?" Wynn asked, watching her stare off into the distance.

Avery turned slowly. Her eyes glittered. "I remember," she said. "Everything. Where I came from. What happened. I see all of it now."

Wynn's pulse jumped. "See what?"

"How it all ended. We knew our land was being attacked by something we couldn't see, and my father felt it was an ancient magic. Others felt our gods had turned on us. Places started to crumble, people started to just fade away... my mother was one of them. We tried to outrun it. Fled on ships into the sea. But there was no outrunning it. It consumed everything." She paused, thinking. "I think I know where to go." Avery turned and began walking with quick, certain steps. The mist parted before her. Wynn glanced at Night and followed, hurrying to keep pace.

They passed through landscapes that never fully formed: a tower built from sand, a staircase spiraling up to nowhere, fields of black flowers that turned to ink as they stepped past. Voices whispered and music played from far in the distance.

And then, through the haze, a shape appeared. They slowed. A tree stood half-formed in the mist, its trunk thick and ancient before them, its roots twisting beneath them into the fog. The base of it split into a cradle of wood, and nestled within that, glowing faintly, was a book. Wynn held her breath.

They approached with reverence.

The cover was worn smooth by time and mist, but the title was still legible, etched in silver script that shimmered as they drew close: *The Book That Controls Your Emotions.*

Wynn felt a chill. Illen had spoken of these *Originals*, books older than stories themselves. Primal, unfinished things. Not made to be read. Made to be borrowed from. Used.

Avery reached out first, her fingers brushing the spine. The book shivered beneath her touch. Then the pages opened, fluttering softly, like wings recalling flight. Inside, words moved as if alive.

On one page, "Love", written in curving letters that bled warmth into the air. On another, "Anger", scorched into the parchment in sharp, black lines. Then "Grief", long and water-stained, as though someone had wept directly into the page. Each emotion connected to a spell. Not to be understood, but wielded.

Wynn flipped through a few, her breath catching. It was beautiful. And dangerous. And wrong. "Not it," she whispered, stepping back.

Avery didn't respond. Her eyes were far away again, her head tilted like she was catching the faintest echo of something calling her name. Night suddenly growled low and deep. Her hackles bristled and her body turned toward the unseen, ears pinned back. Wynn followed her gaze into the fog, but saw only the pale swirl of mist. Then she heard it, a second growl. Not Night's. Something else was in The Margins with them.

Wynn grabbed Avery's arm. "Let's move. Now."

The book snapped shut behind them.

They pressed deeper into the mist. Whispers brushed past them in forgotten languages. A sob drifted by, followed by a muffled scream. Later, some laughter and celebratory cheers.

Then, another book.

It stood upright in the distance, poised like an altar at the end of a clearing. But before they could reach it, something moved. Something *large*.

A shape glided between the book and them. It was scaled and immense, with wings that shimmered in and out of visibility; almost reptilian, but not a creature Wynn had ever seen or even imagined. Its skin was a patchwork of silver and green with ancient, knowing eyes. It didn't walk. It *flowed*.

Night growled and planted herself firmly between Wynn and the beast, fur on end. Wynn drew an arrow with shaking fingers and raised her bow. Then Avery stepped forward. "No," she said quietly. "Let me."

Wynn hissed, "Are you out of your mind?"

But Avery didn't respond. Her arms rose slightly, her palms open. The beast turned to her, lowering its head, curious. Almost... respectful. She said nothing. She didn't need to. There was something in her expression that the creature seemed to recognize. It blinked slowly, turned its massive head, and with one sweeping glide, disappeared back into the mist like it had never been there at all.

Wynn stared, bow still raised. "How did you do that?"

Avery didn't look at her. "Like I said," she murmured. "I've been here before." What she didn't say, what she couldn't quite bring herself to admit, was that it felt like she was meant to be here. She was whole here.

They moved on, hearts pounding. The mist parted once more.

Another book stood ahead.

This one sat alone on a jagged pedestal of black stone, dripping with condensation like sweat. The letters were carved deep and red: *The Book That Will End You.*

Wynn didn't even slow her step. "Nope. Definitely not that one." Something about that book felt all wrong. Its very existence felt wrong. They veered wide, not looking back, wandering into a different area, where it seemed as if they were enclosed by a long hall of ghostly book shelves. They could hear the faint scratching of a quill on paper and on a table at the end, another book sat open on a simple wooden desk.

Embossed into the spine in deliberate letters: *The Book That Will Allow You to Rewrite Things.* Wynn knew she shouldn't, this book wasn't what she was looking for, but curiosity called to her, inviting her to open it.

The pages inside were startlingly blank at first. Then ink bled upward from the page, forming words in slow, careful loops. Each spell had a title, some sharp with urgency, others nearly seductive in their invitation. But one stopped her cold: *The Spell That Will Turn Back Time.* The spell itself was simple and short.

"What?" Avery asked. "What do you see?"

"You can't see it?" She kept her eyes on the page.

"See what? There's nothing there."

Wynn stared at the spell, heart pounding at the possibilities. She could go back. Stop Prima. Save Avery. Save her brother... even her parents. Undo all of it. But, what else would it undo? Everything she'd done to get here? What would happen to The Tarn if she changed even one moment? The book was offering this spell to her, daring her to take it.

She hovered her hand over the page and gently closed the book. "I don't think that's the right one," she said, barely above a whisper.

Then—

A sound in the mist.

A shape moving.

"Wynn..." A familiar voice called her name. She knew his voice, but it sounded different.

Night growled low, muscles taut.

From the fog limped a figure, dragging one leg, a line of blood slipping down his thigh before dripping and vanishing into the mist below. His tunic was torn, his brow streaked with dirt and sweat. But his eyes...

Wynn raised her bow, trembling.

He stopped. Lifted both hands. "No," he said. "Wynn, it's me. Fully me."

She didn't lower the bow. Not yet.

"The lake in front of the castle. That night after the summer storm we were all out in the boat together. Father laughed so hard he dropped the lantern in. You were afraid the fish would catch fire so I jumped in to fetch it."

Wynn pulled the string taught. "What was he laughing at?"

"What?"

"Father. What was he laughing at?"

He smiled, lowering his hands. "You. You were talking about how much the thunder scared you when a bug flew into your mouth. You were so grossed out, but he and Mother couldn't stop laughing. And you got so mad at them."

Her bow dropped. Her mouth parted, but no sound came out. She blinked hard, breath catching. "Turkey?" she whispered. The obsidian ring was around his finger.

"It's me," he nodded, voice thick. "When I came in here, it all came back. Everything I forgot. You. What she did to our family, to me. What I did to others for her. I remember it all."

Wynn looked down, brushing a tear from her cheek.

"I'm sorry," he said, stepping closer. "So sorry, Wynn."

Night stepped forward, cautious, low to the ground. He leaned down and she sniffed his outstretched hand, tail flicking once. Then, tentatively she sniffed his face and licked him on the cheek. Tierney smiled, "She's a pretty good f—"

Wynn fell into his arms and held him as tight as she could. He hugged her right back. She dug her face into his shoulder and sobbed. "I thought I had lost you forever. Then, you came back, but I lost you all over again." She didn't want to let him go.

He pulled her back and looked her over. "I can't believe how much you've grown. I bet you could swim that lake in no time now."

"I hate to interrupt," Avery said softly.

"No," Wynn agreed, pulling back, wiping her face. "We have to keep going. I know."

"What is this place?" Tierney asked, glancing into the mist that stretched forever in every direction.

Avery answered, her voice held more confidence now than Wynn had ever heard it hold before. "The place between stories."

"And what are you looking for?"

"A book," Wynn said. "*The Book That Will Put You to Sleep*. It holds a spell that can undo what Prima has done."

Tierney paused. "I saw it." He pointed, then started limping forward. "This way."

"This way?" Wynn raised a brow. "How do you know any way in this place?"

Tierney shrugged, "I don't know."

She followed.

They came upon it slowly. A pedestal rose from the earth, draped in velvet moss, half-grown from the roots of an ancient, sleeping tree. Upon it sat a deep-violet book. The letters on the cover shimmered in soft, powdery gold: *The Book That Will Put You to Sleep*

Wynn stepped forward. She reached out and ran her fingers over the title. The book felt warm. Tierney, *her brother*, stood beside her. "Do you know what you're looking for?"

Wynn nodded. She opened the book.

The pages turned with purpose, guiding her to the middle. It knew what she was there for. Words appeared on the page, *The Undoing Spell.*

The ink pulsed faintly, old, sentient. A spell that could unravel other spells, stitch by stitch. Wynn could feel the force of it already, like a weight pressing on her chest. She stared at its letters breathing gently on the page. She mouthed the words aloud, her voice barely above a breath. As she spoke them, the letters began to fade, dissolving stroke by stroke as though erased by her voice.

The book stirred again beneath her hands. The parchment glowed faintly as new words formed: "What will you leave in return?" She froze. In her haste she had forgotten what Illen had said.

Avery stepped beside her. "What is it?"

Wynn swallowed hard. "It wants something. Illen warned me... The Margins don't give freely. They take something in return. Something that matters."

Avery glanced down at the page. "What does it want?"

"I don't know," Wynn said, voice cracking. "I don't know what to give—"

But even as she spoke, Tierney stepped forward. He didn't speak right away. Just looked at her, then at the book, then back again.

Wynn turned to him, dread blooming behind her ribs. "No."

Tierney gave a quiet breath, something between a sigh and a smile. "It's me," he said gently. "I can feel it."

"No," she whispered, backing away. "No, I just got you back. Don't you dare—"

He reached out, his hand settling over hers with aching softness. "Wynn. Listen. When I stepped into The Margins... I became myself again. Whatever the Fates did to twist me, it came undone here. But if I go back out there, into The Vast..." He paused, jaw tightening. "...I know I'll be him again. The Hawk. I won't remember you. I won't remember any of this."

Her breath caught.

"This is the only way I can stay *me*," he said. "It's the only way I can help you now. I can't return, not as that monster, not as a weapon. I can't walk among our people knowing I helped put them in chains. But I *can* give you this. I can give you what you need to finish it."

Wynn shook her head, tears gathering. "But I need *you*."

"I'm right here," he said softly. "And I'll be here. Even after you leave."

Wynn blinked hard, fighting tears, fighting everything.

"You're the one who can lead them now," Tierney said. "Not me."

Her fingers trembled in his. "I don't want to lead. Not without you."

He didn't argue. He only reached down and pulled the ring off his finger, pressing it into her palm. "You'll need this to get out of here," he said softly. "I think I was just keeping it safe for you."

The air around them shifted. The mist grew dense, swirling in slow, soundless spirals. The edges of his cloak began to lift as if drawn by invisible threads. Tierney leaned forward, pressing his forehead to hers. "Mom and Dad would be proud of you," he whispered.

"They'd be proud of you too," she sniffed.

And then—

He was gone.

She stood motionless, her hand clenched around the ring, the mist still pulsing where he had stood. Then the book moved again. The pages turned themselves, slow and deliberate, until they abruptly stopped at another spell: *The Last Sleep.*

She hadn't asked for this spell. She wasn't even sure what it did. But the book had chosen. And something deep inside her knew, this was the one that mattered most. It was calling to her. Not in words, but in the way a storm decides where to strike. She didn't have to say the words before they disappeared and in their place, "What will you leave in return?"

"I don't know," Wynn whispered, her voice breaking. "I don't have anything left."

She meant it. Tierney was gone. Her heart felt hollow. There was nothing more to give—

She felt something paw at her leg and she couldn't bring herself to turn around.

Night moved and sat in front of her. Silent. Still. Only... her fur. It was wrong. Already fading at the edges, like smoke thinning in the wind. "No," Wynn called out. Her voice cracked.

"No, no—"

Night stepped forward, nuzzling into her shin. Wynn knelt, reaching out, trying to hold her. Her wet nose, her soft fur, her touch was barely there now. "I didn't choose this," she said to the book, to the air, to whatever power was listening. "I didn't choose *any of this.*" But she understood. Somewhere inside, she understood. The book had chosen for her, already deciding that this spell belonged to her. And it had already named the cost.

Night met her eyes. Steady. Brave. Fierce to the end. There was no fear in her. Only love. She gave one soft huff of breath, and lifted her chin to lick her one more time. And then, she began to disappear.

Her tail.

Her paws.

Her ears.

Her bright, clever eyes.

Gone.

Wynn collapsed forward, reaching for something that wasn't there.

Avery knelt beside her, one hand on her back. "I'm so sorry."

But Wynn didn't answer. She just stared at the place Night had been. They stayed there a long time, the book closed now, silent once more. Eventually, the mists began to thin. The whispers quieted. It was as if The Margins, satisfied with their offering, were gently showing them the way out. Wynn didn't feel triumphant. She felt hollow.

Tierney was gone.

Night was gone.

She had nothing.

A sullen moment went by before Avery gently nudged her. "Wynn... we need to go. You should not stay here too long. Come on." Reluctantly, Wynn stood.

Avery led the way, with Wynn allowing herself to be pulled along. They walked in silence until they saw a blank space. An opening that hummed with something familiar. The Vast waited beyond.

Wynn reached for the ring and slid it onto her finger. Her hand trembled. But Avery didn't move.

Wynn turned. "A?"

Avery stood still, eyes on the space between stories. The mist snaked around her ankles, recognizing her. "I'm not coming," she said quietly.

"What?" Wynn's voice cracked.

"I can't. I mean... I could. But I shouldn't."

Wynn took a step forward, wrecked and exhausted. "Avery, I can't do this alone."

"You're not alone. You never were," Avery said gently. "But this part? This next part? It isn't mine." She glanced around them, like she could see the shape of something Wynn couldn't. "My story's here. Somewhere in The Margins. It always has been. I just didn't know how to look for it until now."

Wynn's throat tightened. "I want you with me."

Avery smiled, her eyes damp. "I know. But I've spent my life being someone else's sidekick. Background. I think it's time I found out who I am when I'm not helping anyone else."

Wynn tried to speak. She wanted to convince her to come with her. Not to stay, but she knew that wasn't fair. Avery never truly belonged in The Vast and she needed to let her go. She pulled her in and held tight. "I'm going to miss you."

Avery hugged her back. "Who knows? Maybe our stories will cross again."

But Wynn knew they wouldn't. This was goodbye.

Avery smiled warmly as she stepped back, into the mist, into the in-between and The Margins took her gently, welcoming her back.

Wynn stood a second longer, then turned toward the opening and crossed the threshold alone.

Wynn didn't have time to mourn or make sense of what she'd lost. The moment she stepped back into The Vast, the air was sharp with shouting, smoke and steel on steel. The grounds around the Tor Castle were alive with movement, banners flying, boots pounding, voices barking orders. Wynn could see that a full-blown battle was in motion. She blinked against the sudden sunlight, disoriented. She had expected to emerge back in the caves, among cold stone and dark shadows. But instead, she was here, thrown into the noise and fire without warning.

She stumbled forward, dazed, drawn by instinct more than direction. Her limbs felt heavy, her mind still echoing with the silence of The Margins. Then she saw the Tarn camp, no longer scattered rebels, but a real force. Organized. Focused. And in the heart of it, giving rapid orders over a drawn map, stood Grace.

Wynn barely had time to register the sight before Grace turned, caught sight of her, and froze. "Wynn?" she gasped.

Wynn didn't speak. She didn't need to. Grace ran to her, wrapped her up in her arms, and kissed her, without hesitation, without question.

Kiernan, nearby in full armor, looked from one to the other. His ears turned red. "Would you two like a moment?" he asked dryly. "Or should I just go fight a few Tor knights for a while?"

Grace didn't let go. "What happened? Where were you? You've been gone a month, Wynn. A month! We thought—"

"A month?" Wynn blinked. "No. That's not possible. It felt like... hours." But then she noticed the snow covering the ground and the winter chill in the air.

Time, dear reader, is a strange and unruly thing. To Wynn, only hours had passed in The Margins. A breath or a blink. But in The Vast, a month had come and gone, dragging behind it the weight of war. Entire lives had unfurled while she was away. Stories written in mud and blood and bravery. Heroes were forged. Villains met their untimely end. And some, like poor General Sorn, who fell off his horse and onto his own sword, met ends so ridiculous they barely deserve a footnote. A tragic death, certainly. Though, as it happens, not as uncommon as one might think. Grace, for her part, feared she would never see Wynn again. Still, she accepted her role with flourish and held the line. She was fierce and commanding in equal measure, directing the lot like she imagined a Valkyrie might, like the ones she had read stories about. I could go on. I could tell you about the midnight skirmish near the cliffs, the broken tower that was taken and taken again... But these are stories for another time. For after the swords have been sheathed and the mead had been poured. These are stories told in memory of the fallen. The rest, the part you've been waiting for, happens now.

Grace stepped back slightly, searching her face. "Where's Avery? Where's Night? What happened to The Hawk? Did you get the spells? Are you okay?"

Wynn could still feel Grace's lips on hers. "Woah," she said softly, "slow down."

Grace did. Barely. Her hands slid down to hold Wynn's.

"What is this?" Wynn asked, looking around. "What's happening right now?"

"So much," Grace said. "Since you left, Kiernan here rounded up an army for you and marched on the Tor. I escaped the prisons, found him, and we've been fighting my Mother and her army ever since. But we ran out of sleep tokens two nights ago,

Wynn. Everyone's running on embers. We're planning our last push."

She looked around the camp, the fading torches, the hollow-eyed soldiers. "You couldn't have shown up at a better time. It's like the Fates..."

"No," Wynn said firmly. Her voice cut through the smoke, the doubt, the fear. "This isn't the Fates," she said. "We control this narrative now."

Grace's smile returned, steadier this time. "Then tell me, Princess, what's the plan?"

Wynn took a breath. "We give Prima what she wants: me."

Grace blinked at her, then took one small step back. "That's the plan?"

Kiernan was quicker. "I don't like it."

Wynn didn't flinch. She stood taller than she felt. "It will work. Because Prima won't expect it," she continued. "Because it's what she wants me to do. To walk right into her hands."

Grace was quiet, thinking. Then she nodded. "You're right."

Kiernan turned to her, incredulous. "Let her just *walk* into them? Give herself up? What have we been fighting for if—"

"K." Wynn's voice was calm, cutting.

He stopped mid-sentence.

"Trust me."

He stared at her for a long moment. Then gave a slow, reluctant nod. "Fine. But I'm coming with you."

Wynn almost smiled. Almost. "I know. You both are."

~ ~ ~

We're reaching the end now. You can feel it too, can't you? The weight of all that's happened, the cost of every step taken. Heroes rarely make it through without bruises, without something broken or left behind. That's the shape of real journeys, frayed and aching and true. So let this be the part where you breathe again. Where the book softens its voice and lets you lean into stillness and grieve the loss of those no longer a part of this story. The world will wait. The next page, too. Let the covers wrap around you like a sigh. Let your breath find its rhythm. Sleep Well.

Unless, of course... oh no, you're too close to the end, aren't you? Can't possibly stop now? Well, if you must go on, then so can I. And if you need to rest, then so can I.

CHAPTER THIRTY-ONE

The Tor Castle still stood proud. Its high black walls and towers were pocked with the scars of battle, but not broken. The banners above hung in stubborn defiance, though many were tattered, the edges scorched and curling. The gate groaned open.

Wynn was marched through, swordpoints at her back. Grace walked on her left, Kiernan on her right. The soldiers surrounding them bore the colors of Tor, armor dented, helms cracked, but grips still firmly on their blades. They walked not with triumph, but weariness. No one spoke. The courtyard lay in ruins, blackened flagstones, splintered beams, the faint smell of char still hanging in the air. Someone had tried to scrub the blood from the stone, but it had been left too long, soaked in too deep. Wynn's boots crunched over the ash and gravel. She kept walking, but her eyes moved restlessly over the piles of armor pulled from dead knights, the crumbling walls and the half-fallen archways.

This place looked like a shell. How had so much changed so quickly? The castle she'd left behind on her way to The Margins had been ominous and terrible, but at least it had been intact.

They passed beneath the great stone archway and traversed the steps. All the while, Tor knights watched them warily, ready to strike if needed. Though they did not lack sleep like the Tarn, they looked equally exhausted.

The great throne room doors swung open.

And there she was.

The Dark One, Queen Prima.

She sat upon her throne as though she had never left it. Her robes were unmarred, dark velvet with golden thread. The world outside was dying and yet she still looked carved from power itself. But Wynn saw through it. She detected the tremor in her fingers, the faint hollowness beneath her eyes, and the brittle tightness in her jaw. She was dangerous, but she was tired.

Prima rose slowly. The silence, the kind that precedes either peace or bloodshed, tightened around them.

Kiernan leaned in just enough to whisper. "I hope you're right about this," he said. "Or this story ends here."

Wynn gave a slight nod.

Prima's voice cracked across the chamber. "Well," she said, and her eyes sparked as they swept over them. "If it isn't the traitors' parade."

Her gaze locked on Grace, and narrowed.

Grace offered a peppy smile, "Mother."

She ignored her daughter and moved to Kiernan. Then, to Wynn. Her lip curled. "I hear you've finally come to kneel."

Wynn took a breath, kept her voice steady.

"This needs to end."

Prima descended one step. "If you're hoping for an epic duel and a satisfying finale where you kill me—" she gestured airily "—I'm afraid that's not how it is going to go."

Nearly twenty knights emerged from the shadows behind the throne, flanking her in silent rows.

Grace stiffened. Kiernan's hand moved subtly toward his blade.

"I know," Wynn said.

"Where is The Hawk?" Prima inquired, looking behind them.

"My brother," Wynn lifted her chin defiantly, "is gone."

Prima's lips clenched tight. "Too bad. He was... useful. And my ring?"

"I have it." Wynn stepped forward. And slowly, she dropped to her knees. "This has to end," she said, lifting her eyes. Her voice cracked, just a little. "Because I'm so bloody tired."

Prima could not have looked more pleased with herself. "I am glad you have come to your—"

Wynn didn't wait for her to finish.

"You bound The Vast in sleepless chains.
But now sleep obeys no master's reins.
The spell you wove, I now unmake.
The Vast will sleep for its own sake."

She stood up.

Prima stared at her, mouth slightly open.

Nothing happened. The throne room was still. The stone walls held their breath. The knights stood frozen. No sound but the distant crackle of a dying fire and the thump of Wynn's heart in her ears.

Prima tilted her head, a slow, incredulous smile beginning to creep across her face. "Well," she said. "That was certainly dramatic."

Wynn's throat tightened. Her chest ached. The words she'd spoken—so sure, so carefully remembered—now hung in the air. Was it too late? Had she gotten it wrong? *Had she just lost everything?* She tried to breathe, but the silence pressed in.

And then... something shifted.

Not a thunderclap. Not a blaze of light. Just... a soft breeze; the kind that might pass through the tops of rustling trees.

One of the knights standing near Prima blinked, slowly. His sword dipped. He frowned, confused, and for a moment looked as if he might drop where he stood. His shoulders sagged under the sudden release of a weight he hadn't known he was carrying.

Another knight beside him let out a sharp breath. A weapon clattered to the floor.

Kiernan inhaled sharply. "I feel it," he said, his voice low. "I feel like I can sleep."

Wynn's throat tightened. "Me too," she whispered, holding back tears. "Me too."

"No," Prima snarled. She took a sharp step forward. Her voice rose. "No! That's not possible. That's not—"

She turned to her soldiers. "Kill them. Kill them all!"

Many of the knights seemed dazed. Some raised their blades toward the trio, but several others turned towards Prima.

Wynn rose to her feet, her voice soft but piercing. "Don't you see, Dark One? Most of your army is Tarn. Loyal only for the sleep you held over them and their families. And now?" She looked at the knights. "Now, your hold is gone."

The knights looked at one another in a stand off, Tor and Tarn alike. Some uncertain, some stunned. The room teetered on a literal knife's edge.

And Grace, Grace did not hesitate.

She stepped forward, lifting her chin, her voice echoing loudly. "Dark Knights," she said, "as Princess of the Tor, I command you to secure Queen Prima and take her to the cells below."

Prima turned, livid. "You don't have that right—!"

But Grace lifted her voice again, louder now. "Do you want this to go on?" she asked, addressing them all. "How much more do you think we can lose? How long do you think The Vast can exist like this? Sleep must be a right, not a privilege to be held by some and abused by others." Her voice cracked, just barely. But she didn't falter. "Aren't you all tired of the darkness?"

It was a strange moment. A shifting weight. A few knights lowered their swords. A few more nodded.

Grace drew a long but steady breath. "I'm ready for something else," she said. "And I think you are too."

An older knight stepped forward. His breastplate bore the mark of Prima's private guard. He looked at Prima then turned, and knelt before Grace. Others followed, some slowly, some all at once. The clatter of swords hitting the floor was a sound Wynn would never forget.

Two knights approached Prima. "I will not stand for this!" she shrieked, struggling as they seized her arms. "You fools! Cowards! Traitors!" But none came to her aid. "Grace?" Prima called out, her tune changed subtly to that of a caring mother. "Grace, you can't do this. You're my daughter. I would have given this all to you."

"You never planned to give me anything, Mother. You just didn't expect I'd take it without asking." Grace gave a soft smile. "What is it you said to me when I was little and you sent me away crying? Oh, yes. *Don't grovel, it's beneath you.*" She nodded to the knights. "Take her."

Prima's protests echoed down the long corridor as the guards dragged her from the room. Her voice was sharp and furious, but growing smaller with every step. Soon, only silence remained.

Grace returned to Wynn's side, breathless. "Was it too much?"

Wynn looked at her, heart thudding. "That was... you were great."

Grace smiled. "I've been practicing that speech my whole life."

They turned back towards the room. The knights of The Tor had their heads bowed before Grace. The Tarn bowed to Wynn. Two princesses, soon to be Queens. The Vast had shifted.

"So. What now?" Grace leaned over to Wynn.

Wynn let out a breath she hadn't realized she was holding. "First, I could use some sleep. I think we all could. Then, I don't know," she said. "I've been making this up as I go."

Grace stepped a little closer. "Then... let's keep making it up?" she said. "Together?"

Wynn nodded, heart full. "I'd like that."

From behind them, Kiernan's voice rang out, dry and tired. "For stars' sake, just kiss already."

So, they did.

There in the throne room, before bent knees and bloody sleepless knights, they kissed. Not because the story was over. But because it wasn't.

When Wynn finally pulled back, she felt herself feeling dizzy yet grounded. "So," she asked, nodding toward the darkened hall where Prima had vanished, "what should we do with your mother?"

Grace gave a little shrug. "Hmm. She might still have the power to enter our dreams. So... kill her? Put her head on a spike outside? After all, it is my castle to decorate now."

Wynn blinked. "You're a little unhinged."

"I know," Grace said, beaming. "But you like it."

And Wynn did. She really, kinda did.

Ah. You were expecting something else, weren't you? A big bang. A final blow. A scream to split the sky. Perhaps even the crumbling of stone and a noble declaration shouted over the ruins. But no. This ending didn't blaze. It *smoldered*. Quietly. A single candle burning low, then guttering out with a soft little *piff* of smoke. A yawn, really. Prima had prepared for a conclusion of epic proportion. She was waiting for swordplay, for a battle and finale worthy of who she thought she was. She didn't see it coming, because Wynn didn't give her the ending she wanted. No fire. No glory. Just a few quiet words. How did you expect my story to end? After all, I am *The Book That Will Put You to Sleep.* Funny, isn't it? With all her efforts to silence stories, it was *words* that undid her. Perhaps she was right to fear the power of books. And now we find ourselves at that familiar refrain again. Princess kissing princess... *They all lived happily ever after*. The End.

Unless, of course... you're still awake.

EPILOGUE

It was fall again. The air tasted like apples and firewood, the trees looked like they'd set the world ablaze in gold and rust and amber. Wind rustled gently tossing the leaves below, carrying the sweet hush of harvest and hearths.

Wynn stood on a mountain ledge, a turquoise-blue cloak gathered around her shoulders. It was soft-lined and heavy, royal in a way she would never fully get used to. A hawk traced a lazy circle high above the forest, its cry distant and bright. Wynn tilted her head to watch it. The ache in her heart had never really left, but it no longer hollowed her out. He had given himself freely. Just as Night had. And Avery... Avery had chosen to stay in The Margins, to find her own story. Somehow, understanding it made it harder to accept.

Wynn looked out over The Vast. It was a softer kingdom now. Since the day Prima had been defeated and The Tor and The Tarn had stood united, something in the land itself had begun to shift. The gray, rocky ridges of the Tor, once stripped bare by bitterness and years of neglect, had slowly begun to green. It was subtle, but steady, like the land was learning to breathe differently. The Tarn ruins still stood where they had always stood, nestled into the valley floor like a sleeping giant; moss still claiming the stone, and ivy curling high around broken towers. Wynn had insisted they remain as they were, a legacy to her parents, and Lorkan, and to what had once been. People, other than her, came to visit now. To remember.

She turned her gaze to the horizon, where the towers of the Tor castle rose above the autumn canopy. Once a place of shadows and fear, it now gleamed with painted shutters, its balconies trailing flowers in pinks and oranges and bold violet-blue. Bright silks draped from the battlements. Paper lanterns floated in the courtyards at night. There were more plush cushions than swords these days. This was all Grace's doing, of course. It wasn't Wynn's style, but in this one respect, she had let Grace have whatever she wanted. Grace deserved color. She deserved to make things beautiful. And she had spent the majority of her time turning the old throne room into a library. This had been a decor change they both agreed on.

It didn't take much to fill it. Despite Prima's campaign to burn every book and ban the written word, the people of both The Tor and Tarn had gone to great lengths to hide what mattered. Stories had survived beneath floorboards, behind loose stones, in secret compartments and under mattresses. When the call went out to "bring your books, your stories, your scraps of poems and forgotten pages," they came in droves. Grace welcomed every one, no questions asked. The once-imposing hall, built for fear and dominance, now overflowed with bookshelves and reading nooks, lanterns and ladders, sunlight and the rustle of turned pages. A free library, open to all in The Vast. Grace knew her mother would have loathed it. That, she admitted with a mischievous smile, was part of the reason she'd done it.

As for Prima, the Dark One herself, what to do with her had been a subject of long and uneasy debate. Grace had meant it when she said she wanted to kill her and put her head on a spike, and more than a few in the newly appointed royal council had agreed. There was talk of exile, of casting her into The Margins, but that only meant she'd become someone else's problem. There was the option of letting her rot in the cells, but even that felt like a gamble; shadows like hers had a way of creeping back through the cracks.

After much debate, it was Grace who made the case that in story after story, evil left unfinished only ever rises again. And being that Prima was Grace's mother, Wynn had decided, quietly and painfully, not to intervene. The only thing that Wynn had insisted on was that there would be no spiked head on the castle wall. Kill her, sure, do what needed to be done, but she had said they could not build a better world by putting heads on spikes. Grace, after some thought, reluctantly agreed. It didn't fit the esthetic vibe she was going for anyway. And so it was that Prima met her end and left this story, officially... I assure you.

Before turning, Wynn took a final breath of crisp autumn air and listened to the quiet hum of a kingdom at peace.

The cave was dark and familiar. But this time, she held a torch, and her steps didn't falter.

This time, she wasn't seeking. She was returning. Her boots echoed softly as she walked deeper, the granite walls closing in cool and close around her.

And at the end of the cavern, they waited. Three ancient shapes, silent as stone, cloaked in shadow. Their veils did not lift, but Wynn felt their attention settle on her, sharp as needle-tips. Their hands, forever weaving, forever unraveling, had stilled. Wynn had spent the better part of a year preparing for this; gathering her courage, untangling her thoughts, remembering all the right words. Grace had asked if she could come, offered more than once to stand beside her, but Wynn had gently refused each time. This was something she needed to do alone. Some burdens, even now, were hers alone to carry.

They smiled, as if they'd been expecting her all along. Or perhaps it only felt like a smile, the way the shadows shifted where their faces should have been, like oil slicking over stone. The flame in Wynn's hand flickered.

"She walks in light yet carries night."

"With heart once lost, now burning bright."

"We greet you, Shared Queen of The Vast."

Their voices echoed softly, reminding Wynn of a scary fairytale Grace had recently read to her. Her fingers curled around the torch.

"On golden leaves the truth shall fall."

"One crown will crack, one voice will call."

"And shadows rise behind the wall."

But Wynn raised a hand. "Ah, no. No, no," she said, stepping forward. Her voice echoed through the chamber, calm and even. "You mistake... that's not why I'm here."

The Fates tilted their heads slightly. Their mechanical movements made the hair on Wynn's arm rise.

"Those who come are those who seek."

"The strong, the lost, the bold, the meek."

"This is the day the Fates may speak."

Wynn could feel the lure of their voice. How easy it would be to hear the answers to any questions she may ask. She remembered Lorkan's words to her, *she would always have a choice.* "I don't need riddles. Not today. Not ever."

The Fates leaned forward in unison, their voices a single whisper.

"Would you like to know your fate?"

Wynn blinked. "Umm... nope. No, I wouldn't."

The three crones hissed, recoiling slightly. No one refused to know their fate. When asked, there was only ever one response.

"And you," Wynn added, brow raised, "all-knowing ones, should really know why I'm here."

"No..." they hissed, unsure now, unsettled.

"Oh, yes," Wynn said, stepping forward, cloak swaying behind. "I lost a good fox for this."

She took a breath. Then, clear and steady, she asked, "Do you want to know *your* fate?"

The three crones hissed again, recoiling slightly. No one ever asked them that. Mortals begged for their fates or fled from them. But none had ever dared turn the question towards them. Curiosity, ancient and terrible, stirred in the dark. Wynn had her answer. She had been counting on it.

"Hush now, hush. The thread is done.
The tale is told, the war is won.
Your needles dull, your scissors rust.
No more names to carve from dust.
So close your eyes, and take your leave.
This land no longer is yours to weave."

She let the words hang for a moment and then followed with, "In other words, *get out.* Weave and meddle somewhere else, you old hags. This story is ours to tell now."

The mountain rumbled beneath her feet, a low groan like something ancient shifting in its sleep. The Fates hissed and trembled with the mountain, their mouths open in a last refrain.

"The thread is gone, The Vast unspun."
"The weave undone by this very one."
"We lose the spool, we drop the knife."
"No hand shall weave the strands of life."

The chamber darkened for a moment, then brightened, softly, as if the torches dared to burn a little braver now. Dust fell like snow from the ceiling, and one by one, the Fates began to fade, unraveling into threads of light that drifted upward and away. It was a lot less dramatic than she had expected.

In the hush that followed, Wynn let out a slow breath. Her eyes were already adjusting when she saw it along the back wall, a narrow crack in the stone, just wide enough to mark the passage she knew was there. She reached beneath her cloak and pulled the ring from the chain around her neck. It glowed faintly in her palm, a steady pull, like a current tugging her toward deep water. She had never quite decided what to do with it. She wrestled between throwing it into the Still River or burying it with her parents near the Tarn ruins. Grace had lobbied hard for the latter option. They'd discussed it many times, usually late, when the candles burned low and their fears crept in with the dark. But in the end, Wynn had kept it. Not because she couldn't let go, but because she couldn't close the door. Not yet. Not to Avery. Not to Night. Not to her brother.

She hadn't told Grace that part. Not fully. But deep down, Wynn didn't believe she was finished with The Margins. Or rather, she suspected, The Margins weren't finished with her.

ONE LAST TURN OF THE PAGE... BECAUSE, BOOKS

Outside the castle kitchens, the world smelled like sweet cinnamon spice and the promise of something warm. Sunlight spilled through the high windows in soft, flour-dappled beams. Kiernan stood covered in a heroic dusting of white, grinning like he'd just unlocked the secret of the universe; and maybe he had, in the form of browned butter. He was elbow-deep in dough, tossing pinches of cardamom and candied ginger into the mixing bowl with the theatrical flair of a man who had finally been allowed to become exactly what he was always meant to be.

The oven crackled and puffed contentedly, working overtime as it birthed loaf after loaf, cookie after cookie. Trays crowded every surface, cooling under clean cloths. The smell had drifted through every corridor in the castle by now, drawing curious noses and castle guards who were "just-passing-through".

"These," Kiernan declared, handing over a neatly packed box tied with a crooked green ribbon, "are my Castle Specials. Brown butter sweet ginger chews. Mostly edible. Definitely experimental."

Wynn took the box and lifted the lid. The warmth hit her first, then the sweet, earthy spice. "These may be your best yet," she said dreamily.

"When you get back," he added, casually wiping a streak of flour onto his brow like a warrior marking himself for battle, "I'll have bread cooling on the windowsill."

Wynn raised a hopeful brow. "Something savory?"

He placed a hand to his heart. "For you? Always savory. And something sweet for Grace."

"Balance," Grace said, appearing beside them, cinching the clasp of her cloak and leaning in to kiss Wynn on the cheek. "It's what keeps the kingdom from falling apart."

Kiernan saluted with a wooden spoon. "Ride well, rule better, and if you come back with mud on your cloaks, I'll consider it a success."

"For Wynn, not for me," Grace cut in, brushing invisible dust off her sleeves. "I have no intention of returning with a single smudge, thank you."

Wynn shook her head, laughing. Grace blew Kiernan a kiss, and then the two of them, rulers of The Vast, stepped out into the wide, golden morning.

They rode side by side, cloaks catching the breeze, their horses' hooves finding a rhythm over the old stone bridge. Two women, so different in manner, but equally stubborn. They refused the easy road. Refused crowns that gleamed too brightly or thrones that asked for blood. They didn't rule with fear. They didn't rule with magic or swords. They ruled with stories and kindness. With wildness and wit. With purpose and laughter and long, slow walks through woods that smelled like cedar and rain. Was it enough to keep a Kingdom together? Only time will tell.

An elf had once made them a promise. And true to that quiet vow, one weekend every month, Grace and Wynn rode south;

past silver rivers and through gold-turning woods, pausing in villages that waved them through like kin, and taverns that welcomed them with warm pies and spicy cider. They rode until they reached a place that could not be found, unless you already knew it was there.

Wynn loved watching Grace as they descended the steps, her face lit by the flames lining the stone walls and the anticipation of finding a good story. This would never get old for her; the way the firelight caught in Grace's hair, the way she walked faster the closer they got.

The library greeted them as it always did. Endless books lining natural stone shelves, sorted in their quiet, particular way. Inviting reading nooks tucked between the stacks, filled with overstuffed chairs and well-loved quilts. A fire that crackled eternally, never needing to be fed, never dimming. It simply burned, warm, steady, and waiting to be enjoyed.

Illen met them at the bottom of the winding staircase, arms folded, eyes soft behind their spectacles. "You're late," they said, reaching eagerly for the cookie box. "I was about to go looking for you myself."

"We stopped for a long lunch and a swim by the falls," Wynn replied.

Grace snorted. "*She* swam. Far too cold for me, thank you very much."

Wynn gave a lazy smile. "You warmed me up afterward."

"Oh, did she?" Illen replied with a coy smile.

Wynn hadn't meant to say it quite so plainly, and the way Grace flushed and ducked her head made her grin widen. Grace was bringing out all sorts of things in her lately.

And Grace, too, was changing in unexpected ways. She was still particular, still orderly, still prone to insisting that shoes be left at the door and spoons arranged by size. But lately, something—or rather, someone—had begun to curl into the quiet spaces of her days.

Like Night, the fox had found Wynn. The pup had emerged soft-pawed from the underbrush while she was out wandering the castle grounds. Golden-furred, with alert ears and sleepy, knowing eyes, she had simply appeared and followed at a distance, then padded a little closer, circling Wynn's feet, until Wynn finally picked her up and allowed her to nestle into the crook of her arm. She dozed there like she'd always belonged.

She wasn't like Night, who had been a flicker in the dark, a flash between trees, untamable, wild, and marching to her very own beat. This one, this sleepy little fox, preferred hearths and cushions and soft spots to nap while the world spun on around her.

Grace, of course, had objected. Foxes, she insisted, belonged outside. She cited hygiene, fur, and of course, mud. Wynn had agreed, mostly to be polite. But the fox, soon named Sunny to match her coat and where she preferred to curl up, had other ideas. And Grace, despite her best efforts, had slowly caved.

Now, it was Grace who left the doors ajar and placed a folded blanket in the corner of her reading nook. Grace who turned a blind eye when muddy little paws left prints on the stone floors. Sunny had slipped into their lives the way warm morning sunlight crawls across a cold floor, intrusive perhaps, but impossible to resist. And Grace, eventually, had let her stay.

All three of them looked forward to visiting the comfortable quiet hug of Illen's library. It was a space that seemed to welcome them back like a favorite passage re-read on a rainy day. Grace was already shedding her cloak, humming as she dove into a stack of texts Illen had set aside. She loved it here: the order, the scent of parchment, the calm rhythm of things set right. Wynn, meanwhile, had her own destination. She padded straight toward the velvet armchair beside the fire and sighed as she dropped into it, the warmth rising up to meet her like a familiar embrace. A mug of apricot tea was already waiting on the side table, steaming gently, as if the library itself remembered her and was glad she'd come. She picked up the thick volume that was resting beside the cup. It was some sea-bound adventure about a swashbuckling princess who charted maps in places no one had dared navigate before; a girl who was always searching for treasure or a place to call home, and something else she couldn't quite name. Wynn flipped through the first few pages.

"That's for you. I think you'll like the main character," Illen said, appearing beside her with a wink.

Wynn nestled in deeper. Sunny, golden and drowsy, curled into the crook of her arm with a soft, contented huff. Wynn stroked her fur absently and took a sip. "Honestly," she murmured, "I'm only here for the tea." But the book rested heavy in her lap, and something about it tugged at her.

Illen chuckled from somewhere among the stacks. Grace was humming again. The fire crackled gently, casting slow-turning shadows on the walls. And for a moment, Wynn just sat there, still and quiet in the warmth. She exhaled slowly, pressing her cheek to Sunny's fur. She wasn't sure she deserved all this. She had everything she'd once only dreamed of: peaceful sleep, love, and a place to belong. And yet, beyond the mountains, beyond the softened borders of their realm, she knew there were still places ruled by shadow. Still lives being tugged and tangled by the hands of crueler Fates.

Across the room, Grace was still humming, half-lost in a stack of books, her curls falling into her eyes as she rearranged titles by moon phase. She looked impossibly focused and impossibly content. Wynn smiled softly, letting the moment settle around her like a blanket. Adventures could wait. At least, for now…

~ ~ ~

And so, dear reader, we've reached the end. I know. I'm a little sad, too. We've been through quite a bit together, haven't we? Daring escapes, stubborn foxes, narcissistic queens, mystical librar-

ians, and at least one cookie breakthrough. You've walked through ruins and danced in taverns. You've explored the misty veils of The Margins and ridden through enchanting forests. You've been on a "literal" adventure. (Yes, I said it. I regret nothing.) But all stories must come to an end eventually. It is our fate, after all. Don't worry. The characters will go on. The fire is still crackling. Grace is re-organizing books in her own completely illogical system, and Wynn has tea in one hand and a sleepy fox in the other while dreaming up her own next adventure. The world is warm, and safe, and still... for now. Which means, maybe, you can let go for a little while. Close the cover. Nestle in. Breathe deep. And if you find yourself missing them... well, this story will be waiting. You can always come back. Or better yet, pick up another. But not right now. Tonight, the adventures can wait. Sleep well.

Acknowledgements

Reader, this one is for you. Yes, you. The one holding me, skimming me, dogearing my pages, maybe even forgetting where you left me. Whether you devoured me over a weekend or wandered through my pages over months, whether you adored me or merely tolerated me, I'm grateful. Because here's the truth: I am only a story, a bundle of paper and words. I come alive because you read me. Without you, I'm just a sleepy little stack gathering dust. With you, I become.

This is for the readers who slip into bookstores like they're sacred spaces, not always to buy, but just to be among spines and ink and possibilities. For the ones who sigh when they crack open a cover, who feel their shoulders drop, who feel seen. For the ones who reread old favorites until the pages fray, who champion the stories the love, and for the brave hearts who try something new. Not every book is for every reader. Sometimes we don't quite click (you and I) and that's all right too. Sometimes a book frustrates you, or challenges you, or utterly wrecks you with a single sentence or the loss of a beloved character (I *am* sorry about that). Stories are strange. They don't always behave. But still, you show up.

And so: thank you. Thank you for keeping stories alive simply by turning pages, dreaming between the lines, and believing that a book, any book, might have something waiting for you inside. Without readers, I'm just potential. With you, I'm a real story. And I liked being real.

Sleep well.

~ *The Book That Will Put You to Sleep*

And now, from the one who heard this story first and wrote it down.

Many years ago, I began writing a classic adventure story, one where the story itself was the narrator. That voice came to me clearly and with a bit of attitude, and then... I let it go quiet. Life shifted and the creative pen was put down for other things. But that voice never fully left me alone. Then one day, I stumbled across a genre I hadn't known existed: cozy fantasy. Reading those gentle, heartfelt adventures sparked something in me, a different way into the story I had once set down and you have now picked up. Whether or not you enjoyed this book, I had a wonderful time writing it, building the world of the Vast, disappearing into libraries I wish were real, and spending time with characters who kept me company when the world felt a bit too loud.

Thank you to my early readers and sounding boards. To my wife, Natalie, thank you for loving me and putting up with me through every creative spiral, and for understanding that sometimes I just need to disappear into the story. To my bestie book buddy and very good friend, Nichelle, thank you for your ear, your encouragement, and your Virgo editing eye. To Janey, thank you for being one of my first readers and a real cheerleader of my words.

To Uluru, my dog, thank you for being the inspiration behind Night's sassiness and spirit.

And finally, to those of you who read all the way through the acknowledgments, who don't consider a book truly finished until every page is read (like my wife), this is for you. Thank you for making room in your world for mine.

For as long as she can remember, Dawn Green has shared her brain with a revolving cast of characters and half-plotted storylines. Every now and then, she lets them out, and occasionally, they become books like *When Kacey Left, In the Swish, and How Samantha Smart Became a Revolutionary*. She lives on the rainy West Coast with her wife and dog, where grey skies mean more time for wandering through bookstores, brewing endless cups of tea (many of them apricot), and getting lost in other people's stories (when she's not wrestling with her own).

Manufactured by Amazon.ca
Acheson, AB